A CHARMED LIFE

Books by Mary McCarthy

THE COMPANY SHE KEEPS
THE OASIS
CAST A COLD EYE
THE GROVES OF ACADEME
A CHARMED LIFE

A
Charmed
Life

BY MARY McCARTHY

HARCOURT, BRACE AND COMPANY
NEW YORK

LIBRARY OF CONGRESS CATALOG CARD NUMBER: 55-10153

PRINTED IN THE UNITED STATES OF AMERICA

A CHARMED LIFE

ONE

JOHN SINNOTT cut his hand trying to raise a stuck window in the downstairs bathroom. They had been established in their new-bought house a month, and John was still doing minor repairs. The summer tenant had left a row of cigarette burns on the upstairs-bathroom mantel, a big grease spot on the rug in the dining room (where he had spilled a platter of steak), a broken windowpane, an ink-stain worthy, as Martha Sinnott said, of Martin Luther on her white writing desk. The tenant was a bachelor lawyer from New York, with a theatrical clientele; and he had paid a very good rent, Martha reminded John, who was inclined to fly into tempers and feel himself misused. You had to expect some breakage, said Martha virtuously. They, too, had broken things in their day, she pointed out, reciting an inventory of their own sins as tenants. But for John it was not the same thing. He declined to compare himself with a tenant who let his friends drive their cars all over the lawn and shoot at bottles when they had been drinking and fall into Martha's herb box, which she had planted in such a fever that spring, when they came up to get the house ready. John did not think that the fact that the tenant had left some liquor in the cabinet compensated for the damage. Nor did he think that the dining-room rug was the place to carve a steak, even though, as Martha pointed out, the table did wobble.

He was angry and he grew angrier all through Septem-

3

ber, as he came upon new scars and scratches, which he no longer mentioned to Martha, for it distressed her to be told of the tenant's misdeeds, partly for the tenant's sake and partly for John's—she feared he was becoming unbalanced. Ever since Labor Day—the day the tenant had vacated—things had not been right between them. Martha, it seemed, had constituted herself the tenant's advocate, finding excuses for him, palliating, appealing for clemency with big sorrowful brown eyes, like a regular little Portia. And in order to excuse the tenant she would gently indicate the house's drawbacks—the wobbling table, the erratic stove, the fact that she had not got around to making curtains for the bedroom. This, for John, was indefensible. He was a young man of passionate loyalties and he would hear no word against the house, any more than he would against Martha. He detested her habit of self-criticism; he wished her and hers to be invulnerable.

He detested it most of all when she was right, or partly right, as she was, he knew, about the tenant. But she did not understand, as if perversely, that his anger at the lawyer was necessary to him, and principally on her account: he could not bear that her house should be treated with contumely. For Martha was in a delicate situation. She ought never to have come back here—and both John and Martha knew it—to the village of New Leeds, which she had left seven years before, when she had run away with John.

The Sinnotts were a romantic couple. Strangers still glanced after them on the street, wherever they went; waiters smiled; butchers beamed—as if they were morganatic, said Martha, who had begun to find the position ridiculous. It was partly their appearance. Martha was a strange, poetical-looking being, with very fair, straight hair done in a little knot, a quaint oval face, very dark, wide-set eyes, and a small, slight figure; she had been on the stage. John, also, was quite remarkable-looking, tall and small-boned, with high coloring, neatly inscribed features, and dark-brown, stiffly curling hair; he was the son of a military family and was often taken for English. Nobody ventured to guess Martha's origins; in fact she was the child of a Swedish engineer and an Italian music teacher, who had borne her in Juneau, Alaska.

On the afternoon of John's mishap, they were wearing matching white wool sweaters. Martha was sitting in the parlor, on the sofa, with yards of heavy white linen on her lap, making curtains for the bedroom; by her side was a box of brass rings. The scene was just what they had desired when they bought the house—the coal fire burning in the grate, white eighteenth-century panelling, deep window embrasures, the old black horsehair sofa, and Martha sewing tranquilly, like some Protestant pastor's wife in an old tale, her mother's gold thimble on her finger. And like the wife sewing in the fairy tale, Martha was wishing for a child. She wanted a center for their life, something, as she said ardently, to live for. Martha was a purposeful young woman; she sought a meaning for everything. She did not understand, yet, why they had come back to New Leeds, and she was waiting, eagerly, for the answer. She could not settle down in the house, as she told her husband, until she knew *why* they were here.

But on this particular afternoon she had decided that it was because they were going to have a child, probably, and her soul drew a breath of relief. John did not want a baby, so he flatly said, but he had never made her do anything to prevent it—he would change, Martha assured herself, if she actually became pregnant. With these thoughts running through her head, she was plying her needle contentedly when she heard a funny sound, a sort of muffled howl, that made her think a wild animal had got into the back of the house. This fantastic surmise permitted her to go on sewing steadily, like a sleeper who dreams an explanation for an alarming noise. She had hemmed nearly half a length before she awoke to the fact that the funny sound was her husband, John, in the kitchen. "What *is* it?" she called out in an angry voice mechanically fending off the knowledge that something bad must have happened to him. She laid aside the material, stabbing in the needle with the resigned, irritable patience of a person who is used to senseless interruptions. A hollow groan answered: "Hurt . . . [gasp] . . . myself." Then she flew to the kitchen.

It was a fairly deep, crescent-shaped cut in the cushion of the field of Mars. The blood was spurting into the sink under a stream of cold water from the faucet. In the cellar, the noisy old pump was hammering as if in its death rattle. Martha resisted the impulse to turn the water down. "Let me see," she begged, but John elbowed her sharply away as she hovered on tiptoe beside him, trying to get a second look at the cut. He kept holding it under the cold water and then licking it, dog style—he clung to the belief that the human tongue was antiseptic. "Bandage," he gasped, gesturing her off with a look of ferocious hatred. Martha obeyed; she fetched gauze pads, adhesive tape, and scissors from the upstairs bathroom, taking her time, though she had the impression she was hurrying. She was no good at first aid, and minor injuries flustered her. She considered them unnecessary.

"Poor John," she asseverated, trying to feel some solicitude as she started down the stairs again. *"Poor* John." But as soon as she saw him, scowling, seated at the kitchen table, sucking his hand, annoyance supervened. His moaning and swaying distracted her as she cut the strips of adhesive. When she tried to get the bandage on, she found that the strips were too short. "For God's sake, let me do it!" her husband exclaimed. Martha's heart quivered. Her delicate brown eyes opened wide and a tear stood in each of them. As she began to cut fresh strips, in silence, the two tears dropped, like gentle reproaches, onto the cherry table.

John Sinnott watched her sullenly. He knew that he had hurt her feelings deliberately, and he felt no remorse. Another time, Martha's honesty and ineptitude would have touched him: she could not pretend to sympathize with what to her was an unseemly display. Appreciative of this—indeed, it was this straightness he admired in her—John nevertheless was enraged. The cut throbbed; he felt sick at his stomach. And he blamed her. Yes, that was the irrational thing. He blamed her, not only for her childish clumsiness with the bandage (she was clever enough with her fingers when it came to cooking and sewing and could make the prettiest tray for you when you were sick in bed with the doctor!) but for the cut itself. The instant his hand had gone through the window, a frantic rage had seized him. He had tried to discharge it elsewhere—on the tenant, the previous owner, the drunken, irresponsible handyman—but it was Martha's toothbrush and lipstick and pale tortoise combs, lying on the window sill, that claimed the blame. Tears of fury had risen to his eyes. His own toothbrush and hairbrush and toothpaste lay on the sill, too. But he could not see them; all he could see was Martha—*her* lipstick, which rolled to the floor, *her* handyman, *her* tenant, *her* window. And all he could hear now was Martha's voice, clear in his memory, murmuring that they ought to have shelves and a medicine cabinet in the downstairs bathroom. He suddenly stamped his foot on the floor and snatched the bandage away.

This was the way affairs had been going ever since they had come back to New Leeds to make a better life. The slightest thing that went wrong made him see Martha in it, though he would not say so. "I didn't think of you at all," he would demur if she protested that he blamed her, whereas in fact she was always in his mind, concealed under the appearance of a windstorm, a bare patch in the lawn, a piece of broken glass, a defective battery. He dwelt in an anthropomorphic world peopled by her impulsive mistakes. Yet the cardinal mistake, which was to come back here at all, he considered his own responsibility. Martha hated New Leeds—that is, its social aspect. This hatred, John had decided, was her safeguard. They could come back here because the place had no temptations for her; she had no wish to be a part of it again. They had come here, he announced, to be alone, so that Martha could write the play that he believed she could do, if she could get the right conditions.

And what was wrong with that, he furiously wanted to know. He had stern faith in Martha. He had seen her through three years during which she acted on Broadway while studying for her Ph.D. in philosophy, and three more years in which she did odd jobs—writing theater notices, recording novels for the blind, making a new translation of *The Wild Duck* for an off-Broadway production—and one year that was wasted in false starts on her play. He was used to making decisions and sacrifices on her behalf. He had stuck to a dullish job in the Historical Society, six days a week, so that Martha could be free not to work on radio or television. He had done this voluntarily and over Martha's protest—she did not altogether like to be believed in. They had come to the country because he had decreed that it was time for them both to be serious, which was impossible in the city, with the telephone going all the time.

8

And, morally speaking, there was no reason John could see why they should not have chosen New Leeds; they had no wish to mingle in the community. Yet ever since Labor Day, from the moment they crossed the threshold, each of them had known that they had blundered, and had known that the other knew. But John's military mentality would not admit of an error once their forces were committed. It incensed him to hear Martha talk blithely of "our" mistake, as she named it. She knew as well as he did that there was no retreat. He had quit his job to come here. Their small capital— the sum of two legacies—was tied up in the house. Every day there were new, unforeseen expenses: yesterday the pump, which Martha had put on the blink by leaving a faucet running; today the window, which would cost a dollar for a new pane, even if he puttied it himself. He had earned no money since they had been here; neither had Martha. She refused to worry about money and kept talking about improvements and additions. After only a month, he was sick at heart and scared. It was ironic for him to think that their seventh wedding anniversary was coming in November; seven years, they had once agreed, was the fatal span for love. At night, he still slept with Martha wrapped tenderly in his arms, but by day, more and more, he sensed that she conspired against him.

What frightened Martha, for her part, was the ebbing of concern. She had caught herself several times forgetting John's existence when he had gone to the village for a few hours. They did not even quarrel the way they used to. Now, for example, once the bandage was on, they were no longer cross, though they had given each other ample provocation. He glowered and she looked sad, but underneath, she knew, neither of them felt a single thing. Martha would have liked to go back to the parlor and pick up her sewing or her book, but it did not seem quite polite to do so while John was in pain. John, she saw, wanted to lie down, away from her insistent gaze. But she could not let him be, because they had once been in love. "Lie down now," she urged, half-heartedly. "I'll put your things away." But he at once smelt a reproach in her offer. "I'll do it," he retorted. "Just go away and leave me alone." Martha glanced out the window. The sun was setting, and wood would have to be brought in for the dining-room fireplace before it got dark; if his tools were not put away, the dew would rust them. She knew very well that if he went into the bedroom, he would not come out for some time, and it exasperated her that he refused to know this simple fact about himself. She did not in the least mind getting the wood—why should she? What she minded was his self-deception. In his place, an honest person would have said thank you, and left it at that. She started to speak and halted herself, taking full credit for not saying what was on the tip of her tongue, but her glance out the window had said it all for her. "I'll *do* it!" he cried, jumping up. He retired to the bedroom and theatrically slammed the door.

Martha shrugged. He had left her in a cruel quandary. Whatever she did now he would interpret as a criticism. If she left the tools to rust, however, *they* would criticize him longer. Therefore, Martha tiptoed resolutely out of the house, found his hammer and screwdrivers and puttying knife, shut up the workshop, loaded a barrow full of locust wood, and wheeled it up to the dining-room door. The beauty of the evening, following on the cut and the quarrel, gave her a sense of solitariness. The single golden quince on the bush by the kitchen door, the virid brilliance of the grass in the locust grove, the flock of birds flying southward had a terrible pathos for her, as if they were orphaned in space. She stood in the doorway a long time, feeling sorry for every natural thing that surrounded them. From this vantage point of desolation, she even pitied herself and her husband, impersonally, seeing them as two wan specks, no bigger than the birds against the greenish-gold sky.

Sighing, she shut the door and laid the fire in the dining room. As usual, immediately after sunset the house turned cold and drafty. She poked up the fire in the parlor, threw on fresh coal, and endeavored to read calmly. But she soon became conscious of the ticking of the unpolished Empire clock on the mantel. She glanced at her wrist watch, which had been losing twenty minutes a day, ever since she went swimming with it in the bay the first week, and at the clock, which gained ten, and tried to get the right time by mental algebra. They were going to miss cocktails, probably, if John did not get up. A surge of fear went through her. Everything in their lives was strung on order and precision. When they had decided to venture New Leeds, they had said to themselves that they must be orderly and dignified; otherwise, they would surely go to pieces, like everybody else who came here.

It was an "artistic" community, beyond the commuting range, and Martha knew its perils, perhaps better than anybody, having got away from it whole and able to tell the tale. She had been telling it for years now, with her gay, floating laugh, to incredulous outsiders who thought she was exaggerating when she related the truly horrible mishaps that befell the various "free lances" and their wives who had come here to gather dust, on a pair of small incomes and the revenue from an August rental. People always said that Martha was exaggerating or that she was "very clever," which amounted to the same thing. But Martha only spoke the literal truth, as John could attest—that was her peculiarity.

And the essence of New Leeds was a kind of exaggeration. Everything here multiplied, like the jellyfish in the harbor. There were *three* village idiots, grinning, in the post office; the average winter resident who settled here had had three wives; there were eight young bohemians, with beards, leaning from their pickup trucks; twenty-one town drunkards. In wife-beating, child neglect, divorce, automobile accidents, falls, suicide, the town was on a sort of statistical rampage, like the highways on a holiday week end. Nothing in New Leeds happened once only. When Martha's house burned to the ground while she was living with her first husband, it was the third house that year to catch on fire. Defective wiring, nodded the old-time winter residents, chewing the fat in the paper store. And while she thought she knew the cause better than the village chorus, the element of repetition still terrified Martha when she remembered the fire; it was as if she had lost, at that time, the principle of individuation and was simply a number in a series.

Every afternoon, now, when she and John went to the pond to swim, they passed the foundation of the burnt house, still standing, surrounded by lilac bushes. John drove past it as fast as he could, but Martha always turned to look, and then dropped into a mood of despondency. It had been a fire-law violation, pure and simple, that had caused the fire, in her opinion. When the workmen were taking down the ugly old overhead lighting fixture in the dining room, she had let them stuff the wires back into the ceiling and just plaster over. She knew it was a fire hazard, but she had done it to save money, at her first husband's insistence. And he had not let her tell where the fire had started when the inspector came from the insurance company. It was normal practice, he averred, to cheat an insurance company—they expected it. That was why they charged such big premiums. It was a neurotic desire to ruin him completely that was prompting her to tell the truth, he said. Martha did not think so, but one never could be sure about such things. (Motives did not matter, John and Martha had agreed, the first day they met, seven years ago, on the beach; you should never be deterred from a good action by the suspicion that your motive was bad.) In any case, it still haunted Martha to think that she might have saved the house, or the clothes, at least, and the books and pictures, if she had wakened her snoring mate when she first smelled smoke coming from the direction of the dining room instead of lying there, assuring herself that it was her imagination. They had had a party that night, and though she had not been tight, exactly, she had had five drinks, counting cocktails, and her first husband had still been drunk and was crashing around stupidly in the hedge, like a maddened buffalo, when firemen came.

Drink, no question, was one of the chief local dangers. Martha said people came here because they wanted to become alcoholics and were looking for a Rome to do as the Romans did in. All artistic communities, she admitted, presented this problem, but New Leeds was worse than most because it had an unusual number of reformed or reforming alcoholics, who threw the drinkers into glum relief. In a village of four hundred souls, there was a strong chapter of the W.C.T.U., to take care of the locals, and a branch of A.A., with regular Wednesday meetings, even out of season, to take care of the "foreigners." Liquor was one of the things, John and Martha had warmly agreed when they first came up, last spring, to get the house ready for the tenant, that you had to be on guard against. Consequently, they made a point of having just one cocktail when they were alone, at six o'clock. In actual fact they often had two, but when they did, they had begun to look away from each other, in embarrassment, as though not to witness the other's fall from grace. The joy of drinking was gone. The slender brimming glass had taken on an aspect of fatality; they looked *through* the pale Martini to the possible future, its precipitate, lying like dark lees in the bottom.

And it was typical of New Leeds that you could not take a drink without wondering whether you might become an alcoholic. Everything here cast a menacing shadow before it, a shade of future perdition. There was something sinister, John admitted, in the fact that you could not get anything repaired. There was nobody to fix the clock; the man who sharpened lawn mowers had died during the summer and nobody succeeded him; the local laundry service could not clean a suit without tearing and discoloring it; the garage-man's only accomplishment was the ability to scratch his head. Everything in the village was relentlessly running down, buckling, warping, mildewing—including the human beings. Or so it suddenly seemed to Martha, coming back like an epilogue to announce the changes that had befallen the inhabitants by slow stages: the town highway superintendent become the titular town drunkard, indistinguishable from his predecessor, in faded blue shirt and lurching overalls; the pretty young girls from the soda fountain staring at her as if helplessly from sausage casings of fat; the gay, smart wives mottled and bedizened, fantastically got up in shawls and peasant bangles—when two of them got together, John said, they made the First National check-out look like a fortune-tellers' convention. New Leeds was, literally, the seacoast of Bohemia. When John looked at the bare patches in the lawn or Martha at her wrist watch, they each felt a stir of terror. The wrist watch, in particular, frightened Martha, for

14

never before in her life had she gone in the water with her
watch on, and she could not explain how she had done
it, for her wrist, as she repeatedly told John, had *felt*
empty. He, too, she knew, was troubled by the watch
incident, just as she today was alarmed and irritated by
the cut, which was really too New Leedsian for comfort.
They had begun to survey each other mistrustfully. Each
feared that if the other let go, for an instant, the
construct of their lives would crumble like stale cake
frosting.

At the outset, Martha had declared that it was too
great a risk to come back, even though her former husband was no longer in the village at all but fifteen miles
off, with a new house and a brand-new wife, with a larger
income than usual, and a baby. She and John, she said,
had all the ominous qualifications for a New Leedsian
residence: two tiny incomes, an obscure fame (Martha's),
a free-lancing specialty (John's), and the plan of doing
something original. Why should they be different from
the others, who were filed away here like yellowed clip-
pings in a newspaper morgue—the ex-lawyer who ran a
duck farm, the oysterman who had gone to Harvard, the
French vicomte who had an antique shop in the summer
and clerked in the liquor store in the winter, the plumber
with his degree in fine arts, the illustrator who had
once been married to a screen star, the former Wash-
ington hostess who now took paying guests? Many of the
New Leedsians had once had talent or ability; you could
see the buried traces if you looked for them, as you could
find Indian flints and stone arrowheads in the debris on
Long Hill. Your typical New Leedsian, as pointed out
in the post office, had a name that rang a bell somewhere,
far, far away; you felt you should have heard of him
even if you hadn't.

Why, then, had they come here, Martha's friends asked her, if the place was as fatal as she said? The answer was that she did not know. Neither she nor John had ever intended such a thing. It had happened by accident. John had been sent by the Historical Society to photograph a house farther down the coast; they themselves had been looking for a place of their own on the seashore. It was a Columbus Day week end, not quite a year ago. The inn they had meant to stay at was closed; they still had friends in New Leeds, and on an impulse they had telephoned them and taken the ferryboat—for the first time in six years. Martha had forgotten how beautiful New Leeds was out of season, with its steel-blue fresh-water ponds and pine forests and mushrooms and white bluffs dropping to a strangely pebbled beach. "There's a house for sale *here*," suggested their hostess, with a shrewd offhand look at both of them as they sat side by side on her sofa. "Oh, no," said Martha quickly. But she had given in, and they had all gone to look at it, just for the fun.

It was, alas, a house she remembered—her favorite house in New Leeds, a pale-yellow eighteenth-century cottage with two red brick sides, set in a green locust grove, with a little avenue of poplars. They picked a single silver-pink climbing rose from a trellis—Mrs. Van Fleet, thought Martha, giving it to John for his buttonhole. There was a spring somewhere back in the woods, the real-estate agent said, and an abandoned house site with lilacs and white old-fashioned double narcissi— thirty-five acres of land and the whole thing dirt-cheap. The agent remembered Martha, very gallantly, and politely gave no hint of remembering John, who had been here only two weeks that momentous summer. It was the nicest house, by far, and the cheapest they had seen anywhere—*early* eighteenth century, John concluded

16

after examining the doors and fireplaces. It was a little shabby, but they liked that. There was an outside study for John, and a workshop, with an old chimney; there were apples, pears, grapes, roses, box; they could rent it in the summer months, if they wanted, and make a very good income. There was no heating, but they could put in an oil floor furnace or get along the first year with kerosene stoves. The woods were full of timber, and every room had a fireplace, which would see them through till Thanksgiving. It had electricity, a bathroom and a half, and some furniture.

Martha had agonized over the decision, for it was hers, of necessity, everybody saw, sympathetically. Three times in two days Martha told the real-estate agent that they could not take the house, and twice she came back to get the key again. They all picked boletus in the woods, and John found the spring; they picnicked and swam in the bay. Their host and hostess pressed and reasoned. New Leeds had changed a lot, they told John. Martha's first husband almost never came here any more; there were some nice new younger people who played chamber music and read plays and poetry aloud. Last week, they had done "Tartufe," in French, with the vicomte. If Martha and John settled here, they could have a little amateur theater. Martha felt herself weakening. Why not? As her hosts, the Coes, said, her first husband did not own the peninsula. She and John would not have to see the old crowd or go to parties. "Give me one reason why not," Warren Coe begged, and Martha could only answer that it seemed in poor taste. But even John thought this was rather silly. Lots of the wives and husbands, too, came back with new spouses, the Coes assured him, and nobody thought a thing of it. Martha nodded, dubiously. The last night, in bed in the Coes' studio, she had waked John up and begged him not to let them buy the house;

17

he had kissed her tearful cheek and promised, solemnly. Two months later, on John's birthday, they had telephoned the realty agency and agreed to send the down payment.

It was fate, they concluded. For good or ill, it was intended for them. Their conventional friends said, "Aren't you very courageous?"—hinting both at the past, for there had been a considerable scandal, and at the fact that the house, as it turned out, was a bargain because the previous owner had committed suicide in the workshop. John and Martha had laughed and shrugged. They liked to be brave; dauntlessness was their medium. The fact that Martha trembled gave a shimmer to their exploits. They had bought the house because, as Martha explained to sundry perplexed listeners, they were afraid of being afraid to buy it. They rose to the challenge. Martha was now thirty-three and John was thirty-two, but they never refused a risk. And they had known perfectly well, despite the Coes' assurances, that they would have to run the gauntlet of the village curiosity.

Martha's story was famous, and not only from her own telling. She had left her first husband's second house in the middle of the night, in a nightgown, driving his Plymouth sedan, which ran out of gas and stranded her on the road to John's cabin, so that she had had to get out and walk, and was picked up by the milkman—tear-streaked, with loose hair and torn mules. He "delivered her to the feller with the milk," and passed the tale on his rounds, wherever a goodwife was up. It was not literally true that she had left the town forever in her nightie, as New Leeds gossip told it; she had gone back the next morning in John's shirt and rolled-up seer-sucker pants, with her hair in a braid, and packed her clothes while her husband was scouring the village for her in the town taxi. Nor was the nightgown transparent.

Nor had she made love with John until that night or uttered a word against her husband during the twelve afternoons they had talked together on the beach; she had been guilty before, but not with John.

Nor—she now said to herself, gritting her teeth—had she stolen the wretched Plymouth, *pace* her husband's partisans; it had been repossessed by the financing company, when her husband, unnerved by the debacle, had ceased to make the monthly payments. Nor, to conclude, had she left a child behind—not her own, at any rate; *his* —a six-year-old boy, whom she had rescued, as a matter of fact, in the fire, when his own father had forgotten him. She was not responsible when the child died the following year, of natural causes, not of his father's neglect, which was a tale she never concurred in, though to those who *knew* the father it had a certain plausibility.

Martha eyed the clock. It occurred to her that John (*dear* John, she murmured to herself, thinking with horror of her first husband) might have fallen asleep. In gratitude to him as her remembered deliverer, she fought down the impulse to go and see whether he would like a cocktail now. He is suffering from shock, she said to herself, tenderly; he needs rest; when he feels better, he will come out by himself. But all the while her nervous demon kept asking whether he realized what time it was. So long as he lay there, shut off in the bedroom, she could not read, she could not even start cooking the supper, for these activities seemed to her discourteous in view of his cut. Under the circumstances, there seemed nothing she could do, appropriately, but muse. She lit a cigarette, feeling even for this a little heartless, and threw the match into the fire.

In the stillness, her critics spoke up. Ever since she and John came back here, she had felt surrounded by criticism—whenever she entered a store, with her head held high and her arm linked through her husband's, not seeking to be recognized. She knew this feeling to be senseless; she had always been popular in the village. But when a storekeeper, wiping his hand on his apron, and shooting it out across the counter, would roar, "Glad to see you back, Missus," she felt a ridiculous gratitude. However, some of the natives seemed to know her all too well. "Notice you're back," said the fish-man softly, gutting a bass in his smelly shop. "Long time no see." She did not even remember him, she protested, and yet he called her "Martha" in a voice that made her squirm. If she had not had John, she said, her bewildered mind would have toppled at the things that had evidently been said about her, about both of them, here in New Leeds, and were still being said, apparently, if the Coes' hints could be trusted. She could almost believe she was dreaming and that the awful stories were true, rather than think the opposite: that people deliberately made them up. They were still harping, for example, on the dead stepchild. John had been furious with Jane Coe for telling her this; he knew how agitated Martha got over such things. It appalled her that the village mind was still churning up the past, tossing the old dirty linen back and forth impersonally, like one of the washing machines in the new laundromat. This was an aspect of their return that neither of them had ever foreseen: that Martha would be thrown back, seven years, into her own ancient history, to start up all the old battles, defensively, as if they had never been won.

She tried now, loyally, to stop thinking about the dead stepchild, for she knew John disapproved. But she could not forgo defending herself. She had honestly—yes, truly —done her best by the boy; the proof was that so many people had thought he was her own child. When she ran away, she had felt dreadful about leaving him; John could support that. Coming back that final morning, she had even had the crazy notion of taking the child with her—a thing quite impossible, of course, unless she and John had been willing to be kidnappers and hide out for the rest of their lives. Nobody, she said to herself, had the right to expect that of her, and was there anybody who dared say that she ought to have sacrificed herself and stayed with her husband for the child's sake? Nobody but that hateful man himself, who in fact had used that as an argument when he wrote to her in New York, telling her that he would not connive at a divorce —a strange argument, forsooth, when he had always been jealous of her affection for the boy, terming it their "unholy alliance." And of *course* it would have been unhealthy for the child if Martha had sacrificed her life to him; the poor babe would have been poisoned by the fumes of renunciation. . . . There was no reason whatever why she should not have done what she did.

And yet, at this very moment, irrationally, Martha was troubled by the thought that if she had stayed, Barrett might have lived. Self-flattery, no doubt, she said to herself with a wry little shrug, stamping out her cigarette. She knew very well, moreover, that she had not hesitated long about leaving him. Martha was not sentimental: just as she was recalling, sadly, how she had grieved over Barrett's death, her memory tapped her sharply, like a teacher's ruler, and reminded her that she had not given Barrett a thought during the months when he must have been sickening; she had forgotten clean about him until she learned he was dead.

This clarity of mind, as she grew older, was more and more wearisome to Martha. She was tired of knowing the truth as it piled up, leaving less and less room for hope and illusions. John, she thought, was the same. He, too, was beginning to see things in this clear, sharp light. They still "loved" each other, but this love today was less a promise than a fact of life. If they could have chosen over again, neither would have chosen differently. Neither of them knew anyone they would have preferred to the other. They could not even imagine an ideal companion they would put in the other's place. From their point of view, for their purposes, they had had the best there was. There lay the bleakness; for them, as they were constituted, through all eternity, this had been the optimum—there was no beyond. There was nothing.

And if this, thought Martha trenchantly, was "maturity," she did not care for it; she would almost rather be dead. It had occurred to her more than once, as a speculation, that perhaps she *was* dead. This was what she would have said, probably, if she had sat by as a commentator and watched herself crawl back here, But, not being a commentator, Martha still had hope. She was just the opposite of John; she would not admit that she had hope, while he would not admit that he despaired. She was afraid to. She feared that this hope might be an illusion, which she had in common with every wreck and derelict who had floated up on the beach. It might be nothing more than the old "free will" of the philosophers, which was a part of the apparatus of consciousness and told nothing one way or the other about reality.

To think that such a hope was still alive in the twenty-one chronic town drunkards, in the barbital addict and the three village idiots, no doubt, as well as in all the beached failures and second-raters of the twenties and thirties, was ludicrous from the outside—Martha could assure them of that—but nobody could see himself from the outside, not even Martha at her most objective, when she seemed to be straining out of the window of her nature, to catch a glimpse of John and herself in the round.

Martha heaved a sigh. She yawned from hunger. The more one knew, the less one could predict, it seemed. In human life, as in palmistry, no sign had a fixed meaning. In the workshop, last week, they had found an old book of the hand, which Martha said, after study, was just as reliable as psychoanalysis; you could make palmistry match your life just as well as Freud's theories, assuming you thought you knew what your life was. John's right hand, for instance—his "made" hand—had no fate line, which could mean that he had entrusted his fate to Martha—they had both seen this, wryly smiling, the minute he stretched out his palms to her. They had found poor Barrett, too, in both their hands, with the bad-luck sign around him, which made Martha say—a thing she half believed—that Barrett was the reason they had not been able to have a child yet, though the doctor had found nothing wrong. It was a punishment laid on her. If she had decreed that they should kidnap Barrett, John, she knew, would have done it; he had had faith in her nobility of purpose.

A deeper sigh escaped her. Then she stiffened on the sofa. She had heard a stirring from the bedroom. There was a loud yawn, a creaking of bedsprings, a slow, dragging step. Her heart bounded. She declined to be hurt because he had slammed the door. Indeed, she had almost forgotten it, which was the way all their quarrels ended nowadays. Another sign—but how to read it? She went quickly to meet him in the kitchen. As he came out of the bedroom door, his hair was rumpled and his face was creased, but his high, boyish color had come back. Evidently he had been sleeping. This at once relieved and slightly irritated her. She looked at his hand; the blood had soaked through the bandage, but the actual bleeding had stopped. "You're better," she said gaily.

"It still hurts," he protested. "But you're better," she

repeated. "You looked awful before. You *glistened* like a sweating piece of store cheese." She smiled, trying to cajole him, as if the "old" John of an hour before were a trying guest they had got rid of and were now ready to discuss. He flexed his hand and made a rueful face. Martha looked at him in alarm. "It *really* hurts?" she cried, with a shiver of sympathy. And all at once she was flooded with penitence. "Do you think you cut a tendon?" she timidly asked. But John seemed to read her thoughts, which were rushing ahead to death and judgment. "Don't be a goose," he said calmly. "Why don't you make us a drink?"

Martha looked at her watch. She was thinking of the doctor's office hours, which were doubtless the same as they had always been—seven to nine in the evenings. She did not like the idea of John's sitting in the doctor's waiting room (if she could get him there) with liquor on his breath. The story would get around that he had hurt himself when drunk, like all the other New Leedsians, who were always catching on fire, falling into open wells or sunken gardens, tripping on stairs, crashing up in their cars. At the same time, Martha yearned for the festivity of cocktails, and John, no doubt, needed it. She suddenly perceived that if she hurried and forgot about the doctor, they could have dinner almost on time and a drink before it too; the day would be almost a normal day, after all, as if the cut and the quarrel had never been. "All right," she agreed. "An Old-Fashioned?" He nodded, approvingly. Martha's Old-Fashioneds were a sign of love. She did them with bourbon, no fruit, and half a lump of sugar, in their best glasses, rubbing the rims with orange peel and lemon peel and putting in a silver muddler. As she set John's drink before him and got a chicken out of the icebox and an onion from the vegetable bin, she was happy again. She had just remembered

24

somebody's telling her that the present doctor here was a penicillin fiend, and her conscience was at rest: John said you could not trust a doctor who trusted to penicillin.

"Talk to me," he ordered, pointing to the chair opposite him. "I ought to start the supper," said Martha, indicating the cut-up chicken. "Let me just put it on," she pleaded. She poured olive oil into the frying pan, turned up the heat, and in a minute threw in the chicken. "Excuse me," she murmured and hurried out the door with the flashlight. She came back with a bunch of thyme and parsley, got out the chopping board and the onion, and sat down across from him with her drink. "I love you," she announced.

But he had sunk into despondency. "I wonder whether you do," he said, frowning, and pulling at the bandage, which was stiff with dried blood. "Sometimes, Martha," he went on, raising his eyes, "I think it's all words with you." Martha's eyes widened. "That's what He used to say," she cried—so they usually spoke of her first husband, as a capitalized pronoun. "So you told Him you loved him, too," observed John. Martha shook her head. "No," she said earnestly. *"Never?"* John pounced. "Hardly ever," conceded Martha. The truth was she could not remember saying it, but she supposed that now and then she must have, when asked, from politeness. "What did he mean, then," demanded John, "by saying it was all words with you?" "I don't know," said Martha heavily. "He might have been talking about Barrett."

There was a strained silence. Ever since they had been back, Martha had been encountering these discrepancies. A phrase or an incident from her first marriage would suddenly crop up in her memory, like a piece in a jigsaw puzzle that seemed to have come from the wrong box. The horrifying thought that there could be a similarity, a common element in her two marriages, had struck her more than once recently. She kept going back to the past for reassurance, to remind herself of the differences.

"Did I ever tell you," she now murmured, "about the time I hit Him over the head with a highball glass?" John frowned and shook his head. "Oh, yes," she said gaily. "Two stitches." she watched him nervously to see what he thought of this revelation. He was shocked. "Of course, I had provocation," she added. "But can you imagine me doing such a thing?" "No," he said in a flat voice, glancing almost suspiciously at her frail figure and candid, innocent face. "That's the way I was then," she declared, sighing. "You can't conceive it, John."

"I don't believe it," he said stoutly, his features becoming very prim and precise. "You were just the way you are now when *I* met you." Martha shook her head. "That was because of you," she explained. "You made me nice. And now I'm relapsing." She glanced at his hand. "Look!" she cried. "It's bleeding again!" And in fact, while they had been drinking the Old-Fashioneds, a little fresh blood had seeped through the bandage.

"It's nothing," said John. "I've been using my hand, that's all."

Martha turned pale. "See?" she said. "That's typical. Up to this minute I hadn't thought to notice which hand it was." It was the right hand, of course. "And the bandage isn't sterile, either," she continued in an excited, self-accusatory tone. "I dropped it on the kitchen table."

John laughed. "Nothing is sterile," he said.

"We must get you to the doctor!" she exclaimed. "I don't trust myself to take care of you. I don't even know any more whether I love you or not. I don't trust myself in anything."

26

He smiled. "You love me," he said "Go on with the dinner." "Do I?" demanded Martha, looking at him eagerly and hopefully. He nodded. Suddenly she began to laugh. "What a ridiculous question!" she said, in her normal, light, clear voice. "How absurd. I sound completely mad. Am I?" "Have another drink," John replied. "I don't think we *should*," said Martha, beginning to slice the onion. He poured a second drink for himself. "Well, half," she said, when he held the bottle over her glass.

She jumped up to turn the chicken in the pan, returned to her seat, and started chopping the onion and the herbs with determination, resolved to be matter-of-fact and cheerful—the way John liked her. "Did I ever tell you," she began, smiling faintly, "about the Young's Assumption Day party? It's the climax of the social season. All the New Leeds irregulars are there with their service stripes and wound badges. It's like a veterans' convention. It happens every year, and every year the doctor is busy from midnight to dawn with splints and bandages. The drugstore lays in an extra stock of Covermark. The ambulance driver used to say that he slept with his clothes on that night. Even the animals get hurt. Sandy Gray threw a knife at Ellen one time and hit their French poodle. There was a big scandal in the town because the new doctor wouldn't sew up the dog's wound. The Grays were furious; the old doctor always treated dogs." "Did the dog die?" sharply interposed John. "No," said Martha. "Of course not. Nobody dies. Hardly ever. That's it; they just get crippled." "It seems to *me*," observed John, "that you're all wrong about the death principle you keep harping on. The inhabitants, from your own account, seem to bear a charmed life." He set his lips somewhat primly, as though he had scored a telling point. Martha ignored the bite in the word "harp-

27

ing." "It could be," she mused, looking up at him with wondering eyes. "Yes, of course, it could be. But you could read it the other way, too. They could be dead already. You can't kill a ghost, you know." She reflected. "That's exactly what I feel like," she confided, elated by the discovery. "A *revenante*. One who comes back." To emphasize the point, she brought the knife down hard on the onion, which slipped from her grasp; her left forefinger slowly began to bleed.

They stared at each other incredulously. "We're just like the others," whispered Martha. They both began to laugh, in loud, resonant peals. The whole house seemed to laugh; the pans rattled on the kitchen walls. "Sh-h-h," said Martha. "Somebody might hear." Though there was nobody for miles about, John modulated his amusement. "Who?" he muttered. "Why, the Fates," said Martha, with a sort of wild gaiety. "They can hear that we're laughing at them. "I thought," retorted John, "that we were laughing at ourselves." "It's the same thing," pointed out Martha. "You're not supposed to laugh at a joke life is playing on you."

She held up her dripping finger ruefully, like an admonishment. "We're just like the others," she repeated. " 'He hath put down the mighty from their seats.' " John nodded. For the first time, he let himself yield to Martha's sibylline wisdom. She was right, he said darkly to himself: they should never have come back here. And at once he felt pity for her, as for any doomed, fluttering creature; he thought of the bird that had been caught last week in the chimney. "Come here," he ordered. He took a gauze pad from its envelope and wrapped it around her finger. "Poor mouse," he said tenderly. "Poor, frightened, jumpy mouse." He put an arm about her as she stood leaning against him. "Poor John," she replied. They smiled sadly at each other; the air was cleansed of reproaches. "So where do we go from here?" he muttered, rhetorically, tightening his arm about her waist.

But Martha had made up her mind. "To the doctor, of course," she said lightly, whirling out of his embrace. She threw the chopped vegetables into the pan with the chicken, poured in some white wine, turned the stove on low, and went into the next room to telephone. "The doctor will wait for us," she reported, coming back. John did not protest. He had decided to trust her. Her own cut was not serious, but it was a warning that his must be attended to; this was Martha's logic. "We'll have liquor on our breath," he said mildly. Martha shrugged. "And people will say we've been fighting," she added. "Don't you care?" inquired John, as he rose and let her put his coat around his shoulders. "No," she said. "After all, it's true—in a way."

They went out into the starry night.

She was happy, he saw, as she always was when she had come to a decision. In despair, Martha found hope. The notion that they were just like the others had lifted her spirits. She did not really believe it, he suddenly perceived. More than ever now, she felt that they were different. She was a little tipsy and she stumbled. "Don't fall into the herb box," she cautioned, with a giggle. John took her arm firmly in his.

TWO

JANE and Warren Coe had asked the Miles Murphys over from Digby for the day. Everybody in New Leeds had been counting on Jane to do it; the community wanted to know how Miles Murphy was taking his second wife's return. "Why, it's simple as pie," Jane had been scoffing, cheerfully, all summer long. "I'll just ask them down. They won't see anything strange in it. We *always* ask them down in October, to go for a walk or something. Don't we, Warren?" "Nearly always," emended Warren, who was a very conscientious person. "Why, if we *don't* ask them this year," yawned Jane, through September, "Miles will be hurt. Miles is awfully touchy. He'll think it's because of Martha."

Nevertheless, when the appointed day came, both the Coes felt uneasy. They were afraid Martha would find out, and though, of course, it was not Martha's business whom they asked where, they now wished they had told her. The most horrible contingency had presented itself to Warren, a poor sleeper, during the night: he imagined Martha and John, out for a walk on the beach, surprising him and Jane with the Murphys. "Wouldn't that be awful?" agreed Jane, in a solemn whisper, when he confided this fear to her at breakfast. She clapped her hand to her cheek and dropped her big, undershot jaw, staring at Warren over the toaster. But secretly she was excited by the prospect; her schoolgirlish heart throbbed to adventure. She liked the plot to thicken, so long as she and Warren could figure in it as innocent spectators. "How could I *know?*" she already heard herself lamenting, her irrepressible giggle starting to make its way up, like a bubble, from her solar plexus. Just the same, she was nervous. She let Warren have his way about the choice of picnic site: even though the cove was tame, compared to walking out on the breakwater, it was safe because Martha hated it. Both Martha and Miles Murphy could be dangerous enemies, she said thoughtfully.

The Coes had no enemies. They were the best-liked couple in New Leeds. Jane was a big, tawny, ruminative girl, now thirty-eight, who played the oboe and the bagpipes. She had a fresh, orangey, milkmaid's complexion and round, curious blue eyes that kept rolling in their sockets; she liked to sit crosslegged and always looked as if she were still wearing a middy blouse and bloomers. Her maternal grandfather, a German chemist, had invented a children's laxative, and her grandfather on the other side, also German, had done very well in the sheet-music business. Unlike the other New Leedsians, she had never had to worry about money. Though you could not tell it from the way they lived, she was said to have a capital of more than half a million very shrewdly invested by her mother's man of business. Besides this, Warren had a tiny income that had been left him by his father's bachelor brother, who was something in shipping in New Orleans: Jane had a multitude of cousins but Warren's family, on both sides, was dying out; his father had died young, and his mother was an invalid.

Warren was an only child. He was now fifty, but you would never guess it. He had an eager, boyish face, rather like a bird's, with a thin, beaked nose and bright spots of color, high in either cheek. He had fair, thin hair, which Jane always cut for him, using professional clippers, so that he had the mazed look of a person just out of a barber's chair. His frame was slight and thin-chested. He smiled a great deal, happily, and had a habit of raising himself on the balls of his small feet, as if he were trying to see over the heads of a crowd. This alert, expectant air was always with him. He seldom sat down, for before he came to New Leeds he had taught for nearly twenty years at a school of design and had spent his days and nights moving about from easel to easel, looking over shoulders. He was a very excitable, forward-gazing person, very moralistic and high-principled; every moment was an adventure to him. Warren loved his relationship with Jane; they told each other all their thoughts, exclaiming over the differences. Jane was indolent; he was full of ginger. Jane was a bit unscrupulous; he was an idealist. Jane was equable; he was easily cast down. But they shared an appetite for life that woke them every morning, greedy for the new day, to be divided, fairly, between them, like a big fresh apple.

This greed for experience was their innocent vice. They did not smoke, except for Jane's occasional denicotinized cigarette; they drank in extreme moderation, often from the same glass: "I'll just take some of Jane's," Warren usually proffered, partly because he hated to waste anything and partly for the fun of sharing. They never touched real coffee. When they were alone, they ate whatever health food Jane had been reading about —yogurt, wheat germ, figs, vitamin soups made in the blender with nine raw vegetables. Yet they were not cranks; like good children, they cleaned their plates when they were out to dinner and came back for seconds. They appreciated fine cooking but thought it unfair to Jane to keep her standing over a hot stove when nature outdoors was so beautiful. They loved long walks, and Warren was a systematic nudist, though he always took pains not to give offense to the neighbors; it shocked him to see some of his friends stripping on the beach, in plain view of an old lady who sat in her second-story window with field glasses.

They seemed utterly different from the other New Leeds people—a thing Jane often pondered on, aloud, in a dreamy reverie, studying her bare toes in her Mexican thong sandals and half-wondering whether she was getting a callous. You would never have thought, she said, that she and Warren would fit in; they were too normal. And yet they were crazy about it; and in ten years' residence—they had come during the war when Jane had been certain the small city they lived in would be bombed—they had become an indispensable fixture. They were the social center of New Leeds; they supposed it was just because they were so normal. They served as a sort of switchboard that plugged in on the various crisscrossed lines. "We're just a public utility," said Warren with his mild, happy smile. In all the years they had been here, they had never had a fight with anybody, not even with Miles Murphy, who had fought with nearly the whole town at the time of his divorce from Martha. They had managed to keep his friendship while refusing to take sides. "I have a lot of respect for Miles," Warren still reiterated, after seven years; he was not afraid to say it to Martha. As he explained to her when he was painting her portrait last month, he liked her because he could say to her the things he really thought. Loyalty to a side, he said, had been instilled in him by his southern mother, but he now thought you had to be loyal to all sides, to the truth *as you saw it,* which, when you came down to it, meant being loyal to yourself. Cleaning his brushes, he watched Martha anxiously to see if she followed his thought. He had a way, he knew, of making things that were simple, darn it, to other people very complex to himself, but Martha always listened, with her absent, encouraging nod. "Probably it's an old idea to you," he said apologetically, and Martha smiled. She never tried to deceive him. "I *value* that quality!" he always cried when her candid tongue was aspersed.

What he valued in Miles was something different— Miles's intellectual equipment. Sitting on the beach, in the noonday sun, he felt thrilled, as always, by Miles's mind. The man was not attractive physically. He was a fat, freckled fellow with a big frame, a reddish crest of curly hair, and small, pale-green eyes, like grapes about to burst. His large face, with its long plump crooked nose, was flushed from the efforts of his digestive tract: lobster shells and the bones of two fried chickens lay piled up, waiting to be buried; two empty Moselle bottles, from Jane's father's cellar, lay on their sides in the sand. As usual, after eating and drinking, Miles was breathing heavily, like a spent athlete: he gave the impression of virtuous fatigue even when he had been overindulging. But he had a brilliant mind, and beside him Warren felt very humble. It was Warren's great sorrow that he had gone straight from a military academy into art school; he had missed the experience of college. Miles had been educated by the Jesuits at Fordham, and from there he had gone on to Heidelberg and the Sorbonne and the London School of Economics. Later on, for a brief time, he had studied with Jung at Zurich. There was scarcely anything Warren could think of that Miles had not done; he had been a successful playwright, with a hit show, about the Jesuit fathers, running on Broadway when he was only twenty-three, a boxer, practically professional, who used to work out with Hemingway, a psychologist, a lay analyst, a writer of adventure stories, a practicing mystic, a magazine editor. He was on that kick, as he called it, when he met Martha, who was just a girl graduate at the time. He was the type, said Jane, that was very attractive to women; he had had three wives and innumerable mistresses and a couple of illegitimate children, besides the present baby and the little boy who had died. And of course, he was a heavy drinker, which proved, according to Martha, that he really cared nothing about women. All heavy drinkers, she had insisted, were sexless underneath—a remark that had been bothering Warren for years. Warren had a very good memory, which he had never thought of as a handicap or an anti-social trait before he came to New Leeds. He used to store up the things his friends said and come back later, if need be, for clarification, after he had turned them over in his own mind. But here, when he reminded people of something they had said five years before, they either did not remember having said it or announced, lightly, that they had changed their opinion. This vagueness and instability put Warren in a dreadful state; he felt as if he held a ring of keys to fascinating cabinets that had had their locks changed privily by some malicious prankster. Looking at Miles now, for instance, brooding and silent, with his scarred chin sunk onto his chest, smoking a cigarette that his new wife had lit and put between his lips, Warren felt as if he might possibly have the key to him in that long-ago observation of Martha's. But when he had recalled it to her, timidly, in another connection (for he did not see quite how it worked, Freudianly), Martha had made a grimace and said, with a rueful glance at John, "Oh dear, did I say *that?*"

Warren hungered for serious conversation, which was one of the reasons he had recently turned from nature to portraiture; he liked to draw the sitter out. On other occasions, he was constantly being disappointed, though New Leeds was full of people who had had interesting lives. "I'd like to get your point of view," he would say, finally, at a cocktail party, to the person he had been waiting patiently to query, but the person, like as not, was tipsy by the time Warren got to him or else only wanted to gossip. Watching Miles today, Warren had the premonition that he was going to be disappointed again. Last year, when the Murphys had come down, Miles had been very interesting; he had advised Warren to read Nietzsche, and Warren had been looking forward to a renewal of the discussion. He had several points he wanted to make; he had underlined passages in the Modern Library *Zarathustra* that seemed to contradict some things Miles had said about Nietzsche's thought. But Miles, when he had arrived this noon, had promptly turned the subject aside. "The translations are all terrible," he said briskly. "You can't understand Nietzsche if you don't read him in German." Warren, for a second, had been mad as a hornet; a few years ago, the same thing had happened with Plato. A point had come up, and Miles had said, "Read the *Republic*," and when Warren had done it and called up Miles in New York, all primed on the cave myth, Miles had told him that you couldn't understand Plato except in the original. Reminded of his earlier admonition, he had said, "I don't remember it. I must have been drunk."

Still, Warren had not yet given up hope of the afternoon. It all depended on chance. Miles, as Jane said, was a moody soul. It was the mixture of blood in him; he was half Irish and half German. Miles himself said it was the devil of a combination; when he was in black spirits, he talked about himself as a mongrel and blamed his parents for marrying. That was his Irish mood. On his German side, he was more poetic and visionary. He had a theory that the Germans and the Irish were all the same mystic people—Celts, and he used Jane's tawny hair to prove it. He got his own red hair, he told them, from his mother's family. He had an affinity with Jane; he liked to get her to talk about her German ancestors. That was why she always brought up the Moselle from her father's cellar for him. Warren was interested in Jane's ancestors too; the family's scientific interests had opened his eyes to a whole new side of life and changed the direction of his painting. But he always felt a little disturbed when Miles got going on Friedrich Barbarossa —it made him think of the Nazis. In another mood, however, Miles would give the Germans what-for and say their trouble was they had never been Christianized properly, except the people in the Rhineland, where Jane's family came from.

Like all the outstanding people Warren had ever known, Miles was inconsistent. Today he might suddenly stand up and shake himself and tell his wife they were going home. Or he might come to the studio, where *Zarathustra* was laid out, and talk for the rest of the day. And the wife and baby would have to wait till he was ready to go, even if it was the middle of the night. One night, last winter in New York, the Coes had heard, the baby had nearly been smothered under the overcoats on a bed at a wild party. Miles had a theory about children; he thought you should treat them rough until they reached the age of reason, which he set at eight or nine, the year the child was able to learn its catechism and prepare for its first communion. This theory, Warren admitted, made him see red. And Miles meant it furthermore; he was not just talking through his hat. For a hard-boiled unbeliever, Miles had a strange admiration for the rules and observances of the church; Mother Church, he said, was a great little psychologist—look at the confessional. And he thought Spare the Rod was sound psychology too, *up* to the age of reason.

The baby, at present, was lying on a blanket, sucking

a chicken wing. Helen Murphy had carried him down the beach on her back, in a sort of fishnet bag that Miles had designed for her. Miles did not believe in sitters, and they had never been able to keep a servant—not for lack of money, for Helen had plenty, but because of Miles's tempers and drinking habits. Warren sat looking at the baby; he loved children and he and Jane were childless. The two women were talking in low voices; Miles had sunk into abstraction. Warren undid the white handkerchief he wore around his head, like a housemaid's dust cap, to protect his brain from the sun. He leaned over to the baby and, smiling, began to wiggle his ears. He knew Miles was watching him, sardonically, from narrowed, slightly bloodshot eyes, but in such matters as these Warren was a fearless traditionalist. The baby, to his joy, smiled back. At this moment, Jane chose to mention the Sinnotts. Warren's heart sank; he slumped into the sand. He felt, as he said later, about as big as a minute. Jane's curiosity, brimming out of her big round eyes, gave the show away. He was cross as the dickens. He and Jane had compacted not to mention Martha unless Miles or Helen did it first, but when it came to gossip Jane was weak and disloyal, like a bad little girl. She was now looking rather shamefaced, her eyes cast down and a tentative grin twitching her wide red mouth; later she would say that Miles would surely have thought it funny if she had *not* mentioned Martha.

Miles sat up, chewing on a spear of beach grass. "How are they getting along?" he inquired, with evident interest. Warren felt terrifically relieved to find that he had been wrong, as usual. There was a slight pause; the Coes eyed each other. "You haven't seen her?" said Jane, looking at Miles curiously. Miles shook his head. "I've *never* seen her," mused Helen. "Of course, I feel I know her from what Miles has said." She said this in a simple, deferential tone that made a great impression on Warren. This tall placid brunette girl simply worshipped Miles, which was what Miles had always needed. Everything about him, apparently, was sacred to her, including his ex-wives; she sounded almost as if Martha were a holy relic of Miles's past, like his first baby shoes. Warren was amazed; he felt he was getting to know Helen finally. "That's funny," he said, sliding over to her, brightly, with his winning smile. "That you haven't seen her, I mean. You'd think you would have run into each other at the Stop and Shop or the Arena Theater or meeting the train or something. It's almost like a reverse coincidence. Mathematically—wouldn't you say, Miles? —the chances would be all the other way. I mean if Helen and Martha missed each other umpteen times . . . ?" His high thin voice halted as he saw that Miles was not interested in a statistical discussion.

"She's changed," said Jane, thoughtfully. "How, Jane?" said Helen, with her warm, interested smile. Despite the fact that she and Miles had been married two years now, she still had a slight, hovering air of ingratiation, as if she were Miles's secretary; she had a long, straight figure and buxom legs, which she wound around each other unobtrusively; she carried her cropped head a little to one side, and kept her lips slightly parted. "Well," said Jane. "More hectic for one thing. Wouldn't you say so, Warren? They laugh a lot at parties. They're both quite witty, you know, and that rather scares people in New Leeds." Miles nodded, with an air of acumen; he had a funny way of listening, not to the things you said, but to something behind them; you could feel him click like an adding machine when a congenial thought was deposited. "She isn't *nearly* as popular as she used to be," continued Jane, candidly, avoiding Warren's eye. "People say they're too critical."

"Ah," said Miles. There was a silence. "They *seem* very much in love," volunteered Jane, slowly. *"Seem!"* reproachfully cried Warren. "You oughtn't to say that, Jane. Of course, they're in love. If they aren't, who is?" Jane giggled. "Warren is awfully loyal," she said to Miles. "Why, that makes me hot under the collar," protested Warren, sitting up and moving his bare thin neck, as if a real collar were confining it. "I'm not loyal. I'm just going by what I see. How would you feel, Jane, if somebody said, 'The Coes *seem* very much in love'? Why, I'd fight the person that said that. Don't you agree with me, Miles? Why, that was an *awful* remark, darling." "They seem to be in love—that's all I said," returned Jane, with composure. "Well, they are," said Warren, fiercely subsiding. He retied the handkerchief carefully round his head. The Murphys laughed.

"After all, Warren," suggested Jane. "There was that story. Last week." Warren's bright face sobered; the spots of color paled; he nodded glumly. The Murphys were all ears. "Should I tell it, Warren?" asked Jane. "Might as well," he answered, folding his arms, with a gloomy, stoical mien and bowing his kerchiefed head. "Excuse me, dear," he added. "Well," said Jane, "the story is they've been fighting. They came to the doctor all cut up and smelling of alcohol. They *claimed* they fell through a window." "All cut up, Jane?" gently inquired Helen. "Well," said Jane. "I haven't actually *seen* them." *"I* have," said Warren. "I met them this morning. I forgot to tell you, Jane. It was just their hands." "But isn't that *peculiar?"* said Helen. "Peculiar is right," said Warren emphatically; he hated to have his close friends involve themselves in a scandal, even if it was just from thoughtlessness—it spoiled his image of them. "Mind you," he added, pointing his finger suddenly at Miles, "I don't think this proves they've been fighting. But I can't see how they both broke a window unless they were spifflicated." "That's the strange part," continued Jane. "That's why everybody's discussing it. They hardly drink at all. Much less than they used to. At least, when they're out in public. Probably they've become secret drinkers." She waggled her jaw. "They say that's very common with romantic couples like that. They move to the country and pull the shades and start drinking and the next thing you know there's a suicide pact." "Have you ever heard of that, Miles?" demanded Warren, his eager falsetto breaking in on Jane's deep, comfortable tones. "Martha says it's quite frequent."

"*Martha* says?" exclaimed Miles. His large frame jerked upward and sideward, as if somebody had stuck him in the ribs. "You mean she talks about it?" "Not about *herself*," qualified Jane. "About other people. There was a case in the papers the other day, people we used to know, and that's how she explained it." "Very interesting," said Miles, nudging Helen's behind with his perforated shoe. "How do you mean?" said Jane. Miles stroked his chin. "Martha is a very sick girl," he said. The Coes glanced at each other, surreptitiously. "I'll give you two examples," said Miles, after a pause. "You remember the fire we had?" The Coes nodded. "Well, she talked about the fire incessantly *before* it happened. She was convinced the house was going to burn down because of some private guilt of her own. And then, by God, it did." "You don't mean you think she started it?" cried Jane. Miles shrugged. "I've been studying some poltergeist cases recently and I recognized the pattern. I don't know how I missed it before. She was the first one up that night and normally she sleeps like a log. She'd rescued the boy before I knew what was what. The boy was asleep too. Nobody smelled smoke but Martha, and she got herself and the boy completely dressed before she called the fire department." "Good Lord," said Jane. "Yes," said Miles. "Notice—she didn't want to hurt anybody. That's typical of these cases. It's an attention-drawing mechanism, primarily." "She felt overshadowed by Miles," elucidated Helen. "But she was quite beside herself," said Miles, "when the insurance people came down to investigate. Wanted to put the blame on some poor devil of a workman who'd done the wiring. Never gave a thought to the fact that he'd be prosecuted if the insurance people believed her. She said it was her fault, really, that she'd instructed him to commit a violation—all poppycock. It was her neurotic way of confessing the truth, of saying, in symbolic language, that the fire *was* her fault; *she* was the firebug. And you know, by God, I remembered something she told me once—that when she was a little girl she used to put her younger brother up to setting fires; he'd get the blame and she'd watch the blaze. The brother never knew it; she was clever, the way she instigated him; he thought all through his boyhood that he was the pyromaniac."

"Whew!" said Warren, running his hand across his brow. He glanced at Jane wonderingly: did she credit this story? He would have liked to argue one or two points in it with Miles, but he hated to let Helen think he disbelieved her husband. His heart, as he told Jane, sank to his boots. The blue day was blackened for him; he knew he would not sleep for thinking of this tale. Either way he looked at it, it was horrible, horrible for Martha, if true, horrible for Miles, if false. And horrible for him and Jane to be listening to it, crouched around Miles on a lovely fall afternoon. "Understand," said Miles. "I don't hold it against her. All that's in the past. I think now I mishandled her. I didn't allow for the fact that she was a very frightened kid when I married her. Helen

42

thinks so too." His wife bobbed her head in quick, sympathetic agreement. "I thought," said Miles, "I could teach her self-knowledge. But when she found out I was on to her, she flew the coop." He laughed. Warren felt deeply shocked. "And she took her revenge. I don't blame her. She has the modern girl's vindictive mania for publicity. She could have left me any time in broad daylight, without any fanfare. But she had to do it in a nightgown, at three o'clock in the morning." Warren caught his breath; this was not the way Miles had told the story before.

Warren and Jane too—he could tell from the look in her eyes—remembered perfectly well the morning Miles had come out to their house in a taxi, his red beard unshaven, fumes of liquor still on his breath, looking for Martha and crying. According to the story he told then he had locked Martha out of the house in her nightgown, in a fit of drunken humor, and gone up to bed fully expecting her to come back in the kitchen door, which was open—that sort of thing was always happening in New Leeds, he had insisted, and the wives did not take it seriously. Martha's story, which Jane and Warren had always believed, was that Miles had waked her up, kicked her out of bed, and pushed her step by step down the stairs and out the front door and ordered her not to come back—John Sinnott had seen the bruises, and the little boy, Barrett, according to the cleaning woman, had been watching over the banister.

"It was another put-up job," said Miles, cool as a cucumber. "*I* was little brother this time. She got the idea it would be nice for me to lock her out, and she set me on to do it. She woke me up from a sound sleep and told me she was in love with Sinnott and dared me to put her out of the house. *I* was the patsy."

"I can *understand,*" finally said Jane, after a very long

silence, "that she provoked you, Miles. But did she actually tell you, in so many words, to lock her out of the house? It doesn't sound like Martha." Warren nodded eagerly. "No question about it," said Miles. "It was the case of her brother all over again, don't you see?" explained Helen. "She put the idea in Miles's head." Warren sighed. He thought Miles was lying, and this depressed him terribly; it meant Miles was a person he could no longer talk to honestly. At the same time, he pitied Miles; he supposed Miles half-believed the things he was saying, though even a rather dumb soul, like himself, could see plumb through them and realize that all that about having forgiven Martha was a lot of hooey. Warren could not imagine that if he and Jane should ever separate—even if it were Jane's fault—he would ever say such awful things about her.

And he guessed that was a limitation, in a way; he lacked the bravado to tell such a big lie. He was old-fashioned. He had liberated himself in his painting, and he and Jane had engaged in some pretty daring experiments in bed, but socially he was no pioneer. Probably, at bottom, he was as big a scoundrel as Miles; in his heart, perhaps he really wanted to beat up women and brag and lie and was just the prisoner of his inhibitions. The psychoanalyst had shown him, five summers ago, that he was full of unreleased aggressions; the cramp he had developed in his right hand cleared up like magic when the analyst proved to him that it was not a painting block but plain muscular tension; the Coes had been having a little boundary dispute with their neighbor, and what Warren really wanted, underneath, it turned out, was to punch the fellow in the jaw. The analyst had opened his eyes to a lot of things; all moral values, to the the analyst, were just rationalizations: ego massage. Warren's own values came from an identification with

44

his mother and from being the class underdog in a sadistic military school, where they used to tear up his water colors and make him do dirty drawings. Any values he had learned that way were probably subjective and specious; no doubt he was just a bottled-up bully who overcompensated in the other direction. And yet you had to live with your values, Warren stuck to that, though he had been awfully interested to get the analyst's point of view. Your rationalizations, darn it, were part of you too. Even if he knew he was a pharisee, he still leapt up when a woman came into the room. And it still made his blood boil to hear Miles spin a theory at Martha's expense, though of course he was just as much of a hypocrite himself to sit there and smile when he wanted to kill the guy. Probably a worse hypocrite, as Jane would be able to tell him, when they talked it over together: the reason he was so hopping mad was probably a selfish one. He did not want to admit that Martha could be dishonest because he *needed* her honesty: she was the only person in New Leeds, outside of Jane, who understood what he was doing in his painting.

"Warren did her portrait last month," Jane was saying. "Oh, I should love to see it," murmured Helen. "Shall we go and look at it, Miles?" Miles made a sound of consent and heaved himself up from the sand. "Is she still so lovely?" Helen asked, arranging the baby in the bag. Warren watched her wanly, almost forgetting to help. She was bound to be disappointed in the portrait— people always were. They looked at his paintings and said, "Oh," in a surprised tone; when he explained the theory behind them, they listened but kept glancing uneasily back at the canvases, as if they could not find the connection. For a moment he suspected Helen of insincerity: did she really want to see the painting or was she only interested in getting Miles moving? The afternoon wind had risen and the little cove was full of wavelets. Miles, warmly dressed in wool muffler, wool shirt, and tweed jacket, might never give a thought to the fact that the baby could take cold. If it had been Martha, Warren reflected, she would have *told* him they had to leave on account of the baby and Miles would have said, "Nonsense," and they would have had a fight. But Helen, the Coes agreed, was a better manager; she tried to lead Miles without his knowing it, but she never argued, they noticed. If he said, "Nonsense," she said, "Yes, dear," as if she honestly welcomed the correction, even when Miles was in the wrong. Warren sometimes wondered whether this was altogether good for Miles; he would hate it, himself, if Jane tried it.

Still, he admired Helen for her selfless devotion, and he undertook to answer her question seriously, as they walked along the beach, back to the house. Helen had the baby; he had the knapsack with the lunch things. Miles and Jane brought up the rear, walking slowly: Jane was looking for driftwood. "Jane could tell you better," he said. "I look at her as a painter. She has a lot of animation in her face. An academic painter, with late baroque light effects, could make her very arresting. That's the way I would have done her in my early phase: a smoldering little saint with fair hair and white skin and black eyes. Some people might call that beauty. But when you study her you see that her face is asymmetrical. One profile's classic; the other's irregular. The eye is narrower and longer; the nose has a little bump; the mouth twists. Personally, I find that profile a lot more interesting. You can see her medical history in it, for instance. She must have had adenoids as a kid and she's astigmatic and she learned to eat on one side of her mouth when she had a tooth out in her early twenties.

The layman doesn't notice these things." He stooped to pick up a sand dollar, examined it, and put it in the pocket of his canvas trousers. "In the old days," he continued, with a sideways glance at Helen, "they used to think they could tell a witch if the profiles didn't match. Jane would have been burned. That's what got me started noticing. One side of Jane's face is reflective; she even has a tiny cast in that eye, and there's a funny droop to the mouth. The other is active and practical. It's awfully interesting stuff when you get onto it. Women, I find, are more two-faced than men, which is what the human race has always thought anyway." Helen smiled vaguely. Her own parts were rather curiously assembled —small, round head, small ears, large legs, large, full long neck—though she was a pleasant-looking woman, taken as a whole. "John Sinnott," added Warren, "has the most regular features I've ever seen. His profiles exactly match, which is frightfully rare. And the features are small too, cameo-cut, though he's a tall man. It's a French Renaissance face. Probably Norman blood." "You're interested in ancestry?" said Helen. "Oh, terrifically," said Warren. "I suppose it's the southern side of me. Ever since I started these new portraits, I've been studying anthropological types. Jane took her major in anthropology. We've been looking up some of the old books on phrenology too—wonderful stuff." He sighed. "Those old boys knew a lot that we moderns have forgotten. Have you ever gone into phrenology?" Helen shook her head. "Try it some time," advised Warren, over his shoulder, as he began to scale the sand cliff, holding out his left hand for Helen after he had got a foothold. "Of course, I know you're busy," he added apologetically, pulling her upward, "with the baby and the house. But I'd love to know what you and Miles thought of it. I have some heads and charts in the studio;

47

I'll show you, if you'd like." And he hurried ahead, bending back the briars to make way for Helen and the baby.

The Coes lived in a modern house that had been designed for them by a cousin of Jane's. It stood on a bluff, overlooking the open ocean; the Coes now wished they had built in a hollow, the way the old settlers had, for the situation was very windswept, and nothing but dune grass and dusty miller and wild beach peas could get a footing in the whirling, shifting sand. In their early years, they had tried to keep a goat there; Jane had read that goat's milk was terribly good for you and they were going to write to the Trappists for their receipt for cheese. But the goat was not happy; the reindeer moss, Jane concluded, was bad for it, and they had had to give the poor animal away, before she perished, to an eccentric old lady, one of the local characters, who was a zoophile and ran a sort of pound for all the discarded animals of the neighborhood, chiefly the half-wild cats the summer people abandoned. Yet the windy, barren, desolate setting had, it turned out, one unexpected advantage. Beaten by the storms, the house had weathered, so that it now seemed to belong to the landscape. The squat rectangular building, with futuristic hardware, painted gray originally and topped by a roped-off sundeck, now looked like an old-fashioned wooden icebox that had been wintering for generations on a New Leeds back porch. The Coes liked this effect and assigned credit to themselves for not having fought Nature. Everything fitted in, the worn tarpaulin covering the sundeck, the goat's post—even the cylindrical bottled-gas tanks by the kitchen door, which looked so unsightly against a traditional house—harmonized with the main structure and with the sand heaped around it and the patches of reindeer moss and the gray sea birds circling above.

Warren's studio, into which he now showed the guests, stood fifty feet away from the main house. It had a two-story window with north light, which at present was obscured by three army blankets tacked up to keep out the cold. There were cushioned benches around the walls, lamps, a station-stove, and bookcases put together with bricks and planks. Warren was a very tidy man, and the corner in which he painted—pinning back the blankets—was impeccably neat; an oblong of floor around his easel had been swept with a hearthbroom he kept for the purpose. But the rest of the large room was a dusty, cobwebby jumble; he never heeded it unless they had company, but then he felt a quick embarrassment, seeing the shamble through their eyes: Jane's mother's piano, which they never used, blocking a side window; the pair of rusty English bicycles propped against the wall; the ping-pong table, covered with a stained sheet of canvas; the broken washing machine; the deep-freeze that had proved impractical because the electricity was so uncertain during the stormy season; the electric doughnut-maker and the combination waffle iron and sandwich grill, the roto-broiler, the mixmaster, the special pizza machine—all the gadgets sent Jane by her gadget-minded family perishing here as in a boneyard; the sun-faded draperies from the big living-room window; the badminton set. It was a comic spectacle, Warren ineluctably knew; Miles could hardly keep from guffawing, and he did not blame him. Smiling apologetically, he got out the whisk broom and began to brush off the cushioned benches so they could put the sneezing baby down; he used the feather duster on the piano. Removing his kerchief, flushing, he explained for the hundredth time that a modern house did not have much storage space. "Damn fool," he said, vehemently, "pardon my French, I ought to have had the sense to build a two-story garage." He knew the Murphys were thinking that it was Jane's fault and he hated them for thinking it; at the same time, he mildly and politely desired to share their mirth. Miles was prowling about the room, studying the derelict objects with the air of a scientific connoisseur. "What, for God's sake, is this, Warren?" he demanded, pointing to the infra-red broiler that Jane had got last Christmas, when they were trying a high-protein diet. Warren explained how it worked or, rather, he gamely joked, how it *had* worked. Jane was in the house, getting a tray of drinks, and it gave him a queer feeling to be jesting so boldly without her, almost like an escapade.

"Why, it's a regular cemetery of their hobbies," Miles expatiated to Helen. Warren gently smiled. "That's what John Sinnott told me," he agreed. "He says I should do a painting, 'The Artist in His Studio.' Only he thinks I should call it, 'The American Artist in His Studio.'" "Ah," said Miles, nodding. All at once, his belly began to heave. "That's good," he cried, slapping his thigh. "Damn good!" He shook his handkerchief open and wiped the tears from his eyes. Dust flew. Warren waited courteously till the temblor of mirth had subsided. Thanks to Martha's explanation, he was able to see what John and Miles saw: a satiric canvas, after Titian, in which he himself, the artist, a tiny dusty figure, was pushed into one corner, while his wife's scientific gadgets and games and decorative fads monstrously took over the foreground. But to him, as he had tried to make clear to Martha, the objects in the room were not ridiculous, though he could see how in the aggregate they might appear so, to an outsider. To him, they evoked exciting memories, of midnight feasts shared with Jane, bicycle trips, skating on winter ponds, ping-pong rallies, doughnuts and cider; the piano made him think of Jane's mother, and the deep-freeze recalled the hurricane two years ago when the electricity had been off three days and the road blocked, and they had lost nine gallons of assorted ice creams, which he and Jane had poured into buckets and taken on foot to the goat-lady. And it was not Jane's fault that the appliances broke down; it was partly the climate—the sea air was bad for machines. She was not a good housekeeper, but, darn it, he admired her for that. All the women in her family had been fanatic housekeepers, and Jane had had the gumption to rebel. Martha had shrieked when Jane admitted that Warren had not had an ironed shirt in three years, but if he did not mind, why should Martha object? He would rather have Jane's companionship than a stiff shirt any day. So he always said, and what was more he *meant* it. In his young days, he had been quite a dandy: he had carried a stick and yellow gloves and had his clothes made by a Turkish tailor. But those days were over. He had let Jane give his things away to a refugee without batting an eye. You could not dress like a stuffed shirt in New Leeds unless you were a dodo. It was John Sinnott, actually, that New Leeds chuckled over, when he came to parties in a dark business suit and white shirt. And Warren did not go to the city often enough any more to make it worth while to own a city suit. For those rare occasions, his gray corduroy, with a necktie, looked perfectly all right, especially if Jane touched up the shirt collar for him. In fact, as Jane told him, he looked much more the artist in that soft material.

The only thing that gave him anxiety was the thought of his mother's funeral—what would he wear? She was past seventy-five now, living in a boardinghouse in Savannah; her sister wrote that she was getting very frail. He was resigned to the prospect of her dying, except for that one thing—the suit to follow her to her grave in; he still had his bowler hat, which Jane had overlooked.

This absurd worry preyed on his mind sometimes during the night, even though he assured himself that when the fatal telegram came, Jane would think of something. She was awfully resourceful.

He knew some people thought he was dominated by Jane. Miles, for instance, this minute, was saying to him in a grave undertone: "If it was my wife, Warren, she'd clean this place up." Miles, of course, thought only about his own comfort; he ate and drank like an Elizabethan, dressed in a florid style, with loud shirts and tweeds and silk socks, never considering for a minute that it was a human being who waited on him and catered to him and kept his things in order, laying out on a silent valet—Jane had seen it—everything he was going to wear, right down to the handkerchief and the necktie, while she had the baby and all the housework to think of. There was a sound at the door, and Warren hurried to open it. Wrapped in a shawl, Jane stood there with a tray of ice and bottles and glasses. "Let me help you, dear," smiled Warren, taking the tray from her and urging her into the warm room. He noticed that she had forgotten the fizzy water and he skipped out to the house to get it, before she could realize and try to go instead. And he was glad to do a little service like that to help her, for he knew blamed well that she had a lot to put up with from him; he was a selfish cuss to live with, preoccupied with his painting, abstracted, not dry behind the ears yet, intellectually. For a girl who had grown up in a big family and who could have married anybody she wanted—or a darn sight better anyway—it was not a normal life.

And when Jane had married him he had not been nearly the person he hoped he was now, thanks to her. It tickled him to think of his outgrown self—a conventional, safe little water colorist and pen-and-ink man, doing the usual stiles and cottages and dilapidated mansions and wrought-iron gates and Paris roofs and doorways; he had liked architectural themes and hoped to be a modern Piranesi or Callot. He had had to unlearn all that, bit by bit, like tearing your skin off piecemeal—some job for a man over forty. He could never have done it if Jane and her family had not stood by, financially *and* morally.

He came back into the room quietly, carrying a pitcher of water; they seemed to be out of fizzy. "Oh, Warren," exclaimed Jane, who was putting wood in the stove, "you didn't need to do that. I brought water." And sure enough, to his embarrassment, there *was* water in another pitcher on the tray. He felt like two cents. "We're out of soda," said Jane, with an awkward laugh. "I guess that's what Warren went for." "I'm sorry, dear," said Warren. "I thought you'd forgotten it." "I did," confessed Jane. "I forgot to order it at the store. I *always* forget something." "Never mind, never mind," said Miles, with an air of testy magnanimity. Jane poured the drinks and Warren got ready to show the portrait.

It was a big picture, like all his recent work—six by eleven. He hauled it out, unwrapped the outer canvas, fixed the lights, and then stood back to see what they would say. "Oh," said Helen, after a moment. "Ah," said Miles. "Do you see anything of Martha in it?" queried Warren, looking up at the portrait. He himself saw nothing but Martha, refracted all over the canvas. He had been trying something new, a dispersed, explosive cubism, in dark, smoky colors, in which the sitter's personality-nucleus was blown apart into its component solids. There was a geyser of smoke in the middle representing the moment of fission; he was trying to get time, the fourth dimension, into his painting. "I think I see her nose," Miles said finally, when he had backed up against the farther wall.

53

THREE

MILES was nonplussed by the portrait. It reminded him a little of science fiction and a little of old-fashioned movie music and, most of all, of Jesuit sermons on Hell. It conveyed fury and conflict. It was, he supposed, what you might call program painting. "It represents fission," said Warren. "I'm using that as the theme for this whole series of portraits." Miles made an impatient gesture. Warren had explained the theory behind his painting before; he was trying to express the fourth dimension or the general theory of relativity or something of the kind—Jane's father, a scientist, had put him up to it. This sort of talk did not interest Miles. Theory, in artists, did not matter to him, only results. "By their fruits, ye shall know them," he always said, sententiously. He had first known Warren in his so-called quantum phase, which was succeeded by his galactic phase: Warren seemed to think that progress was mandatory in art and bubbled about advances and setbacks—he had lost three years, he had once confided, when he let Picasso lead him up the garden walk. Most artists talked that way nowadays—perhaps they had always done so; and most of them had a father-figure in the background who supplied the motor-ideas. They were all boy scouts in their corduroy fashion, eager beavers, following the leader, some jackleg critic or straw-boss philosopher.

But the work was something else again. Whatever

nonsense he spouted, Warren was an able draftsman. He had got the hair just right—a fair skein of silk streaming across the canvas. In Miles's desk drawer, at home, among the keepsakes of his previous marriages—a pair of tiny gloves, a ribboned garter, an old packet of fish-skins—there was a tress of Martha's hair, now dulled, that had once shone and rippled like the hair in Warren's picture. And Warren had caught something of Martha's temperament in the blunt tilt of the nose and the tiny, staring eyehole of the nostril. "Why, it's the best thing you've done," Miles suddenly decided. The other three looked at him, wonderingly. Miles read Helen's questioning gaze. "Isn't it rather dark?" she murmured. She meant academic. There were two opinions in New Leeds on the subject of Warren's painting—the one that called it too modern and the one that called it academic. Among the summer crowd, Warren's quest for the fourth dimension was considered rather a joke, a sad joke, because he was a nice man. There was a lot of irony in the position, Miles had often reflected. If Warren had been a carpenter or a plumber, he could have made his marks as a *naif* painter with a scientific "vision," but his art-school training rendered him funny ha-ha to the cognoscenti, among whom Miles did not number himself. In the days when the poor devil used to have exhibitions in the rug-and-craft shop on the village green, everybody turned up, out of friendship for the Coes, and quietly snickered into their sleeve at the sign hand-lettered by Warren—"Prices on Request." He had never sold a canvas in all his years up here, which, Martha used to claim, was a sort of achievement, considering the local taste. He could not even give one away: people protested that they were too big or too dark for a seashore house.

Miles began to pace up and down. His present wife's

55

attitude annoyed him—she was too conventional in her responses. He stopped by the liquor tray and poured himself a fresh drink. He was thinking of Martha. He had always had a weakness for intelligent women, though he knew them to be bad for him, like drink or certain kinds of food. They disagreed with him, in both senses of the word. Now that he was older, he knew enough to leave them alone. He had organized his life sensibly, and the proof was that he was writing again, after fifteen years. But he had bouts of dissatisfaction, when he resented the choice that had been made for him. That was how he felt about it on his glum days, as if an authority had chosen for him, though the authority had been no other than Miles Murphy: he had prescribed for himself, as his own therapist, studying his character structure and deducing from it the qualities he required in a mate. He had given a woman friend his specifications—a girl approaching middle life but not too old for childbearing, not previously married, unencumbered by family, possessing an independent income and an open mind, with a sense of her own dignity, submissive, pleasant-spoken, and moderately pleasing to the eye. And his friend had produced Helen the first crack out of the box.

Helen was all woman, and he was damn lucky to have got her. They did not make them like her any more. Her father was a Greek wholesaler in Chicago, with a big import trade; Helen had stayed home to nurse her mother when the old man died and the older brother married. She had helped run the family business for a time, done her bit for war relief, and studied ceramics at the Art Institute. The family was cultivated; she had an uncle who was a Metropolitan. When the old lady passed on, finally, she was practically alone in the world, except for a raft of suitors—Penelope waiting for Odys-

seus. And she had had the patience to hold out till crafty
old Odysseus came. She was not stupid, though stupid
people thought so, but she had learned how to efface herself, in the European way. For the first time in his life
(his mother had never favored him), he discovered that
he came first. She could take his abrupt dictation and decipher his manuscript notes and hold the dinner till midnight if he did not feel like eating. She could keep the
child quiet in the morning when he had been sleeping a
binge off. When they read Aeschylus together in the evenings, as they were doing this fall, she looked up the
hard words in the dictionary and put them down on a
list for him. She kept the household accounts and never
bothered him about money. If he felt like talking, she
listened and asked intelligent questions. If he was
nervous and morose, she left him alone. She never
turned on the waterworks, like Martha; a little bird
must have told her that he could not stand women's
tears.

She did not stimulate him—that was her only draw-
back. He did not notice this, he found, unless he had
been drinking. Then, in a disgruntled frame of mind,
after he had sent her off to bed, he would open the desk
drawer, stare at Martha's little gloves, and set himself to
recalling her clever remarks. Martha always hated this
habit of his—the desk drawer, she said, and everything it
contained of him. She hated his remembering things she
said. "You turn everything into the past," she would tell
him sharply. And she also used to complain that he remembered her worst *mots,* accidentally-on-purpose.
"That isn't funny," she used to say coldly, when he was
chuckling over one of her satirical strokes. "Please,
Miles, don't quote me." It was all part of her general
pattern of rejection and self-hatred. She could not stand
to hear anything said twice. One habitual phrase of his

used to drive her crazy: "I'm inordinately fond of pickles," "I'm inordinately fond of potatoes." "You're inordinately fond of saying that!" she had cried out once. "I know you like potatoes. Don't dwell on it." Today, whenever he used the expression, it tickled him to think of Martha.

She was awfully good on people. He had to hand it to her, even when he was the target. And every time he saw the Coes, nowadays, he remembered the night when everybody was saying that Warren was too intellectual in his approach to painting and Martha had retorted that he was just as intellectual as Barrett, who kept asking "Why?" all day long. That had hit Warren off to a T, though Miles had not appreciated it at the time. He was not as noticing as Martha; she was very feminine that way. He used to tell people, confidently, that Warren had a genuine epistemological bent. He groaned, now, to think of what he had started when he had put him onto Whitehead and Russell and Sullivan.

This, he felt awesomely sure, was a deed he would have to answer for on Judgment Day. He had not dreamed, when he first undertook to supervise Warren's reading, that Warren was utterly innocent of the nature of an abstract concept: he took everything he read with a happy literalness and supposed that modern science had fixed it so that two and two equaled five. He had pounced on that notion in Dostoevski, and came bearing it to Miles like a retriever, a few years back. "Haven't the scientists proved that?" he had asked, with startled eyes, when Miles tried to unscramble him. The poor fellow could not get the idea of proof out of his noodle. Science and philosophy had deranged his common sense. "How do you know that?" he kept challenging when you let drop the most casual observation. And since he could not understand the only two fields in which proof was possible—logic and mathematics—he had fallen back, despondently, on the notion that everything was false. He had even, for a time, lost faith in his painting. His work, he had discovered, was a lie, just as big a lie, he said bitterly, as Rembrandt or Titian, who at least *thought* the world they were painting was real. The fact that you could never see time—the fourth dimension—had hit him amidships halfway through a volume of Kierkegaard; he realized he was a faker and illusionist and probably ought to be put in jail. This revelation had made him sick; Jane vouched for it. He lay in their outsize bed, shivering, under the electric blanket, for nearly three weeks, baffling the doctor and the Freudian analyst, who was piped in daily from New York.

And then, *deo gratias,* he had recovered. He had telephoned Miles to tell him the glad tidings. He had been cured, he confided, by relativity—the hair of the dog that bit him, as Miles remarked aside. Under the electric blanket, he had thought about outer space and reasoned that a lie could be true there, just the way parallel lines could meet. Miles had not had the heart to gainsay him. What was the use of explaining to him that a lie existed only in discourse? The little fellow, he saw, had fallen in love with the concept of outer space. He visualized it as a sort of scientific heaven in which all the false appearances of this earth were corrected by curving back on themselves and becoming their opposites. For him, in his current phase, relativity (which he identified with philosophical relativism) was a new and blissful absolute, the absolute topsy turvy, like a kid's picture of China. If everything was relative, as he now felt assured, then his painting might be just as true as Rembrandt; truer, perhaps? What did Miles think, he inquired eagerly, a year ago on the breakwater. Miles had shaken his head. Given

59

Warren's premise, he pointed out, it would not be truer —let it go at just as true as Rembrandt.

And pragmatically, Miles now admitted, the idea seemed to be working out. Warren was feeling no pain. He had come a long way since last year, he had explained to Miles during luncheon. The fear that he might have to wait till after his death for recognition no longer troubled him, he declared. It was not really a postponement, if you thought of time as curved. "Just a question of time, eh?" said Miles, chewing on a chicken breast, and Warren had nodded, joyously, blinking his soft eyes like a bashful lover and wiggling his bare toes in the sand. Miles, to tell the truth, had felt a little disturbed by this new packaging of pie in the sky. And yet, like all religions, it had done something positive for the true believer; here in the studio, Miles could see that. Warren's work, certainly, had taken a leap into freedom, or a plunge into necessity, if this portrait was typical. It had entered a domain in which you could not tell whether it was good or bad.

Which, he supposed, was in a way what Warren was aiming at.

"It's supposed to represent an equation," proffered Warren. "The one the atom bomb is based on. It's Martha in a state of fission. In my next series, I'm going on to fusion—the hydrogen-bomb formula." Miles nodded—he had begun to get the drift of the painting—but Helen had a little frown, like shirred chiffon, between her dark brows. "Would you like to see the figures?" said Warren, hopefully. "I got them from a mathematician who was staying in the Hubers' cottage this summer." "Oh, Warren, that's *boring*," said Jane, in a flat, comfortable tone, looking sidewise at Helen, who was sitting up, with an air of determination, on the old sofa and tightening her knotted scarf about her throat. "Isn't your idea rather literary?" she said to Warren in an anxious voice. "Almost like illustration?" She had an air of helpfulness. "All painting is literary," Miles corrected. "It makes a statement about the world. What we used to call the artist's vision. The rest is wallpaper." Helen pursed her lips and narrowed her eyes, tilting her head from one side to the other, as she strove to see the canvas from Miles's deeper perspective. Miles nursed his chin and watched her. He repented his rudeness. Evidently, she did not like the painting, but this was a wholly natural reaction. Nobody, to Miles's knowledge, had ever liked Warren's painting, with the exception of Jane's father, who, so to speak, was its onlie begetter and owned examples of every period. And people trained in the arts, like Helen, were positively upset by it. "Shall I take it away?" volunteered Warren, with a solicitous, inquiring look at Helen, as if a guest had shown uneasiness of a pet dog or cat. Miles was touched. "Leave it," he said, shortly, raising a hand. "I want to think about it." He flung himself onto one of the benches.

A strange temptation was assailing him. He wanted to buy the portrait. There was a stifled impresario in him; he liked to think of himself as a Renaissance tyrant-patron commanding his goldsmiths and his limners. He had a number of portfolios of drawings, chiefly of erotic subjects and strange beasts and mythical monsters; before the old house burned down he had owned a half-dozen paintings done by artist cronies from the Village bars he used to haunt. Yet all his wives, even the gentle Helen, disparaged his taste in art. He liked "magic" realism, Dali, the Gothic scenes of Max Ernst, the color of Reginald Marsh—paintings that gave him something to chew on—but his wives were always trying to educate his eye with Braque and Juan Gris and Mondrian. Ever since he had closed up his consulting-room, he had not had a free hand. Draftsmanship, a fine line, appealed to him, and despite what his wives said he felt himself to be a connoisseur of drawing. Moreover, he was a gambler—the year he had had a hit on Broadway, he had owned a piece of a race horse—and the fact that Warren Coe was a hundred-to-one shot played powerfully on his fancy. He was a little drunk and he relished it.

Staring at the painting, he gave himself up to reverie. With a certain somber irony—for he knew himself full well—he heard himself showing a visitor through his Coe collection. "Interesting little fella; lives up here all year round, in New Leeds; never had a real show or a criticism; doesn't know himself what he's up to; got a science bug; dominated by his wife's family, scientists, Germans, from the Rhineland. Extraordinary draftsman, though; used to be a drawing teacher. Not a primitive; an isolate. Got a spot of Blake in him. I was the first to discover him. . . . That's my second wife, the picture that got me started—my last Duchess, you might say, if you still remember your Browning. 'There's my last Duchess hanging on the wall, looking as if she were alive.' " A short chuckle broke from Miles. The humor of the purchase nudged him in the ribs, sardonically. Martha, he remembered, used to say that he would like her if she were stuffed and mounted, like a dead bird.

"Helen didn't care for it at first," he went on in a more serious vein to his fancied guest. "She's got more taste than I have. But people of taste are at a disadvantage when it comes to a long shot like Coe. It's what I like to call the fallacy of the trained eye. Art historians pretend that it's the philistines that scoff at the new men. Pardon me if I say that's horse shit. The philistines aren't interested in art unless it's called to their attention as something they ought to get sore about. It's the boys and girls with the trained eyes that come to smile at the Armory show and the Salon of the Refusés—the ones who *know* better than the painter. Who laughed at Whistler? Ruskin. Who laughed at Socrates? Aristophanes. Who laughed at Racine? Molière."

A hard green light glittered in Miles's eye. His narrow lips compressed like scar tissue. He had a sense of astuteness, cunning, and clarity. Every analogue in the history of culture told him that Warren Coe was hot. Coe was an idiot, but most of the masters were simpletons, like Monet, or had a screw loose somewhere. Yeats's spiritualism was just as balmy as any of Warren's notions; the plan of *Ulysses* was nuts and academic as hell; pointillism, as a theory, was drivel. Your typical genius, of today, was some modest little goof, like Warren, plugging away in solitude at a mad scheme or invention that no reasonable person would give a nickel for: Duchamp, the early Schonberg, Ives, that fellow who was a doctor in New Jersey. The more, in fact, Miles pondered the case, the more unaccountable it seemed to him that Warren had not been discovered already. And this, all at once, gave Miles pause; a morose suspicion overtook him. Somebody, he felt, was trying to deceive him; the wool was being pulled over his eyes. Some unidentified force was trying to maneuver him into buying a painting that nobody else would have as a gift. Or was it the other way round? Was a hidden force trying to dissuade him from answering the knock of opportunity? He heard his wife and the Coes talking and shot a mistrustful look in their direction. It seemed to him that they might be ignoring him for some purpose. All his ideas began to seesaw; he could not tell which side of the inward debate he was on. More and more, in recent months, he had found it difficult to think in his customary rapid, purposeful style. The more clear his ideas became, the less he could choose between them; it was as if he had floated into Warren's relativity and hung, confused, over vast profundities.

"How much?" he said suddenly, in a thickened voice, jabbing a thumb at the portrait. The others turned and stared. Warren's soft, driftwood-colored hair seemed to rise slowly on his scalp. They had not understood him, evidently. "Much?" Miles repeated, with an effort, pointing to the picture again. The liquor had half-paralyzed his tongue but he did not allow this to deter him, for he understood that art-collecting was conducted in terse signs and monosyllables. "You mean the price?" asked Jane. Miles nodded, heavily. They all sat there, goggling. "Why, gee, Miles, I don't know," said Warren mildly. "It's ten years since I've put a picture up for sale. Mr. Carl—Jane's father—is the only regular Coe buyer. And that's in the family. . . ." He went bubbling on, but Miles interrupted him. "Set a price," he said. "You don't mean you're thinking of buying it?" cried Jane. "Why, Miles, where would you put it?" murmured Helen. "In the gymnasium," retorted Miles. Last year, they had bought an old windmill and turned it into a gymnasium for Miles to work out in; up above, he had a study, where he wrote.

Roses bloomed in Warren's fading cheeks; boyish tears stood in his eyes. "Golly," he said. "Golly, Miles," and he came over and shook Miles's hand. "I don't know what to say," he added, staring bashfully up at the portrait. Jane intervened, with a sharp glance at Helen. "Why, Miles," she cried, "you don't want to buy a picture of *Martha!* People would think you were crazy." Miles's tongue loosened. "They wouldn't know it was Martha," he said playfully, with a fraternal wink at Warren. Jane was aghast. "I shouldn't think Helen . . ." she began, but her voice faded away, uncertainly, as

64

Helen, beside her, merely smiled and picked up the baby. "Why, you'd get *awfully* tired of it," Jane resumed. "I mean *I* would, if it were my ex-spouse. I wouldn't want Warren around to haunt me if I were happily married to another man. Why don't you take something else? Get Warren to do a portrait of Helen and the baby."

Miles thought he saw what Jane was up to: she was trying to obstruct the sale. Like so many of the New Leeds women, she wanted to keep her man in a state of financial dependence. Painting Helen and the baby, as Jane very well knew, was out of the question. Helen was far too busy, as a wife and mother, to give time to the sittings. "Helen has her hands full," he said sharply, with a meaningful look about the studio, "taking care of her house and family." He set his drink down, unfinished, and pulled himself to his feet. "Name a price," he said to Warren. Warren looked at his wife. "You'd better think it over, Miles," he said, smiling a manful smile. "Are you ready to go, dearest?" asked Helen, getting up. They were all trying to obstruct him; they thought he was in his cups.

"I don't think Warren should let him do it," Jane was saying to Helen, in her loud, schoolgirl whisper. "Martha wouldn't like it at all. Why, Miles might be tempted to deface the picture." Miles got the point: once, years ago, when he and Martha were first married, he had cut up one of her dresses with the kitchen scissors; he still had a piece of it, somewhere; it was among the things, ironically, that they had saved from the burned house. "All that's in the past," he said gruffly. "I don't hate her any more." Jane giggled. "I don't know why you laugh, Jane," said Helen. "Martha means nothing to Miles. He forgave her long ago." Both the Coes were silent. Warren drew a deep breath. Under Miles's eyes, he had turned into a wan little old man. "Jane's right," he said. "I have

Martha's friendship to consider." "You mean Martha would *mind?*" Miles said to Warren, incredulously. The thought completely sobered him and he felt strangely hurt. In his own heart, he had repented. If he had not driven her away, she would never have gone off with Sinnott, he often told himself, tenderly, now that he was married and the bitterness was gone. *"Mind!"* cried Jane. "They both would. You should hear the things they say." "Shut up, Jane," squealed Warren. "You shouldn't tell Miles that." "I'm telling him for his own protection," went on Jane serenely. "Why, if he took that portrait, John Sinnott might come down to Digby with a knife or a gun." "Stop it, Jane," begged Warren. "John Sinnott is a friend of yours. And you don't *know* that about him. Why, John was a pacifist during the war." "They can be the most violent," said Jane. "After all his father was a brigadier general in the army. And his mother was from West Virginia. He's very primitive underneath. He's the type that harbors a grudge—anybody can see that." "You've got it all twisted up," said Warren. "His father was in the Medical Corps and he was only a colonel." "Probably a surgeon," replied Jane, astutely. "And everybody knows about surgeons."

"This is ridiculous," said Miles, lighting a cigarette. "I don't give a frig about Sinnott's heredity. Stay out of this, Jane. Sit down, Helen. I've asked Warren to put a price on the picture. Naturally, I'm not going to insist on it if he honestly thinks Martha would object. Not Sinnott. Martha." He looked steadily at Warren and spoke in a calm, patient tone. He was much more interested, now, in eliciting the real state of Martha's feelings than in the picture, which he looked on coldly as bait for Warren to rise to. The conversation, for him, had taken on the character of a judicial inquiry, but he hid this from the others behind a casual mien. "It's true," admitted Warren, with a peaked smile. "She might not like it. You never know how people will react. And, darn it, she has a stake in the painting. After all, she sat for it as a favor to me." "We all have a primitive streak," put in Jane, eagerly. "Why, you know how Indians are about having their pictures taken." "Why, yes, Miles," cried Warren, excited by Jane's analogy. "In Mexico, they'll break your camera if you try to take a picture of their dances. They believe you're stealing their soul. And there's a lot of that in all of us, let me tell you."

Miles laughed. "And if I stole her soul?" he suggested. "If I know Martha, she'd be flattered. She's probably still attracted to me, at bottom. Helen thinks so. Why else do you think she came back here?" The Coes eyed each other. This question, Miles perceived with interest, had been the subject of controversy between them. Warren forestalled Jane's answer. "Maybe," he said, defiantly, "because she doesn't care any more. That's why she *could* come back. After all, she loves the landscape here." Miles pondered this thought. He was selfish and egotistical, but not, he believed, vain. He considered it possible, psychologically, that a woman could cease to respond to him. "But Jane says she talks against me," he observed. "That argues a residue of feeling." Helen nodded. "Miles never talks against her," she explained. Warren clenched his hands. "Excuse me, Helen," he said, "but that makes me blow my top. I'm sorry, everybody, but I can't let that pass. What was Miles doing, just now, on the beach? Do you realize what you did, Miles? You accused her of arson. Why, she could be arrested and tried if that was brought to the authorities." He whirled about, like a little prosecutor, and pointed his index finger at Miles, who would have been taken aback if he had not been familiar with the mechanism of transference. Poor Warren was merely discharging his pent-up aggression against Jane; he must have wanted to sell the painting badly. "Arson?" mildly drawled Miles. "I don't think I said that, Warren. I was talking in analytic terms; perhaps I didn't distinguish clearly enough between fantasy and reality." Warren clapped his hand to his mouth. "Pardon *me*," he said. "Excuse me for living, but that's not what I heard. From what *I* heard, let me tell you, Martha could sue you for slander. And *win*. Amn't I right, Jane?" "Yes," said Jane, thoughtfully, rubbing her jaw. "You ought to be careful, Miles. You know how people carry things back here. Why, she could have Warren and me for witnesses."

The complacent, calm stare of Citizeness Coe, arranging her shawl on her shoulders, sent a chill through Miles. He recognized that Jane, fantastic as it seemed, was quite serious in what she said. If Martha were unbalanced enough to charge him, Jane and Warren would step responsibly in the box to witness for her; and not because they disliked him; they would do the same to Martha or to each other. Between them, he thought, staggered, they made a dangerous couple: Jane was a tale-bearer, and Warren had total recall. For the first time, Miles perceived that Martha's return was going to be a limiting fact in his existence. As long as she was here, he would have to watch his Ps and Qs, even in little things he let drop to Helen about her, lest Helen repeat them to Jane or one of the other local busybodies. And yet her return was a sort of provocation, needling him to tell the truth, if only to defend himself against the things she and Sinnott might be saying. He was between two stools and every eye would be on him to see how he was "taking" it; that, he suddenly realized, was why he and Helen had been asked down here today. "Jesus, Mary, and Joseph," he whispered, remembering his remarks on the beach. The fat was in the fire already, if Warren could not be persuaded to keep Jane's eager tongue still.

"Don't worry," said Warren, kindly, as if divining his thoughts. "We all say a lot of things we don't mean. We're not going to tell Martha, I promise you." "OK, old chap," said Miles, feeling moved. He drew out a paisley handkerchief and wiped his brow; the room had become quite warm. "Another drink?" said Warren. Miles declined. "You're not going to stay and *talk?*" asked Warren sadly. Miles shook his head. "Another time." "Come back next week," proposed Jane, "and we'll take a long walk, out to the point."

Miles shook his head again. Once in a season was all he could take of the Coes, as a general rule, unless brutal loneliness overtook him; there was nobody to talk to in Digby, except Helen and an old Marine boxer, the real-estate agent and a stripling with a crew haircut who got out the weekly newspaper. "Or come and read *Bérénice* next Friday with the vicomte," urged Jane, with a funny look in her eye. "We'll have some drinks and music afterwards." "Martha going to be here?" queried Miles, sharply. "I don't *think* so . . ." said Jane. "Don't say that, darling," expostulated Warren. "You don't *know* that. They said they might come, after all." And they began to bicker, excitedly, as to what John Sinnott had said, on Tuesday, and whether it contradicted what Martha had told Warren in the post office. Miles watched with a saturnine grin. "No," he said flatly.

"You don't want to meet her?" Jane's round blue eyes grew big and naively wondering; she jerked her head back on her neck. "No," said Miles. This decision had just matured in him, and he caught Helen's troubled, surprised gaze. "That's awfully unusual," pronounced Jane, waggling her jaw and looking up sidewise at the portrait. "I mean, why would you want to have her *imago* in your study if you won't see her socially?" "Yes," chimed in Warren, "where's the logic in that, Miles?" He had a look of profound disappointment on his bright features, like a child who sees a treat wafted away from him. "Gee," he said, "it would have been fun to get you and Martha together again. I thought, down deep you really wanted that when you took a shine to the picture." He turned a sweet, pleading face to Miles. "Please," he begged. "Come do *Bérénice*. Come to dinner first. A week from tomorrow." "No," said Miles, curtly. "It wouldn't be fair to Helen." Rebuked, both the Coes directed their widened eyes to Miles's better half, who smiled serenely and murmured, "Whatever you say, dearest." Warren sank his cheek into his palm. He was torn, Miles could see, between his sociability and his sense of delicacy toward a woman's feelings. But Jane was staring boldly at Helen. "You don't *want* to see Miles's ex?" she exclaimed. "I don't mind," said Helen, in a faint voice, looking to Miles for guidance. "I mind for her," said Miles, grandly, letting the cat out of the bag; he took it for granted, as a mere matter of propriety, that Helen would feel jealous of Martha, and he saw no harm in letting the Coes know this. In his opinion, it reflected credit on her.

Jane cogitated, looking from one to the other. "Everybody does up here, you know, Helen," she chided. "I mean divorced couples meet their ex-mates. They all go to the same parties, and nobody thinks a thing of it. There wouldn't be any social life if everybody felt like Miles." "I am different," said Miles. And in truth he felt a million light years distant from the New Leeds people. Old, soured, boiled as an owl a good deal of the time, bored to desperation except when he was working, he nevertheless had passions, he told himself, that let him know that he was a man still, among senile adolescents. Like an old lion, he nursed the wound Martha had given him because, as Jane ought to realize, he held sex sacred. "Why, Jane, isn't that funny?" he heard Warren twitter. "What?" said Jane. *"You* remember, darling," her husband prompted reproachfully. "Martha said the same thing, right here in this room. Only she said, 'I'm different.' Remember that?" Jane nodded. "When they first thought of buying the house," she mused. "She didn't want to meet *you*, Miles," she continued, with a giggle of innocent malice. "That was the reason she gave for not buying it. We all told her she was a nut, that everybody met their ex-spouses here. But she claimed she was different. . . ." Miles smiled disbelievingly. "Martha," he observed, "is a woman of words." "Oh, she meant it all right," averred Warren. "She *fought* buying that house, let me tell you."

Miles's face reddened. He felt a ridiculous stab of pain. She refused to meet him while he, sentimental fool, had been on the verge of buying her portrait! The anger that had been accumulating in him during the past discussion suddenly boiled up and he wanted to hurt somebody. "Let's go," he said harshly. "Forget about the picture." As he took a step toward the door, a knock sounded. There was a stark moment of silence; no one moved. The conviction that it must be the Sinnotts was graven, Miles saw, on every face. "It *can't* be them," whispered Jane. "It might be," whispered back Warren. Another knock came. "They know we're here because of the cars," whispered Jane. "Answer it, man," said Miles, in his normal voice. As Warren skipped to the door, Miles turned aside, steadying himself. Very likely, he said to himself, it was not Martha at all.

But it was Martha, in a gray cloak, accompanied by

71

her husband and a strange tall girl with short blond hair, wearing slacks. As soon as the door opened, Miles felt a release of tension in his belly. Now that she was here, he could say it: He had known they were going to meet today, ever since he got up this morning, and all his talk of not wanting to see her had been a protective mechanism, against disappointment. Wise Helen must have guessed when she saw him before his mirror, clipping the hairs in his nose while he was shaving, for she had said nary a word when he put aside the old coat and tie she had laid out for him in favor of the new tweed and the paisley. Jane Coe must have known that it was in the cards too as she sat there like a witch in her black shawl, urging him to stay. He would not put it past her to have cooked the whole thing up with Martha; he had never trusted the two of them when they got together.

Martha herself, he noticed, was very formally dressed, for New Leeds. She had on a pair of smart black walking shoes, stockings, a black skirt, and some sort of white silk blouse, under the cloak, which he moved forward to take from her, doing the honors, while the rest of the party milled about in confusion. Sinnott was the only one who retained his self-possession, coming forward to shake hands briskly, ignoring the portrait—a very considerable feat, for, the sixty-six square feet of canvas had magnetized every eye but his. Nobody could miss the fact that Martha had been the chief topic of conversation. It was, as they said, a situation. Martha was shaking all over. Miles could feel it, as he lifted the cloak from her shoulders; he remembered that she had trembled, the first time he saw her, on the stage of a hapless summer theater production, so badly that the scenery shook.

Her nervousness put him at ease. "I'm glad to see you," he announced, taking her frightened hand in his firm, friendly grip. And he meant it. Whatever he might have expected to feel, seeing her at last, pleasure and cordiality were his prime sensations, as if he had caught a glimpse of a familiar face in a crowd. "It's good to see you," he reiterated, looking her over. But she, in a characteristic movement of rejection, began to apologize. They had thought, outside, that it was the Hubers' car, she said; the Hubers had a new Cadillac too. Otherwise, the inference was, they would not have come in. Miles suppressed a smile. Wild horses, in his opinion, would not have kept her out, once she had guessed that he was inside: she had had to see him, just as he had to see her. But she was alleging that they must go, that they had dropped in, just for a minute, to have the girl in slacks meet the Coes, who were going to be her neighbors. Dolly Lamb, she explained, with a jerky nod at the tall girl, was a painter who had taken the house on Tern Pond for the winter; she did not know anybody up here; that was why they had brought her.

Miles patiently listened, looking down into Martha's eyes, like brown topazes, he used to say. There were faint wrinkles around them now, and she had a distrait, slightly careworn air. "Cool off," he felt like telling her. "You don't have to account for yourself to me any more." As she named Tern Pond, she colored and hurried on with her exposition, for she and Miles used to picnic there, at this time of year, and once or twice, after bathing, they had made love, over her protests, on the sand, by the deserted house that this girl must now be occupying. Martha had claimed that somebody would come and catch them; she had had a lot of sexual defenses, though she always liked it, in the end. Her look, now, kept dodging his and flying nervously to her husband. Miles turned his head to examine him—a thin, high-colored young man in old flannels and a whipcord jacket with leather-patched elbows; not the New Leeds type. He had never paid him much heed in the days when Martha used to talk to him, before she ran off; there were always young men, on the beach, actors or poets or anarchists, that the young wives liked to gab with. Sinnott, the women used to say, was exceptionally good-looking, which was why Miles had not bothered to notice him. But he now conceded that he had been wrong. There was something in the tall, scowling fellow that was out of the common run, something of the old-fashioned gentleman, a kind of knightly quality that Miles found appealing. To his surprise, he felt no jealousy. From his vantage point of seniority, he found, he could look on Sinnott and Martha almost paternally, as if he had sired this marriage. He found himself wishing them well and hoping, for Sinnott's sake, that Martha was behaving herself. She seemed, as Jane Coe said, to be genuinely in love, and the Coes evidently liked him. Whenever Sinnott spoke, Jane Coe giggled responsively and Warren Coe beamed, as he had at the baby on the beach. Yet there was something unstable there, underneath the nice manners and the glowing cheeks of the *chevalier de la rose*. If Miles had had him as a patient, he would have diagnosed an hysterical fixity, very rare in men, nowadays.

Martha had changed a great deal. She was more unsure of herself and at the same time she had more dignity. There was less of the wayward modern girl and more of the bohemian lady in her. She had even changed her hair-do; that little knot at the nape was new. In the old days, she had had braids, wound around her head, unbecomingly, and she had worn peasant skirts, sometimes, and stripes and bright colors. Sinnott must have taught her how to dress. She had a frail look that Miles had never associated with her before, despite her small hands and thin waist. During their marriage, he had always been conscious of her tensile strength and durability—her Scandinavian side. Now it seemed as if the poetic side— the Italian mother—had got the upper hand. She appeared to be living constrainedly in some sort of romance: a projection of Sinnott's, probably, a borrowed ego-ideal.

The fact that she had changed so was an eye-opener to Miles. It troubled him to think that he, in the past, might have handled her wrong, on the theory that what she wanted was a strong father-figure, whereas perhaps all along it had been a brother she was looking for. . . . And yet she was tenser than ever, he was disturbed to see. When he refilled his glass and brought her a strong drink from the table, to encourage her to talk, he was startled by the laughing sharpness with which she spoke of the local people. He would have said shrill, except that she spoke in such a low voice that he had to lean closer to catch the anecdotes she was relating. He was a critical man himself, but she made him feel old and tolerant, by contrast. Yet it puzzled him to remember, as he listened, that it was Martha's arrogant intolerance that he had loved most about her. He shook himself a little as it occurred to him that it was he who had changed, grown soft and torpid from age and creature comforts. Listening to Martha now, he had the same unpleasant sensation that he got from leafing over his early plays when he was alone in his windmill with a gale blowing and a glass by his side. Is this I, he asked himself, or was that I, back there?

"Let's sit down," he said, interrupting her. He drew up two chairs and arranged them, a little apart from the group. On the couch, just to the right of them, Warren had cornered Miss Lamb, who sat upright and edgy, with a scared look, while he, leaning forward, his head to one side, was explaining the theory of his work to her. Miles motioned to Martha for silence. "Picasso," they heard Warren's modest voice say, "uses a succession of images, like the animated cartoonists to express linear time. I've gone a long way beyond that. Last year, I showed the continuum by painting both sides of the canvas. You get the idea? A mathematician up here suggested it to me. What you have is a continuous painting that curves back on itself. It's the real break with easel painting." "Why don't you try sculpture?" the girl interposed, in a demure murmur, edging back from him on the couch. Mentally, Miles slapped his thigh, but Warren took the question literally. "I may," he said, thoughtfully nodding. "I never thought of that. I guess it's pretty obvious to an outsider." The girl said something indistinct. Warren's high laugh rang out. "Of course," he cried, "I know it's absurd that I should be ahead of Picasso—ever read Kierkegaard, by the way? Oh, you should, darn it; he taught me to accept the absurd. I've learned to accept a lot of things since I took up science and philosophy. The first thing I found out was that just about everything I thought was true wasn't. Ever have that experience? I owe it mostly to Miles here."

Miles turned his head and deliberately winked at Martha. "You remember," he said in a whisper, "what you used to say about our host here and a six-year-old child? 'Why?'?" Martha nodded. She smiled, like her old self. Then, all at once, she turned pink and dropped her gaze to her lap. Miles felt himself flush too. He knew what she was remembering. It was impossible, it seemed, to find a subject of conversation that did not contain an oblique reference to their common past. He decided to take the bull by the horns. "Thank you," he said, in a low voice, "for writing to me about Barrett. I ought to have answered." "Oh," she said, hurriedly. "It was nothing." Her glance scurried off to her husband, who had paused in the midst of a conversation with Helen to watch Miles and Martha laughing and whispering. Helen was looking the other way. "I'm glad," said Martha, loudly, "that you have a baby. It's a boy, isn't it?" "Yes," said Helen from across the room, picking up the child and dandling it on her lap. There was a silence. "What are you writing?" said Martha, with a desperate look, again in a voice that was meant to carry.

Everybody turned to hear Miles's reply. "A philosophical work," he said, shortly. "It would bore you to hear about it." John Sinnott raised an eyebrow. "Not at all," said Martha, with a queer little smile; a strand of fair hair had escaped from its knot and fallen across her forehead. For a moment, she looked strangely like the portrait, dissociated, fissionized. She had come apart, poor girl, Miles said to himself, as he watched her raise her hand to brush the stray lock back. There was a bandage on her finger and, stealing a look at Sinnott, he observed that he too had a bandage, a fairly large one, on his right hand. What was wrong between them, he wondered. Was it her failure to have children or the failure of her work as an actress? He looked shrewdly at Sinnott. Had he forced her to leave the stage?

"Why, Miles," said Jane, goggling, "didn't you know? Martha is a philosopher too." "Not a real one," said Martha, as Miles turned to stare at her. "I never took my degree." "We told you about that, Miles," put in Warren. "Don't you remember?" Miles shook his head. "Oh, yes," said Jane. Miles frowned. Either he was losing his memory, what with the drink and age, or people had ceased to interest him, except perfunctorily. He could see from Helen's face that he had just had a bad lapse; the Coes *must* have told him about this development in Martha, and yet he had clean forgotten. "You don't say?"

he muttered, and began to ask her whom she had studied under. But he scarely heard her answers for thinking how strange it was that any detail about Martha could have eluded his notice, when he had once put detectives on her, not even to get evidence—for he had plenty—but just to learn what she was doing and whether his friends were seeing her. "What are you up to now?" he interrupted. "You doing your dissertation?" Martha smiled. "You just asked me that," she pointed out. Miles pulled himself together. "The answer is no," said Martha, with a pert little twinkle. "I decided not to do it two years ago." Miles nodded. His curiosity stirred. "What *are* you up to?" he demanded. To his surprise, Martha colored. "I'm writing a play," she confessed.

Miles gave a start. For a moment, he was violently angry. There it was again, that pattern of imitation. She had not changed in the least; she had come back here to compete with him again. He no longer considered himself a playwright, but that was how the public remembered him. She must have read his thoughts. "I'm *not* going to take up boxing," she murmured, twitting him, with a little air of apology, which he thought was in poor taste. He rose on his dignity. "Don't apologize," he said. He had always been a magnanimous man and he took comfort in the thought. He had always told Martha, he recalled, that she had a wonderful ear for dialogue. He had no doubt, once he thought about it, that she could write a very clever little comedy. "That's great," he said, warmly. "You've found yourself at last. I always said you could do a play." "I remember," said Martha.

"And you'll bring something to it that I never had," he continued, his friendliness increasing, for he truly loved the arts and suffered here in this sterile region from the absence of young shoots of talent to spring up around him. He was nearly fifty-five, now, and Warren

Coe, who was close to his own age, was the only bud of promise he had been able to detect in the area; the rest were all blasted. Everybody was "artistic," and nobody was an artist. "Yes," he nodded. "Practical experience of the theater. That's the thing. I don't mean exits and entrances—anybody can manage that side of it. I mean a feeling for the medium—the grand imposture of the whole thing. It's a make-believe world that the layman doesn't get the hang of. Nobody can write a real drama who hasn't smelled the grease paint; it's like somebody composing music who's never played an instrument." Martha gave a deprecating shrug. "I don't know," she said. "Actors and actresses have written some terrible plays. Bernhardt, remember?" "Ah," said Miles, "but there was Shakespeare, and Molière and O'Neill." "On the other hand, there was Shaw," she answered. "And Congreve and Wilde." "Wilde was a lifelong actor," protested Miles.

The others had turned again to watch them. Unconsciously, they had both raised their voices, as if they were alone together and the rest of the room were blocked out. "What was that, Miles?" wondered Warren. "Say that again." "Yes, let us in on it," pleaded Jane. But Martha had risen, with a little grimace. "We must go," she said. "Oh gee," sighed Warren. "Just when it's getting interesting." But Martha shook her head. John Sinnott had fetched her cloak and was on his way to her with it like a galleon. Dolly Lamb stood up. Miles frowned as he watched young Sinnott put the cloak on Martha's shoulders. He himself, he thought sourly, ought to have been the first to leave. Yet he had been having a fine time, sparring with Martha, before the others broke it up. It was like a bit of the old days. But it was frustrating to talk to her like that, with Jane Coe's big ears flapping and Warren's nose twitching for crumbs from the banquet, Helen looking tense and worried on his behalf, and John Sinnott's warrior's eye on them and his biceps flexed to defend Martha. Miles rose and stretched. "Maybe I'll come to see you one of these days," he said to Martha, with a slight yawn. Martha seemed taken aback. Was it possible that she was afraid of him still? "Umm," she said, noncommittally.

Everybody was on the move, all at once. They were picking their way out to the cars, guided by Warren's flashlight. Miles stood in the parking space, waiting for Sinnott to move his old open Ford out of the way of his Cadillac. Helen and the baby were in the car, and Miles was watching the girl painter drive off first in her jeep, when, in the glare of Sinnott's headlights, he became aware that Warren Coe was beside him, batting his eyes and wiggling his eyebrows and smiling an urgent question in the direction of Martha. For a minute, Miles could not divine what had got into him. Then he remembered the portrait. What Warren was saying in pantomime was that Miles should ask her, now, if it was all right for him to have it. Miles inwardly shrugged. Sober, he was not sure whether he wanted the painting, but he did not mind asking, just for the hell of it. He strolled up to the Sinnotts' car and indicated to Martha that he wanted to speak to her. Martha rolled down her window. "I like that portrait of you," he said in a casual tone. Martha's eyebrows rose; she turned to her husband, who merely raced the engine. "Seriously?" she said in a lowered voice, looking back to where Warren was standing. "Seriously," agreed Miles. "It's far the best thing he's done. In fact," he continued, leaning his elbow on the little car's window sash, "I've had the notion of buying it." Martha stared. "You're crazy," she said. "Where would you put it?" She bit her lip. "Excuse me," she corrected herself. "It's none of my business." "Warren tells me," said Miles, "that he'd have to have your permission to sell it."

Martha looked at her husband. "Why not?" he said lightly. "You don't want it." "This isn't a joke?" demanded Martha. "No, of course not. Why should it be?" returned Miles, rather irritably. "You really think Warren has something, then?" Miles nodded. "Why, then," said Martha, gaily, "I think it's marvelous. John, wouldn't it be wonderful if Warren could be discovered after all these years?" John smiled briefly. "Yes," he said. Miles had the feeling that Sinnott was inwardly laughing at him, and that Martha too would burst into merriment, the minute he turned away. She was peering at him critically as if to make out whether he was drunk. "Sleep on it," she suggested, after a moment. Her voice was gentle and solicitous, but he felt the old rage rising in him at the notion that she was trying to manage him again, the first chance she got. In the eyes of this superior pair, he was nothing but a maudlin jackass. "Good night," he said abruptly and moved away from the car.

FOUR

THE VICOMTE had come to call on the Sinnotts just after Sunday lunch. He was sitting in an easy chair, by the fireplace, holding a small earthenware dish of Martha's pot-de-crème, vanilla, in his square, seamed hand. By his side rested his walking stick, and he was still puffing a little from his walk up the hill. Nobody knew his age. He had a large red face and dark-blond, straight, pomaded hair of a hue that could scarcely be dyed; he wore it combed back, without a part, and longish, like a woman's short bob. His suit was a faded tan silk, cut rather loose, which looked as if it had been made for him in Japan many years back. The vicomte had a much-traveled mien, like a stout suitcase with frayed hotel stickers; today, he suggested the Orient-fans, a kimono, verandahs, matting. John had not recognized him, as he made his way up the driveway, with a basket of field-mushrooms, a house-gift, in one hand, and the stick, which he paused to rest on, in the other. He had the air of a meditative pilgrim toiling up to a monastery with an offering. "Why, it's M. de Harnonville!" cried Martha, peering out the window, astonished and somewhat pleased that the vicomte had dressed to pay them a visit. For ordinary use, behind the counter in the liquor store, he wore a dark-blue T-shirt, a green eyeshade, blue jeans, and sandals. On his feet, at present, were a pair of high shoes, recently blackened,

82

evidently, for the shoeblack was coming off on the chair's white slipcover while John frowningly watched.

Martha had put a little table down, for the custard cup and spoon, but M. de Harnonville ignored it, holding the cup in his hand and letting the spoon dribble custard onto his napkined lap in the most aristocratic fashion. He had come, it slowly transpired, to buy an early Seth Thomas clock that the Sinnotts had inherited with the house. He was also interested in a sundial, a birdbath, and a painted rocker, which he believed to be stored in the workshop. The previous owner, he said, coughing, had promised him these things, but since the poor bloody old chap had killed himself without making a will, M. de Harnonville stood ready to pay.

John and Martha glanced quickly at each other. The thought flashed between them that the vicomte was in cahoots with the former handyman, who had already carried off a truckload of stuff in deference to the late owner's supposed wishes and had nearly got away with the clock and a pretty silk-and-velvet patchwork quilt, worth over a hundred dollars, which he had stowed in an old bureau drawer. But the instant the suspicion entered her mind, Martha quashed it, shaking her head slightly as a warning to her husband to do likewise. She hated suspecting people, and the vicomte was popular in New Leeds, where he was known as "Paul" to everybody, from the bank president to the village idiots. Though he lived in a single, bare room back of his antique shop and ate his meals sitting at the counter of the local grille, reading a Boston tabloid, he was held to be an authority on everything going—world politics, wines, cooking, gardening, how to arrange your furniture. She and John, it seemed, had already got off on the wrong foot by sending to Boston for a shipment of reasonably priced, decent wine, after one look at the vicomte's stock. You could not do that, the Coes hurried over to tell Martha when they heard about it via the express man: everybody here went to Paul, who got a percentage—how else would he live in the winter, when the antique business folded up?

"You'll have to get used to the folkways," Warren told John, with one of his peaceful smiles. But John chafed against the village and the village chafed against him. "Be nice," Martha kept feeling impelled to tell him on the brink of every occasion. "Be nice," she had pleaded, just now, as she recognized the vicomte approaching. Callers took up too much time, he contended, and wasted Martha's energy. He could not forget that they had come here for a purpose and he watched Martha's outlay of energy with a sort of fanatic jealousy, as though there were only so much of it, a diminishing stock. He was still angry with her, she knew, because she had sat for the portrait. It was getting "involved" in New Leeds, he said—which she had promised him she would not do. And he was cross with Warren for having asked her. Just as he had predicted, she had come home worn out after each sitting, for Warren had taken advantage of the occasion to make her talk philosophy with him for three hours at a stretch. And he still kept popping around with what he called "unfinished questions."

"That's life in the country," Martha explained, patiently. In the country, she said, you had to be *disponible*. Otherwise, people would say you were a snob. So much the better, argued John: then they would leave you in peace. But Martha would not consent to this. It was bad for your character, she tried to show him, to hoard yourself like a miser: openness and hospitality were the basis of ancient virtue, like Abraham entertaining the angels, unawares. Abraham was not writing a play, John retorted. For John, the village was an enemy silently waiting to infiltrate as soon as his back was turned.

Last week, he had gone up to Boston, to do some research in the library, and came home to find that Martha had let the plumber and his helpers drive their truck over his freshly seeded lawn. It was not her fault, actually: she had heard the truck too late, and opened her study window and screamed at them like a harpy, pointing to John's barriers and a big "Keep off the Grass" sign. She was proud, for John's sake, that she had done that much, though the plumber went off in a huff and would not come back to fix the pump he had botched up. He was very sensitive, it seemed, about being a plumber, because he had gone to college, and Martha, the Coes told John, should have thought of that before she yelled, "Can't you *read?*"

Martha was not tactful, despite all her theories of hospitality and neighborliness. She could never remember the things you were supposed to remember about the people up here—who had had a lung removed and who was impotent and who was drinking and who was on the wagon this season. And yet, as she knew, in New Leeds such facts assumed a great importance and even conferred distinction. Right off the bat, she blundered, for example, with the vicomte by offering him coffee and a brandy. "Dear lady," protested M. de Harnonville, "I am an alcoholic." How was she expected to know that, she demanded of John later. She hardly knew the vicomte. He had come here after the war, to stay with some moneyed summer people, just before she left Miles. He seemed to know her very well, but all she could remember of him, from that period, was that he was said to be writing his memoirs of the Resistance: his hosts liked to tell how he had been parachuted, disguised as a businessman, back into his native province, where he had worked for the Allies. Martha had thought this remarkable—because he was so fat—and she was greatly surprised to come back, after all these years, and find him still here, a placid institution, like the new high school. His name was on the town roll of honor, in the square, but everybody seemed to have forgotten about the memoirs. Jane Coe, in fact, now claimed to know that he had really spent the war years in New York, acting as a paid courier to rich refugees: a cousin of the Hubers had seen him, she declared. And she added her own cheerful surmise, that he had probably been working for the Germans too—he looked, she thought, a lot like Goering.

"You oughtn't to say that, dear," Warren had interjected mildly, but Jane pooh-poohed his fears. Nobody up here, she said, would mind what Paul had done, not even the FBI, who only cared about Communists now. Why, Hitler himself could come here and set up as a house-painter and nobody would mind; that, in a *way*, agreed Warren, was the nice part of New Leeds.

It was the vicomte's rich air of fraudulence that took Martha's fancy today; he appealed to her sense of theater. She did not even object to the shoeblacking coming off him; it was a part of his makeup. He sat in the chair like somebody playing the roll of an impostor nobleman, fat, florid, seedy, with a plaintive blue eye—a compendium of myths and history, with his darker pages open, almost ostentatiously. And yet the Coes attested that he was a real vicomte; *strangely enough*, observed Jane with a toss of her shawl. He had really traveled a great deal, the Coes said, and spoke a great many languages and their dialects. The liquor-store window, in the winter season, was papered with a collection of educational photographs, of the Upper Nile, the Ganges, a Chinese riverboat, a Russian cruiser of the tsar's day, a fjord, a cork plantation, an American oilfield, in all of which M. de Harnonville was standing, looking exactly the same, and surrounded by a swarm of natives, just as he was here. Yet if he had spent six months, as he claimed, in all the places he had been caught by the camera, he would have to be a hundred and twenty, according to Warren's count. Jane declared that the answer was simple: Paul, who was probably about sixty, had lived a double life, she said thoughtfully.

He was a bit of a bore, Jane contended; he talked too much about *mon oncle, le duc* and society people, whom nobody was interested in, nowadays. But Warren disagreed; he had learned a lot from Paul, he insisted. John, Martha could see, was of Jane's opinion. He barely concealed a yawn as the vicomte began to relate the history of alcoholism in the Harnonville blood: *mon oncle, le duc,* it seemed, had been a famous toper. For Martha, however, the vicomte and his uncle were interesting just because she doubted their reality. To call her husband's attention to this point, she gave a gay little laugh. "I don't believe it," she said flatly. The vicomte frowned. "I assure you," he said. "It is all in the memoirs." Martha saw that her jesting tone had offended him. "Still," she persisted, "I never heard that *you* were a drinker." The vicomte shrugged. "Oh yes, my dear girl," he affirmed. "You would not have known me. I was a shocking sight. In the gutter. Six months. Positively." He began to rummage in his pockets. Martha giggled. She feared, as she told John later, that he was about to produce a snapshot of himself in the gutter, but it was only a cigarette case. He lit a mentholated cigarette, waving aside John's match. He had, Martha observed, a very bad cigarette cough. "When was this?" she said, skeptically. The vicomte meditated. "Oh . . . during the war . . . I cannot say now the exact date." Martha was silent. She did not want to press him, rudely, but it was he who had introduced the topic. And she still did not believe him, as she tried to indicate to John, though she could not think why anyone should *pose* as an alcoholic. The vicomte met her look. "You're seeking the stigmata?" he said. "Stigmata?" cried Martha, alarmed; she suddenly remembered hearing that the vicomte was *très catholique.* "The signs," said the vicomte, with an air of impatience. "The signs of alcoholism." Martha nodded. "They are there," he assured her. "My doctor could tell you. The blood sugar is never the same." "But you don't drink any more?" "No," said the vicomte. He pulled himself out of his chair and selected a small bronze from the mantel, turned it around, and set it back in silence.

"It must be hard on you, working in the liquor store," said Martha, at a loss for another topic and getting no help from her husband, who sat looking intently at the vicomte now, as if the old fellow were a foreign particle that had intruded on his field of vision for the first time. " 'Ard?" said the vicomte, blinking. Martha repeated her remark in a louder voice. M. de Harnonville turned wonderingly to John. "My wife means the temptation." "Ah," said the vicomte. "But that is part of our method." " 'Our'?" queried Martha, uneasily mindful again of the vicomte's religion; John was a perfect Roundhead who held popery in aversion. "A. A.," said the vicomte. "You know what it is?" "Alcoholics Anonymous," chorused the Sinnotts. The vicomte nodded. "A wonderful society," he said. "Truly missionary. In the spirit of Vincent de Paul. I give them what little time I have here. They call me and I come. It is very moving. Last week, in the woods, a little girl, abandoned by her husband—oh, *la pauvre.*"

He bowed his head. "Isn't there a clash of interests?" said John, with a cold little laugh. He disapproved of Martha's taste for pious frauds and he refused, despite all her merry glances, to find the vicomte amusing. "Interests?" repeated the vicomte, picking up a little china figure, replacing it, and shading his eyes frowningly against the afternoon sun. "He means the interests of your work in the liquor store as against the interests of your work in A. A.," interpreted Martha. "But where is the problem?" said the vicomte, resuming his chair. "As an alcoholic, I know wines and whiskeys very well." Martha opened her mouth to explain further, but at John's impatient signal she closed it again. "Besides," mused M. de Harnonville, in a franker tone, "it is like the pleasures of the eye and the hand for a man who is past the age for the other. . . . A little perversion, I suppose." He tilted his big bobbed head. Martha jumped up. "Let me take that," she said and hurried out with the empty custard cup to the kitchen.

Left alone with John, the vicomte leaned back in his chair and looked shrewdly at the tall young man opposite him, in white shirtsleeves and black sleeveless sweater, perched rather nervously on the black sofa. "I understand you very well," he said, unexpectedly. "You are a young American, of good family; very high-principled, like your wife. You are thinking of *la question morale*. But you must remember that 'moral' in French has a somewhat different meaning." He got up and went to the window, where he stood looking out onto the lawn, with his arms behind his back. "You should prune that rose tree," he observed. Under his authoritative stare, John felt their property blanch; the sandy patches on the lawn grew bigger and whiter; the box withered; briars raised their stalks. "If you fix it, it will be very nice," he heard the vicomte sum up. "But it will cost you $20,000—a fortune." The old man shrugged and turned away from the window. "We like it shabby," protested Martha, in the doorway, seeing her husband's woeful face. The vicomte threw out his hands and gave a short laugh. *"Chacun à son gout,"* he conceded.

There was a disturbing finality about him—a mixture of positiveness and indifference, as if being French and a swindle had given him the last word. And it was indeed the *last* word he seemed to articulate, in his hoarse, choking voice. He dismissed his own words, like useless servants, the minute they were spoken and paid no attention whatever to the sounds that issued from the Sinnotts. Each of his abrupt summations was succeeded by a "profound" silence. In the workshop, where they had gone to inspect the things, his connoisseur's eye had wandered straight to the beam from which the suicide had hanged himself. "You're not superstitious?" he ruminated. He seemed more interested, really, in the mechanics or workmanship of the tragedy than in the business he had come to transact. He measured the drop, thoughtfully, with his fat lower lip protruding, and hoisted himself onto the bench, which, he explained to the Sinnotts, nodding, the dead man must have used. In fact, Martha, watching him uncomfortably and clutching her husband's arm, began to feel that the antique business was only a pretext for getting into the workshop. But all at once he made a grimace of boredom and clambered down, brushing dust from his trousers. He looked over the furniture, briskly, and offered what to the Sinnotts seemed a very fair price—the idea that the stuff had been promised him appeared to have been given its *congé*.

John Sinnott could not hide his surprise. The clock, though ugly, had a certain collector's value, but twenty dollars for the birdbath? He and Martha exchanged wondering looks. "You're sure you're not cheating yourself?" he felt driven to ask, as he peered for the third time at the figures M. de Harnonville had scrawled out on a page from his notebook. This concern, which filled Martha with wifely pride, appeared to nettle the vicomte. "My dear fellow," he said with an air of patience, "these garden things are very desirable." "But it's hideous," protested Martha, running her finger over the birdbath. "It isn't even old." The vicomte blew his nose. "Each to his own taste," he said, stowing away his dirty handkerchief. "I find it quite pretty." A pall of silence fell. They began to walk slowly across the lower lawn. Martha was vexed. Solely in the interests of accuracy, she wanted to dispute with him the value of those knickknacks. Thanks to John's work in the Historical Society, both the Sinnotts knew a good deal about furniture, and Martha was vain of the fact. She was also proud of their taste. And, despite all indications to the contrary, she had been hoping to find a fellow-spirit in the old *antiquaire:* somebody who had standards and was a purist in this uncorseted place. Yet every time she spoke she had the feeling that she was screaming, across a gulf of petty misunderstanding. The sound of her own voice, childishly positive, like a college girl's, cut into the still afternoon and made her resolve not to speak again, until she could master the desire to argue.

But the vicomte himself reopened the subject. "The sundial and the birdbath," he said, stopping and leaning on his stick, "I can understand they are not to your liking. But why sell the clock? Excuse me if I say you were foolish." "We don't like it," said John, crisply, like a manifesto. "But it's very good," objected the vicomte, raising his voice and tapping his stick peremptorily on the ground. "Very old, relatively. Very rare." "We don't like Americana," explained John. "Americana!" cried the vicomte, pointing at the house. "But that is Americana." "No, it isn't," said Martha, abruptly. "But of course," said the vicomte. "What else would it be?"

"When we say Americana," replied Martha, in tones of forbearance, "we mean something quaint, what you call *folklorique*." The vicomte tapped his stick again; his big seamed face grew redder. "Excuse me," he said. "I understand very well the distinction. But to me, if I may say so, your house is Americana. It was not a house for a wealthy merchant, but a simple cottage. And inside, on the old chimney piece, you have put an Empire clock, marble and bronze, very nice in its way, but in a different spirit altogether. In your place, I should have kept the clock you sold me and got rid of the Empire one." "But the Empire one is handsome." "Handsome?" The vicomte raised a shoulder. "But they are very common, you know."

With another shrug, he took out his pocketbook and handed John the money. The Sinnotts glanced wonderingly at each other as John stuffed the bills into his pocket. This was a windfall for them; they were very low at the bank, and a mortgage payment was due. Yet their pleasure was discolored by the vicomte's irascible manner, which seemed to insist that he had "done" them, against his inclination. "Count it, count it!" he exclaimed, as if speaking to a child, and John, shrugging himself, obediently leafed through the bills, while the old man watched him. Martha felt dissatisfaction in the air, as if they had all been weighed in each other's scales and found wanting. She knew what she had expected of the vicomte, but how, concretely, he had found *them* a disappointment she could not make out.

Yet he made no move to go. He seemed rooted to the spot, tracing a pattern with his stick on the stubbly lawn. "You could sell off some of this," he suddenly proposed, pointing down the locust grove to the old apple orchard. "You have more than you can manage. By the road there, you can cut off two house-lots." John Sinnott's brows drew darkly together; he stiffened and threw his chest out, like an equestrian statue of one of his military ancestors. "I can find you a buyer perhaps," their visitor persisted. *"No,"* pleaded Martha. The vicomte slowly turned his head and regarded them in rheumy astonishment. "You are romantic," he divined. "Certainly," said Martha. In her lexicon this was a term of praise. But the vicomte made a *moue* of boredom and returned his blinking gaze to the ground. In the silence, they heard a quail call. The feeling that there was a defeated purpose in the vicomte's visit oppressed Martha's spirits; she hated the inconclusive. Her common sense told her that he had come simply to satisfy his curiosity, like so many others who had "looked in on" them since John's accident the other day, only to be disappointed, apparently, to find everything in order, the bed made, the floor swept, the dish towels on the line. But she felt something more here, as if he had something to say to them that he had thought better of when he saw them together, for the first time, on their home ground. Disturbing ideas floated through her head: that he had come to proselytize them, for A. A., for the Roman church, or to warn them, like one of Abraham's angels, away from New Leeds. Her eyebrows queried her husband, over the vicomte's bent head. There was still time to go swimming, if their guest would only leave.

"You'll send for the things?" prompted John. The vicomte absently nodded. "I have a man with a truck who works for me sometimes." He seemed lost in reflection; the Sinnotts waited. "I'll give you a lift," proposed John. The vicomte did not appear to hear him. "My truck," he said, bowing to Martha, "has just had the honor of transporting you to Digby." *"Me?"* cried Mar-

93

tha. "Your likeness," said the vicomte. "Oh, the *portrait!*" She turned a dismayed, startled face to her husband and felt her neck redden. "Oh, *no!*" she cried.

But John showed no surprise. "I *told* you," he said, interrupting her exclamations and giving her a baleful look. "You knew?" the vicomte said, coughing. "Martha knew," said John, curtly. Martha shook her head violently. She had *not* known, she said to herself. She had really believed what she had been telling John for the past three days: that Miles would not even remember the portrait when he woke up the next morning. A pain gripped her heart: for the first time in their knowledge of each other, John disbelieved her. "You were right," she admitted with a timid, placatory smile. "You *see?*" he said, poking her with his elbow, meaning that it was her fault, for having sat to Warren.

The vicomte watched them. "A strange whim, don't you think," he said, seating himself on a garden bench, "on Murphy's part, to want to possess a likeness of his ex-wife? Something abnormal, I find—a little in the manner of Bluebeard." Martha lowered her eyes. She agreed with the vicomte, but she had made a rule with John not to discuss Miles openly, here in New Leeds. She was burning to know more; after the first moment of perturbation, her natural inquisitiveness reasserted itself. But John, she saw, was truly upset. He sank onto the grass, wrapped his long arms, in their white shirtsleeves, glumly about his knees, and stared straight ahead of him. She settled down by his side and patted his knee lightly. It embarrassed her to have the vicomte see how hard John took things. At the same time, she was sorry for this gentle, moody being, her husband, who dropped more and more into himself, the more he disapproved of her, nowadays. And yet she could not see—as she would have said, but for the vicomte's presence—what she had done that was wrong, except in its unforeseen consequences. Nobody could have predicted that Miles would buy the portrait. She could scarcely believe it, even now, on the vicomte's word. The only thing that persuaded her, inwardly, that it was true was the fact that it had befallen her, almost like a punishment, for yielding to Warren's entreaties.

The vicomte was continuing his speculations, addressing himself to John. "After all," he mused, "it's a distorted vision, poor Coe's. A mutilation. *Quelle horreur!* Your wife's eye rolling about the canvas like a marble. I wonder you permitted it." John raised his eyebrows but said nothing.

"So you delivered it," hurriedly put in Martha. She did not want the vicomte to find out that John had objected to the sittings; if it got back to Warren, his feelings would be hurt. "Yesterday," agreed M. de Harnonville. "As a favor to Jane Coe, who came to ask me at the store. She had it tied onto the top of her station wagon, but it started to fall off in the village." John suddenly laughed. "Badly damaged?" he said hopefully. Martha frowned and seized his hand. "A little," said the vicomte. "I fixed it for her. I know something of picture-restoring. In a way, the accident was fortunate. It enabled her to reduce the price." John turned his head to the vicomte, with an expression of dawning interest. "What *was* the price?" queried Martha. "Eighteen hundred dollars," said the vicomte. *"What?"* cried the Sinnotts, in unison, sitting straight up and staring at each other. "Eighteen hundred dollars," repeated M. de Harnonville, cautiously smiling. "A bit steep, eh?"

The Sinnotts began to laugh, immoderately; John Sinnott rolled over on the lawn and bounced about, like a young boy. "Why, that's crazy," said Martha with feeling. "Mr. de Harnonville, you don't mean to say that Miles *paid* that?" "My dear," sighed M. de Harnonville, "you should know. Murphy is not a man who pays easily. I have been at law with him myself. . . ." "What time of day was it? Was he sober?" Martha demanded. "Sober?" said the vicomte. "I can't say. He was not in a good humor when I came. I wanted my man to put it up for him. But he called out to his wife to tell the baron to just leave it and go. Ever since our lawsuit, he speaks of me as the baron."

"And Mrs. Murphy?" said John, with a sidelong look at Martha. Their eyes sparkled at each other, as if they were at a play. "She was very nice," said the vicomte. "It was she who had arranged it with Jane Coe. She telephoned Jane to bring it, as a surprise for Murphy's birthday." The Sinnotts fell back on the ground. "Poor Miles!" sighed Martha. "He always hates his birthday presents. . . ." She did mental arithmetic. "Why, he must be fifty-five. . . ." "Who set the price?" interrupted John. "Jane, surely?" said Martha. "No," said the vicomte. "It was Warren. Jane herself was a little troubled about it; she asked me several times did I think Miles would think it was too high." Martha gave a fresh shriek of laughter. "How did he arrive at it, do you think?" she wondered, turning to her husband. John reflected. "By the yard," he ventured. "Actually, it's not a big price, by Fifty-seventh Street standards. A dealer would want two thousand, anyway, for a Pollock or De-Kooning of that size." "But Coe is an unknown," virtuously objected the vicomte. "It appears to me that he took an advantage of his friend."

"Why, it's shocking," agreed Martha. "The Coes are rolling in money. Not that you could tell it, from the way they live. It's typical of rich people to do a thing like that to a poor man like Miles." "Helen has money,"

John pointed out. "Not like Jane," said Martha. "Jane told me once that her family lived on the income of their income. And Warren has something of his own." The vicomte's blue eyes dilated. "Why, just think of it, John," continued Martha, sensing some sudden disagreement in her husband. "It's black ingratitude. After all, it's the first picture Warren's sold!" "You're mistaken," retorted John. "He's been selling his paintings for years, to his father-in-law." "A-h-h!" acknowledged the vicomte. "You have explained it. The father-in-law is a rich man." He nodded approvingly at John.

"Still," murmured Martha, "those aren't *bona fide* sales. Warren must know that underneath." Her brow wore a severe ruffle; she was angry with Warren for implicating her in something preposterous. The two men shook their heads. "No, my dear," said the vicomte. "He cannot permit himself to know. People cannot live with such knowledge. They go and hang themselves in the workshop. The proof that he doesn't know is just what your husband said—the price he felt obliged to charge Murphy." "Obliged?" Martha gave a sharp laugh. "Obliged," repeated John. "You can see that, if you want to. If Warren asked Miles less than he's been asking Mr. Carl, the inference would be that he'd been taking charity all these years from his wife's father." "Oh, come!" said Martha. "I always thought Mr. Carl liked his work." "Perhaps he does," said John. "It is more convenient for him that way," suggested the vicomte.

"You horrify me," cried Martha. "Both of you. You sound so cynical." And she looked in amazement at her husband. "What do you want?" wondered the vicomte. "That Coe should know that his work is valueless and his *beau-père* should know it too?" "I'm not talking about value. I'm talking about price," objected Martha. "But it's the same thing," said the vicomte. "Value is the price we will pay for what we want. Until yesterday, your portrait had no value. Today it has its price—that is to say, it exists, where before it was only an idea. Now it has been recognized; it is born." "Oh, stuff!" said Martha. "You just said yourself that the painting was horrible—didn't he, John?" "To me, it *is* horrible," agreed the vicomte, equably. "But I am not of an age to appreciate modern art."

Martha flung up her hands. "I can't argue with you," she said. "You keep shifting. 'Appreciate'—what does that mean?" "To set a price on, silly," said John. Martha frowned; she felt entangled in the discussion, and yet somewhere, in this cat's cradle of verbiage, there was something that seemed to her important to say. "Am I so wrong," she demanded, turning earnestly to John, "to expect Warren to know a little bit of the truth about his work? Just a little bit? I don't ask the impossible." "And what is the truth, madame?" said the vicomte. "Can you tell us?" Martha nodded, ignoring the buttery satire in the vicomte's voice. "Why yes," she said. "At least a part of it. The truth is that Warren's work is absurd, in the world's eyes. And I expect him to take that into account, when he sets a price on it. You think so yourself or you wouldn't have laughed at him." "Perhaps Warren will have the laugh on all of us, in time," said the vicomte, sagely.

Martha smiled. "That's what every undiscovered artist hopes for—the last laugh. But Warren is all too serious when he puts that ridiculous price on his paintings. He really thinks price *is* value." "Naturally," said the vicomte. "Other people value us by the price we set on ourselves. Coe was right; he got away with it." He gave a barking laugh and ran his hand over his pomaded hair. "No," said Martha. "That won't do, in the arts. You can't 'make' value by high-pressure methods, like a business men's price-fixing syndicate." "They all *do*," observed John. "Not all," said Martha. "The typical 'new' artist, of legend, had no idea what his paintings were worth. He was always giving them to his landlady." John cited exceptions; Martha countered; the vicomte looked bored. "Tell me," he said, abruptly, flexing his brows at Martha, "you do not have faith in your own work?" Martha felt John's eyes on her. "No," she said. "I don't. *He* does." She jerked a thumb at her husband. "For my part, I alternate between hope and despair." She gave a rueful sigh. The vicomte slowly rose and stretched. "Ah well," he said, "you will never succeed, then. In this world, everything is relative."

Martha stood in the kitchen, washing the vicomte's custard cup and humming a hymn tune. The two men had gone; John had insisted on driving the vicomte back to the village. Outside, the sun was sinking. It was too late to go swimming, and John, when he came home, would probably be cross at her for letting the vicomte stay so long. On the kitchen table stood the vicomte's basket, which she had forgotten to empty and return to to him. "Oh hell," she said, staring at the basket and knowing that this meant that they would have to see the vicomte again. Moreover, she had forgotten to thank him a second time for the mushrooms, which he had gathered with his own fat hands on the deserted golf course. "Oh hell," she repeated, beginning to tote up the record of her errors for the day. She had let him stay too long; she had been rather rude in the discussion; she had criticized Warren in a way that was bound to get repeated; she had paid no attention when John tried to deflect her by taking Warren's part. She could not learn, apparently, to strike a middle course between indulging a person like Warren and lambasting him to the first stranger who appeared.

99

And, in John's eyes, of course, she had betrayed him by announcing that she had no faith in her work. It was true, though not in the sense that the vicomte had understood. "You didn't have to *say* it," she heard her husband's voice proclaim. "I was upset," she mentally defended herself. "How would you feel if he had just bought your portrait?" And she *had* been upset, she supposed—more than she had consciously realized. Everything Miles did unnerved her, every word she heard of him, though she did not always feel it straight off. "That horrible man," she said aloud, remembering his drawling voice, and his elbows, in their hideous hairy tweed, resting on their car door, the other day at the Coes'. If he came to see them, as he had threatened to do, she would not, she clearly foresaw, have the force to prevent him. Neither would John; they were both too polite. She would never have the boldness to tell him that he had no right to come there.

She heard the car door slam, down the hill by the garage, and ransacked her mind for something to tell John that would divert him from the subject of the portrait—something amusing or very serious. But as she watched him, coming up the hill, with a determined, purposeful step, there were only words running through her head: *value, posterity, truth.*

FIVE

I T WAS Martha's theory that people, whatever they said, did in the end what they wanted. The only exception she knew of was her relation with Miles. With Miles she had done steadily what she hated, starting from the moment she married him, violently against her will. "You wanted to, all right," he used to growl at her, but she knew that it was not true. She had no explanation for this strange fact about herself. She was timid but not supine; nobody, except Miles, had ever browbeat her successfully. It was her youth, her friends had told her: when she met him, she had been an untried girl, who had not found herself, as the phrase was. If that was the case (and even John seemed to think so), she should have outgrown her fear of Miles during the intervening years; she *felt* much stronger, certainly. Yet, to her horror, the other day at the Coes', when she was face to face with Miles, the years between vanished and she had begun to tremble again, as she had not trembled since the night she had left him. This awful weakness in herself she dared not confess to John, chiefly for fear of troubling him with something that was inexplicable. She did not like Miles, but she did not dislike him either, apart from his effect on her. Now that she was free of him, she saw his good points and his drawbacks in her customary clear perspective. Here in the New Leeds region, he had a certain stature, compared to the other men; he had a canny mind and read a great deal, seriously. He might yet produce something worth while in the new field he had roamed into—the history of ideas; he was forceful and energetic, with a gift for amassing information that was like his prodigies at the table. . . . His trouble, Martha had decided, was that his talent was crushed by his ambition; he had wanted to be another Goethe and had ended up as a rolling stone. And he had no facility of expression. She herself, she now perceived, had qualities Miles envied: a sharp ear and a lively natural style. There was therefore no reason why she should tremble before him, when she knew him, moreover, to be selfish, brutal, and dishonest in his domestic life.

Her weakness in his presence must, she supposed, be explained by that mysterious entity known as power. But this did not take her much further, because she did not understand power, either the desire for it or the yielding to it. She could not imagine, except when she was near Miles, obedience that was not based either on rational consent or on rational fear. But she had obeyed Miles, when she was married to him, without knowing why.

This irrational element, this bewilderment before her own actions, had been present from the very beginning; she had ceased to know herself from the moment she met Miles. She was just out of college then, where she had been voted "most literary" as well as "best actress." Her teachers said "Martha can do anything." She herself was not sure yet whether she really wanted to try to be an actress, which was what her class book predicted, or to write poetry, her earliest interest, or to plug ahead and do graduate work, which was what her favorite teacher advised. Her father was sending her an allowance so that she could take her time. She was engaged to a young man who had two more years, still, of architectural school; she had just had a rather squalid abortion, which another young man had paid for; she was acting small parts in a shoestring summer theater—when Miles, a friend of the producer, drifted in one terrible evening, after a bad performance, and started bulldozing her into marriage before she really knew him. It was what she needed, he assured her, appraising her with his jellied green eyes when she woke up, for the second time, in bed with him, after a lot of drinks. And because she had found herself in bed with him, against her natural inclinations (for he seemed immensely old to her, being well over forty while she was not yet twenty-one), she had concluded that he must be right. He knew what was best for her, doubtless—she needed a steadying force, a man, as he said, with a mind. She went back to the theater dormitory and sat on her bed, stoically, like a lump. She did not understand what had happened. She had only, she bemoaned, wanted to talk to him—a well-known playwright and editor, successful, positive, interested in her ideas and life-history. And yet he must be right; even her teachers would think so. She would never, surely, have yielded to his embraces, shrinking, as she did, from his swollen belly and big, crooked nose, if some deep urge in herself, which *he* seemed to understand, had not decreed it. The fatalistic side of her character accepted Miles as a punishment for the sin of having slept with him when she did not love him, when she loved, she still felt, someone else. Nevertheless, she had naively sought a compromise. She had begged Miles merely to live with him, as his mistress. But Miles had held out for marriage, instanter; he needed a mother for his son. She was still hesitating when the knot was tied and Miles was sitting beside her on the train, his chin sunk on his chest, morosely silent, a stranger, as they journeyed to pick up the boy, who was living with Miles's sister. He would not let her telegraph her presumptive fiancé, in Cambridge, until the ceremony was over.

That was Miles. He would not let her give notice to the theater people, either, but made her pack her bags while she was still rehearsing next week's part. The rest of her marriage, which had lasted four years, was in a way simply a catalogue of the natural things Miles would not let her do. He would not let her fly to Juneau to her father's funeral, though her mother was ill and wired her the money. He would not let her see her brother off to the war or have him in the house when he came back wounded. He made her change her hair and turn over her small capital to him, after her mother died; he would never give her an allowance for the household or herself. He held the checkbook and hired and fired the servants, when they had them. He would not let her go to New York, once they had moved to New Leeds, unless he accompanied her. She could not get the child vaccinated or inoculated against diphtheria because Miles objected. He refused to have her practice birth-control and when she did it, privily, he made terrible scenes at night. He would not let her see her friends or accept an invitation without consulting him first. And, finally, he would not let her leave him.

There it was again. She was afraid to leave him, though he had no means of preventing her from doing it at any moment, had she dared. But, improbable as it seemed now, she had felt she could not leave him without his permission. When she finally ran away, it was partly because of John, whom she had secretly fallen in love with, but mainly because Miles, by pushing her out of the house, had seemed at last to give her license. That was why she flew out to the garage, in her nightgown, before he could revoke it. And even at that moment, as she turned on the ignition, she had the uneasy sense that she was taking advantage of Miles: he had not really meant for her to go.

This unaccountable fear she had often discussed with John. It was exactly, she said, like a phobia, like the fear of dogs or snakes or high places; reason had nothing to do with it. To tell herself that Miles could not hurt her had no more effect than pointing out that a snake was harmless or a dog did not bite. She *knew* he could not hurt her, seriously, and she used to force herself to oppose him, on small points, like an acrophobe who makes himself look over a parapet. But it did not work. The more she nerved herself to differ with him, the more fear she felt. It was only a sort of social shame or conscience on Barrett's behalf that drove her to take stands. She resisted him because she thought she ought to, in a flurry of hysterical defiance. And the mere act of controverting him made her lose her head. She would find herself arguing excitedly when she knew she was in the wrong, or the issue would get away from her and turn into something else. Their penultimate quarrel, for example, had exploded in the middle of the night, after a party, when she was carrying out two overflowing pails of garbage and he refused, with a sardonic bow, to hold open the screen door for her. There she was, manifestly, the injured party, but instead of leaving it at that and taxing him with it the next day, when he was weakened with a hangover, she immediately distributed the guilt by setting down one pail of garbage and slapping him across his grinning face. She never knew how to make him feel sorry for what he had done.

The first night of their marriage, when he had suddenly struck her, for no reason, as she was climbing into bed, she had looked up at him in mute amazement, too startled even to cry. So far as she knew herself, Martha was one of those people who were naturally reasonable, like an open-minded child who listens unsuspiciously to what is told him and expects no evil. And Miles, from the outset, with a sort of blind purpose, like a mole, had set himself to undermine her sense of credibility: she could not believe what was happening. If she were a real woman, Miles used to tell her, she would learn how to handle him. But something obstinate in her nature refused to be indoctrinated; her passion for the normal rebelled. She would not exploit his "good" moods, and fear and nervous excitement caused her to fumble their quarrels. The sound of his tread, coming up the stairs, at night, when he had been drinking, made her heart race with terror, even when she had the door locked against him. In fact—here again was an oddity—she was more frightened on the nights when she had had the courage to turn her doorkey, softly, while he was still downstairs, than when she had left the door unlocked. It was her own guilty temerity, in the face of him, that held her palpitating, waiting for the knob to turn, the heavy knock to sound, rattling the whole house, and the step, finally, to lurch away into the guest bedroom.

It still made her shiver to think of those nights. She had not been able to get to sleep, even after he was gone and she could hear his snores, like regular paroxysms, coming from down the corridor. Fear would be succeeded by remorse, another form of cowardice; she always flinched from offending anyone, as if from a blow at herself. She could not bear the picture of humiliation, even in an enemy, even in Miles. The thought of the maid and Barrett listening in their beds, while Miles pounded uncertainly at the door, a suppliant, made her relent, as often as not, and tiptoe across the room to let him in. It was better, on the whole, to be kicked out of bed and to retreat herself to the guest bedroom than to listen to his exiled snores and be sorry.

A psychiatrist, of course, would say that she had wanted Miles to beat her. Miles himself used to contend this, in his seignorial style; he convinced himself that he was doing her a service by letting her have a black eye. It was on the strength of such "insights," she supposed, that he had begun to take paying patients after she had left him. But even discounting Miles's opinion, Martha herself had often wondered whether there could be a grain of truth in the charge. Yet if there was anything she knew about herself, it was that she hated violence. She had never received it from John and never, as she assured him wryly, missed it. He objected because she screamed, sometimes, when he came upon her unexpectedly, and her hand sometimes flew up to her face, as if to ward off a blow, when he raised his arm casually, in the midst of a discussion. But she was hoping to get over these reflexes, the last trace of Miles's influence, as she had got over her bad dreams and the other fears, of automobiles, of falling, that he had left in his wake. With John, she was a different person, and she was proud of it. She had even been looking forward, secretly, to meeting Miles again, to confront him with her new character.

The strange thing was that nobody seemed to have noticed her trembling the other day at the Coes', though the pounding of her heart, when Miles came to take her cloak, had been so loud that she thought the whole room must hear it, like a rumbling in somebody's stomach. She had not seen the Coes since, but John and Dolly Lamb had assured her that she was fine when she asked them, "How did I seem?" in an apprehensive voice. And John, when she reiterated the question, adding, "Tell me the truth," appeared a little surprised.

"You were fine," he said again, absently: his only criticism was that she had been *too* natural and friendly. This alarmed Martha. Either, she reasoned, he was withholding his real view, from tact, or else, she possessed, unknown to herself, the power to deceive him. And the last thing she wanted was to have such a power.

She had always been able to deceive Miles because he did not know her. He had mistaken both her faults and her virtues. He did not reckon with idealism as a serious factor in life and judged, as he used to say weightily, by actions. He had supposed that she must love him because she had let him seduce her on the very first meeting and because she did not leave him though she continually threatened to do so. This refusal to listen was a form of stupidity that Martha especially abhorred, and she considered Miles well punished for it. If he had ever taken seriously her passionate desire to leave him, she might not (she now believed) have been driven to show him in practice how little indeed he knew. To *pay attention,* for Martha, was the prime human virtue; without it, there could be no dignity and no reciprocity. The alertness of this faculty was what she prized in John. She wished nothing to be hidden from him, not even the bad parts of her nature. She respected his privacy, because he was a man, but for herself, if she could not be transparent, she did not want to love.

It seemed to her, therefore, ominous that the minute Miles re-entered her life, a slight deception began, almost automatically. She was able to conceal again, like that *other* person, whom she was supposed to have outgrown. She was both glad and sorry that John had not observed the turmoil she had been thrown into. It cut her off from him; he no longer knew her, which was perhaps for the best, since she did not know herself. Looking at Miles, she felt the old central question turned on her like an artillery piece. In the twelve years since she had met him, he had not changed at all. She could explain, in a way, how she had come to marry him, under the circumstances, and how, under the circumstances, she had stayed with him so long. But why she had let this man make love to her in the first place remained totally mystifying. Just at this point, when she looked at him and then looked backward, there was a terrifying blank.

"Yes, why did you?" said Dolly Lamb, gently, with a quizzical look at Martha, who had driven over to see her the day after the vicomte's visit. She was used to Martha's irruptions into her orderly life and had come up here, only the Saturday before last, to paint the marshes, because John and Martha had written to tell her that they had found a house she must live in, like Thoreau's, on a pond. It was a shack, really, that had been used in the fall by duck-hunters—two tiny rooms and a kitchen, with only a fireplace to heat them and a kitchen range. At night, in her bunk-bed, Dolly protested, she was cold, but John and Martha had laughed and told her to sleep in woolen socks and sweaters. Dolly feared that she would offend them if she went to Digby and bought an electric blanket; they were very set in their notions of what was fitting for her.

Dolly was a year younger than Martha and still unmarried, which had resigned her to being prescribed for by everybody, as if she had an ailment. She was a distant cousin of John's and had been at college with Martha, in the class below. She was tall and long-legged and curiously flattened out, like a cloth doll that had been dressed and redressed by many imperious mistresses. She had a neat round little face that came to a point unexpectedly in a firm, slightly jutting chin, short crisp blond hair, of a silvery cast, a silvery quiet laugh, and bright silver-blue eyes that shone with a high gleam, as if they had just been polished. Her pink cheeks and ears had a faintly angry, scrubbed look. In her unusual style, she was remarkably pretty—like a china shepherdess, said some people; like a gray nun, said others; like a mermaid, like a scalloped Spode plate, like a heron, like a shingled, weathered cottage, like a Swiss clock with bells and a maiden inside. It was Dolly's fate to evoke fanciful comparisons, to be, as Martha said, a *posse* rather than an *esse* to everyone who knew her. She was too inscrutable, said Martha; that was why she had not got married—men did not think she was real. John said it was her shyness and the fact that she had been brought up by two eccentric aunts, who had died and left her their money. An orphan, he said, was just a figment who was sentimentalized by the whole world, like the heroine of a storybook; Dolly had never had any real privacy to develop herself in. Ever since Martha had known her, she had been under trustees.

She was now giving Martha tea and English muffins, which she was toasting with a fork over the fire. Her face was bright with the heat and puckered with a frown of concentration; this thoughtful, anxious, winsome look was typical of all the serious, clever girls she and Martha had been friends with at college. They bent their soft brows in continual perplexity, as if a teacher had just asked them a probing question. Dolly was gentler and more reserved than Martha; she was ironic where Martha was satiric and modest where Martha was vain. But just these differences, as in two sisters, pointed up the likeness between them—a likeness that reassured them, even though they affected to deprecate it. Martha today had come to talk to Dolly about Miles, and she felt a little guilty about it because it was the first time, in seven years, that she had reposed her confidence in anybody but John. "I'll just stop and leave Dolly some tarragon," she had called out to him, as she drove off. "Have a good time," he advised, and Martha could not make out whether this meant that he saw through her excuse.

"Well, I was tight, of course," she said now, watching her friend butter a muffin. Dolly gave a faint, embarrassed smile. "Oh, Martha!" she said. Martha laughed; she had always liked to shock Dolly. "I've slept with lots of men when I was tight," she continued. "You'd die if I told you how many." Dolly's eyes widened in a question. "Not now, of course," said Martha, quickly. "Years ago. Before I knew John." Dolly nodded; she handed Martha the muffin and sought to change the subject slightly. "Miss Prentice," she said, naming their favorite teacher, "always said you married Mr. Murphy for security. She had seen his picture once in the paper." The two girls smiled. "Poor Miss Prentice," murmured Martha. Dolly frowned. "But you never cared about security," she pondered. Martha nodded gloomily. "I know," she said. There was a silence. "He seemed so *old*, Dolly," Martha exclaimed suddenly, setting down her cup and passing her hand across her brow, as if to calm herself. "He hasn't changed a bit. I'd forgotten what he looked like. It gave me a turn to see him and remember myself yielding to his charms." "I thought you were tight," objected Dolly. "I was *conscious*," cried Martha. "I wasn't that tight. I remember everything about it, except one tiny little bit—the bit where *he* says I kissed him. I can't remember that at all. The next thing I knew he was taking me into a motel, on the old Post Road. I was afraid we were going to get fleas. I remember thinking about *that* all the time. Do you suppose I really did kiss him, Dolly?" "I don't know," said Dolly. "If I did," said Martha, "it wasn't meant to be that kind of kiss. If it was, I *don't know myself at all,* Dolly. All I can remember of my feelings is a sort of vague surprise, as if there were a big misunderstanding going on that ought to be cleared up, before it was too late, but I was too tight and tired to explain it to him. Up to the last minute, in the cabin, with all my clothes off, I was still trying to tell him that he was acting on a mistaken premise. I think I went through with it, as a sort of concession, to get him to listen to what I was trying to say." She gave a little laugh. "Did you mind, Martha?" said Dolly, sympathetically. "Not specially," said Martha. "It just seemed to me beside the point for him to be making love to me. I wasn't either drawn or repelled—till the next morning, when I was horrorstruck. And then it happened again." "In the morning, you mean?" said Dolly. Martha shook her head. "No. The next week. I thought it was all over and I could forget about it—treat it as an aberration. But then he turned up again, at the theater, and the same thing happened again, in practically every detail. . . ." Dolly scratched her head. "You *must* have been attracted to him," she concluded. "But I *wasn't,*" said Martha. "I *had* a man I was attracted to, more than one, in fact." She shrugged and took another muffin.

"It was an awful mistake to come back here," she continued. "Don't tell John I said so; he doesn't like to hear it. He knows it too but he won't say so. I can't tell him what I feel any more. He wants us to be brave and indifferent." "But why not?" said Dolly. "Why should you let Miles affect you?" "I don't know," acknowledged Martha, sighing. "But he does. I can't help it. He casts a long shadow. I don't want to live in it. I feel depreciated by him, like a worm, like a white grub in the ground." She jumped up and began to gesture with the muffin, conscious of acting a part; yet what she said was quite true. Again, as with John, she found that she could not be herself and describe the feelings Miles aroused in her. "I don't understand," said Dolly. Martha nodded; communication seemed hopeless. "Look, Dolly," she said. "Between Miles and me, there's a permanent war of principle. He claims to know what I am, to interpret me according to his authorized version; I'm sure he pretends to know why John and I came back here and why we married and what we 'get out of each other,' as he'd put it in his nasty grasping vocabulary. And I claim to know about him; thanks to my experience, I have the 'lowdown' on Miles. Two claims like this can't exist side by side, in balance. One has to crush the other. And I'm the one to be crushed, inevitably." She waved the muffin. "Why do you think that?" murmured Dolly, knitting her brows. "Because I doubt," said Martha, rather grandly. "It occurs to me that I may be wrong. Miles has never had that experience." Dolly inclined her head. "I see what you mean," she said, thoughtfully. "Meeting him the other day. . . ."

Martha's face brightened. "You thought he was awful?" she demanded, sitting down with a thump. "Yes," said Dolly, in decided tones. "In what way?" pressed Martha. "So *heavy*," said Dolly. "Like a stone-crusher. He made me nervous too. He reminded me of everybody's father." "Good!" exclaimed Martha. "You want people to dislike him?" asked Dolly. "Of course," said Martha. "I rejoice in it. What did you think of *her?*" Dolly screwed up her forehead. "Rather nice, I thought, really. Very sweet face. Attractive in her way." Martha bit her lip. "More so than I am?" But before Dolly could answer, Martha withdrew the question. "No," she said. "Don't tell me. I don't want to hear, either way. Why should I care if she's attractive?" "You're jealous," said Dolly, with a troubled countenance. "I must be," ad-

113

mitted Martha. "But not in the way you would think. I stayed awake all last night, examining my conscience. I can't bear to have such feelings. They're unworthy. And I have no right to them. It isn't as if I wanted him for myself. Perish the thought. I would die, I think, if he started after me again. That's what I keep telling myself." She closed her eyes and sat leaning back on the canvas-covered couch, looking all at once very pale and exhausted. "I always told him," she said, slowly, "that he ought to let me leave him, for his own sake. I thought I meant it. I thought I had enough generosity to want him to be happy, apart from me." She took a deep breath and set her lips. There was a silence while Martha brooded and Dolly watched her affectionately. "Don't tell me if you don't feel like it," she murmured. It frightened her a little to see Martha like this, a waxen effigy of resolute misery; she had always considered her a gay, resilient person. Martha made a grimace. "I'll try," she said. "In a minute." She closed her eyes again and reflected.

She was the worst wife he could have married, she used to tell Miles. It would be best for both of them, if he would let her go. "You're the one I want," Miles always retorted, comfortably. "No," she would answer, resting her head on his arm, in the big bed (this would be one of their "good" mornings, when Miles was on the wagon); another woman, in her place, she said, would submit to his moods and make him happy. But though she allowed for this contingency in theory, she really did not think it likely. A saint, she meant, would put up with him. Hence it had greatly dismayed her, the other day at the Coes', to see that this hypothetical other woman actually existed, smiling and tender, obeying him gratefully, murmuring, "Yes, dearest," when he gave the sign

to go. The notion that Miles could be "dearest" to anyone struck Martha as preposterous. It was still more fantastic to hear from the vicomte that it was *Helen* who
had sent for the portrait. Such abnegation seemed to
Martha unnatural and almost wicked. She could not, as
she said to John, get over it. Yet it had a certain ring of
familiarity. *That,* she declared with a sigh, was exactly
the crazy kind of thing Miles tried to exact from a
woman who wanted to live with him in peace. There was
method in his madness; he made his wives choose between him and common sense, between him and ordinary decency.

He made his wives his accomplices; that was why they
could not escape him. They had to stand by and watch
him abuse the servants, hold back their wages, eat their
food, accuse them of robbing him. He insisted that his
wives lie for him, to his creditors, to the insurance company, to the tax people. He had no sense of limit or of
other people's rights. Nothing was safe from his mean-
dering appetites: the maid's time off, her dinner, her
birthday box of candy, the cooking sherry, the vanilla.
He slept in every bed and commandeered every bathroom. He even, Martha remembered, used to eat Barrett's lollipops.

There was method in it, Martha had reiterated, to
John, only last night: mere lack of consideration could
not have carried him so far. His outrageousness had a
purpose; by a campaign of calculated "frightfulness" he
broke his wives' spirits. She herself could never live
down, in her own mind, not what he had done to her,
but what she had consented in—their treatment of her
brother, the beatings he used to give Barrett. It was *his*
child, she used to tell herself; she could not interfere
every time; it would only goad Miles on, etc., etc. These
arguments were sound; she was justified; she had done

her utmost. There was only one thing—a thing she had never quite brought herself to confess to John. Hearing Barrett cry, she had sometimes experienced pleasure. For an instant, before she could stop herself by pressing her fingers to her ears, she gloated that Miles was revealing himself in his true colors to his son. And, to be honest, she often felt something of the same kind when he ate the servants' food.

If she had not felt this, she might have managed him better. She had seen this suddenly last night, in bed, clear as a vision or an unexpected refraction of her face from a street mirror. Miles had been right. It had satisfied her, in some part of her soul, whenever he behaved badly to herself or anyone else. It had proved, so to speak, a point. "You *see?*" she had felt like exclaiming, to Barrett, to the servants, to her doubting self. "That's the way he is!" Martha was too fair-minded to incite him to any of his crimes, and indeed she *had* done her best to protect other people from him and to cover up his traces, so that the world would not know. But if despite all her efforts he demonstrated *what he was,* some part of her was well content and nodded to itself, as though a prediction had been verified. He would not *let* her love him, she used to tell herself, in gloomy triumph; he would not let anybody love him, including his own child. Now it dashed her to recognize that somebody else had succeeded in doing what she had always defined as the impossible. "She loves him," she had said aloud to herself, wonderingly, sitting up in bed and feeling a strange pang of jealousy.

Her own love, beside this, seemed a paltry, commonplace thing—why should she *not* love John? It took no special virtue; he was a lovable person. She had turned on the light softly and looked down at him, a coil of limbs in the bed; he slept like a child, his lashes quivering

gently on his cheek, his curly hair disarrayed pic-
turesquely. He was beautiful and good, and yet as she
looked down on him, curiously, she had a hollow sense,
as though those very qualities had deprived her of an opportunity, the opportunity of loving against the grain.

"I'm envious of their marriage, isn't that ridiculous?"
she said to Dolly, now, with a light, forced laugh and a
grimace. "I can't bear the idea that anybody might
think that it was happier than mine." Dolly poked the
dying fire. The pine wood was green; Martha and John
had told her that she ought to have locust. She felt a
little shocked, as usual, by Martha and wondered
whether Martha was different from herself or simply
more honest—a question Martha had often provoked
among her college circle. "You mean," said Dolly
thoughtfully, trying to understand, "that if he's happy,
it casts a reflection on you?" Martha nodded. "But why
should it, Martha?" pleaded Dolly. "You weren't the
right person for him." Martha laughed. "Dear Dolly,"
she said, "you sound so sensible. But I'm not. I'm an ab-
solutist. I want to be a paragon uniting all the virtues.
You remember that speech of Iago's about Cassio? 'He
hath a daily beauty in his life that makes me ugly.'
Well, I feel that in reverse. I'd like to say to Miles: 'I
have a daily beauty in my life that makes yours ugly.' In
fact, I'd like to say it to every single person here in New
Leeds, except you. All these tawdry people. That's why
we came back here—to show them how tawdry they are
in comparison to us." "Why, Martha, that's horrible,"
said Dolly, with her hand to her cheek. "I told you," said
Martha. "No wonder I feel like a worm. I hate this in
myself and I can't cast it out. And once I've discovered
it I find it everywhere—all over me, even in my best actions. I suddenly feel that that's why John and I got

married: to show the rest of the world how to do it right, a sort of star turn, calculated to excite envy." "I don't believe it," said Dolly, resolutely, shaking her head. "I know you both better than that. John was always a bit of a show-off, in his reserved way, and so were you, Martha. But you both admire lots of people—your friends. I've heard you. You're both tremendous enthusiasts." Martha reflected. "Yes," she said. "You're right. In a way. I always prided myself"—she laughed—"on the notion that I knew when to be humble. It must be this place that's brought out the latent worst in me. Because of Miles. I feel I'm living in a showcase. Everybody is looking up to Digby and making comparisons. Or is it my imagination? It seems to me that it's inevitable, that the human mind, given two similars, weighs them against each other. The principle of balance." Dolly inclined her head. "I see," she murmured. "But can't you stop thinking about it?"

Martha lifted a shoulder. "You might as well tell me to stop thinking about myself. I can't. If I think about him or her, I think about myself. If I think about myself, *they* pop into my mind. It's degrading. Do you think about yourself a lot, Dolly?" "Constantly," smiled Dolly. "In terms of reprimand." "I know," said Martha. "I wonder if these other people do. I can't make out. If they did, you'd presume they'd make some effort to improve their messy lives. So probably they don't. I like your shells," she added, examining an arrangement of graduated seashells that Dolly had picked up on the beach. "You did it for pleasure, I imagine. If it were I, I would do it to make somebody admire my ingenuity." She sighed and got up. "And the irony is, Dolly, that nobody here cares. They don't know the difference. All my silly efforts are wasted on them. You should have seen the vicomte yesterday: the soul of phlegm. And I

was hurt. Imagine. I wanted him to like our furniture."
"Why *shouldn't* he?" said Dolly indignantly. Martha
laughed. "I love you, Dolly," she murmured. "You're so
loyal." She hesitated. "Thank you for coming up here,"
she said quickly. "I know you did it for us. Forgive us for
bullying you." "All my friends bully me," said Dolly
cheerfully. "Anyway, Martha, *I* admire you. You don't
have to force me to, either of you. But you do make me
feel inferior. You always have. When you're here, I burn
the muffins." She pointed with the fork to the charred
remains on the hearth. Martha's fair skin colored. "I
didn't will that to happen," she said. "Honestly. I'd
much rather you didn't burn them. I love perfection
in my friends. I don't grudge you the seashells or having a better character than I have. It makes me happy."
She pondered. "Isn't there such a thing, any more, as a
healthy rivalry, a noble emulation, like the Olympic
Games or a contest of bards? Does it all have to be
poisoned, nowadays? This horrible bohemian life you
see up here, with lily cups and beards and plastics—it's
real leveling, worse than suburbia, where there's a frank
competition with your neighbors, to have the newest car
or bake the best cakes. I can understand that. I'm like
that myself. But here nobody competes, unless there's
a secret contest as to who can have the most squalid
house and give the worst parties. It gives me the strang-
est feeling, as if I were the only one left in the world
with the desire to excel, as if I were competing, all alone,
on an empty stage, without judges or rivals, just myself—a solipsistic nightmare. 'That way lies madness,'
as old Dr. Hendricks used to say, remember, in fresh-
man philosophy. In Juneau, Dolly, there used to be
a madwoman who rode up and down the streets on a
bicycle, wearing a sort of circus costume, tights and a
red jacket, and white paint and rouge. I feel just like

her when I walk down the main street here, in a dress and stockings; everybody stares—I'm anti-social. The other day, in the First National, one of the local beldames actually plucked at my arm and asked me why I wore stockings. 'Nobody does up here,' she informed me.'"

"You always were a rebel," said Dolly. "You'd be the same if you lived in Scarsdale." "No," said Martha. "If I lived in Scarsdale, I wouldn't care what the neighbors thought. And I wouldn't want to reform them." "You want to reform these people?" asked Dolly, with a quizzical smile. Martha nodded. "Of course. I'm trying to set an example. It's not only vanity; there's also a corrective impulse. 'Let your light so shine before all men.' That's the very height of my folly. John and I are making ourselves ludicrous with our high-toned ways. I know it but I won't desist. It becomes a form of fanaticism. They can kill me, I say to myself, grandly, but they can't make me be like *them*."

Dolly remained seated on her stool by the fireplace, watching Martha arrange her gray cloak. "You won't believe it," said Martha, "but I don't want to have a selfish life. I hate this obsession with myself, these odious comparisons. I want to live for somebody else, for 'humanity.'" She gave a droll smile. "You have John," pointed out Dolly. Martha frowned. "That's just the trouble," she said. "He won't let me live for him. He wants to live for me. It leaves us at a peculiar deadlock. I keep telling myself that if we could only have a baby, everything would be changed. I felt certain that when we came up here, I would 'conceive,'" The habit of speaking in quotation marks was one the two young women had acquired in college; Martha had trained herself out of it, professionally, but when she was with Dolly the mannerism reasserted itself.

"Maybe you will, Martha." Martha shook her head. "I'm thirty-three. A little too old really, for a first baby. And years ago I had an abortion. It may have done something to my insides. Anyway, it's probably wrong to have a baby as a 'solution.' One ought to have it for no reason, just for itself." Her hand was on the doorknob, but she still lingered. "Come to dinner to-morrow. I'll cook something vainglorious for you. Maybe we'll go mushrooming first. John has found a new kind. And we have some beautiful poisonous ones, waxy yellows and exotic carmines, that we thought you might like to paint. The poisonous ones, naturally, are the prettiest." She was speaking, all at once, very rapidly, in a disjointed manner. Dolly looked at her wonderingly. "Thank you for the tea," added Martha. "Thank *you* for the tarragon," said Dolly, slowly getting up. "I really must go," said Martha, still not moving. "John will worry. That's the disadvantage of your not having a telephone. Dolly, *are* you lonely here?" "I *like* it," said Dolly.

The two young women's eyes slowly canvassed each other. "One more thing," said Martha, hurriedly, in an offhand tone but holding her friend's gaze. "About the baby. It occurred to me last night that the reason I wanted one was because of them." Dolly dropped her eyes. "You mean the Murphys," she muttered, staring at the floor. Martha nodded. "They have a baby. I want a better one. It stands to reason. I never thought seriously of having one till we came up here." Dolly's figure stiffened, as though a pain had shot through it, as she listened to this abrupt confession. "You mustn't say that," she admonished. "I know," gravely agreed Martha. "If I ever *should* have a baby, you must promise to forget that I told you. It may not even be true." She tossed the last phrase off lightly and stood on tiptoe to give Dolly a kiss. Dolly received the kiss absently and remained where she was, leaning slightly forward, like a pillar, as she heard the door shut and Martha's quick, lively step crackle the twigs in the path outside. The horn played a flourish, in farewell, and the pond sent the sound back, a distant airy cadenza.

Dolly drew her thumb slowly across her jaw. She frowned. Her neat dish face wore a mazed look of consternation. She shook herself, dog style, and went, still frowning, to pick up the tea things. "You must not be *shocked*," she said to herself aloud, in stern bell tones, as she headed toward the little kitchen.

SIX

"YOU MUSTN'T be shocked by anything. That's the first lesson for the artist," said Sandy Gray, seriously. He was a tall Australian with a brown beard who had formerly been an art critic on an English magazine. He was wearing a black wool shirt, black dungarees, and black wading boots and was knocking out a black pipe on Dolly Lamb's table. It was mid-morning. Dolly had been painting, on the ridge outside her house, when she saw a strange man striding through the pond toward her, cutting down the pickerel weed with a hunting knife as he went. She shaded her eyes to watch him, but he ignored her anxious figure, while making straight for the spot where she was standing—like a guided missile, she fancied. A mild, half-humorous fear crinkled her forehead. She was readily dismayed by the most ordinary encounters; everything for her was numinous—the butcher with his cleaver, the hunter in the woods. Her virgin heart feared the Angel Gabriel in the milkman, bumping along the road in his truck, and did not dare refuse the milk, cream, eggs, and butter he offered her, far beyond her small wants. Behold the handmaiden of the Lord—she lived meekly in the age of fable, amid powers that had to be propitiated. The intruder today, in a black visored cap, swashing through the pond, advanced on her like a superman from a comic book or the man from the telephone company; in either case, the same perplexity presented itself: who

123

was to speak first? "Hello," she called out bravely, when he was twenty feet away. "Hi," he retorted and flailed his way up the slope to her easel. He studied her painting in silence, scratching his ear. He then walked into the house in his wet boots, followed by Dolly. "I'm Sandy Gray," he stated, in a voice that took her aback by its softness. "Have you got a cup of coffee?" "Only instant," confessed Dolly. "That'll do," he answered. "Fix us a couple of cups."

Out in the kitchen, as she put on the water to boil and measured out the coffee, she could see him, hunched on her studio couch, reading her copy of *Art News,* his black cap pulled down and his hunting knife stuck in his belt. Dolly was perturbed. Apprehension had told her who he was even before he had introduced himself: a typical backwoods blowhard, according to John Sinnott; a horrible boor, said Martha. He was a former Communist, it seemed, who made sandals in the summertime, for the tourist trade, and rode a motorcycle and used to feed his children on peanut butter and send them to school barefoot, till the S.P.C.C. stepped in. On no account, warned Martha, was Dolly to give him any encouragement, if he dropped by to call on her. His fourth wife had just left him, and he was on the prowl again. He would want to be neighborly and to advise her about her painting, but he was only after liquor and somebody to cook his meals for him.

He did not *need* any encouragement, Dolly inwardly cried. He seemed so at home that it was she who felt like the interloper. When he had finished his coffee, he took his cap off, tossed it on the couch, and walked up and down her small living room, his thumbs stuck in his belt, examining her effects just as if he were alone in the house. He opened and closed the door to her bedroom, glanced up the chimney flue, picked up a picture postcard and scanned the message on the back of it. He stood for a long time staring at the books in her makeshift bookcase, lifted out one, riffled through it, and replaced it, upside down. During this inspection, not a word was spoken. Dolly's soul was outraged, but her tongue refused to move. She did not know how to forbid him the extraordinary liberties he was taking. He behaved like a higher authority with a warrant to search out evidence of her personal tendency. As she sat, meekly watching, a thread of silvery humor wove in and out of her thoughts, tracing a delicate embroidery. At the same time, suspense began to mount in her; her heart beat faster under her pale-blue shirtwaist and golden chamois jacket. She could not escape the thought that he was here to pronounce a judgment.

On the driftwood table, by the window, there was a bowl of poisonous mushrooms, brought her by the Sinnotts, which she had set up to paint. He bent down to smell them and made a noise of disgust. "Corrupt and dainty," he said, in his soft, breathy voice. "Throw them out. They stink." And before Dolly could protest, from her footstool by the fireplace, he had taken the dish from the table, opened the screen door, and flung the deadly mushrooms out into the pinewoods. "Damn you!" cried Dolly, jumping up indignantly. "You've just ruined my still life." She confronted him, quivering, her arms akimbo, while he watched her, unperturbed, from his greater height. In a minute Dolly fell back, discountenanced by the grave look of his deep-set eyes, which swept back and forth, slowly, across her face, like two searchlights set in the bushy camouflage of hair and beard and brows. Having lost her temper and sworn at him, she found herself mysteriously translated onto a plane of intimacy, and she listened, a little bemused, as he proceeded to give her a lecture on decadence, with illustrations drawn from what he had found in her dwelling. The fact that he claimed to "know" her without even knowing her name imparted a sort of dreamlike solemnity to the home truths he was telling her; he descended on her like some meddlesome old prophet twitching the sleeve of a busy monarch with a message from on high.

"Stop hoarding," he said gently, pointing to her collection of seashells and to the starfish arranged in a graduated series on her mantelpiece. "It's your own shit you're assembling there, in neat, constipated little packages." Dolly's cheeks suddenly flamed. She was as a matter of fact given to constipation and she felt as if he had peeked into her medicine-cabinet and found the bottle of Nujol. Moreover, she detested coarse language. The British, she told herself dutifully, were less nice in their speech than the Americans. But even as she strove not to mind, not to be insular and puritanical, tears sprang to her eyes, and she had to wipe them away hastily on the sleeve of her jacket. "*Are* you shocked?" he asked with a face of polite inquiry. When Dolly nodded mutely, he stood pulling his beard and frowning. She expected that he was going to leave, in disgust with her, and she found that now, contrarily, as always seemed to happen, she wanted him to stay. "You're angry with me," she ventured in a small voice. He shook his head. "I try to be honest," he explained, "and I hurt people, like an abrasive. I want to sand them down to their essentials, scrape off the veneers. When I saw your picture, out there, I knew I had something to tell you." "You *liked* it?" she said wonderingly. "No. I hated it. It made me want to spew." Her work was sick, he told her—cramped with preciosity and mannerisms. Underneath, he discerned talent, but it was crippled, like some poor tree tortured out of shape by a formal gardener. She needed to be bolder and freer.

Dolly frowned. She had heard this from every one of her teachers and she supposed that it must be true. But it wearied and confused her to be assured that there was a vital force imprisoned inside her that was crying to be let out. How did they *know,* she used to mutter to herself in secret outrage. If there was anybody else inside her— as far as *she* could testify—it was a creature still more daunted and mild and primly scrupulous than the one the world saw. For years, she had been trying obediently to be bold and free in her work, and the results had always been discouraging, even to her counselors. When she "let herself go," her paintings got big and mechanical; she painted drearily, in the style of the teacher who had advised her to be herself. She was tired, moreover, of being told she had talent. She had come to feel that it was like a disease that she toted from doctor to doctor, seeking a new opinion, a new treatment. Her last teacher, whom she had stayed with a year, had been a neo-romantic; before that, she had had an intra-subjectivist and before that, a magic realist. And it was always the same story. Each began, enthusiastically, by undoing the errors of his predecessor. That was the easy part, but what came next, supposedly—the leap forward, the breakthrough—never was accomplished. She parted from each master sadly, with the knowledge that she had disappointed him. Perhaps it was her money, Martha had lightly observed; perhaps she was like the rich young man in the Bible, who could not accomplish *his* breakthrough unless he sold all he had and gave to the poor. . . . Dolly resented this suggestion; she had been thinking about it in the last few days, pacing up and down the wooded path with her hands dug in her pockets. Everybody, she felt, had been trying to change her, to take something away from her. For the first time, all alone here, with her teeth gritted, she had dared think that it was *she* who had the right to be disappointed. In the silence of her house, her heart murmured against her teachers and well-wishers; *they* had promised miracles and then let her down.

As she listened to Mr. Sandy Gray, echoing the familiar cavils, this resentment suddenly exploded. "But I *am* precious," she exclaimed, leaning forward on the footstool and striking a blow on her chest. "I'm inhibited. I'm afraid of life. I'm decadent. That is *me*. Why can't I paint that if I want to?" Sandy Gray smiled. "You can't paint a negation," he said. Dolly clenched her fists. "What about Bosch?" she demanded, seizing the name arbitrarily as a standard to rally to. "Bosh, my dear girl," he answered. "You know better than that. Horror isn't a negation. Only fear. You mustn't be afraid." Dolly sighed. She could not tell him the truth: that every moment of her life was shot through with terrors; peril stirred all around her, whimsically, in the rustling of the trees, in the sound of the icebox running or the gurgling of kerosene in the tank. This was what she was straining to show in her painting: the absurd powers that were bending her to their will—nature as animate and threatening and people as elemental forces. But what her critics saw in her small canvases was only "meticulous craftsmanship," "timid conceits," "quaint charm." If they did not urge her to break through, they advised her to illustrate children's books.

"Are you afraid of me?" Sandy Gray queried. Dolly considered and then shook her head, smiling. Strangely enough, she was not; she was only afraid of what the Sinnotts would think of her for letting him stay so long. He was so much like one of her bogeys that she could deprecate his terrors. He had come out of the pond just like a myth, she said to herself with amusement. She was far more fearful of what she called normal people: John and Martha, for instance.

Even if they had not told her, she would have known how her visitor looked to them. She could borrow their sharp eyes, alas, as easily as she could have put on Martha's severe, horn-rimmed reading glasses. To the normal vision, Sandy Gray was just another rusticated bohemian, solemn and loquacious and self-vaunting, a not-very-intelligent and pretentious bore. And yet, to Dolly's eyes, there was something Christlike about his appearance. His hair and beard were a soft, delicate brown. His skin was white, and he had deep-set, light-brown eyes with strange bluish whites. He carried himself stiffly, almost as if he had a spinal injury, and his long arms were frail. The black shirt and jeans and boots and gruff manners were deliberately misleading. He was really a gentle person.

As soon as she had said this to herself, Dolly felt a defiant quiver of pleasure. She had two kinds of friends: those she described to herself as "gentle" and the others. The second kind was always criticizing the first kind and saying they were unworthy of her. The more the second kind criticized, the more she clung to the first. Her aunts, who themselves were oddities in the New England manufacturing town she came from (one of them smoked cigars and was deaf and enormously fat), always used to complain that she had odd, unsuitable friends. They would never let her choose her pets either, and all her life Dolly had felt herself in the position of a little girl in a big house stealing out to give a saucer of milk to a stray cat, which, as her aunts used to warn her, was probably diseased. She had loved her aunts; she loved John and Martha and all the other sensible, sharp-spoken people who had succeeded to her aunts' place in knowing what was right for her—her trustees, her teachers, and their European-born wives, who fixed her hair for her and put mascara on her quivering lashes, before an art opening, and told her when to let her hems down and how to walk into a room. These rational guardians of her interests were all somewhat alike; the world admired them, and so did Dolly. Her "gentle" friends were all different, resembling each other only in the stubborn quaintness of choice that had selected them. She had the queerest collection, picked up on her travels, priests and nuns, elderly doctors with tropical diseases, destitute baronesses, progressive high-school principals, housewives, young soldiers, broken-down artistes; many of her friends were children. A psychiatrist once told her that she was afraid of being overrun by strong people and sought out weak ones, whom she could protect. This was not quite exact, Dolly herself recognized. *Everybody* wanted to tyrannize over her, the weak far more insistently, she had to admit, than the strong, who sometimes had other things to think about than telling her what to do.

She was taken in too easily, her trustees said, examining her check stubs. But that was not the case. She knew very well when she was being exploited by the kind of person she called gentle, and she claimed the right to be exploited, hugging it to herself like a toy that somebody was trying to wrest from her. Down deep, in the bedrock of her soul, there was a mistrustfulness of good sense. Behind every caution, she suspected a deprivation; something was being withheld. The demand to see *for herself,* ever since her thirtieth birthday, had been developing into a secret mania; she wanted to *live.* Outwardly, she was just the same, quiet and decorous, but in her soul she pioneered obstinately, inverting every notion that was offered her, especially where people were concerned. Much as she loved John and Martha, whenever she was with them she had to fight off the suspicion that her judgment was being constrained.

The first night she had arrived here, they had had her to dinner and put her to bed afterward, in their guest bedroom, despite her insistence that she wanted to sleep in her own house. The water was not turned on yet, John pointed out, and the house would be damp and cold from having been shut since Labor Day. In the morning, he would settle her in and see that everything was in order. He and Martha were extraordinarily helpful; they loved preparations and bustle and giving advice. After dinner, in their parlor John had handed Dolly a list of all the people she might need: the plumber, the electrician, the laundress, the odd-job man, the woman who would clean, if Dolly wanted her. Her garbage, he said, she would do best to take to the dump, and, for one person, it was wiser not to have the milkman; better buy milk when she needed it from the store. Between them, they had thought of everything. They told her the best places to swim at this time of year and where to get the freshest eggs. John drew a map, showing where mussels were to be found, on the old pier, and where you could dig clams and collect oysters; he marked some painting sites on it in red pencil, with stars. Martha made him show where the Indian pipe grew and where a file of cigar-colored boletus marched down a sand road, like a Mexican army on parade. They did everything, Dolly felt, but paint the pictures for her, so eager were they to be useful and anticipate her needs. It was a sign of love, and she knew it; moreover, it was a sign of intelligence. She was pleased (or had been, until today) with the painting ideas they had given her, which suited her painstaking brush. The frail Indian pipes, gray-white shading into pink, with a delicate black fringe on the petals, like a glass-blower's flowers, had turned out awfully well; the boletus picture was not finished, but the conception was splendid.

And John had done everything for her, without being asked. He had come to put back the screens when the late mosquitoes bothered her and he had dug her a garbage pit when he saw that she did not like to take the can to the dump, which had a horrible smell and rats and human scavengers, eagerly picking over the refuse. He chopped some pine wood for her and found out what was wrong when the chimney smoked. Martha had come, with extra pots and pans and dishes. She had brought Dolly a cook book with the best recipes marked. And she always knew the best; that, to Dolly was the worst of it. If Dolly followed instructions, everything came out right; and if she tried a different recipe from the one recommended by Martha, the result was a disaster. The Sinnotts always knew; it was an instinct with them. And they never compromised or pretended that anything was other than it was. This quality had never failed to amaze Dolly, in all the years she had known them—their sense of life's topography. Everything in New Leeds was where they said it was and looked precisely as they had described it, the good and the bad, the wilted lettuces and withering carrots in the grocery-store bins, the sunset from Long Hill. When Dolly, hopefully, would find that they had been wrong in some particular, it would turn out that she had not followed the directions. John, especially, was a born guide. After a day in Hell—Dolly felt certain—he could conduct a guided tour of all the circles, walking ahead with his long, bounding step, commenting on the architecture and pointing out the denizens whom it would be worth while to meet.

This trait, to Dolly, was both wonderful and terrible. It was the distillation of all she feared and mistrusted, admired and envied. John and Martha were like parents to her, though they all three were nearly the same age. They could not help thinking for her (no one could, apparently), and if she let them, everything sparkled with high spirits and certainty. In these bright October days, they were living, the three of them, in a sort of idyl, full of games and laughter. They made a charming picture —Dolly had studied it, as though in a mirror or in the still glass of one of the roseate ponds: the dark young man and the two fair-haired girls. In the mornings, John worked on a brochure he was doing for the Historical Society, while Martha wrote and Dolly painted, on a schedule he had devised. Nearly every afternoon, they met for a swim or to go musseling or mushrooming. On especially good days, they picnicked on the beach, with a hamper of fried chicken and a cranberry pie. They often had dinner together, cooking over Dolly's fire or eating, more formally, in Martha's pink dining room. They read poetry and argued heatedly about books and pictures; Martha spun theories out of John's and Dolly's perceptions. Late at night, armed with a star book and a flashlight, they went out to have Dolly identify the stars for them. There was the promise of a French play-reading at the Coes', about which the Sinnotts appeared to be squabbling.

John did not want them to go, and Martha protested that it would be unkind not to. She had already cast Dolly in the role of the queen, Bérénice, and was sketching out a costume for her, though there was no plan of dressing up. Dolly was troubled by these arguments between the Sinnotts, quick and laughing as they were. In the ten days she had been here, she had become aware of a change in their relation. She could see, behind the screen of persiflage, that John was worried about money and that Martha's play was not going well. Several times it had been on the tip of her tongue to offer them a loan, but the fear of intruding kept her silent. They were going, she sensed, through a period of testing, in which no outsider, even a second cousin, could help. Dolly often wondered, especially since Martha's visit, whether it had not been a mistake on their part to try themselves out here, of all places, where there were so many bad memories for Martha to live down. But it was precisely like the Sinnotts to seek out the severest conditions. They would not compromise, Dolly knew, any more than they would drink instant coffee; they demanded the supreme test.

She herself had no doubt about their power of survival; it was her own she questioned as she lay awake at night in her bunk-bed, listening to animals that John assured her were only squirrels. Influenced perhaps by their example, she too felt that she had reached a point of decision. But her own little bark was not even launched yet on the unknown waters that beckoned her, while John and Martha were already at sea, having chosen to sink or swim. It was an awful choice; Dolly could see why they were scared, even though, for once, she thought she knew better than they did and could promise them that it would be all right for them in the end. But they would not believe her if she told them. "You only see the surface," Martha had said once, gloomily, when they had all had a lot of red wine at dinner and Dolly had been telling them what a beautiful life they had made here. "Are you different when you're alone?" Dolly had asked in alarm. No, said the Sinnotts; they had fights, sometimes, but it was not that. It was something else, said Martha. "All this," she declared, with a sweeping gesture that took in her long, shadowed dining room. "We made it, but I can't believe that it's real."

She did not want Dolly to stay on here. Only till

Thanksgiving, she told Dolly firmly. After that, Dolly would not like it. The winds would begin to blow and it would be too unpleasant to go sketching and the people would get on her nerves. But it was just here that Dolly disagreed with her. Despite what Martha said, she felt determined to extend her stay through the winter. She did not want only the "best part," as Martha called the fall season; she wanted the whole thing. And it distressed her to be told, repeatedly, by both John and Martha that it would be fatal for her to get to know the people here. She had heard it from them the first night, in their white parlor, when her head was swimming with the information that was being pressed on her. Sandy Gray's name, she ruefully remembered, had led the list of persons especially to be avoided, if, as Martha said, she had come down here to *work*. That was the point, both the Sinnotts had averred, talking very fast and underscoring each other's words. If you came here to work, there were only a few people you could safely see: the Coes, a couple called the Hubers, who were much older, and one or two others whose names Dolly could not remember. The rest were *death*, said Martha, stamping out a cigarette.

"But why?" Dolly had murmured, sleepy and confused. "They don't work," said the Sinnotts, with an air of having explained the universe. Dolly did not understand. There were lots of nice people who didn't work, she protested, feeling a wayward loyalty spring up toward this criticized group. The Sinnotts shook their heads. The local drones were different, they explained: they had turned New Leeds into a hive of inactivity. They not only did not work but they proselytized for sloth. They had even converted the natives. "Do you know," cried John, "what the carpenter told me the other day when I called him in to look at some sills? He said, 'Believe it or not, we try to do a good job.' " Dolly laughed dubiously; she could see that the Sinnotts were very much excited. These people here, they continued, had no object in life except to see each other incessantly, over a bottle. They did not read; they did not travel, farther than Digby or to Trowbridge, the county seat, when one of them was arrested for drunken driving or had to appear in a divorce case. They did not even keep house or take care of their children any longer. Their wants were reduced to a minimum—shelter, something to eat, blue jeans and a Mackinaw, and a bottle of Imperial. They were like people of the future, said Martha —a planner's nightmare of what the world would be like when work had been abolished and everybody took a vitamin pill instead of bothering to cook.

"But why *shouldn't* they live like that if they want to?" Dolly had been saying to herself, over and over again, in a plaintive voice, alone in her shack, as she answered the Sinnotts on behalf of these New Leedsians whom she had never been permitted to meet. "Why *should* they work if they don't have to?" She herself was industrious, even in her pleasures, like a sober little girl making mud pies, but it seemed to her that it was unfair of the Sinnotts to expect the rest of humanity to be like *them*. Moreover, she was curious, which was, she felt, her right as a woman. She was restive, living in an idyl, with two omniscient beings cautioning her not to open Pandora's box, not to light Psyche's taper, not to eat the apple.

"Yes!" she cried, jumping up, when Sandy Gray proposed that she come for a walk in the woods with him. "Why *shouldn't* I if I want to?" she said aloud, rubbing her pale curls thoughtfully, as if she were just waking up. She let him lead her off up a hidden trail, leaving her easel where it was and her brushes unwiped. It was a wonderful walk. He knew the woods better than John and Martha; he showed her foxholes and deer tracks and where a skunk had its den. They explored an old logging trail, very much overgrown. He helped her climb over trees that had been blown down by the last hurricane. Brambles tore her stockings and a hornet stung her, but he hurried down to a little stream and made a mud plaster to put on her cheek. They scaled a high ridge, going cross-country, and found a place where you could look out and see seven ponds. Outdoors, he was a different person, courteously doing the honors as if nature were his home. His hand was always ready, at her elbow, to guide her up a steep spot when she needed it, and he looked the other way when she had to stop to take the stones out of her shoes. They talked about the difficulties of painting from nature, which was always changing just as you got your colors set, and about chess and the Great Barrier Reef. Just before lunch-time, they saw a fawn.

"It looks like you," he said, turning to scan her with a short, gusty laugh. "The startled fawn." Dolly colored; it was not the first time she had heard this allusion made. Nevertheless, she *liked* him, she said to herself, as she peered into the little mirror that was tacked up over the kitchen sink. She was a sight. There were burrs in her hair and her face was streaked with mud, but her cheeks were glowing. He was still there, in the living room, drinking a glass of white wine while she fixed them some lunch: Portuguese bread and hard salami and tomatoes and cheese. He was telling her about his children, who had been handed over to his third wife by a court order when his fourth wife left him. He was suing to get them back. His lawyer was going to show that she was living with a French Canadian truckdriver, down on the bay front, in a house made of cement blocks, and using the maintenance money to buy her paramour presents.

"Which one?" called Dolly, slicing the salami. "You mean the fourth or the third?" He meant the third, he said, but the fourth wife was here too, working at the counter of the grille. All his wives were here, except the second one; the first was in the graveyard, up by the high school—a very fine woman, he observed, used to be a singer, older than he was, one of the pioneer artists to settle in New Leeds. For some reason, the dead woman's presence seemed obscurely shocking to Dolly. Remembering the Sinnotts' stories, she did not dare ask what she had died of, lest she hear that she had burned up or fallen down a stairway. "What about the second one?" she murmured, setting down the plate of bread and cheese before him and slipping into the place opposite.

A dour expression darkened his face. "Ellen," he said, slowly, munching a piece of bread. "You've heard about Ellen?" Dolly shook her head. "You must have," he exclaimed. "Your friend Martha must have told you." Dolly shook her head again. Fear tightened her throat; it was the first time Martha had been mentioned between them, and there was something ugly, a sneer, in the way he pronounced her name. Yet why *should* he like Martha, she asked herself; after all, Martha did not like *him*. "That beats all," he remarked. "Why?" said Dolly, faintly, after a silence. "They were best friends," he said. "Thick as thieves." "Oh?" Dolly quavered, filling his glass with wine and pouring milk for herself. "I loved Ellen," he said, chewing. "She was the only one I loved." "But what happened?" said Dolly. "She left me," he retorted. "Seven years ago." Dolly drew a quick breath. "Martha Murphy," he said, "put her up to it. I have proof. I found the letters. I pieced them together from the wastepaper basket." "Letters?" "From Martha to Ellen—general delivery," he said impatiently. "Urging her to leave me, for her soul's sake. Ellen was weak.

She didn't want to leave me. She did it because she was told she ought to. Everything Martha did, she copied." Dolly bit her lip; she could see the possibility of this all too clearly. On the other hand, she could see that Martha might have had reasons. The more he spoke of Ellen, who had been young and blond and beautiful and was disowned by her parents when she married him, the more Dolly felt that the marriage had been unsuitable. "Where is she now?" she inquired, pushing a bowl of grapes toward him. "In Mexico." She had gone through her own money, it seemed, and was living with a Mexican on the alimony from her second husband. But Sandy Gray still loved her and still wanted her back. Now that he was between marriages, he had started writing to her again, and she had answered. . . .

Dolly glanced at him thoughtfully from beneath lowered brows. Here was a man, she perceived, who was living on hope. Ellen, his children—he expected to get them all back at once and start a new life. He had no idea, apparently—she thought with pity—that anything was ever finished. He was still toying with the notion that he might have sued Martha for alienation of affections, along with his mother-in-law, who had also written letters. Miles Murphy had told him he should have done it when he went to him as a therapist. The word, *therapist,* prickled Dolly's sensibilities. He had a number of jargon terms that embarrassed her and she did not care for his Americanisms, which sounded awfully queer in his Australian voice. And his table manners were disturbing. He talked earnestly, with his mouth full, and particles of food kept falling into his beard. All that was unimportant, she said to herself, watching him spit the grape seeds out onto his plate. He had a fearsome sincerity that made good manners seem false.

This sincerity appalled Dolly, for his sake. He was

living here in the woods like a mole in a tunnel. The outside did not exist for him, evidently. He was utterly free of self-consciousness—the consciousness, that is, of how he might look to others. It made Dolly feel guilty even to question his hopes, to peep at him through the eyes of the judge in Trowbridge or through the eyes of the woman, Ellen, whose snapshot he took out of his black breast pocket to show her. She held the snapshot at arm's length, narrowing her eyes to appraise it in the light of his expectations. It was a pretty blond girl, thin, with a long bob and a pearl choker, wearing a sun dress. Dolly felt as if she knew her; she had known the type in college—the strained, squirrelly debutantes who dropped out in the sophomore year to make a reckless marriage. *She will never come back to you,* she said to herself, remorseful for her percipience. "She's lovely," she said aloud, handing back the photograph. He nodded, stowing the picture away with a little pat of satisfaction.

He remained, musing, at the table, drawing on his pipe, while Dolly washed the dishes. He did not offer to help her, and she was grateful for this. There was not room for two in the little kitchen, Dolly had found; when John Sinnott washed up for her, they kept bumping into each other. She did not want to be at such close quarters, indoors, with Mr. Sandy Gray. In the house, his clothes gave off a slightly sour, musty smell, like that of an unaired closet. His fingernails were clean—she had looked to see—but she could not rid herself of the notion that his white soft skin was dirty, underneath his clothes, which she could not imagine ever going to the cleaners' and coming back on hangers, like middle-class apparel. If he bathed at all, she conjectured, it must be in the pond. She could picture his long white form immersing itself naked, as if in a baptism, with a cake of Ivory soap.

"Would you like a swim?" His voice came suddenly

from the sitting room. Dolly started. More than once, she had had the uneasy feeling that he could read her thoughts. "No, thanks," she answered, in a muffled voice. He would expect her to take her clothes off. Even the Sinnotts had been surprised, the first afternoon, when she produced her gray wool bathing suit. "You don't need that here," said Martha, but John had been more tactful and left his underdrawers on, in the water, while Martha had swum nude. After that, they had both brought bathing suits, whenever they came, which Dolly felt was an imposition on them, for the whole point of New Leeds—she could hear Martha saying it—was that you could go in naked.

"Good!" came the voice from the sitting room. "Most people swim too much here." Despite her relief, Dolly again was troubled; she felt that her friends were being criticized. And what was wrong with swimming? She dared not ask. "The natives never swim," the voice answered her silent inquiry. "It's a city person's fad, like cooking in the fireplace." "Good Lord!" said Dolly, raising a stricken hand to her cheek. "Wasn't that what they were used for, originally?" she ventured, hanging up the dish towel. "Hell, yes," he said. "They did it from necessity. Now it's phoney, an artifice. 'Oh, I adore these old fireplaces,' " he quoted in falsetto.

Dolly came reluctantly into the sitting room. Her fireplace was not old, but her two wire broilers and an asbestos glove stood beside it, bearing witness against her. She could not make out whether he had seen them. And his point of view was mysterious to her; she could not locate where he stood, with such an uncompromising air. New Leeds, he declared, was being ruined by an influx of smart people with money and artificial standards. Dolly rubbed her eyes. Who did he mean, she asked herself wonderingly. The Sinnotts, if he meant them, had no money. And who else could answer to this description? She could only suppose that he must be referring to her. "Who?" she interrupted. "Who are you talking about?" He smiled. "My dear girl," he said. "You must have met them and been entertained in their homes." Dolly shook her head. "I don't know who you mean," she said stubbornly. He puffed on his pipe. "The Coes," he said finally. "The Hubers." And he named off the very people whom Martha had said she could see. Dolly pressed her lips firmly together to stifle the laughter that was bubbling up. "The Coes!" she cried faintly. "You're dreaming." She started to add that she had been served a drink in a jelly glass in their establishment, but prudence closed her mouth just in time; she did not want him to find her with an artificial standard showing. "The Coes are all right," he conceded. "But they're rich people and they want to set the tone. They've formed a choice little group: your friend Martha, of course, and poor old Miles, when they can snag him."

Dolly laughed uncomfortably. "I thought you liked Mr. Murphy," she protested. Sandy Gray nodded. "Miles was my friend," he said somberly. "Now I don't know him any more. Or he doesn't know me. It's this damned change. He's got a new woman and he's gone respectable. He drives around in a Cadillac, wearing a sports jacket. If I ask him to drop in to see me, he explains that his white-wall tires won't take these back roads or his wheels will get out of alignment. Or he's busy with his philosophical work. There's something slick and hard about the guy now that he's got his life fixed up. 'First things first,' I said to him the last time we met and he stared at me like a boiled lobster." Dolly smiled bleakly at the comparison; she felt touched and troubled by what she was hearing. "Perhaps he *is* busy," she suggested. The fact that she herself had seen him the other day at the Coes' weighed heavy on her conscience. "First things

142

first," Sandy Gray repeated. "Let me give you an example. I went down to see him last month, on my motorbike. I had the idea that I might get him to testify for me, professionally, as a psychologist, about the kids' condition. Miles knows Clover, my third wife, from way back; she grew up here; her father wrote for the pulps. He knows she's an unfit mother; she used to take care of his kid for him when he was living with Martha. I figured he could drop in to see her now and report what he found to my lawyer." Dolly's brows furrowed; a deep sense of horror overcame her; her stomach felt queasy. Her sympathies, by instinct, flew to the mother's side and repelled the idea of spying on her. But she immediately felt rebuked by another inner voice that told her she was being conventional. Many fathers, she knew, made better parents than many mothers; it was only tradition that shrank from the facts. Moreover, there was spying and spying; in a good cause, she supposed, it was justified. "I told him the whole story," Sandy Gray was relating. "And he sat there at his desk, in that damned windmill, listening, tapping his foot and doodling on a piece of paper. "So what happened?" said Dolly. "Did he refuse you?"

Sandy Gray snorted. "He never gave me the chance to ask him. He cut me short in the middle of a sentence. 'Well, well,' he said, getting up and looking at his wrist watch, the way he used to do when the hour was over. 'Interesting case, Sandy. It will make a judgment of Solomon when it comes to the court in November.' " Despite herself, Dolly laughed. "And that was all?" she murmured, sobering her face. "That was all. He had an engagement, he told me. He went to the door and rang a bell for his wife."

A silence fell. Dolly herself became conscious of the passage of time. She dared not look at her wrist watch, but the sun had left the windows and it must be, she realized, at least three o'clock. In an hour, the sun would set, and nothing was accomplished. She had not gone for the mail or bought her groceries; her brushes and paints and easel were still outside. Yet she tried not to think of these things, which were mere details, she told herself. Her work, her life, her mind were cluttered with detail. "First things first," she muttered under her breath, like a lesson. An hour ago, she had been on the edge of something—a straightforward relation with a man. And now suddenly it was spoiled, by her having, so to speak, underthoughts. The silence, as it continued, propagated trivia; she looked about her and saw crumbs and tobacco everywhere, which she could not wipe up because it would be conventional. The need to make conversation became an uncomfortable urgency, but she could think of nothing to say but something about the weather. Moreover, she was afraid that John and Martha might come. And on top of everything else, she had to go to the bathroom.

She jumped up and lit a match to the fire laid in the fireplace. He turned to watch her, crouching at the hearth. "How old are you?" he said abruptly. Dolly told him her age. "Are you a virgin?" he demanded. Dolly's spine stiffened; she rose, slowly, and backed up against the fireplace wall. Nobody had asked her this question since she had been in college. She had often yearned to discuss what was the central fact in her life, but everybody steered shy of it, even her closest friends. Yet now that she had been asked, finally, her tongue remained paralyzed. She stared at him speechlessly, trying to feel indignation.

"Well?" he said. "Are you or aren't you?" Dolly looked at him in anguish. "Don't you know?" he said, ironically. This, in literal fact, was the case. She had had a single experience, five years before, on a boat, at night, on the deck, behind a stack of steamer chairs. A sailor had interrupted them, and she had fled in shame to her cabin, not sure whether or not the act, as the books said, had been completed. The next morning they had landed, and she had never seen her partner, a young student, again. Since that time, men had made love to her, and she had responded, even while resisting. But they got discouraged too easily; they gave up, like her painting teachers, just when she might have let herself go. Several times, she had nearly made the plunge. She had permitted what her aunts used to call liberties and was ready to give the final favor, though she still weakly pushed and struggled, when the man, straightening his necktie, would get up and say he was sorry. *"Don't* be sorry," she had several times cried out, but they took this as mere courtesy on her part. The older she got, the more men hesitated to tamper with her, because they thought she was a virgin, and she could not correct this impression, because she was not sure.

As she stood gazing at Sandy Gray, she felt the gates of her speech miraculously unlocking. She was going to tell; his wish to know was impersonal. After all, she reminded herself, he was in love with another woman. Recklessly, she opened her mouth and took a deep breath, but at that moment he got up and yawned, stretching his long arms. "All right," he said. "I'm sorry. Don't tell me." He picked up his cap from the studio couch. "But I'll tell you one thing," he observed thoughtfully. "You've never been in love."

Dolly's rueful gaze rested, startled, on him. It was true, but how did he know it? Her stubborn nature had known many passionate attachments—to animals, to her teachers, to her friends. But she had never loved a man, in the sense that he meant, except in daydreams. "How do you know?" she said. He shrugged. "I see it every-where," he replied, gesturing with his cap. "In your work. In the way you stand, backed up against the wall. In your books. *Noli me tangere.*" Tears came to Dolly's eyes for the second time that day. "Don't cry," he said. "I like you. You're a good little child in your pinafore. You love Mummy and Daddy and Nanny and little brother and sister and your teddy bear. Some day you may grow up to be a woman."

He put on his cap. "Drop over to see me," he said. "I live on the other side of the pond, behind that pine grove." Dolly stood watching him go, the way he had come, striking with his knife at the pickerel weed. She felt shattered. A long-sought opportunity had been missed. Another time, if she saw him, everything would be different: she would know him too well to speak openly. It was because he had come to her as a stranger, out of the pond, like a water god, that she had nearly confessed herself. She was tempted to run after him, but another feeling, a sense of proud umbrage, held her where she was. He was wrong about her, she said to her-self triumphantly. He had missed the point altogether. She had no Mummy or Daddy or brother or sister. She was an orphan. He was stupid not to have seen that. And John and Martha were right. Thanks to him, she had lost a day's painting. Perplexity smote her. She struck herself a violent blow on the forehead. "Oh damn," she cried. "Damn, damn, damn!"

SEVEN

IT WAS Friday morning. Jane Coe had set the alarm
clock for eight, so that she would be sure to get hold
of the electrician before he went off for the day. The
icebox had been on the blink since Tuesday, and every
morning she had missed him. It was no good leaving mes-
sages with his wife, to give him at lunch-time, for he was
a lazy loafer who hated to come all the way out the back
roads to the Coes' house and risk getting stuck in the
sand with his new low-slung car. You had to coax him, in
person, using all your womanly wiles; if he once promised, he would not go back on it. Jane understood his
point of view. Why should he come and waste his time
here when he could go bass-fishing instead? He did not
need the money; he made his killing on the summer people. Warren begged to differ; he and Jane had had quite
a discussion on the subject only the night before. According to Warren, Will Harlow had a duty, as the only
electrician in the community, to come when he was
called, like a doctor. When Will went off to Florida last
winter for a vacation, leaving everybody stranded and
children's milk spoiling in the iceboxes, Warren had
seen red. But Jane said that just living was more important than fussing with other people's electricity if you
didn't have to; Will's customers could have put the milk
out the window and waited calmly till he came back. She
did not think it was fair to consider the texture of life
the most important thing, for yourself, if you didn't ap-

ply the same standard to poor Will, who came when it suited him or when he needed the money. This debonair statement had made Warren explode. "You mean Will Harlow comes here just for the money?" he had cried, setting down his cup of Sanka with a bang on the table; they did not bother with saucers. "He comes here because we bribe him," he added, breathing fire.

"Of course," replied Jane, yawning. This was truer than Warren knew. Jane had made a study of Will Harlow's psychology, and in the summertime, when everybody was competing for him, she would put something extra out of commission to make it worth his while to come fix the stove or the icebox. She had a defective mixer that could be counted on to blow the electricity in the whole house if necessary. This was one of the little things she hid from Warren, on account of his high principles, but last night she had told him, just to shake him up. She had been reading an article in a medical magazine, explaining that anger was good for you; it kept you from getting cancer. They had had an awful fight, and Jane, sure enough, had slept like a log. She had slept so well that when the alarm clock rang, she had turned it off and burrowed back into her pillow, forgetting why she had set it. At nine o'clock, she had waked up with a start to realize that it was the day of the *Bérénice* reading and that the Hubers and the Murphys were coming for dinner first, and after dinner, the others, Miss Lamb and Paul and the Sinnotts. They would all be awfully put out if there were no ice for their drinks. She plodded out to the telephone, in her furry scuffs and bathrobe, but it was too late: Will Harlow had already left, for his workman's day.

It was a dark rainy morning. Warren reported, after a look at the weathervane, that they w re in for a three-day blow. That was why she had overslept, of course;

everybody overslept on overcast mornings. In the bathroom, Jane drew a long face and thrust her lower lip
out, staring at herself sternly in the mirror to keep a
furtive giggle down. There was a funny side to it, her
owlish reflection agreed: John Sinnott would tell her she
had missed the electrician from perversity. Every time
he and Martha came, something went haywire. Either
there was no ice or else there was no soda water, like the
last time, or she had forgotten to get salt, for the dinner,
or sugar, or there were mouse-droppings in the flour.
These things did not matter, Warren assured her, but
Jane had felt a little bit embarrassed, a few nights before,
when they had had Miss Lamb to dinner, and they had
found they were out of paper napkins and paper towels
and kleenex, so that they had had to give her toilet
paper, folded neatly by Warren, for a napkin. They used
to have linen, Warren told Miss Lamb, with a tender
glance, like a hug, at his rosy spouse, but Jane had given
it all away, except for the sheets and pillow slips, which
did not have to be ironed. When they first came up here,
they had a whole trunk full of Jane's grandmother's
beautiful embroidered linen from Germany, stored out
in the garage. Jane had never used it, and they needed
the storage space for Warren's pictures. Martha had
some of the napkins now; they looked lovely on her
table, with the big Ws in heavy scroll embroidery—it was
a lucky coincidence that both Martha's maiden name
and Jane's grandmother's had begun with W.

Jane did not grudge this gift. She was naturally open-
handed, and it also satisfied her thrifty side to see that
the things were being used. She thought Martha was
crazy to bother with the washing and the ironing and
keeping the table polished, and it gave Jane pleasure to
think of the hours she herself was saving *not* doing these
things. When she looked at her napery gleaming on

Martha's dark table, she felt the same way she felt when she saw their goat munching a tin can in the zoophile lady's back yard: she was glad she had found it a good home. She had a genius, she admitted, for finding people who would take things she did not want. Last year, she had even discovered a man who was delighted to have their garbage to feed to his pigs—which saved her going to the dump. As it turned out, he insisted on having it sorted and he complained about broken glass and coffee grounds, so that idea had to be chalked up as a failure. But sooner or later, Jane was confident, she would solve the garbage-disposal problem, in a way that would make everybody hold up their hands in astonishment and wonder why they had not thought of it. She and Warren had tried everything: expensive chemical devices buried in the ground; a gas incinerator that functioned in the kitchen; burning the stuff in the fireplace or in Warren's studio stove. But nothing as yet had worked out to suit her; unless you went to the dump, you always had the labor of sorting.

Labor-saving schemes of one kind or another played a large part in Jane's thoughts. It was something she had inherited, probably, from her inventor-grandfather; Warren said that her bump of inventiveness was very much enlarged. Recently, she had been pondering putting in some sheep to act as lawn mowers around the house and fertilize the ground with their droppings, so that some time she could have a vegetable garden—according to the latest theories, it was better not to weed. And she had heard of a place where you sent the sheep's wool, which came back woven into blankets. That was what had got her started: she and Warren needed some new blankets; the moths had got into their spare ones. Last fall, when John and Martha were staying with them, John had said, "What is this, Jane—a blanket for an octopus?" Warren had agreed that they needed blankets, but he wanted to just buy them in a store, like other people. The sheep, he pointed out, would have to have cover, in the wintertime, and be fed, the same as the goat. And if he and Jane wanted to go away some time, during the winter months, to see some exhibitions and picture galleries, they would be stuck here, because of the sheep. Sheep lived outdoors, Jane argued; all they needed was a little sheepfold that they could huddle in, during a storm; you could just put some oats or whatever they ate out for them. But Warren was too tenderhearted. In the summer, yes, he conceded; but he would not take responsibility in the winter. "If you can find somebody who will have them for the winter, dear," remained his last word.

Jane was very foresighted when she had her mind set on something. She would not get the sheep until spring, when she could buy them cheap, as lambs, but she had already sounded out the goat-lady and the butcher at the First National. They had both turned her down, as she had feared. And yet she still felt that there must be somebody in the community who would be glad to take care of the sheep for her. There was a balance in human psychology, she had always reasoned, like the balance of Nature; and just as snakes were useful to kill rodents and weeds to put vitamins in the soil, so there had to be somebody who would find a use for those sheep during the winter months. She had been turning over the problem every night before going to sleep, visualizing the lambs, one black, one white, and the blankets she would have woven to her own design, in a modern zigzag pattern. She had read about mathematicians who put their unconscious to work on a difficult equation and woke up with the solution. And this morning, as a matter of fact, as she was dialing a number where his wife

thought she might reach Will Harlow, inspiration
smote her. The public high school, she exclaimed to
herself, widening her eyes. In a modern school like
that, they must have a course in zoology or natural
science, for which a pair of sheep would be perfect. And
the school year exactly coincided with the months Warren did not want the sheep.

"Wonderful, dear," agreed Warren, somewhat absently, from the kitchen, where he was coddling some
eggs for his breakfast. He had slipped out of bed ahead
of her, as he sometimes did when he wanted to start
painting early. "Did you get Will?" he added, gazing
sadly at the toaster, which did not seem to be working.
In the doorway, Jane shook her head, recalled to the
day's agenda. "They didn't answer," she said. "I'll have
to try and find him. He can't be fishing in this storm.
I'll bet he's down at Snow's Bungalows; all his cronies
are working there, putting up some new cabins. . . ."
She added some water to last night's coffee and turned
the heat on high. "Say," she said, thinking, "maybe I
could get a piece of ice from the iceman and we could
put it in the guest-room bathtub." Warren's face
brightened obediently, and then a shadow fell on it.
"There's wood there, dear. Remember?" Jane frowned;
the bathtub was full of driftwood that they had carried
up from the beach. It had seemed to her an excellent
storage bin for keeping the wood dry; last year, they had
left their wood outside, under a tarpaulin, but it had always got damp. "We could put the ice in *our* tub," she
proposed. "You don't need a bath." Warren apologetically
opened the dark icebox; there was a smell of mold and
spoilage. "Don't you think it would be better to try to
get Will?" he queried. "That's just penicillin," said
Jane briskly, but after a moment's thought she acqui-

esced. It would be less work, she calculated, to find Will
Harlow than to go to the iceman and have to lug the ice
out of the station wagon, dump it in the bathtub, and
then chop it, by hand.

She was eager to go talk to the high-school principal
during the morning recess; it did not do to postpone
things and let your enthusiasm peter out. But she over-
rode the impulse. The sheep could wait; Warren was
anxious for tonight to be a success. He was full of gratitude to Miles, for buying the portrait, and he wanted
everything to be nice for him. This meant that Jane
would have to go and get the cleaning woman, put her
to work, and drive her back home, when she was
through. She would have to find Will Harlow and take
the carving knife to the butcher to be sharpened; they
were having a joint for dinner. She would have to stop
at Martha's and get some herbs for the salad; there was
a torn slipcover on the sofa which she could fix in a
jiffy, if she could remember to buy mending tape. They
had been planning to spend the afternoon at the cove,
gathering oysters—her mother had just sent them a
patented oyster-opener—but the weather precluded that
now. Nevertheless, it would be a busy day for her, and
she would be bound to forget something important if
she got distracted by the sheep. For one thing, she ought
to wash her hair, and for another, she ought to get Paul
to open up his antique store during his lunch hour so
that she could buy some stem glasses for the wine. She
still had a last set of goblets stored away up above the
beams in the studio, but it would be more trouble to
look for them and get them down and have Mrs. Silvia
wash them than it would be to get new ones, which
Paul could dust out in the shop for her. That was the
difficulty about a party; everything landed on you at
once. Most people here didn't care what you served it

in, so long as they got their booze, but tonight's guest list was a little different, more bourgeois, she supposed you could call it, though to somebody like her family Miles Murphy would be pretty startling.

Warren, moreover, had been funny lately, ever since the Sinnotts had arrived. "Why can't we have something like this?" he had said wistfully, holding up a thin glass at Martha's dinner table. For years, he had been setting the table with cottage-cheese glasses for the wine and had never seemed to notice. He was different from Jane; other people's possessions stirred something in him, evidently—memories of his mother's house. Jane almost thought he was envious, which was silly because they could afford anything the Sinnotts had, if they wanted it. It was a question of practicality. Martha's fragile glasses would be broken in a week in the dishwasher— as Jane knew from experience—and nobody nowadays wanted to take the trouble to wash glasses by hand and dry them.

Nevertheless, she was going to let Warren have his way. He would soon see for himself that it was not worth it to have a breathless, perspiring, frazzled wife flop down at the dinner table across from him. What he really prized was her intellectual companionship, and she could not spend the day perusing current books and magazines or just thinking, curled up on the sofa, if she was going to be a compulsive housewife, like her mother, always "over" the servants and arranging flowers and looking for dust. Germs were good for you; they built up immunities; Jane had not had a day's sickness, except during her periods, since the vacuum cleaner broke.

"I wonder whether the Murphys will come," said Warren, peering out the window. The weathervane on the studio was whirling about wildly; gusts of rain struck at the house; the gutters ran. "They'll come," said Jane. It was the kind of dismal day that made people want to be together. "All the way from Digby?" Warren said doubtfully. "They know I'm expecting them to dinner," answered Jane, who never worried. "They would have called by this time, if they weren't coming, so that I wouldn't go ahead and do the marketing."

In the station wagon, on the way to the village, Jane herself began to wonder. She could hardly see to drive, down the wet sand road. In the village, the main street was deserted. As she turned into the parking space, she saw the Sinnotts' car, which still had its New York license plates, speeding north, out of the village, toward Digby. She could not make out who was in it, but it was burning a lot of oil, she noted; they ought to get it fixed. Where could either of them be going, she wondered, on a morning like this? Could they have had another fight? Her speculations ceased as she hurried across the street to the post office in her plastic raincoat and hood, which were no protection, really. Her long full orange cotton skirt was flapping wetly around her bare ankles, and her ballet slippers were soaked.

She opened her mailbox and found a telegram. "Western Union man just brought that around," said the postmistress. "Your phone's out of order; somebody on your line left the receiver off the hook." The smallest village idiot stood watching her with a grin as she broke the seal with her forefinger. "Somebody die," he repeated in his high, loud gabble. Jane shook her head. "Telegrams don't mean death any more," she said to him, kindly. She made it a policy to spread reason wherever she could. Nevertheless, her heart missed a beat; she was afraid it was from the Murphys, begging off for tonight. Her eyes ran over the message: Warren's mother was dead, of a stroke, yesterday, in Savannah.

Her first thought was of the roast she had had the butcher cut specially the day before. Death was peculiar; it made things like that pop into your mind. Still, it was a problem whether she could return it; being an only child, Warren, of course, would have to go to the funeral. She would have to cancel the play-reading. A deep disappointment took hold of her, as she tried to tell herself, by way of comfort, that at least the day would be simplified. It would not matter now about the wine glasses or trying to get Will Harlow. But it was a cheerless comfort; without the plans to fill it, the day seemed bereft. And Warren would have to be away for three days at the very least; when he came back, he might want to go into mourning. They would *never* have the play-reading, she said to herself sadly, stuffing the telegram into her Mexican leather pouch. She would have to call the Murphys and tell Paul, in the liquor store, and call the Hubers and Martha, who could tell Miss Lamb. They would all be let down just because one old lady had happened to die the day before. It made her think of the time when her fifteenth birthday party had to be canceled because her brother had come down with polio. The Greeks had a better idea; when somebody died, they feasted, to show that life went on.

All at once, she realized that the idiot and the post-mistress were both watching her, avidly, she thought. Wrapping her raincoat about her, she started down the street to the drugstore to telephone. They would have to know right away, so they could make other dinner plans. What a waste, she said to herself. But as she trudged through the rain, two thoughts struck her. What was the matter with her? Obviously, Warren could not take the plane; all flights would be canceled. According to her car radio, the storm was general throughout coastal New England. She could drive him to Trowbridge, to get the afternoon train, but he would not reach New York till nearly midnight, too late, probably, to catch the sleeper for Savannah. He might just as well stay here and wait to get a plane in the morning, when the weather would doubtless clear. He could go to Boston, of course, in the hope that flights would be resumed again this afternoon or this evening, but he might not get a seat; Friday was a bad travel day. And there was a second obstacle. What was he going to wear?

Jane had been considering this question ever since they had heard that his mother was failing. In the south, as she knew, people were stuffy about the ceremonial of mourning. A black band sewn on his corduroy sleeve would not be enough, probably, to satisfy Warren's cousins and his aunt. He could stop off in Boston and get a ready-made dark suit and a pair of black shoes; but it seemed crazy to spend the money on something he would wear only the once. Moreover, there was the time factor. He would have to have the suit altered. Ready-made pants were always too long for him and too baggy in the seat. Even if he took the suit to some little tailor, it would take a couple of hours for the alteration to be done, what with the pressing and everything: he might miss the plane, if there was one, hanging around and waiting. Last week, however, Jane had had a brain wave. Seeing John Sinnott walk into a party in his dark-blue suit, she had realized that he and Warren had much the same build. John, of course, was taller, but his shoulders and waist were narrow, like Warren's, and he had a small behind; she had checked on this point when they were in swimming, in the nude. The blue suit would be just right for Warren, if she turned up the trousers; there was a steam-iron put away somewhere in the studio that she could press them with. Black or a dark oxford would have been better, but there no point in repining. It was a piece of luck that the only dark suit in all New Leeds—except the bank president's—should have come here with the Sinnotts in September. If Warren's mother had died last year, there would have been no suit for him at all. The blue was very dark, almost midnight, and it would look very nice with Warren's blue eyes. And John had a lot of neckties; she had seen them hanging on his bureau, some of them in dark, conservative colors. Warren had only two: bright wools woven by the New Leeds Craftsmen. The shoes Warren would have to buy, in Trowbridge or Digby. John's feet were too long, though narrow, and Paul's black shoes, which he wore for state occasions, were short enough but too broad. Even if Warren were to wear several pairs of wool socks, he would not be comfortable, and foot comfort was important, psychologically—that was why they went barefoot so much.

Sitting in the drugstore phone booth, with her wet skirt and petticoat bundled about her, Jane took out a coin and hesitated. There was no use trying to get Warren yet, if their phone was out of order. It came to her that it must be she who had left the receiver off the hook, while she was calling Will Harlow and thinking about the sheep. And even if Warren had replaced it in the meantime, he would be in his studio now, out of earshot of the phone. With the planes not flying, there was no hurry about telling him. She decided to call Martha first and ask about the suit. But just then she remembered seeing the Sinnotts' car heading out of town. What was she going to do if they were off somewhere for the day? She dropped in the coin, and Martha answered. She had been trying to get Jane, she said, to tell her they could not come to the play-reading because John had had to go to Boston this morning to finish some research. Jane heard her out, without interruption; she could have saved Martha her breath by telling her about Warren's mother, but she was curious to know what explanation the Sinnotts had cooked up between them: any fool could see that John had gone to Boston to avoid having to meet Miles tonight. For herself, Jane wanted to find out diplomatically, before asking straight out, whether the blue suit was here or whether it had gone off too. "I thought I saw John," she said. "Dashing out of the post office. What was he wearing?" "A raincoat," said Martha. "And that good-looking blue suit?" persisted Jane. "Why yes, I think so," said Martha. "Yes, he was," she added, more positively. Jane caught her breath. "How long is he going to be gone?" "Just today," said Martha. "He has to see somebody for dinner. He'll be back late tonight." "Oh," said Jane.

A new idea was forming in her mind. It was clear now that Warren could not leave till tomorrow in any case; he would have to wait on the weather *and* the suit. There was no reason, therefore, why they should not have the play-reading. Warren himself had been looking forward to it for a week now. He and Jane had read the play, together, in Masefield's English translation, and he wanted to discuss with Martha the peculiar philosophy behind it. He would be horribly disappointed if the project fell through. But of course, with his mother dead, he would think that they ought not to have it, not for any real reason, but just because of the forms. He had been expecting her death anyway; after all, she was seventy-nine, and when he had gone down to see her last year, he must have realized it was good-bye. And it was not as if his knowing, today, could do any good. If the telegram had said, "Mother dying," that would have been different: he would have wanted to telephone and start off as fast as he could, even though she would be unconscious and incapable of recognizing him—that was how she had conditioned him. But since the old lady was gone, what could be the harm of letting him have the play-reading before he found out?

It was only an accident, actually, Jane suddenly perceived, that she had got the telegram this morning. There were some days when they did not go for the mail at all, and she often left the receiver off the hook for twenty-four hours without noticing it. Actually, if it had not been for the party tonight, the telegram could have stayed there in the box without their knowing it until tomorrow at least. So to all intents and purposes, it was as if she had not got it yet. And how much better it would be, from everybody's point of view, if she had not happened to stop in at the post office just now. . . . If Warren was going to grieve, in spite of having worked through his mother-attachment with the psychoanalyst, he might as well begin tomorrow, Jane said to herself in her practical voice. There was nothing he could do anyway, and useless suffering was the worst kind; that was the good part about funerals—they gave the relations something to put their minds on. If she were in Warren's place and it was *her* mother, she would want him to spare her until she could get off on a plane and start making the funeral arrangements. She would *want* him to have the play-reading for her.

Absently listening to Martha, Jane made her decision. The play must go on, she said to herself with a grin and a hollow feeling in her stomach. For one wild instant, she considered taking Martha into her confidence, but prudence intervened: if she was not going to tell Warren, it was better that nobody should know until tomorrow morning. And Martha might disapprove. She was telling Jane now all the virtuous reasons why she too could not come to the play-reading: she had some letters to write; she had bought some green tomatoes and was going to make a pickle; she had no car and it was too far for Dolly to come for her. "I'm sorry," she wound up. "But after all you don't need me. There are only seven parts. Dolly can do Bérénice; her French is much better than mine. And you can do the confidante." "Don't be a nut," said Jane, feeling cross with Martha. "Of course, we need you. You're the only professional. Warren will *die* if you don't come." It was true: Warren's expectations rested on Martha's presence; he was happy in the thought that she and Miles could be friends again, thanks to the portrait. But Martha kept sounding reluctant. She would rather not, she insisted. "Is it because of Miles?" Jane demanded, boldly. Partly, Martha admitted. But it was not only that, she pretended; she had all those things to do and she wanted to be home, for John, when he got back from Boston: he would have an awful drive in this weather. Jane made a face. "Why, you don't want to stay there all alone, waiting for him," she exclaimed in scoffing tones. "If he has dinner in Boston, he won't be back till one in the morning." "Yes," acknowledged Martha. "You'll be home by that time," Jane pointed out. "Warren will come and get you and bring you back afterward. You might as well come to dinner; I've got a big roast."

There was a tiny pause. "I couldn't," said Martha faintly. "Not to dinner." "Because of the Murphys? Don't be crazy," said Jane. "You don't have to be afraid of *them*. Miles is still in love with you. Everybody says so. That's why he bought the portrait." "That isn't *true*," Martha's voice protested. "And if it were, it would be all the more reason. . . ." "Not to come?" said Jane. "I don't see that at all. He's settled down now. He's not going to *do* anything unless you encourage him. Anyway," she added, "they may not come. Because of the weather. And *somebody's* got to eat that roast." "No," said Martha. This firmness was not like Martha, Jane said to herself. "Is it John?" she ventured. "Did he tell you not to come?" Martha remained silent. "He doesn't have to know," remarked Jane. "You'll be home before he is." "Oh, I couldn't do that," cried Martha in a horrified voice. "Well, then, tell him after he gets back. Tell him you felt lonely. Why shouldn't you go out to dinner if he does in Boston?" "I don't know," said Martha. "I must say, it does sound rather silly when you think about it." "Then you'll come," said Jane. She felt Martha hesitate. "No," Martha said finally. "I'd better not. He might call me, from Boston, and it would worry him if I weren't here." "He calls you up," exclaimed Jane, "when he's just gone for the day?" "Sometimes," said Martha, proudly. Jane considered this strange; to her mind, it argued a lack of security. "Oh, come anyway," she said. "He probably won't call. I'll have Warren stop by for you at seven. Don't forget to bring your book; we've only got two copies, unless Harriet Huber finds one. And bring some herbs from your garden." "No," pleaded Martha, but Jane rang off. She was certain Martha would come, to the play-reading, if not to dinner, and probably to both.

But as soon as she felt satisfied that she had won her point, a slight uneasiness beset her. She was not sure that Warren would approve of Martha's coming to dinner; they had agreed that it would be better for the Sinnotts to arrive afterward, so as not to embarrass the Murphys. To Jane's mind, John's absence altered everything: Martha would just be an extra woman who could be slipped in next to Harold Huber, like somebody you were having for charity. But Warren might

not see it that way; he might feel that Jane had betrayed him. And if he ever found out about the telegram
. . . ! In the stuffy phone booth, Jane felt suddenly
queasy; she rested her head against the telephone and
tried to collect herself. Her eyes wandered sidewise out
into the drugstore; the druggist had his back turned and
the soda-fountain girl was reading a comic book. But Jane
had the conviction that they had just been watching her
and listening to her conversation. Against all reason, the
notion fastened itself on her that the whole village
knew that Warren's mother was dead. She drove her
station wagon very slowly out toward the cleaning
woman's house; two cars passed her, as she crawled along,
and again she felt that eyes had turned to study her.

There was nothing unusual in that, she assured herself; she was a bit of a curiosity in the village and people
always stared. They thought she was a character, just
because she was sensible and easygoing. Her ideas made
people laugh, and she did not mind; all her brothers
had teased her, and in boarding school and college, she
had been looked on as a card. People laughed at her
because she was innocently logical. She was being logical,
now, about Warren's mother; she had thought it out,
step by step, reasonably, as she did all her ideas. Nobody
could possibly know about the telegram (that was all her
imagination); the Western Union man was a typical
closemouthed Yankee who would not tell anybody anything, not even the time of day, unless he had authoriza-
tion. There were dozens of stories about him.

Jane's heart began to race. She had overlooked one
factor. Supposing the Western Union man telephoned
to make sure the telegram had reached them? She had
no way of knowing whether the phone was still off the
hook. Faintness overtook her. She was not used to deception, she realized, except in small things; up to now,

she had only told white lies and did not mind being caught in them. In fact, it was rather fun to let Warren catch her in an untruth; quite often she would give herself away, with giggles, like a kid playing hide-and-seck, just to let him pounce on her, the way he had last night.

But now, for the first time, she recognized, she had done something that Warren might take a grave view of. He might not think it was funny or delightfully in character for Jane to be suppressing this telegram. And once she started lying, she would have to keep it up. If she did not produce the telegram the minute she got home, she would have to claim she had never got it, no matter what, assuming she was questioned. Her original plan had been to "discover" the telegram in their mailbox early tomorrow morning, when she could come to the village on some pretext. Warren, she reckoned, would be too busy packing and trying on the suit to press any inquiries about why it had not been delivered earlier. And by the time he got back from Savannah, it would be too late to follow it up; nobody would remember. Only two people, Jane reasoned, had seen her get the telegram this morning, and one of them, after all, was an idiot, who did not know one day of the week from another. The real problem, she now decided, was the Western Union man, who was the old-fashioned, conscientious type. If the phone was still off the hook and he kept trying to get them, he might send a man out from the phone company or even drive out himself in his old Ford to deliver it in person. Or would he check with the postmistress, to find whether the Coes had got their mail? That would make three people who knew. And what if Warren's relations, down there, got worried when they did not hear from him and put a tracer on the telegram?

Jane stopped the car by the roadside. She was shivering all over. This was what it felt like, apparently, to embark on a career of crime. It was not worth it; she could see that at once. Honesty was the best policy. Whoever said that was right. She marveled, sitting there, at the women who made a practice of deceiving their husbands. How did they do it? She thought of the New Leeds wives who had had clandestine love affairs: Ellen Gray, in the old days, and Martha, when she was married to Miles. She could understand their doing it once, but to keep it up, as a regular thing? Her teeth began to chatter, as her mind stole amazedly back over the course of romantic history: Queen Guinevere, Mary Stuart—living every hour in the fear of discovery. How had they done it? She had never approved, much, of adultery; the fun of marriage was sharing things with your mate. But she had never before considered how much courage adultery took, far more than the act repaid—days of suspense for a few seconds of pleasure. She had always thought of herself as a hardy soul, but now she saw that she had never really dared. Daring, she cogitated, was a matter of taking chances. It was like statistics or gambling; you had to compute probabilities. And there was always the unforeseen, the little thing you overlooked that would catch you up in the end—what they called contingency. She herself already felt like a different person, just for thinking of deceiving Warren, or rather she felt the same, but everything else had changed and become somehow slippery, like when Alice went through the looking-glass—into the fourth dimension, Warren said; that mathematician had explained it to him.

Devoted as she was to Warren, she had always found his mathematical theories a little bit boring, and she noticed that other people did too. But now she perceived that there was a human side to all that: people who were afraid began to count and reckon, just as she was doing, and they were faced, straight off, with infinity. And when you were afraid, something queer happened to time. Looking at her watch, she found that only ten minutes had passed since she left the drugstore, though it seemed like an hour at least. Her thoughts, evidently, were racing like her pulse; that was what it must mean to live a double life, like Paul.

And yet, she reflected, it was not anything wrong she was contemplating. To keep Warren in ignorance was the kindest and most sensible thing. It would be almost a sacrifice, on her part, to go through all this anxiety so that he could have a few hours' peace. The only way it could hurt Warren not to know would be if the story got out that he had had a party the night after his mother's death. But he could always say that he didn't know, which would be true. Furthermore, it was not a party, exactly, but something educational. After all, it was a *tragedy* they were going to read, which would put Warren right in the mood.

A smile twitched at Jane's lips; her eyes goggled. She felt tickled by her own power of reasoning. Other people would say she was outrageous, but it was only the truth she was thinking. Wasn't tragedy supposed to be a cathartic? She put on an innocent expression and arranged her plastic hood attractively over her tawny hair. A brand-new idea had come to her. She was going to the Western Union office and send a telegram for Warren to his old aunt: "Impossible leave today because of storm. Taking plane Savannah tomorrow morning. Grief-stricken. Love to all." But as she considered this message, she saw that it would not do. It would satisfy the Western Union man, but the dating would give her away. Warren's aunt would be bound to let the cat out of the bag by asking Warren about the storm; old people like that were always interested in weather

166

conditions. Jane pondered. Lying was not easy, when you had to cover your tracks. But it stimulated your brain, like doing a chess problem: you had to think ahead to all the possible moves on the other side of the board. The easy thing would be to go home and tell Warren now and get it over with, but she could not bear to give up, now that she was started. A solution would come to her; solutions always had. The point was to word a telegram so that it could sound as if it had been sent tomorrow, in case Warren ever saw it, and at the same time to fix it so that the Western Union man would not wonder. . . . Just as she was despairing, the light suddenly broke: she would send a night letter! "Warren taking plane. He will arrive Savannah, today, Saturday, p.m. and will phone you from airport. Both of us very sad to hear of mother's passing. Condolences to all. Signed, Jane Coe." She counted over the words to make sure it was long enough not to surprise the Western Union man that it was going as a night letter; luckily, her small economies were famous in the village. He would not think a thing of it, unless she started explaining. "Never apologize, never explain," she said to herself sagely, starting up the engine.

Tomorrow morning, when she brought Warren the bad news, she would tell him that she had just sent that message for him, from the Western Union office, and he would say, "Wonderful, dear," as he always did when she thought ahead for him. Then, even if his aunt should happen to show him the telegram, Warren would be too hot and bothered to notice the NL, for night letter, up among the symbols at the top. If he did, he would think it was a mistake.

In the little telegraph office, heated by a station-stove, Jane lost her usual aplomb. The Western Union man in his brown buttoned sweater unnerved her; he was so silent and poky. He did not make a sound as she wrote out the message for him, printing in big letters. She felt she ought to say something as his cracked brown finger moved laboriously over the yellow sheet she handed him, marking each word while she waited, sweat breaking out on her brow. Finally, he looked up over his glasses and scratched his head. "Sure you want to send it this way, Mrs. Coe?" he said, with a sharp look. Jane nearly passed out; she felt just as she used to when she was called into the head mistress's office. "As a night letter, you mean?" she blurted out. "Yes . . . I think so. . . . It's cheaper, and the person it's going to will be out all day anyway. When they get it, you see, today will be tomorrow, or the other way around." She could have killed herself when the telegrapher, nodding his old head slowly back and forth like a rocker, finally saw fit to reply. "That's your business," he observed. "Tweren't that I was thinking of." He got up from his stool and meandered over to the window. "Looks to me," he said, "like a three-day blow. Doubt Mr. Coe will get a plane tomorrow morning." Relief made Jane giddy; she nearly laughed aloud. "Why don't you add, 'Weather permitting'?" she suggested brightly, pointing to the telegram. "Put it after 'plane.' 'Weather permitting, he will arrive Savannah . . .'?" The telegrapher considered. "That's it," he nodded. "Don't cost you no more."

Jane bolted out of the office. He was a rare one, all right, she said to herself, and he held her in the palm of his hand, if he only knew it, like that awful creature in *Madame Bovary*. She was still shaking when she drove up to the cleaning woman's house and parked for a minute to steady her nerves before having to face another native. The way they watched you steadily, without saying a word, seemed to her suddenly sinister, like being surrounded in the jungle. She longed for a confidante, to whom she could explain herself, but Warren was the only person who would understand and sympathize. Some day, she decided, she would tell him what she had gone through this morning, and they would laugh about it together; it would become one of Jane's exploits. "Do you remember the time your mother died?" she could hear herself begin, and her face, in the car mirror, at once assumed a sheepish bad-girl look, with the lower lip thrust out and the long chin dropped, while the big blue eyes rolled appealingly, ready to dance, if only a partner invited. She was two people, really, as Warren had delightedly discovered, first on their honeymoon, and then again and again, just as he thought he had her settled. There were big Jane and little Jane, stern Jane and guilty Jane, downcast Jane and blithe Jane—she knew this from scolding herself as she used to scold her doll. And it was bad Jane, she recognized, who had the upper hand this morning. She had just done something *awful*. But now that she admitted it boldly, gazing hangdog at herself in the mirror, she promptly felt much better. Fear left her; some day she would confess to Warren and that would take care of remorse. She honked the horn for the cleaning woman and waited, at the wheel, unflurried. There was plenty of time for everything, so long as she took it easy and reminded herself that nothing mattered, really. She could still get Will Harlow, and if she didn't, so much the worse. Moreover, if she was lucky, she might catch the high-school principal at lunch, when she went to get the glasses.

EIGHT

T itus reginam Beronicen, cui etiam nuptias pol-
licitus ferebatur . . . statim ab Urbe dimisit
invitus invitam." Miles cleared his throat and
looked around the Coes' living room. The dinner dishes
were cleared, and the play-reading was about to begin.
Warren and Jane Coe sat by the fireplace, sharing a book
and a hassock. They had elected not to take parts; it
would be more fun, they said, just to listen. The rest of
the company was paired: Martha was looking on with
the vicomte; Dolly with Harold Huber, a thin white-
haired man in a red flannel shirt who used to be a lawyer
and now ran a duck farm; Miles with Harriet Huber, a
big pink woman with a gray pompadour. Helen Murphy
had not come. The child was sick, and Helen had been
calling all day, to try to change the date to next week,
but somebody on the line had left the receiver off the
hook, so in the end Miles had driven over alone, not to let
the Coes down. Martha was alone too, and for a while, at
dinner, it had looked as if she and Miles were going to
play opposite each other, as the Emperor and the Jewish
queen, but Martha had insisted that Bérénice be given
to Dolly. Martha was quite high; the gin-and-french,
without ice, before dinner, had evidently gone to her
head, and she had gulped a lot of claret. Warren had not
seen her that way for years, not since she had been married to Miles, and he had felt troubled as he repeatedly
filled her empty wine glass. Her dark eyes glittered in

her pale oval face, and she spoke very positively, interrupting Miles in the middle of his harangues. At the same time, she looked very pretty, with her tapering neck and gold knot of hair, like a girl in a locket; she had not reached the usual New Leeds state, where the eyes would narrow and the features slip out of drawing, like a loose mask—a thing Warren hated, no matter how many times he saw it happen. He was apprehensive for Martha, knowing her as he did and sharing her nervousness about Miles. An outsider might not have realized that she was tight, but Dolly Lamb, Warren noticed, when she came in after dinner with the vicomte, had given her a quick, quizzical look, the minute she heard her laughing, in clear, sharp peals, at something that was not awfully funny. Martha had noticed the look too and hastily set aside her glass of B and B. She asked for more coffee, but unfortunately it had run out, and Warren did not want to bother Jane, who seemed tired and preoccupied, with making a fresh pot. Instead, he hopped out to the kitchen and brought everybody a glass of water.

"*Titus reginam Beronicen,*" Miles began again. "*Reginam,*" murmured Martha to the vicomte, with a grimace, making the g hard. "I hate that soft, squelchy church Latin; after all, it's *Tacitus* he's quoting." The vicomte furled his lower lip, like a little flag, and shrugged. "A matter of taste," he said. "Who knows how the Romans pronounced?" "We *do* know," whispered Martha. "*Quiet!*" Warren begged. "I want to hear Miles translate it." "Say," said Harold Huber, "include me out on the Latin. We came here to *parler français,* the way Harriet got it." "It's just the preface," explained Dolly in an undertone, pointing to the text. "Racine gives the *locus classicus* he got the plot from." "Oh," replied Harold Huber. "Shoot," he said to Miles. " 'Against his will and hers, Titus sent Queen Bérénice, whom, it is said, he had even promised to marry, away from the City.'" Miles glanced at Martha for confirmation. She nodded. " 'He, unwilling, sent her, unwilling, away,'" she said dreamily. " *'Statim'*. 'At once.'"

"Pronto," Miles chuckled. "Forthwith. *Subito*. There you have it, boys and girls. Yet in Racine it takes five acts to bring off." He took out a handkerchief and blew a trumpet blast on his long nose. "Racine's a microscopist," he explained. "A slow-motion camera trained on the passions." "Precisely," said Martha. "Unlike Corneille," continued Miles, "he's intersted in *process*. Racine's a kind of scientist—bear in mind that this is the seventeenth century, the great age of French science and invention." Warren nudged Jane. "Gee, this is interesting," he said. "Racine," Miles went on, with a gimlet stare at his audience, "is a scientific observer of human behavior; he takes a single action and enlarges it, under his microscope, the way you might study a plant or the organs of an animal." "Yes," put in Martha, excitedly. "How clever of you, Miles. That's why the unities were necessary to Racine. People think the unities were arbitrary and artificial—a convention of academicians. But I can see that you could look at them as scientific, as if he were setting up a laboratory, for a controlled experiment." "Excuse me for living," Warren bashfully interjected, when he saw that she was through, "but what are the unities?" The vicomte sighed and laced his broad red hands over his belly; Harriet Huber yawned. "Time, space, and action," ventured Dolly. Martha nodded. "The action takes place in one day on a single set. Here it's the *cabinet* or closet, as they used to call it—Titus's glorified private study, where he transacts his personal business. Next door, on one side, stage right, I think, are his imperial apartments; stage left, on the other side, are the apartments of the queen, Bérénice.

Rome and Jerusalem, and the parley-ground between."
"What's she doing there, anyway?" inquired Harold
Huber. "She's his guest," said Martha. "She and her
suite. In history, her brother Agrippa was with her."
"Isn't she Titus's mistress?" Jane wondered. "Evidently,"
said the vicomte, widening his blue eyes. Miles and
Martha exchanged an interrogatory look. "I don't *think*
so," said Martha. "No," said Miles. "She isn't. Racine
doesn't set it up that way. For five years, they've been
engaged, but he hasn't tampered with her. Racine makes
that plain in the preface"—he tapped the book—"where
he compares her to Dido. Bérénice, he says, doesn't have
to die in the end because she, unlike Dido with Aeneas,
hadn't gone the whole way with young Titus."

"Oh, I bet they slept together," said Jane airily.
"Everybody knows about those long engagements. You
can't tell me they didn't have intercourse." She giggled.
A look of amusement passed between Miles and Martha.
"Not in Racine, Jane," said Martha. "He says they
didn't, and you have to suspend your disbelief for the
purposes of the play." "Maybe they did in history, dear,"
said Warren. "But this is a work of art, and you have to
accept the artist's convention." "Oh, pooh," said Jane.
"If they didn't sleep together, that was the whole trouble.
That's why their affair fizzled out. If he'd had them sleep
together, he could have had a happy ending." "Maybe
that's why he didn't," suggested Dolly gravely. "He
didn't want a happy ending, you mean?" put in Warren.
"Right," said Miles.

"Will somebody please tell us what this is all about?"
Plump Harriet Huber querulously patted her pompadour. Except for her batik robes and the priests' vest-
ments she sometimes wore, she was a very ordinary
woman, who had formerly been a singer. Harold Huber
was brighter than she was and keen as a whip, Warren

had found, on his specialty, which had been railroad law. He had come a cropper through some arbitrage deal and nearly been put in jail, but he had a sharp head for business and had made good, up here, with his duck farm, which he had bought up cheap from a derelict writer who had mortgaged the ducks to go to Paris. Everybody ate ducks, to help Harold, but poor Harriet always seemed a little out of things, like somebody's mother. "All you people," she complained now, "seem to have read the play ahead of time." "Yes, Miles, give us the story," chimed in Harold Huber. "I think Paul should do it," said Jane with a hostess's eye on the vicomte, who sat blinking drowsily in his canvas chair. "Let the baron tell it," Miles conceded grandly. "Ah well," said the vicomte, opening his eyes, "it is many years since I have seen it performed. *Mon oncle, le duc,* took me when I was a little shaver, to see Bernhardt in the role. It was before her break with the *Comédie Française.* He had a mistress, I believe, who was playing the part of the confidante—your part, my dear girl," he added, to Martha. "Later, there was a quarrel between her and Bernhardt." "Let's get on with the story," Miles said impatiently.

But Paul was offended. "You tell it, my friend," he said. "It's nothing. A *ficelle. 'Marion pleure, Marion crie; Marion veut qu' on la marie,'* as Voltaire wittily said." He broke off into a fit of coughing. "I don't believe he knows it at all," Jane whispered to Warren. "Not Voltaire—" began Martha. "Ssh," said Warren. "Titus," commenced Miles, "the new Emperor of Rome, loves Queen Bérénice of Judaea." "What you would call today a puppet queen," interjected the vicomte, smoothing his long bob. "Titus," said Miles, "has conquered Jerusalem." "The Arch of Titus," whispered Dolly, to Harold Huber. "Quiet!" implored Warren. "Titus," Miles resumed at a brisker pace, "has brought the vassal queen to Rome, where he conceives the notion of marrying her. His father—" "Vespasian," announced Martha. "Damn it, Martha," exclaimed Miles. "Stop helping me. Tell the story yourself." He folded his arms and scowled. "Shall I?" Martha appealed to the company, as Miles remained stubbornly silent, his narrow lips set. "Go ahead, Martha," said Jane. "All right, then," said Martha. "When the play opens, it's Titus's wedding day. His father, Vespasian, has died, just a few days before, I think, and Titus is now Caesar. In her apartments, Bérénice is waiting to be married. She doesn't realize (dramatic irony) that Titus has decided to renounce her, because Roman law and custom forbid Caesar to marry a queen and a foreigner." "Why?" said Harriet Huber. "Prejudice," said the vicomte, looking at them over a large pair of glasses, which he had produced from his pocket. "It is the same as with us in France. Ever since they threw their own kings out, the Romans *détestaient les rois.*" "The Senate," resumed Martha, "has reminded Titus of his duty and he comes to tell Bérénice that he's going to send her back to Judaea—unwillingly." The vicomte looked up from the text. "But Bérénice is naughty," he supplied. "She takes it in a bad spirit—not nobly—protests that he is tired of her and threatens to kill herself. *Eh bien,* Titus, who loves her still, becomes a bad boy too and threatens to kill *him*self. When the lovely Bérénice hears this, she knows that he loves her and rises to her full height." The vicomte sat up in his chair, threw his chest out and held himself at attention. "She renounces Titus, of her own volition, and sets sail for Judaea, promising not to die. Titus stays in Rome and takes up his job as Emperor."

"And that's all?" said Harriet Huber, curiously. "That's all," said the vicomte, settling back in his chair with a somewhat triumphant expression. "You forgot

Antiochus," prompted Martha. "Ah yes," said the vi-comte. "The king of Comagena. It is the part I will take. Another Oriental, like Bérénice. Another barbarian. He is Titus's rival. He loves Bérénice and hopes to get her, what do you say, on the rebound. But in the end he too renounces. He gives up his crafty design and becomes like a Roman." There was a silence. Dolly frowned. "It's rather like an Austen novel, isn't it?" she timidly observed. "All the characters become educated; they grow up and buckle down to their duties, like Emma marrying Mr. Knightley." She screwed up her brows. "It sounds awfully uncomfortable," she added, with a little shiver. "But naturally," said the vicomte. "The characters have growing pains. That is what tragedy is."

"Let me ask you a question," said Warren, who had been waiting dutifully for an opening in the conversation. "Why doesn't Titus give up the job of Emperor and just marry Bérénice and live like a plain citizen?" "Like the Duke of Windsor," exclaimed Harriet. "I knew it reminded me of something. 'The woman I love.'" She laughed a little and looked at her husband. But Jane, who seemed out of sorts for some reason this evening, turned impatiently on Warren. "Oh, Warren," she said, "you know the answer to that. It's right there in the play." "I forget," confessed Warren.

Miles opened the book. "Act V, Scene 6," he noted, and began to declaim, addressing himself to Dolly:

> "Oui, madame, et je dois moins encore vous dire
> Que je suis prêt pour vous abandonner l'empire,
> De vous suivre, et d'aller, trop content de mes fers,
> Soupir avec vous au bout de l'univers."

"Isn't that just *like* the Duke of Windsor?" cried Harriet. "'To sigh with you at the ends of the earth'? Wasn't there something like that in that record he made?" She hunted in her text. "*Je suis prêt pour vous abandonner l'empire . . . ?*" She turned a questioning glance on her husband. "Probably the Duke of Windsor copied it out of Racine," declared Jane, rounding her eyes and dropping her jaw. "Hardly," said Miles, with a curt, silencing nod in her direction. He continued, his green eyes fixed on Dolly:

> "*Vous même rougieriez de ma lâche conduite*
> *Vous verriez à regret marcher à votre suite*
> *Un indigne empereur sans empire, sans cour,*
> *Vil spectacle aux humains de la faiblesse de l'amour.*"

Dolly colored, as if in character, under Miles's stare. "There, you see, Warren," said Jane. "Think of poor Titus giving up his empire, trailing around after her, and with all those trunks. . . ." "What trunks, darling?" Warren turned to her anxiously. "I don't get your point." "Why, the Duchess of Windsor's, of course," retorted Jane. "Everybody knows about her traveling with seventy trunks of dresses. In Titus's day, probably, in Palestine, it would have been on camels." Harold Huber guffawed. "But Jane is quite right," interposed the vicomte, with an air of virtuous reproof. "That is what Titus would have become if he had married the queen for love—a flunkey." " '*Un indigne empereur . . . vil spectacle aux humains de la faiblesse de l'amour,*' " quoted Miles again in a sonorous voice; his French was extremely fluent, but he spoke with a rolling accent that made it sound like an Irish brogue. The vicomte and Martha smiled. "But is love a weakness?" cried Warren in alarm. "Does anybody here think love is a *weakness?*" "In a king, certainly," said the vicomte, folding his hands. "Do you agree with that, Miles?" Warren turned to his friend. "Not only in a king," he said finally, in his drawling voice. "In any man, I would say. Love is for

177

boys and women." Martha's fair brows made two skeptical arcs, but she said nothing. Warren looked hopefully around the circle, but nobody rose to love's defense. "What about Plato?" he said to Miles, in a tone of diffident reminder. "That isn't what Plato says." "Plato meant something different," Miles replied brusquely. "The concept you're thinking of—romantic love—was unknown to him." "That's not what *I* got out of him," protested Warren. "If that isn't romantic love in the Symposium, what is it?" he said. "Transcendence. Idealization," said Martha. "Plato despairs of love, mortal love, as we understand it." Miles tapped his foot in its fancy shoe. "Oh, excuse me," she said, demurely. "I interrupted again." "I agree with Miles," Jane suddenly proclaimed. "In a man, love *is* a weakness." Warren jumped up from the hassock. He was quivering all over. "You don't mean that," he said incredulously. "Oh yes," said Jane. "Well, all I can say—" he began, and then words failed him. "I could eat that *rug*," he finally announced, pointing to a cotton string rug of a tattletale gray shade that lay in front of the fireplace. Dolly's humorous eyebrows lifted inquiringly as she examined the rug and then Warren. "Not really?" she murmured. *"Really!"* replied Warren fiercely, clenching and unclenching his jaws as if he were about to bite into it. "Calm down, dearie," said Jane. "Why not get on with the play?" suggested Harold Huber. "Let's postpone the arguments of counsel till after the case had been presented."

The play-reading proceeded. Warren, choking back his emotions, acted as monitor. He and Jane—he explained to the newcomers, with a bitter glance at his mate—had read aloud so many times, both to each other and in groups, that they had worked out a set of rules for it. Nobody was to interrupt the reading during an act;

at the end of each act, questions of translation could be asked. Questions of interpretation were to be deferred until the whole play had been read, and no side remarks were tolerated. Laughing was strictly forbidden except in the case of a comedy. Drinks were served *after* the reading. As he enunciated these rules, hollow laughter echoed in the chambers of his heart. He felt like that French schoolmaster giving the Last Class in conquered Alsace-Lorraine. His marriage was over, probably, after tonight, now that Jane had let him know how she really felt about things. He loved her, and she considered it a weakness. To go on after that would be hypocrisy.

Rules, he said to himself wanly. He and Jane made them together, and then she broke them. It was just like these play-readings, where he, poor simp, tried to keep order and everybody laughed at him. And the regulations they had made—except the one about ' drinking— were harder on him than anybody. When an interesting point came up, he could hardly hold himself in; waiting till the end for a discussion was agony, especially since by the time they had finished, nobody else ever seemed to remember the passage he had in mind. But it was not fair to the author, he and Jane had agreed, to pick a play to pieces before it had had a chance to say its whole say.

Yet she was always one of the worst offenders, giggling and interrupting and popping her eyes or making trips to the kitchen during the most significant parts. Every time they read aloud, he constantly had to remind her that the play or the poem had the floor. But tonight, as he slowly became aware, she was more subdued than usual, as if she knew what she had done to him and the reckoning that lay ahead for both of them, after the others had gone. She did not poke him when Miles gave a funny reading or when Martha overacted her part. She sat listening, thoughtfully, her chin sunk in her hand.

Her mind, he could suddenly tell, was a million miles away from him, though he could feel the comfortable warmth of her big vital body next to him, on the hassock. She had no idea how she had wounded him, evidently, and, soothed by her physical presence, he gradually let himself relent toward her, even though he knew that this was the worst crime one human could commit against another: not to take their words seriously. When she turned and smiled at him, vaguely, during the first intermission, he smiled back and wiggled his ears slightly, feeling like Judas Iscariot.

He turned his attention to the play. He had hoped he would like it better in French than he had when the two of them had read it in English, but instead it let him down even more. Unlike Jane, he was not musical, and that, he guessed, was the trouble: the jingling alexandrines sounded monotonous to him, even when Paul was reading. He liked Dolly best; her accent was neat and pretty, though she did not put much expression into her lines. Martha and the vicomte were frowning over their text when Dolly came to the big scene of despair and jealousy in the fourth act, where she was supposed to be waiting for Titus in a state of extreme disorder. Martha, as her waiting woman, read her own lines with unnecessary urgency, as if she were trying to push Dolly into the proper mood:

> "Mais voulez-vous paraître en ce désordre extrême?
> Remettez vous, madame, et rentrez en vous-même.
> Laissez-moi relever ces voiles dédachés,
> Et ces cheveux épars dont vos yeux sont cachés.
> Souffrez que de vos pleurs je répare l'outrage."

This sounded very comical, in Martha's quick, passionate voice, while Dolly sat there, cool as a cucumber, not a silvery blond hair out of place. Even Miles looked up and chuckled when Dolly replied, in her circumspect tinkling bell-tones: *"Laisse, laisse, Phénice; il verra son ouvrage."* Warren had to call twice for silence before Dolly could go on with her part. She was at her best, Warren thought, in the final passage, when she turned to the vicomte, with imperturbable dignity, like the senior prefect in her boarding school:

> *"Sur Titus et sur moi, réglez votre conduite.*
> *Je l'aime, je le fuis; Titus m'aime; il me quitte.*
> *Portez loin de mes yeux vos soupirs et vos fers.*
> *Adieu. Servons tous trois d'exemple à l'univers."*

It was a pretty poor example they were going to set the universe, in Warren's opinion, but at least Dolly gave him the idea that a person *could* feel that way.

Unfortunately, he missed the first part of the discussion, because he was busy fixing drinks for everybody. Even Jane wanted one, to his surprise; she asked for a bourbon and fizzy, and drank it straight down when he brought it. "I was thirsty," she said. All the dinner guests were thirsty, it turned out; there had been a mite too much salt in the roast. Dolly took a glass of port, and the vicomte joined her. "I thought you didn't drink," exclaimed Martha, tactlessly, for the vicomte often drank, in moderation, since his reform. The Hubers and Martha had Scotch; Miles had a big drink of bourbon, to wet his whistle, as he called it. Warren himself had a glass of plain fizzy, when he finally joined the circle. Martha and Miles, on good terms again, were talking about the influence of Port Royal on Racine, and the Hubers seemed rather out of it. They had had the smallest parts —Titus's and Antiochus's confidants—and people always forgot that they were not intellectuals. Warren brought the subject back to the play, which they could all share.

"How terribly Protestant it is," said Dolly, making a little face. "But naturally," said the vicomte. "Port Royal was Jansenist. That is a Protestant heresy. Racine had it in his bones." "Why do you say 'Protestant,' Miss Lamb?" demanded Harriet Huber. "What's the difference, Miss Lamb?" Martha answered for her, taking a long drink. "Setting a good example. Renunciation. Training the will. Scruples." "But don't the Catholics have those?" Harriet asked the vicomte. "We are not puritans," said the vicomte, sipping his port. "Miles," said Martha suddenly, "how would you distinguish between the Corneillean will and the Racinian will? There're the same conflicts, in Corneille, between passion and duty, between the state and the family, between the family and the single person. Yet you couldn't say that Corneille was Protestant. . . ." Warren's head kept turning eagerly, back and forth, from face to face; it made him feel as if he were watching a tennis match. "Well," said Miles, cautiously, "in Corneille, I would say there was more feeling for power. It's an imperial will, in Corneille, swelling out to world-domination. He wrote a *Bérénice* too, you know." "Maybe we ought to read that next," proffered Warren conscientiously. "To get both sides—" "A Renaissance will," broke in Martha. "The difference between setting an example, like Titus and Bérénice, and dominating through your will, like the people in *Cinna* or the *Cid*. *'Je suis maître de moi comme de l'univers. Je suis, je veux l'être.'* Do you remember that, Dolly, from college?" "I hated it," said Dolly, with feeling. "It's more Faustian in Corneille, wouldn't you say, Miles?" persisted Martha. "And isn't there something else? In Racine the conflict of passions is more internalized, within the soul of the character— his famous 'psychological realism.' The soul, in Racine, is an arena, full of sinuous savage beasts leaping at the whip." "Good Heavens," said Harriet Huber. " '*Vénus toute entière à sa proie attachée,*'" quoted Miles. "If you remember your Phèdre. The beast within. A thoroughly Protestant vision, I agree, Miss Lamb." Dolly colored. "Love, in Racine," pursued Martha, with a significant glance at Dolly, as if reminding her of some earlier conversation, "love is seen as a sort of diabolical possession —witchcraft. Poor Phèdre. Racine made her a great heroine by giving her a bad conscience. It's more sensual that way too. She hates herself and this passion that fastens itself on her, like a bird of prey."

"Let's get back to *Bérénice* for a minute," urged Warren. "I'd like to hear what the rest of you think about the philosophy in there." " 'Philosophy'?" questioned the vicomte. "There is no philosophy in *Bérénice.*" "Warren means a philosophy of life," said Martha. "Isn't it the same thing?" protested Warren. "No," said Miles. "Gee, I'd like to discuss that with you," said Warren. "Later, my boy," said Miles. "Let's stick to the subject." "Well, but . . ." said Warren, hesitantly. He wanted to point out that no discussion could be worth anything if you did not go back and define your principles, but he could see the impatience in both Miles's and Martha's faces. He conquered his disappointment. "What I want to know," he began, "is whether this play makes you as mad as it does me. It makes me want to eat nails." "Why, Warren?" said Martha gently. "The way I see it," said Warren, "that Titus is a prig and a hypocrite. He was no gentleman, if you'll pardon my French." "Why?" said Dolly. "He was engaged to Bérénice, darn it," cried Warren, "and then he broke his promise to her, just for reasons of state. I call that pretty cheap. He owed it to her to marry her, when he'd been engaged to her for five years." "And she wasn't getting any younger," said Martha, with a laugh.

"But his father died, dearie," said Jane. "When he got to be Caesar, he couldn't marry her, because of that old law." "He should have thought of that before he got engaged to her," Warren said hotly. "He knew the law and he knew his father was going to die some time. And it strikes me," he continued, emboldened, when nobody answered, "it strikes *me* Racine was pretty much of a faker not to have *made* that point in the play. If Shakespeare wrote that play, he darn well would have showed what a son of a bitch Titus really was." Miles looked at Martha, who looked at Dolly. Warren could tell from their expressions that they thought he had made a point. "You're right in a way, of course," said Martha finally. "Don't you think so, Miles? In a play by Shakespeare, Titus might have been shown up a little, like Prince Hal. It's the same plot, really, when you think about it. A playboy prince and his boon companions. The education of a king. When the prince's father dies, the prince, rather priggishly, sends his companions away. The rejection of Falstaff isn't too different from the rejection of Bérénice, only in Racine it's called renunciation. Probably Shakespeare," she went on, with an apologetic smile at the vicomte, "is truer to the way things happen. One never knows, in real life, exactly how much self-interest or surfeit there is in these great renunciations."

"That's all old stuff," said Jane. "People don't renounce any more, unless they're compulsive or something." "There was Kierkegaard," said Warren. "*I* gave up my singing career for Harold," observed Harriet. "Probably you wanted to anyway," said Jane, candidly. "I mean, would you have given up Harold for your singing? I'll bet Prince Hal was bored stiff with Falstaff. He sounds just like some of the people around here. And I'll bet Titus, underneath, was anti-Semitic. It says right

184

here in the play that he doesn't want to get mixed up with Bérénice's Jewish relations." Laughter shook the room. "Jane's right," said Warren, stoutly. "Act II, Scene 2. Shall I read it?" "We remember," said Harold Huber. "Those two queens, wasn't it, of Bérénice's blood, who married a slave or something?" Warren nodded. "But that isn't anti-Semitism, Mr. Coe," protested Dolly. "Something pretty darn close to it," said Warren. "It shows what kind of a guy Titus was that he'd listen to an argument like that."

Miles sighed. "Racine wasn't interested in character," he said. "You have to get that through your noodle. You can't judge him the way you do Shakespeare. Shakespeare was interested in politics and political types, which means he was interested in motive—the thing that makes people move, the way they do, in society. Underneath, of course, you'll find the archaic patterns. The death of the father alters the Oedipal constellation; the son, so to speak, intromits the father, swallows him, and assumes his primordial role. That's what we see happening underneath the surface of both these plays—the *Henry IV* sequence and *Bérénice*. The renunciation of Bérénice may involve a belated rejection of the mother, the feminine component, in Titus; you see the same thing with Falstaff, whose relation with Prince Hal was suspiciously homosexual." Jane adjusted an earring. "That's what I always told you," she said to Warren, who nodded sadly.

"What about the death of the mother, Miles?" inquired Harold Huber. "That doesn't have the same importance," said Miles. "Not for the normal man, in his prime. The normal man outlives the mother while she's still hale and hearty. It's only in pathological instances that you find a son coming into manhood, finally, when the mother passes on." Jane sat picking at a spot on her skirt. For some reason, she kept staring at Miles's shoes, which were black and very shiny looking, cut almost like a pair of slippers. "Still, Miles," she said casually, "in our culture you'll find a lot of fuss about the death of the mother. Or do you think that's all commercialized, like Mother's Day and Christmas?" "Purely ritualistic," said Miles. "Contrary to popular opinion, the mother doesn't count in the American scene. I used to see it in my practice. She lives too damn long. Of course, there's a certain amount of guilt among the descendants when they eventually get rid of the old girl. Half racial memory; half social uneasiness. They think they're expected to feel something."

There was a silence. If Warren was a fair sample, they were all thinking about Harriet, who was three times a grandmother and devoted to her two sons. "An angel just passed over," she said brightly. "The angel of death," said the vicomte, crossing himself. Harriet turned to him. "I was just reading an article," she said. "By a Protestant minister. About how people are going back to religion. I never felt the need of it myself, but perhaps that shows I'm a back number." "Like all of us," said Martha, sharply. "None of us, except the vicomte, are religious." "But what about church attendance figures?" ventured Harriet. "Aren't modern people supposed to be feeling a lack in their lives that they need religion to fill?" Martha shrugged. "An advertising gambit," she said. "First you convince people they lack something and then you sell them a product to remedy it. People 'need' religion to 'deepen their awareness' or give them 'tragic irony'—the way I 'need' a facial cream to make my life more glamorous." Warren felt a little embarrassed, on account of Paul; if Martha were completely sober, she would not have flared up like that. "But if

186

there is a lack, Martha?" said Dolly. "Then it ought *not* to be filled," said Martha. "If it's a real lack, it's a necessary hollow in life that can't be stuffed up, like a chicken. Insufficiency. Shortcoming. I don't need God as a measure to feel that. Do you, Dolly?" "God, *no!*" said Dolly.

"But you two are superior people," said Jane thoughtfully. "Take the average person; take Mrs. Silvia, my cleaning woman—" "I refuse that," said Martha. "I *am* an average person." Everybody laughed at the haughty air with which Martha said this. "Oh, come on, Martha," said Jane, yawning and rearranging her hair. "We all know we're superior to the ordinary person, mentally, anyway, and we all live more interesting lives. We don't need religion; we've got books and pictures and music. We don't have to go to church for spiritual stimulation. It's just like in Rome; Christianity was a slave religion. A person like Titus was above it, the way he was above marrying Bérénice, because he was the Emperor. Love's a form of slavery too; an Emperor couldn't be a slave to love—that's what the play is saying." "But what about his promise?" squealed Warren, anxious to get the conversation back on the main track. "Do you think some people are superior to promises?" "Oh, Warren," said Jane. "Promises in love don't mean anything. Look at all the people who get divorced." She clapped her hand over her mouth. Warren felt about the size of a pin. But Dolly rescued the situation. "It seems to *me*," she remarked, "that there isn't any 'ought' or 'ought not' at issue in the play. It's really taken for granted what Titus ought to do. The interest is in whether he *can* do it." The vicomte nodded. "Quite right," he said. "It is not a modern problem play. The standards are there, for Titus and Bérénice; no one in the play doubts them. The question is whether the characters can rise to conformity with them."

"Conformity!" Warren hopped on the word, which was the one he had been seeking all along, he joyously realized. "You've put your finger on it, Paul," he announced excitedly, waving his hand for silence. "That's what I hate in this play. It's all about conformity. The characters are a bunch of conformists. Bérénice, for about two minutes, is a rebel, and then she throws in the sponge and conforms like the rest of them." "But that is tragedy, my dear fellow," said the vicomte. "The principal figure learns to be *sage*." "Not for me, it isn't," said Warren. "Oh yes," said the vicomte. "The old Oedipus, for example, has learned to be wise." "To me, that's just horror," exclaimed Warren. "Oh no, it isn't," said Harriet. Everybody, suddenly, began talking all at once, the way they always did when a discussion got promising. Warren could hardly hear himself think. "Life *is* horrible," said Harold Huber, dryly. "Oh no, it isn't," cried Dolly. "It's beautiful!"

"Oh, I know life is horrible," Warren interrupted, with a happy smile. "I learned to accept that long ago. Everybody's a bastard, including me and Jane. But that doesn't stop me from being mad as all hell about it." Every eye turned on him in bewilderment. "Excuse me, Warren," said Harold, "but I don't get you. What's the argument? If you've learned to accept the facts of life, what's eating you about Racine?" Warren looked miserably about him; nobody understood him, not even Jane. He caught Martha's eye imploringly. "I see what he's getting at," said Martha, after a moment's thought. "What Warren misses in Racine is the bitterness. Isn't that it? In the Greeks you get bitterness and you get it again in Shakespeare. There's acceptance without resignation—a kind of defiance, in the end, like Othello's last speech: 'I have done the state some service and they know't.' There's none of that in Racine—none that I remember. The characters are too subservient to official morality, *serviables,* like courtiers." Warren bobbed his head up and down, exultantly, in dumb show, while she was talking; this, he presumed, was what he had meant to convey. Pleased with herself, manifestly, Martha smoothed back a vagrant lock of hair and sank back into her chair with a sigh. They had finished with *Bérénice.*

The conversation broke up into dialogues. Miles went to make himself a drink and brought Martha one. He sat down beside her. "That was fast work," he commented, mopping his brow. Martha smiled at the tribute; her face wore its mischievous look. "Still," Miles went on, in a low voice, "between you and me, what is it they accept, d'you think, in the Greeks and Shakespeare? Not a social code of morality or manners, as the Frenchies understood it." Warren took a seat on the floor near them. "They accepted the way things *are,*" said Martha. "Inevitability. The way things happen, regularly. The laws of geometry of the universe." "I'll buy that," said Miles. "There's one big exception," he added. "I know," said Martha. *"Hamlet."* "You think so too?" inquired Miles with a genial start. He was always surprised, Warren had noticed, when anybody had the same thought he had. "In *Hamlet,*" Miles continued, "everything has gone screwy. No more laws. No more regularity. A ghost is masterminding the action, and nobody's sure whether he comes from the good place or the bad place. In *Hamlet*—Martha, you'll appreciate this —ambiguity raises its ugly head. Is Gertrude's marriage unnatural or isn't it? Is Claudius a villain or just the fall guy? Is Hamlet crazy? That question never gets settled. You can read it that he *is* crazy, like a lot of loonies that pretend to be mad, thinking that they're fooling their keepers. Or you can read it the other way.

Hamlet himself isn't sure whether he's crazy or not. He keeps pinching himself, like a person trying to find out whether he's dreaming. That's the famous doubt." Martha smiled. "I agree," she murmured. "But doesn't that open the question of whether *Hamlet* is really a tragedy? Or a pathetic case history, which is what some actors make it seem?" "Ummm," said Miles. "Jones's interpretation—too narrowly psychoanalytic. Those categories are all right for the groundlings, but I don't find them too helpful in my own thinking nowadays. If Hamlet's just a neurotic, the problem loses interest. For me, *Hamlet* initiates the crisis in epistemology. If it's clinical, it's a case history in the annals of philosophy. A hero questions, for the first time, the whole apparatus of cognition. He sees differently from the 'normal' people in the play, from his mother and old Polonius and Uncle Claudius and Ophelia. Is his vision distorted by the ghost's revelations? Should he trust the ghost or mock him? And this doubt is involved with the whole epistemological puzzle, with how do you know what you know." "Exactly," cried Martha. "The mistrust first of our senses and then of our moral perceptions. That was what I was working on, for my doctorate, the history of that. The two mistrusts are related, as Kant saw when he tried to reorganize the whole subject: how much do we know and how?" "I always said you had a head for philosophy," observed Miles, blowing his nose.

"The same thing in ethics," pursued Martha. "Raskolnikov's question: if there is no God, how do I know that I shouldn't murder a useless old woman? Raskolnikov's question was Kant's question." "Why shouldn't Raskolnikov?" burst in Warren. "I've often thought about that. Jane and I read it two years ago, and it seemed to us that Dostoevski stacked the cards at the end there. He never gives you a reason why Raskolnikov should feel sorry at the end. Raskolnikov was right, according to his lights. I wouldn't want to murder an old woman myself, but that's probably because of the way I was brought up—my conditioning. Logically, there's no reason." "Logic doesn't answer those questions," murmured Martha, with a side glance at Miles. "You have to start with a datum. Put the question the other way round. 'I wouldn't want to murder an old woman; what are my reasons?' You'll get further that way." Warren rubbed his head in perplexity. "But gee," he said, "that's a pretty big assumption you make there. I mean, why should I assume that my own private preferences hold good for the rest of us humans? I don't want to murder old women, but some other fellow might be made differently. It seems to me you've got to consider that. You've got to give *that* fellow a reason. Don't you think so, Miles?" Miles looked down into his pleading eyes. "The electric chair," he said. "That's the reason we give him." Warren felt deeply hurt; Miles was only playing with him. "But you can't do that," he protested. "You have to show him *why* you're giving him the electric chair." "He's right, in a way, Miles," intervened Martha. "You have to make universals. 'Behave so that thy maxim could be a universal law.' I agree with Kant." Miles frowned. "Kant's effort failed—too mechanically monistic. Listen, Warren," he said thickly. "For you, it's an academic question. If you don't want to murder old women, let it go at that. Don't worry about the other fellow. Live selfishly."

A snort of laughter broke from him. Martha smiled too. Warren could see that she disagreed with Miles, but instead of arguing with him, she changed the subject. "He's like Shaw," she said to Miles, with a teasing look down at Warren. "A doubt-spreader. He wants to marshal the logical reasons for every conceivable villainy, even though he himself wouldn't hurt a fly or touch a cup of coffee. That's why poor Shaw couldn't write a tragedy even when he tried. The tragic action turned into a discussion group, with everybody putting forward his point of view, for debate. Just like you," she said to Warren, who was snuggled at their feet.

"But isn't that what the Greeks thought, Martha?" objected Warren, sitting up. "We saw the *Antigone* this summer at the Arena Theater and, golly, it seemed to me, that all the characters were in the right there. Just like *Saint Joan* or *Don Juan in Hell*—we have that on records. I mean, everybody has his point of view. Creon is right, the way he looks at it, wanting to uphold the law, and Antigone is right, the way she looks at it, wanting to bury her brother. It's awfully interesting if you compare that with *Saint Joan,* where Joan is right in her way, and the Archbishop, Cauchois, is right in his. If you compare the texts, you'll see what I mean." A happy thought struck him. He jumped up. "Let me just run out to the studio and get them, and I can show you." "Sit down. We can remember," Miles said curtly. "It'll only take a minute," pleaded Warren. "No," said Miles, looking at the watch on his freckled wrist. Warren complied. He knew Miles's irascible humors and he was afraid that if he disobeyed him, Miles would be gone when he returned. "Tell me the difference, then," he said, scrambling back to his place on the floor, by their side.

"You tell him, Miles," said Martha. "After you," said Miles, with a courtly bow from the waist. "No, please, you do it," cried Martha. "Well," commenced Miles, "in Shaw, it's a matter of logical demonstration. Each character 'proves' the validity of his position, sometimes by paradox, like Candida's father. In Sophocles, it's different," he broke off, rather irascibly. "For God's sake, War-

192

ren, get me a drink." Warren could hear them conferring as he fixed them both drinks. His conscience troubled him a little, for he felt they had both had plenty, but he knew they would go on talking as long as he supplied them with liquor. "In Sophocles, Warren," said Martha, when he came back, "the characters don't set up a debate. They act. And it's shown that action itself is ambivalent. An action like Antigone's can be both right and wrong simultaneously—not right from her point of view and wrong from Creon's but right and wrong absolutely, in the chain of consequences it sets off. Her brother gets buried, as piety demands, but her lover, Haemon, kills himself, as the result of her deed and its punishment. You can see it better with Orestes. Orestes's action in killing his mother, Clytemnestra, was both right and wrong—enjoined on him by the gods and yet accursed. He had to purge the action of its wrong aspect by penance and madness before reconciliation could take place, and the Erinyes become the Eumenides. Did it ever strike you," she interrupted herself, turning to Miles, "that Hamlet is Orestes in reverse? Hamlet pays for his murder by suffering and madness ahead of time, while Orestes kills his mother on credit and has to pay the bill in the sequel. In *Hamlet,* by the time Gertrude drinks the poisoned cup, all passion has been spent." Miles laughed. "I always thought of Hamlet as an early bohemian," he said. "A student, frequenter of actors, constantly philosophizing and living off his uncle. That's why the poor devil couldn't make anything happen, till the end, when he balled everything up and killed the wrong people."

Martha giggled. Warren had seldom heard such an interesting discussion, but he wished they would stay on the subject, instead of making fun of it. "What did you mean," he said, hitching himself closer to Martha, "about Antigone being right and wrong at the same time? You mean she shouldn't have buried her brother if some innocent third party was going to suffer for it?" Martha shook her head, rather crossly; all at once, she looked dead tired. "No," she said. "She *had* to bury her brother. There's no should or shouldn't. Or right or wrong, in the modern sense. There's only the tragic perspective: the eye of eternity or the Greek measure of limit, which everybody oversteps, by a sort of fatality. Nobody can stay in the right—I mean in real life—that's the terrible thing, Warren. If you think you're in the right for more than a few seconds, you'll find that you're in the wrong. Nobody can have a permanent claim on being the injured party; it seems horribly unfair, but there it is. As soon as you feel injured and begin to cry for justice, you discover that your position has gotten undermined; the ground has shifted beneath you, in a slow sort of landslide, and you find yourself cut off."

"You mean you become unpopular—you're talking about martyrs? We see a lot of that in the law courts," said Harold Huber, easily. For some time, everybody had been listening to the conversation; Martha's tone had become rather dramatic and personal. From Jane's saucer eyes and Dolly's worried frown, Warren could see that everybody must be drawing the same inference he was: that she was alluding to herself and Miles. "Unpopular—that too," said Martha. "Though that isn't what I meant. But it's the same thing. You can joy in unpopularity, and that becomes evil too, very quickly. It's another form of righteousness, of that fatal feeling that you're triumphantly in the right." "I get that fatal fe-e-ling," sang Harriet Huber.

Just then, the telephone rang—two longs and a short. Alarm crossed every face; it was so late, after midnight.

Warren moved to answer it, but Jane, swift as an eagle, in her black shawl and black skirt, darted across the room and pounced on the phone before he could get to it. "Who? Who?" she said, warding him off with her elbow when he tried to listen too. He was sure it must be bad news of some sort, but then her tall figure relaxed a little, and she motioned to Martha. "It's John," she announced. The others tried to make conversation while Martha talked, but Jane stood beside her, with a face of unabashed curiosity, taking in every word. "No, I'm not," Warren could not help hearing Martha protest. "Not very, anyway. Do I sound funny? . . . Of course not. Dolly's here. . . . All right, all right. Good-bye, darling." "He says I sound tight," she remarked, ruefully, to Jane. "Where is he?" Jane demanded. "In Boston." "In *Boston?*" Jane stared. "You mean he's spending the *night?*" "Curiosity killed the cat, Jane," observed Harriet. "No, no; he's just leaving," said Martha. "He's at an all-night garage. He had to have the car fixed."

Jane seemed strangely concerned. "Why, he'll never get back tonight," she prophesied. "In all this storm. He should have started sooner." "It's only three hours," said Martha. "Four, in this weather," said Jane, dourly shaking her locks. "I'll bet he stops for the night at one of those little road-places and doesn't get home till noon tomorrow. He'll be so exhausted he'll oversleep." Martha laughed. "You don't know John," she said. "He'll be here, a little after three." But Jane continued to take a gloomy view. "He'll probably have an accident," she said. "Hurrying. On these slippery roads." "*Jane!*" said Warren sharply. She had always had a tendency to pry, which he accepted in her, because she was a woman, but now the thought crossed his mind that she might be a little demented. If so, it was his fault; he was too absorbed in his work and left her with nothing to think about but other people's doings. "Calamity Jane," chuckled Harold. "Why don't you let Martha do the worrying? He's probably had a date with a blonde." Jane recovered herself; she shook her big body like a collie dog. "Martha's a blonde," she pointed out, in her practical way. "A brunette, then," emended Harold.

Dolly rose. The good-natured Hubers seemed to bore her. "I'll take you home," she said to Martha. Warren's heart sank. "Oh, stay," he pleaded, offering her another glass of port. But Dolly was adamant. She was painting from nature, she explained, and had started a picture for which she needed the early morning light. "Oh," said Warren sadly. He turned to Martha. She could stay a little longer, he argued. It was out of Dolly's way to take her; Dolly lived just over the dunes and Martha was on the other side of the peninsula. The Hubers would take her, when they returned Paul to the village. And she had not finished her drink yet. "I'll take her," said Miles, peremptorily. Martha hesitated, glancing from face to face. "A *little* longer," she said nervously. "Are you sure, Martha?" said Dolly, with a keen look into her friend's brilliant, excited eyes, which veered away from her. "I might as well be hanged for a sheep," said Martha, settling back in her chair. Warren beamed. "Wonderful!" he said. "Gee, it's funny you should say that," he added, after a moment's consideration. "What?" said Martha. "About a sheep," confided Warren. "Jane and I are going to get some. She fixed it up today, with the high-school principal. I *knew* I had something to tell you. Remind me when I get back." He took the flashlight and led Dolly out; Martha turned back to Miles.

NINE

A N HOUR and a half later, he was making love to
her on the Empire sofa in her parlor. She would
not let him carry her into the bedroom, where
they could have done their business in comfort. Straining at a gnat and swallowing a camel, as the Good Book
said—that was milady Martha. He settled a small sofa
pillow firmly under her hips, but the position was still
not right. The sofa was too short and narrow and slippery as the devil—covered with some horsehair material
that was probably all the rage now. It groaned as his
bare knees sought to get a purchase on it, and moreover he was cold. Their little house, which was pretty
enough, did not have central heating, and the coal fire,
glowing in the grate, cast romantic shadows over the
white paneling without giving any real heat. The room
temperature, he reckoned, must be about 62°. There
were no shades that could be drawn—only some white
ruffled curtains of a thin material. He had turned the
lights out when he had finally persuaded her to take her
clothes off, but the fire illuminated the room so that
anybody, looking in the window, could have seen their
shadows, playing the beast with two backs, enlarged
on the wall.

Sinnott could not possibly be back for another hour
and a quarter. Miles had looked at his watch, to check,
before having at her, when he had downed his highball.
He could have done without the drink, but Martha,

being what she was, had had to go through the pretense of having asked him in for a nightcap, and they had wasted fifteen minutes, making polite conversation, looking over the house and admiring the big old fireplaces and the wide boards of the floors. He had been curious, as a matter of fact, to see how they lived: she was still a good housekeeper, evidently, and the rooms reflected her personality, at once gay and austere; he could see Sinnott's influence in the number of art books scattered about and in the nice old Victorian sets in the white bookcases. He would have preferred, however, to prowl around on some other occasion, without Martha at his heels, explaining the history of everything. There was nothing here he could identify as belonging to the period of their marriage; the few family things her mother had sent her, old Swedish stuff mostly, had gone up in the fire. Yet he had a queer sense of recognition. Some of the chairs, the wallpapers, the frying pans hanging in the kitchen, the wire lettuce basket, a violet cushion, all looked like old friends to him. She had built her nest again, like a bird, out of the same materials. It agitated him to see this. "You had this before," he said, almost accusingly, picking up a little bronze Italian figure and turning it over in his hand. "No," she averred, but when he pressed her, she admitted that she had had one something like it.

As he stood in the kitchen doorway, watching her make the drinks (he and Helen had a bar in the living room, with a vacuum jug that was kept full of ice cubes), her familiar tussle with the ice tray plucked at the strings of his memory. "Let me do that," he said, when she started trying to open the soda water. He took the opener and the bottle from her, noting her quick flush of surprise. She was thinking, of course, that he had never helped her before. He followed her back into the parlor, observing the motion of her hips, which pranced a little as she walked, with short, incisive steps, in her high-heeled shoes. Up to that moment, he had not been sure whether he wanted to dally with her or not. But now the old Adam in him sat up and took notice. They were alone, hubby was gone—why not? He stood by the fire-place, pretending to examine a picture. She sat down on the sofa opposite him. There was one of those pregnant silences. He tossed off his highball, wiped his lips, took a quick look at his watch, and started across the room for her.

She had struggled at first, quite violently, when he flung himself on top of her on the sofa. But he had her pinioned beneath him with the whole weight of his body. She could only twist her head away from him, half-burying it in one of the sofa pillows while he firmly deposited kisses on her neck and hair. Her resistance might have deterred him if he had not been drinking, but the liquor narrowed his purpose. He was much stronger than she was, besides being in good condition, and he did not let her little cries of protest irritate him as they once might have done. The slight impatience he felt with her was only for the time she was wasting. She wanted it, obviously, or she would not have asked him in. The angry squirming of her body, the twisting and turning of her head, filled him with amused tolerance and quickened his excitement as he crushed his member against her reluctant pelvis. He had no intention of raping her, and it injured him a little to feel how she pressed her thighs, which she had managed to cross, tightly together to protect the inner sanctum, when all he wanted, for the moment, was to hold her in his arms.

Her hair slipped from its pins, and he seized the long tress eagerly in his hands, pressing his mouth into it and inhaling deeply. From the sofa pillow came a muffled cry of disgust; when she turned her head, finally, to mutter "Stop," he planted kisses on her cheek and ear. Breathing in the fragrance of her hair, nuzzling in her neck, he grew almost worshipful and ceased to hold her securely. Seeing this, she at once scrambled over onto her stomach and lay taut, as if waiting. Encouraged, he sought the zipper on the side of her dress—women's clothes always bamboozled him—but she took advantage of his preoccupation to struggle up to a sitting position and began to push him away, with her small hands against his chest. She was wearing a high-necked black dress of thin wool; he could see her small, full breasts, like ripe pears, straining against the material, and he bent down to taste them through the wool. But she would not permit this; her hands sprang up, blocking his approach, as he bore her down again. He kissed her white neck and the hollow of her throat, but whenever he tried to reach her mouth, she turned her head away sharply.

He began to get the idea. The thing was to respect her scruples. She did not seem to mind if he kissed her arms and shoulders; it was her breasts and mouth she was protecting, out of some peculiar pedantry. And yet she was not really frightened. She did not scream or try to hit him or scratch him, as she might have, and he, on his side, did not try to raise her skirt. The struggle was taking place in almost complete silence, as if they were afraid of being overheard. There was only the sound of their breathing and an occasional muffled "Stop" from Martha. They made him think of a pair of wrestlers, heaving and gasping, while taking care to obey the rules. A string of beads she was wearing broke and clattered to the floor. "Sorry," he muttered as he dove for her left breast.

He heard Martha laugh faintly as she pushed his head

away from her tit. The humor of it was beginning to dawn on her, evidently. She was too ironic a girl not to see that one screw, more or less, could not make much difference, when she had already laid it on the line for him about five hundred times. His hunger for her now, when he was so well fixed up at home, was a compliment, which she ought to accept lightly. That was the trouble with intelligent women; there was always an *esprit de sérieux* lingering around the premises. They lacked a sense of proportion. But she was commencing to see it from his angle; her struggles were becoming more prefunctory. "You want it, say you want it," he mumbled in her ear. He was getting exasperated, foreseeing that he would be nervous during the act itself if she did not stop procrastinating.

She shook her disheveled head and wrenched away from him, but just then he found her back zipper. He tugged, and the steel moved on its tracks; the back of her dress fell open. He could feel her stiffen, as he moved his hand, carefully, under her slip, up and down her spine and over her smooth shoulder blades. He bent down to kiss her there, and she did not try to stop him; her back, apparently, was not covered by the ground rules. She lay almost torpid, and he ventured to try to pull her dress off the shoulders in front. "Don't," she cried sharply, as the material started to tear. She sat up in indignation, and his hand slipped in and held her breast cupped. "Take it off," he urged, speaking of her dress in a thick whisper. "I can't," she whispered back, as his other hand stole in and grasped her other breast. They began to argue in whispers. She mentioned Helen, the Coes, New Leeds, but not—and this was curious— her husband. "Please don't," she begged, with tears in her eyes, while he squeezed her nipples between his fingertips; they were hard before he touched them; her breath was coming quickly. She had caught his lower lip between her teeth, and there was a drawn look on her face, which meant that she was ready for it. "Stop, Miles, I beg you," she moaned, with a terrified air of throwing herself on his mercy. "It won't make any difference," he promised hoarsely. She shook her head, but as they were arguing, she let him slip her dress off her shoulders. He freed her breasts from her underslip and stared at them hungrily. Martha's eyes closed and she took a deep breath, like a doomed person. "All right," she said.

Glancing at her wrist watch, she got up and took her dress off and put it on a chair while he hastily undressed himself and turned off the lights. But to have allowed this interval was a mistake. Women were funny that way —give them time to think and the heat goes off, downstairs; he had often observed it. Now he found, once he had got well started, with her arms and legs where he wanted them, that she was no longer responding. She had a lot of will power and she had probably figured out, while she was undressing, that she would not "really" be unfaithful to Sinnott if she did not come to climax. Or else she had begun feeling remorseful. She was nice enough about it; she went through all the motions, trying to give him a good time. But he could not really rouse her, and it took the heart out of him. He regretted the whole business before he was halfway through. He detected that she was trying to hurry him, which made him stubborn, though he was colder than a witch's tit and anxious to get home. Her movements subsided; her limbs became inert. It occurred to him, with a start, that she was actually very drunk, though she had not showed it especially. Compunction smote him; he ought not to have done this, he said to himself tenderly. Tenderness inflamed his member. Clasping her fragile body brusquely to him, he thrust himself into her with short, quick strokes. A gasp of pain came from her, and it was over.

She got up, staggering a little, and disappeared, with her clothes—into the bathroom, presumably. He dressed himself hurriedly by the fireside and stood, warming his hands, waiting for her to come back. He could not hear a sound, except the gurgling of the fire; in the stillness, the house seemed deserted. Alarm overtook him. He turned on the lamps and at once felt conspicuous, as if in a show window. The room had a sordid, disarrayed look. There were scattered beads everywhere and big bone hairpins; the sofa had skewed around, out of position, and a small rug was caught in the casters. For two bits, he would have gone home, *subito,* but he was afraid to leave without knowing what had happened to her. It struck him that she might have passed out. He glanced at his watch and at the clock on the mantel, which had stopped, evidently forever, at a quarter of three. He remembered her talk at the Coes' and he felt as if the eye of eternity were on him, as he paced up and down, irresolutely, smoking a cigarette. When he finished it, he said to himself, he would go and look for her. Suppose he had injured her? Or supposed she had cut her wrists or taken poison, in a fit of self-dramatization? The veins stood out on his forehead. He was tempted, to make himself scarce, while the coast was clear. He stamped out his cigarette, impatiently, and opened his mouth to call "Martha!" in his peremptory baritone. But his vocal cords failed him; he was afraid to make a noise. He waited a little longer.

Just as he was at his wits' end, she came back, wearing a pink dressing gown and a pair of slippers, with her hair, combed, down her back. This domestic image made him feel awkward and remorseful, like the sight of his mother in curlers and wrapper, waiting for him on the stairway of their Yonkers house when he had been out roistering with the gang. "Are you all right?" he said, finally, staring into her pale face. Her eyes had turned black, like two big raw prunes, and she looked a little the worse for liquor, though she had put fresh lipstick on. She nodded, smiling faintly. He wanted to assure her, from the bottom of his heart, that what had just occurred would never happen again, but he felt it would sound impolite to say so. "Good-bye, Miles," said Martha gently. He could not make out whether that was meant to be symbolic or whether she was impatient to get him out of here. He took her hand and kissed her hastily on the forehead. "You'd better clean this up," he jerked out, with a blunt gesture around the room. Then he turned and beat it. But as he started down the hill to where his car was parked, he stole a look back at the house, and to his relief he could see her through the thin curtains moving about the parlor, busily straightening up.

Miles had not enjoyed it much either, Martha said pensively to herself, as she picked up the beads from the parlor floor. It had been like an exercise in gluttony; they had both grasped for a morsel they did not really want. But she did not feel especially bad for what they had done. Now that it was over, it appeared to have been inevitable. She had thought it all out while she had been lingering in the bathroom, dousing her face in cold water to sober herself up and hoping that he would leave, so that she would not have to talk to him again. She had brought it on herself, she supposed. She ought not to have asked him in, knowing that it was a risk, even as they stood in her doorway. But it had been one of those challenges that she always rose to, like a fish to the bait—the fear of being afraid. And she still did not think that Miles had brought her home with the set purpose of seducing her. It had happened all by itself, *invitus, invitam.* In the end, he had done it, she reckoned, just because it was obvious; it was a kind of strength in him not to fear banality but to step right up to it like a man at a free-lunch counter.

She could not deny that she had asked for it, if only by her imprudence. Yet when he had first landed on her, she had felt like laughing. She could not take it seriously. All the while she was struggling, she had been suppressing a smile, at his ridiculous searching for her zipper (he had never been able to find anything), at the blunt simplicity of his onset that took her consent for granted. Her chief worry, at first, had been that he would break the sofa. She had not been alarmed for her virtue, feeling certain that she could free herself once he grasped the sincerity of her objections. She was disgusted with him for slavering over her hair, but since she could not stop him, she resigned herself—that was the way he was, and his enjoyment could not harm her. This inability to feel outrage was of course her undoing. Even when her dress was open, she could not summon wrath sufficient to warrant scratching him or kicking him to keep him from exploring her back. Then, once he had touched her breast, she no longer, so it had seemed to her, had the *right* to refuse him. It was like that thing in law, where if you let somebody cross your property without hindrance, they finally secure a right of way. A drunken notion of equity had been beating at her mind, even as she pushed and parried—the idea that one more time could not possibly count and that she was being preposterous.

And she still felt the force of this reasoning, even now, as she methodically filled the ice tray and carried it, spilling, across the kitchen to the icebox. The only thing that shamed her, looking back on the encounter, was the fact that her senses had awakened under Miles's touch. She would have liked to blot out that part, which was only a minute or two, from her memory. But honesty compelled her to remember, with a half-desirous shudder, that moment when his hand had first squeezed her expectant breast and languorous delight had possessed her, like a voluptuary.

She made a face and proceeded unsteadily to the bathroom. But as she stood there, brushing her teeth, her sensuality relived those few moments, and she longed for John to come home. Disgusted with herself, she rinsed out her mouth and spat into the basin. Nothing, she thought angrily, could be more immoral than utilizing your husband, whom you loved, to slake the desires kindled by another man, whom you detested. Moreover, her practical side added, she would be very unattractive to him in her present condition, still half-tight, swaying a little, and smelling of stale alcohol. He would be cross with her, anyway, for going to the Coes' and getting drunk and seeing Miles again. And he would be right; it could not have come out worse if he had predicted it himself.

Misgivings overtook her. He would be bound to find out that Miles had driven her home. Should she admit that she had asked him in or not? Tomorrow he might notice that there was an inch or so missing from the bottle of Scotch. She took three aspirins and drank two glasses of water, revolving the problem in her mind. She could say Miles had come in for a drink and made a pass at her, which was true enough but hard on Miles; or she could say he had come in for a drink and not made a pass at her, which was kind but hard on John's credulity. Or she could say that he had left her at the door and blame the missing whiskey, if John noticed it, on the handyman, who was notorious for taking liquor whenever he came into a house. Martha steadied herself on the wash basin and stared at her flushed face in the mirror. She would never have thought that she could entertain such wicked ideas even for a second.

A shiver ran through her. She had not realized how cold the house was. Poor Miles, she thought, picturing his big white perspiring body, clad only in socks and garters, exposed to the drafts of the parlor. And it would be a miracle if she herself did not get sick from lying naked on the sofa in late October, with only a coal fire going. John would never forgive her if he knew of this piece of heedlessness. If she died, he would be furious and blame it all on the Coes. She smiled fondly, thinking of John's oddities, and hurried into bed. He liked to assign blame, arbitrarily, in military style. And he would be more annoyed if she caught cold than at any other feature of the seduction. *Dear* John, she said to herself. He would doubtless find a way of making New Leeds the villain of the whole episode, assuming she were to tell him. But she could not risk telling him, and precisely for that reason. Being intelligent and perceptive, he might forgive her and Miles and even see the absurd logic of it. But he would have to find some target for his stores of blame.

She sighed, hugging the blankets to her. The best thing would be to say that she had had Miles in for a drink and then gloss over the next part. If he asked whether Miles had made a pass, it would be wisest to say yes, just a little one; if she denied it, he might doubt the whole story. The one thing to fear, aside from her getting a cold (for which he would certainly hold the Coes' play-reading responsible), was that he would discover that her jet-and-crystal necklace had been broken. He had given it to her, two years ago, for her birthday, and though it could be restrung, he would never feel quite the same about it, like the watch, which was a gift too. John had a peculiar attitude toward fragile, delicate things—among which he included herself. He loved them angrily, foreseeing their destruction, and did not want them to be used, except on the highest occasions. This attitude always vexed Martha. It seemed to her somehow undemocratic. She believed firmly in use. That, in a sense, was what had got her into trouble tonight—with Miles, she could not treat herself as a precious vase to be kept on a top shelf, like their Bohemian glass, which she insisted on using too. And yet look what had happened. Her dress was a wreck—she would have to mend it and iron it the next time John went away; her necklace was broken; she had started lying and deceiving and thinking of implicating the poor handyman. And she would probably have an awful hangover.

She buried her head in the pillow and resolutely went to sleep. When she woke, it was daylight and the place beside her was empty. She came into full consciousness instantly and sprang up in bed, her heart pounding with terror. Her watch said eight o'clock. He should have been home five hours ago. She listened; the house was silent. Not even the pump was running. Flinging off the covers, she vaulted out of bed and sped in her bare feet across the cold floors up to the guest bedroom. There was no one there. A ringing scream came out of her. It smote her with utter certainty that he had somehow come home and seen them there through the window and quietly gone away forever. She tried to reason with herself. After all, she had looked at her watch before Miles turned out the lights, and it had been only a quarter of two. Nobody could have made it from Boston in that time. And she had looked again, at two-twenty, after Miles had left. John must have been killed in an accident.

But her common sense refused to credit this. The police would have called her. A hideous thought came to her. Perhaps her watch had been wrong. Suppose it had started losing more than its allotted twenty minutes a day? And now that she thought about it, she could not remember setting it ahead yesterday morning, as she usually did, right after breakfast—the day had been upset with John's leaving early. Another memory jogged her. When Warren came to fetch her last night, she had been surprised: she had not expected him so early. "Oh, my God!" she heard herself cry. Her watch said eight-five now, but it might be much later. The clock in the parlor had stopped last week, when John tried to fix it himself; he could not get the pendulum back right. She stumbled to the telephone. But the operator said: "I am sorree; we are not allowed to give out the time." She tried the Coes' number; it was busy. Dolly had no telephone, and she and John had no radio. Outside, it had stopped raining, but the gray sky did not reveal whether it was morning or afternoon. A peculiar inhibition checked her when she thought of calling the Hubers; she did not know them well enough, she considered, to call them and ask them the time. She could call the vicomte and ask the time casually while ordering some liquor. She picked up the phone and set it down again irresolutely, stricken with shyness, like stage fright. She perhaps did not want to hear what time it was, for then she would know the worst for certain.

The only thing that mattered was to find John and try to explain it all to him. But she did not know how to set about this. Her hand went out again to the telephone, but she shrank from calling the police. If he had been killed in an automobile accident, she did not want to know. The only course that seemed really feasible was to go back to sleep. Numbly, she started to the bedroom. Someone, eventually, would come and find her there, hiding under the covers. She got into bed and closed her eyes but opened them almost at once as another cry escaped her. "I can't *stand* it," she moaned. And indeed it seemed to her that she could not endure another moment of existence. She began to sob aloud, as if from a physical pain.

Unable to stay in bed, she wandered into the parlor and wanly commenced to rebuild the fire, and as she knelt crouched by the hearth, weeping, she noticed that black and crystal beads were lying in the cracks between the floorboards and that two bone hairpins were in plain sight on the sofa. A strange relief swept through her. What if John had come home and seen this, she said to herself, forgetting that he had already, so she believed, seen everything. She poked out the beads and swept them into the dustpan, marveling at how tight she must have been last night to have presumed that she had cleaned them all up. And yet—as she now noticed for the first time—she did not have a hangover. She remembered reading somewhere that fear did something to your adrenalins and that pilots, during the war, never got hangovers on a flight, no matter how much they had drunk the night before. A wild laugh broke from her. What a price to pay for not having a hangover!

Just then, down the hill, she thought she heard a car's motor. But she went back to building the fire, reluctant to look out the window, lest it not be he. In a moment, there was a knocking on the kitchen door. Nearly fainting, Martha went and pulled it open. It was only Jane Coe.

"Where's John?" she demanded at once. Martha could not speak. She threw herself, sobbing, onto Jane's bosom. "Gone," she finally said. "Gone!" Jane hurried into the bathroom and got a wet washcloth to wash the tears and coal dust off Martha's face, which gave Martha time to recover herself. In the first instant, she had wanted to confess everything and be comforted, but now caution intervened. "What time is it?" she asked huskily. It was quarter of nine, Jane said. Martha's heart leapt with incredulous joy. Her own watch said eight-thirty. Therefore, *therefore,* she said to herself, her fears were groundless: he could not have seen anything. But then it came to her that he must be dead or injured, and though, two minutes before, she would have felt this was the lesser evil, now this new horror struck her with re-doubled force. She moaned. "What happened? Did you have a fight? Why aren't you dressed?" said Jane. "Or didn't he come home last night?" Martha nodded, speechlessly, and burst into fresh sobs. "What did I tell you?" said Jane. "He probably spent the night in some tourist place, just the way I said." "No," retorted Martha. "He would have called me." Jane looked grave. "Have you called the police?" Martha smiled sadly. "I was afraid to."

Jane herself called the police and the hospital in Trowbridge. There was nothing. But they were sending out an alarm, though Martha was not much use there: she could not remember the car's registration number or the year of the make. All she could say was that it had a New York license plate and was an old black Ford convertible.

Jane put a pot of coffee on and made Martha dress. Then she told the news she had brought with her: Warren's mother had died. He was off to New York this morning on the little plane from Digby, and then on to Savannah, taking the afternoon plane. There was only one difficulty: he had no suit. "No suit?" exclaimed Martha, from the bedroom, trying to take an interest. Only his corduroy, it seemed, and that, agreed Martha, fighting down her tears, would not do for a funeral, not in the South, anyway. *You must think of others,* she said to herself. *Jane is thinking of you.* And she put her mind on the problem. "Well," she suggested, coming back into the kitchen, "when he gets to New York, he can take a taxi in from the airfield and pick up something off the rack at Brooks Brothers. The fitter can probably baste the pants up while he waits." But Jane did not take to this notion. She had had a better idea, it seemed. "What was that?" said Martha, absently. Jane lowered her eyes. "That blue suit of John's," she acknowledged. Martha buried her head in her arms on the kitchen table and began to laugh hysterically. "It's gone," she gasped. "Isn't that ironical?" Jane gave her coffee, and she grew a little calmer. "Is that why you came?" she asked at length. Jane nodded. "Oh, dear," said Martha. "Oh, dear. I'm sorry."

She reflected. Actually, there was an old suit of John's in the wardrobe, a dark gray, almost black, which he had never worn up here because it was too formal. The trousers were frayed at the bottom, but that would not matter, for Warren, since they could be turned up. She went to the bedroom and came back with the suit on a hanger. "Will this do?" she asked. Jane could not hide her delight. It was perfect, she declared, examining it as it lay draped over a kitchen chair on its hanger. There would just be the sleeves and trousers to fix. "Take it then," said Martha, wiping her eyes with a paper napkin. It occurred to her that she was a monster to be lending John's suit this morning, but she could find no reason not to, except a superstition, and the idea, too horribly practical to contemplate, that he might need it to be buried in himself. The gruesomeness of this interview was making Jane uncomfortable, and it was not Jane's fault, Martha pointed out to herself, that John had not come home. "Go on, take it," she said. Jane hesitated. "He'll be all right, Martha," she said, with real kindness, patting Martha's shoulder. "I know," lied Martha. She took a sip of coffee to show how brave she was going to be. "I ought to come and help you," she added, uncertainly. This feeling was partly sincere. Jane needed somebody to help her get the suit ready; one person could work on the trousers and one on the sleeves. But she had expressed the wish aloud to show Jane that even *in extremis* she was capable of disinterestedness. If John were here, he would scold her for this.

She could not help feeling that Jane was being selfish, as she watched her hurry down the hill with the suit over her arm. It never occurred to Jane, apparently, to offer to go and get Dolly, so that Martha would not be alone. Martha closed her eyes, waiting for Jane to be gone. She knew she was going to scream again, as soon as the station-wagon drove off. When she opened them, she saw their convertible. "JOHN!" she heard Jane yell, and in a second there he was, climbing out of the car, smiling imperturbably as he always did after an absence; the knowledge that he was lovingly awaited made him matter of fact—he looked away, so to speak, from his arrival, as if it were a present he was bringing.

He had spent the night, he told them, by the side of the road, in the car. The driving had been terrible, and he had been sleepy. He had not called Martha because every place along the road was closed. He had not expected her to be silly and fearful, he added, tipping her chin. If he had known that, he would not have brought her a present—a white rose tree he had found for her at a nursery garden, next to the place where he had had breakfast. Martha studied him. He seemed rather strange and artificial, as he produced the rose tree from the car. If she had not herself had a bad conscience, she would have suspected him of being unfaithful. His story sounded very odd (though like him in a *way*) and she had good reason to be annoyed for the horrid suspense he had caused her. Yet it was lucky (if he only knew) that he had not come home last night and found the mess in the parlor. Everything, indeed, about his return was fortunate, even the fact that Warren's mother had died, for they all went off at once, with the suit, to the Coes' house, where Warren was packing and putting away his painting things. John did not ask her about last night; they were all too busy concentrating on getting Warren off on time. They tried the suit on him, and Martha shortened the sleeves and moved the buttons, while Jane did the trousers, which John then pressed with the steam-iron; he did it better than either of the girls. With all these hands working, the suit was ready in an hour, which left fifteen minutes for Warren to stop in Digby and pick up some black shoes. They did not talk much, out of respect for Warren's mother; even Jane was quiet. It was Warren himself, finally, who brought up the subject of the play-reading. He asked Martha whether she and Miles had had a chance to go on with the discussion. "No," said Martha, shortly, busy with her needle. She heard the iron pause. "Miles took you home?" John, in his shirtsleeves, his head bent over the ironing board, dropped the question casually. Martha, on the telephone, had promised him to go home with Dolly. Yes, she now acknowledged, in a slightly defiant voice; and she had asked him in for a drink. "You asked him *in?*" cried Jane, opening her mouth wide. "Why, you're a nut,

Martha. What happened? Did he make a pass at you?" They all turned their heads. Martha took her courage in her hands. "Of course not," she said, smiling broadly. She held up the suit-coat and blushed. "Look at her," said Jane. "Of course, he did. Confess, Martha." Martha shook her head, stoutly. She put on a merry expression. "My lips are sealed," she proclaimed. Warren, who was standing in his underclothes waiting to put on the trousers, had a grave, concerned look—what Martha called his jury face. But John let the matter drop lightly. "She doesn't want to tell," he said. "Martha is a gentleman."

Afterward, in the car, on their way home, he asked her, with his eyes forward, on the road. "My lips are sealed," she repeated, and added in a more serious tone, "Don't ask me about it. It was nothing. For a minute, he misunderstood the invitation. One can't really blame him." John nodded. They drove on in silence, but she could see that he was satisfied. She put her hand over his on the steering wheel. "Did you spend the night on the road because you wanted to punish me for going to the play-reading?" "Maybe," he said. "I thought so," she replied. "But you're not cross any more?" "No," he said. "But we can't have him dropping in all the time," he added. Martha smiled. "He won't." She did not understand why he had decided not to scold her, but she accepted it as final. Men were like that; her father had been the same. They had tact at critical junctures, which was a sort of omniscience. And their mysterious decisions were final; she would not hear any more about the play-reading unless she brought it up herself. She essayed another subject. "Wasn't it funny—about the suit?" she murmured. John laughed. "It was awful," she went on, "when Jane came and I thought you were dead and I went and got out the suit anyway. It made me think of that poem of Yeats's: 'Twenty-one apparitions have I seen. The worst a coat upon a coathanger.'" She had not meant, by this, to reproach him, but he evidently thought she had, for his hand reached out and gripped hers tightly, in commiseration.

TEN

THE FALL days known as "glorious" were over. Warren Coe's mother's death and the storm that accompanied it marked the annual break in the weather. A black frost followed, putting an end to Martha's herbs and Dolly's swamp foliage. There were no more fairy-ring mushrooms on the golf course or boletus in the woods. The sky clouded over by noon every day, and the wind whistled about the boarded-up summer cottages. The borders of the ponds grew sodden, with only a fringe of wild cranberry. The bay was gray and choppy. Blue jays and woodpeckers kept desolate house in the woods. It would be like this, said Martha, until May, though there might be days in late November when you could swim heroically in the ponds, and days, if you were lucky, in January, when you could ice-skate through the dark afternoons, coming home to hot rum toddies and big fires.

But in an ordinary year, there would be only a perpetual March, from the first black frost till the shadbush bloomed in May. Winter here was a limbo—a windtorn parking area, closed shops and inns, vandalism, and divorces. Nearly everybody who could afford to got away, as the phrase went, after Christmas; the rest stayed on creakily, like a skeleton staff. Already, in early November, the village had a forlorn, rejected look. The last permanent summer people had shut up their houses;

the last canned luxury items disappeared from the gro-
cery shelves; the ferry from Trowbridge to the main-
land had made its last run for the season—to get off the
peninsula, you had to go all the way round. Town boys
were breaking into summer houses; police and care-
takers made their rounds; mice came in from the fields
and big rats from the dump. The fish-man from Digby
stopped delivering; the laundromat closed up. The
sirens of the ambulance and the fire engine shrieked
through the night.

It was the best time of the year, Sandy Gray told Dolly:
with the outsiders gone, you finally got the feel of the
place. He had been opening scallops, along with the
native women, getting $1.50 an hour. Next month, he
was going to decorate bureaus for the New Leeds Craftsmen, on a cooperative basis. In January, he would start
work at the fish-storage plant, over at North Digby. He
was not doing this for the pay check but for the sake of
the kids. With the custody case coming up and their
whole future at stake, he had pocketed his principles,
temporarily, and put himself in the hands of his lawyer,
who told him to find a job and make his peace with society. On the advice of his lawyer, too, he had shaved
his beard and had his hair cut. First things first, he told
Dolly, who regarded these changes with bewilderment.
Would you hire a doctor to save your life and then refuse to follow his prescriptions? "But I liked you better
the way you were," she said doubtfully. "That's because you're afraid of change," he explained, in his
gentle, gusty voice. "The true individualist has the
courage to wear a mask."

When she came in her jeep to pick him up the morning the case was scheduled, he was wearing a leather
jacket, a pair of dark trousers, and a white silk evening

scarf wrapped about his neck in lieu of a necktie. His lawyer, he said, had warned him to appear on time at the courthouse in Trowbridge, in conventional dress, and to see that his witnesses did the same. Dolly's costume Sandy had chosen himself from her closet—an unbecoming gray tweed suit she had had made up in England. But it worried him that she had no hat. All the way down in the jeep, he kept fuming with impatience and cursing the stop lights and the midmorning traffic in the villages. The judge, he reminded her, was a stickler for punctuality, and his case was third on the docket. "We have plenty of time," she shouted, repeatedly, over the noise of the jeep. His fretfulness alarmed Dolly. This was not the Sandy she knew. The loss of his beard had done something strange to him. Whenever she glanced at him, sideways, she had a sense that she was intruding. At the same time, she could not help noticing that his chin was recessive.

She was going to be a character-witness for him. How this had come about she scarcely knew now. How could she testify to his character when she had been in New Leeds exactly one month? But it was not the length of the association but the frequency that counted, Sandy had assured her. For the past two weeks, she had been with him every day. She had ridden pillion on his motorcycle and washed his hair in her basin and helped him deliver furniture, down the peninsula, for the New Leeds Craftsmen. They had gone to see Miles Murphy, while Dolly had waited outside, in the jeep, because of Martha, and they had taken a bottle to call on Sandy's fourth wife, to persuade her to testify. They had been sharing a Sunday paper and doing the crosswords together. The fact that she had come here as a stranger, said Sandy, would make her testimony more impressive. She had no axe to grind, and the judge would see at a glance that there was no sexual involvement.

It was true; there was nothing between them. His second wife, Ellen, was coming back in December; he talked about that constantly, when he was not talking about the children and Barney, his lawyer. Her return, he said, could only mean one thing—she wanted him back. Her second husband had finally made a settlement on her, so that she was free now to remarry. Sandy was fixing up his house, to be ready for her; Dolly had been with him to buy curtains and look at some linoleum for the kitchen. He had even had the plumber around, to get an estimate on putting in heat, which he could pay for by selling some pond frontage to a developer. His excitement touched Dolly almost painfully. She had never been so close to a man, on the one hand, or been so disregarded, on the other. After the first day, he never even glanced at her paintings; as soon as he got to know her, his abrupt honest mind had simply dropped the idea that she could ever do anything serious. And after his first enquiries, he paid no heed to her sex. It never occurred to him, apparently, that Dolly could be jealous, or sad that their relationship would end when this "real woman" came back. He never considered her feelings, which made Dolly feel safe with him, though somewhat depreciated, like a thin dime nestling in his pocket, while he reckoned his future in gold. And yet it was wonderful—upsetting and enlightening—to be treated so objectively. Being with him, she had decided, was like posing naked for a life-class: you had to forget the *you*.

But now, as she climbed the courthouse steps, looking up at the huge granite columns of the neo-classic front, she felt as if she were awakening from a dream. She had a slight hangover, and her eyes, which had sunk back into her head, had a bleary glazed look; she kept blinking them to focus on her surroundings, as if she had been playing Pin-the-tail-on-the-donkey. It was the first time she had had any contact with the law, and the courthouse, with its Civil War cannons, inspired her with terror. It belonged in a dark mill town of the nineteenth century—the kind of town she had been born in. Her sense of proportion protested at its presence here, overlooking a village green, a general store, and a double row of clapboard cottages, advertising rooms for tourists, home-made jellies, and sea-captain's chowder. "Probate court" they were going to, and the very name evoked her childhood, her two aunts, wills, trustees, tombstones, granite faces.

With her coat-collar turned up and her hands thrust in her pockets, she stood under the portico, alone, taking no notice of the other people passing in and out, her eyes smarting with tears from the bitter wind. Sandy had hurried inside, to confer with his lawyer. When he came out and joined her, lighting his pipe, he was in jubilant spirits because his ex-wife, Clover, was late. Everybody else—the two lawyers, the witnesses—was present and accounted for, inside the gray building. Clover's lawyer was pacing up and down the corridor and telling Sandy's lawyer that he had half a mind to throw the case up. She had missed the morning bus, it seemed, and somebody had called the clerk of the court to say that she was hitchhiking. Her ex-stepmother—one of the old-timers here—was trying to calm the lawyer down by explaining Clover's character. Sandy's lawyer was very hopeful; he had finally got an affidavit from the New Leeds dentist about the state of the kids' teeth. She had been feeding them on candy bars and cookies— too lazy to open a can.

Dolly put her hands to her ears. She did not want to

hear any more. It was all true, no doubt; Sandy had convinced her. But these dreadful details, hammered home, had the effect of dividing her sympathies. "Why shouldn't she hitchhike?" she said suddenly, in a clear stubborn voice. "My dear, *I* don't mind," said Sandy, smiling. "It's what the judge will think. Hitchhiking is illegal in this state." "But she can't *afford* a taxi," argued Dolly, striving to be composed and reasonable. "She should have thought of that before she missed the bus," Sandy replied. "Everybody else got here. It's no good feeling sorry for her. We're all sorry for her; we've all tried to help her. She's a tragic kid, really—a natural delinquent; no mother, father a drunkard, four step-mothers in a row. The leopard can't change its spots." He turned up Dolly's coatsleeve and glanced at her watch.

"Look," he said softly. "There she is now." On the highway below them, a Nehi truck had stopped. Two children and a woman clambered out, waving to the driver. "Watch!" said Sandy, gripping Dolly's arm, as the boy and girl raced across the road, without looking either way to see whether any cars were coming. "I wish the judge could have seen that," he added, when they had safely crossed the road, followed by their mother. An afterthought struck him. "*You* saw it!" he cried, elatedly, tightening his hold on her arm. "Put it in your testimony. I'll tell Barney to ask you about it." "I couldn't," said Dolly faintly. Sandy had made her believe that she would not be harming Clover if she merely testified to his character; some of his best friends were going to be character-witnesses on *her* side, and he did not hold it against them. But now he wanted her to go further, and he dropped her arm impatiently when she tried to explain that she could not magnify this little incident on the road into criminal negligence.

"I know, I know," he said. "You 'don't want to take sides.' "

Hurt, Dolly made her way into the building; the court was sitting on the second floor. "Barney" had told her where to go, but she took the wrong staircase and got lost. She hated the lawyer and the effect he was having on Sandy. He kept warning Sandy that the courts favored the mother, and that Sandy would lose the case if he did not "get in there and fight." He had been very short with Dolly, when Sandy had brought her to his office, to be rehearsed in her testimony. As soon as he heard that she had known Sandy only a month, he had slammed down his pencil. He pretended that Sandy had given him the impression that they had known each other before. When Dolly said no, firmly, he shot her a peculiar look and suggested that they *might* have known each other "in the big city." "You being a painter and him being an art critic, it would stand to reason that you'd met." "No," Dolly had repeated, lowering her gaze. "I'm afraid your testimony won't be of much help then," he said irritably, shutting up a folder. "I *told* him that!" cried Dolly, indignant. "Oh, well," sighed the lawyer. "Let's take down what you've got. You never know what the judge will stand for. Unmarried, I take it," he said, pulling a pad of yellow paper to him.

Contempt for her scruples, Dolly felt, underscored those last words and the measuring, smooth look that accompanied them. He *diagnosed* her, she inwardly protested—as if telling the truth were a symptom, like being unmarried, like, if he only knew it, her dainty, faint-hearted canvases stacked against the wall, unfinished. She began to feel guilty, as though she had to explain herself. He wanted to know what she was doing here, out of season. Mentioning the Sinnotts, Dolly flushed.

Because of Sandy, she had hardly seen them since the play-reading. She did not dare think what they would say if they knew she had let herself get involved in the custody suit. "Sinnott?" said the lawyer. "Oh yes, the girl in the nightgown. She's back again, I hear." Dolly nodded. "Come to think of it, you look kind of alike. Same type." "We went to college together," murmured Dolly, as if in extenuation. "Uh huh," said the lawyer, writing. By the time she left the office and joined Sandy outside, on the motorcycle, she felt she had done wrong not to stretch her testimony a little. But when she told Sandy what had happened, saying that she was sorry, he wearily cut her off. "Why should you lie for me?" he said. "Barney didn't expect that. It was just a misunderstanding."

A janitor showed Dolly into the courtroom. Another case was being heard. She settled herself on a bench and peered around. On her left, at a little desk, was a man in a blue uniform with a star. High up, on a platform, at a long table, was the judge, a long-nosed man in a black robe, like a college professor's. The witness stand, at his right, was empty; the judge was whispering with two men, who, Dolly presumed, were lawyers. On the far side of the room, by the window, stood Barney, looking out. "Divorce case," a man next to Dolly informed her. When the testimony resumed, and a big black-haired woman took the stand, nobody paid any attention, except the judge and the two lawyers. People kept passing in and out, in desultory style, rather, Dolly thought, like tourists in a European church, where a droning mass was being said in one of the chapels. The proceedings seemed very lifeless; she had to strain her ears to catch what the witness was saying, in a monotone, like a lesson learned. It was a case, apparently, of wife-beating. "Two beautiful big black eyes," she heard the witness intone, and the lawyer picked up the phrase and repeated it, like a chant. Then, before Dolly knew it, the case was over, and the man in the blue uniform was calling their case: Alexander Gray against Clover Gray. Nearly everybody in the courtroom moved forward, past a brass railing, and Dolly moved with them and took her seat on a wooden bench at the right. Sandy was not yet in the courtroom, and all these people, at first glance, were strangers to Dolly. She found herself sitting next to a tall white-haired man in a sort of cowboy costume, with a sombrero on his knees. Across the room, to her surprise, she recognized the milkman, in a pink shirt and Windsor tie.

The courtroom door swung open, and Clover sauntered in, accompanied by a small gray-haired man with a briefcase. She had little bright blue eyes, like Christmas tree bulbs, lit up. Her brown hair was pulled up in a horse's tail, with a big plaid ribbon tied around it. She had on a great deal of rouge, and her lipstick had come off on her front teeth. She wore an old, shapeless winter coat, red knee socks, moccasins, and a plaid skirt and vest. The skirt was much too big for her, and to Dolly's eyes, she looked pathetically unreal, like a child painted up and dressed in adult clothes to beg on the street at Thanksgiving. The two children had disappeared. She was walking straight toward Dolly, who lowered her eyes and laced her fingers on her lap. "Aren't you in the wrong pew?" Clover said, in a deep husky voice.

Dolly started and looked about her in perplexity. "You're his witness, aren't you?" said Clover. "These are my witnesses." Dolly reddened and jumped up, dropping her pocketbook. The uniformed man, the sheriff, was hurrying toward her. Somebody handed her

her pocketbook. The whole courtroom stared while Dolly changed places. She stumbled into a seat at the end of the front row, by the witness stand, while across the room Clover took the seat she had vacated. The two "teams" of witnesses, facing each other, made Dolly think of a spelling bee or a give-away program on television. She could not imagine where they had come from, where the lawyers had found them; they were like professional mourners, too, or like floaters rounded up to vote in an election. She could not remember seeing any of them, except the milkman, before. But gradually she began to recognize faces. At the end of the back row, on her side, was Sandy's fourth wife, Margery, the girl who worked in the grille. Across the room, on Clover's side, was the oysterman. Next to him was one of the New Leeds Craftsmen; Dolly had not known him, with his hair combed and a shave. All of them were transformed for the occasion; that was what had confused her. In their ordinary gear, she had been seeing them every day at the post office or the First National check-out. But now they wore "city clothes" or, to be exact, parts of them. One man had on striped trousers over bare feet and sandals; another had a necktie and pearl stickpin with a pea jacket. Ancient waistcoats, long earrings, tarnished metal blouses, old fur pieces, a gold watch chain with a Phi Beta Kappa key, velvets, nodding plumes, a motoring veil, proclaimed the community's notion of a solid respectable front. The man next to Dolly wore a white suit, like Mark Twain. But his feet, she could not help noticing, were in leather bedroom slippers. It was the same all along the row: an uneven satin hemline ended in bare legs and tennis shoes; a black tailleur, in a set of espadrilles. A kind of defiance, evidently, had set in with the feet, which refused to render unto Caesar.

A strange smell rose from the witnesses—a combination of stale alcohol and mothballs. Dolly could still taste last night's liquor on her own breath, and she wondered whether these perfumes could be wafted up to the judge. Just below her, near the sheriff's desk, sat a small woman in a plain suit, with a notebook and briefcase. The man next to Dolly leaned over. "S.P.C.C.," he whispered, cupping his mouth with one hand while his elbow nudged Dolly in the ribs. "S.P.C.C.," he repeated, opening his red-rimmed eyes very wide.

Dolly stared miserably at the network of empurpled veins in his cheeks. To her horror, she had begun to feel ashamed of these New Leedsians and to look upon them with the eyes of an outsider—the caseworker, the judge. Nearly all of them seemed the worse for drink, swollen and dropsical, or lean and red, with popping eyes and stiff veins and shaking hands. Several of the men had bits of dried blood on their faces, where they had cut themselves, apparently, while shaving. One young man—he could not have been more than thirty—had stone-gray hair and a face as white as leprosy; his arm was in a sling. And yet they were all in good spirits. It was only she who was depressed and self-conscious. Dolly could hear them discussing the judge. "He always favors the woman," said a young man in a corduroy coat and turtle-necked sweater. "I had him when Carol divorced me." "You're wrong, darling," said an old woman in slacks. "I had him and he cut off the maintenance."

A woman with dyed red hair and a face like a monkey suddenly addressed Dolly. "Did you hear about my case?" Dolly shook her head; she had never met this person, who seemed to be drenched in the perfume called *Femme.* "I've seen you in the liquor store," the woman went on. "I'm a friend of Paul's. Do you know what happened to me last year? They brought me into court for lowering the birth rate." Dolly looked perplexed. "I ran into a car carrying three pregnant women. They all had miscarriages and sued me." The woman's voice was loud and laughing. The caseworker looked up and frowned. Dolly reddened. "I'm a sort of jinx," her new friend continued. "Last year, a man dropped dead on my sofa. I thought he had passed out."

Sandy slipped into the seat next to Dolly. He had been talking with the children. "She has them coached," he said angrily. "Her lawyer's got it rigged up for them to talk to the judge in chambers." Dolly indicated the sheriff. "I don't give a damn if he hears," Sandy muttered, lowering his voice. "She has no right to bring the kids into a thing like this. It's criminal, having their feelings pawed over. 'Do you love Mother best or Daddy? Come on, tell the Judge.' Imagine what that will do to them twenty years from now." He sat back with an air of dark satisfaction, then jumped up, in response to a signal from Barney, who had been talking with Clover's lawyer by the window. Dolly rubbed her forehead. He was right, she thought remorsefully; such a decision was horrible for a child.

"They want to make a stipulation," volunteered the man in the white suit, nudging Dolly again, to direct her attention to Sandy, who seemed to be arguing with his lawyer. "What's that?" said Dolly, uneasily; she could see that Sandy was getting worked up, by his gestures. "The lawyers get together," said the young man behind her, eagerly, "and try to agree to shorten the testimony. Clover doesn't defend, and they fix it up with the judge to award divided custody. They always try to pull that." The man in the white suit nodded. "But wouldn't that be the best thing?" timidly suggested Dolly. "After they've got us all down here . . . ?"

said the man in the pea jacket, looking at his watch. "If they don't start soon, damn it, I'm going to step out for a drink." "Oh, please don't," cried Dolly. "The town's dry, Jack," said the man in the white suit. "Local option." The man in the pea jacket settled back on the bench. "Oh, it's all a farce," declared the man in the white suit. "We're all wasting our time. We come down here to be nice, to do a favor. Who knows the rights and wrongs of these things? *I* don't. I'm just a character witness. You too?" Dolly nodded. "I don't judge between 'em," said the man, dropping his voice, as Sandy started back to his place. "In my opinion, the best thing would be to give the children to the state. Let the town bring 'em up. The town spawned 'em, you might say."

"Barney's sore," reported Sandy, sitting down. "He wanted me to compromise." "And you wouldn't?" said Dolly. Sandy shook his head. All at once, the courtroom grew quiet. The judge sat up, under the American flag; a woman (the assistant registrar, said Dolly's neighbor) took her place at the other end of the judicial bench, under the state flag. Spectators tiptoed into the rear benches. The first witness was being sworn: Mrs. Mary Viera, a cleaning woman who worked by the day. "Our star witness," said Sandy. She was a small, black-eyed person in a dark suit and white blouse—the only respectable-looking person, thought Dolly, in the whole array of witnesses. Her English was surprisingly broken, and she had a voice queerly pitched, like a parrot's. She worked, it seemed, occasionally for Clover, and she testified to the state of the house, on the days when she came to clean. It was very dirty, she agreed, under Barney's questioning. Cat pee ("Excuse me, Mister,") in the corners; children's beds dirty; food stuck on the table; food on the walls; icebox dirty, food with beards inside; grease burned on pans; dog food all over, on floors, no vacuum cleaner; old smelly mop; no light bulb in toilet.

Dolly tried to shut her ears. She hated Mrs. Viera, with her spying black eyes. The man in the white suit cupped his mouth. "Worst damn cleaning woman in New Leeds," he whispered, with a wink, to Dolly. Sandy frowned. He was following the testimony intently, leaning forward and nodding as Mrs. Viera spoke. Bottles, yes, bottles everywhere; garbage spilled outside; children barefoot. The S.P.C.C. woman was writing in her notebook. A pair of spectators moved closer, and Mrs. Viera, obligingly, raised her parrot-voice. Barney's voice, prompting, had a smooth, smiling tone. "And what about this fellow that lives there?"

To Dolly's surprise, Mrs. Viera became guarded. "What fellow? I don't know." "Oh, come on now, Mrs. Viera," Barney said impatiently. "You know there's a man living there. The whole town knows it." Clover's lawyer rushed in with an objection. The judge leaned forward. "Is there a man living with Mrs. Gray or not?" he said to Clover's lawyer. "Does your client deny this?" Everyone looked at Clover. "We don't deny it," said Clover's lawyer, easily. "We will show that he is a paying guest."

Barney took a step backward; the judge raised his eyebrows; even Clover's witnesses appeared to take this as news. Sandy half-started to his feet, but Dolly pulled him down, by the leather jacket. "Proceed," said the judge, rapping lightly with his gavel. "Have you seen this man there?" Barney demanded of Mrs. Viera. "Sometimes." "Where does he sleep?" Mrs. Viera did not know. She was asked to describe the layout of the house. There were two bedrooms, a living room, a kitchen, and a little room, with a couch in it. "Maybe he sleep there," she volunteered. Barney frowned. Had she ever, he wanted to know, seen that couch made up, with sheets on it? No, agreed Mrs. Viera, but most of the times she had been there, the fellow had been away; he worked, she had heard, as a truckdriver.

Sandy made a soft, groaning sound. "She's changed her testimony," he whispered angrily. "They all do it—these damned Portuguese. You get them in the courtroom, and they get scared." "Where does he keep his clothes?" said Barney. Mrs. Viera did not know. Had she ever seen his clothes in Mrs. Gray's bedroom? The courtroom seemed to catch its breath while Mrs. Viera reflected. She was not sure, she answered finally. Barney protested: this was not what she had told him when he came to her house to talk to her. "What do you mean—not sure?" he said in a hectoring tone. "Not sure," mumbled Mrs. Viera. Sandy's witnesses looked wonderingly at each other. The judge intervened. It was an important question, he said, and she could help the court clear it up. She must try to search her memory. "No good, Judge," said Mrs. Viera, simply. "When he"—she pointed to the lawyer—"come to my house, he ask me if I ever see man's clothes in Mrs. Gray's bedroom. I say yes." "Well?" prompted the judge. Mrs. Viera grinned. "But Mrs. Gray wear man's clothes herself—man's shirt, pants, old coat. This the first time I see her in skirt."

Laughter shook the courtroom, led by Mrs. Viera. "And is that why you've changed your story?" Barney demanded sternly. "My daughter explain me my mistake," said Mrs. Viera serenely, turning to the judge. "She tell me I not understanding questions." "You mean," said the judge, "that you sometimes saw men's clothes in Mrs. Gray's bedroom, but you are not sure, now, whose they were?" Mrs. Viera nodded. "Maybe hers. Maybe his." Barney mopped his brow. Surely she knew the difference, he insisted. But Mrs. Viera would not be budged. "Maybe hers. Maybe his," she repeated, with a gleeful look at the judge.

When Clover's lawyer's turn came, he started on a fresh tack. He asked Mrs. Viera how long she had lived in New Leeds and how many residents she had worked for and whether she kept a clean house herself. "Oh yes," said Mrs. Viera proudly. "I believe you, Ma'am," said Clover's lawyer, who spoke with a slight southern accent. "But now tell me. The conditions you describe in Mrs. Gray's residence—are they unusual?" Mrs. Viera looked puzzled. "I mean the dirt on the floors, the dog food, the moldy icebox, and so on—do you often see these things when you come to clean for your ladies?" Mrs. Viera brightened. "Oh yes," she said happily. "All the time. All the time. Summer people too. Everybody live like that here in America. Like pigs." There was a movement of recoil on the benches; the sheriff stiffened and fixed his eyes on the Stars and Stripes. "Watch what you're saying here," the judge commanded, sharply. "You don't mean everybody." "Everybody I working for," explained Mrs. Viera. "Not poor people—Portuguese people, Finnish people, Yankee people. They keep clean house; don't have cleaning woman." She appeared to search for her meaning. "Rich people, college people, famous people, lawyer, writer, painter— just like Mrs. Gray. Live like bootlegger." Another laugh rose. "I think she must mean me," giggled a woman in Dolly's row. "She's pathological," said another woman, with bitter emphasis. "*I* wouldn't have her in the house." The judge rapped for silence. "Have you ever worked for Mr. Gray?" continued Clover's lawyer. Mrs. Viera shook her head. "But Mr. Gray just the same. I have friend who tell me—" The judge cut her off. "You can only testify to what you've seen yourself," he told her. "I don't know what this testimony proves," he went on, in tones of irritation, to Clover's lawyer. "The general standard of living that prevails in New Leeds," the lawyer went on, undaunted. "I'm trying to set Mrs. Gray's housekeeping in its context, your honor. Many of the older ladies here, in our permanent winter colony, are famous housekeepers, but the breed is dying out. Other times, other customs."

"Proceed," said the judge. "Would you say that Mrs. Gray was a good mother?" Clover's lawyer asked Mrs. Viera. "Kind, considerate, thoughtful?" Mrs. Viera scratched her head. "Mrs. Gray very nice woman. Very friendly. Good mother, I don't know." She turned to the judge. "It's the same like I was saying, Judge. All the women I work for, not like poor women. Easy with the kids, not strict, not scolding. But not paying attention. Not mending clothes, ironing, fixing hair, cooking, sending to church, sending to Sunday school. 'Listen to radio,' 'Go away and play now.' Open can. 'Here, eat.' Mrs. Gray, I think, have big heart, play with the kids, cut out magazines, draw pictures, play the guitar to them, sing. But not careful for kids. Not worrying." "Do you think a worrying mother is a good thing, Mrs. Viera?" demanded Clover's lawyer. "Sometimes," she said, turning thoughtfully to the judge. "I don't talk so good in English. What I mean, Mrs. Gray not bringing them up, not teaching, not feeding right, not putting to bed—" "And all your employers are like that?" cut in Clover's lawyer. "Oh yes," beamed Mrs. Viera. "Oh yes."

Dolly's head was aching when they went across the highway for lunch at a counter. Barney came to sit with them; most of the other witnesses, on their side, had finished their testimony, and gone off to eat at the hotel in the next township, which had a cocktail lounge. Dolly's testimony, Barney said, was going to be very crucial, as things were shaping up. Mrs. Viera had turned the whole case upside down. There was nobody else who could swear that this truckdriver actually slept with Clover—nobody but the children, who would probably not be asked in chambers, unless the judge could find a way of doing it delicately, by indirection. And Clover had undoubtedly warned them not to tell what they knew. "Oh, it's all so ugly," sighed Dolly. She half-agreed with the man who said it would be better to hand all the children of divorced people over to the town. "Human nature," said Barney, munching on a hamburger.

The trouble was, he continued, that you could never get the natives up here to come into court and tell what they'd seen. Clover never drew a shade, but her neighbors down by the bay acted as though they were blind if you tried to get an affidavit out of them. The ones who were willing to talk always turned out to have a screw loose, like Mrs. Viera, or like the milkman, who was stage-struck and saving up to go off to drama school. The kid loved to testify, but he would only describe the state of the kitchen when he brought in the milk in the mornings. He swore that he'd never looked in the bedroom window, though he walked right past it every morning. " 'I mind my own business,' he says, with a flounce of his tail." "I don't see why you have to bring sex into it," Dolly said suddenly. "I don't think Sandy ought to do that when he believes in sexual freedom himself. You've got plenty of evidence to show that she's a bad mother. Why worry about proving 'immorality'?" "Because that's what the court likes to hear about, Miss Lamb," retorted Barney, reaching for the ketchup. "Besides—let's be frank—the S.P.C.C. has a record on Sandy. All right"—he raised a hand to forestall Sandy—"I'll agree. That was different. That was a health fad. You kept the kids barefoot to develop their feet. And you didn't toilet-train them, to develop their character. And you fed them on peanut butter because of something you read in a book. But the court looks at the *record,* damn it." "You know what happened," said Sandy, in a low voice, to Dolly. "The boy went to school barefoot, and the other kids threw knives at his feet. The teacher had the S.P.C.C. after me. There's an irony for you. It was those ruffians and their parents that ought to have been investigated." Dolly gave a gasp of pain. "But you went right on sending him," protested Barney. "After the teacher told you to get shoes." "How did I know?" cried Sandy. "The teacher sent a note. 'Please put shoes on Michael.' Nobody gave me the reason. I'd taught Michael to be brave and he wouldn't squeal to me on his little classmates. I was damned if I'd put shoes on him, just to appease the local bourgeois." He banged his knife down on his plate.

"Easy, boy," said the lawyer. "We don't want you making speeches to the judge. You used to be a Red, remember?" "Clover can't use that," declared Sandy. "She was in the Party herself. I broke long before she did. Miles got me out of it during my analysis. He showed me I was really an anarchist." Barney laughed. "Oh, balls," he said. "You're a property-owner and a registered voter. But don't forget: there's a lot of hostility to you artistic folk up here still. You could see that in old Viera's testimony. She was getting her own back, after all the stinking messes she's cleaned up for you geniuses. Now, Miss Lamb," he said, picking up his bill and a toothpick, "when I call you to the stand, speak up. We want the judge to hear you. And don't be afraid of stressing what you've got to tell. Let it ring out. We want to make the court realize that Sandy's turned over a new leaf. Describe what you've seen yourself—the things a woman notices. Is the house clean? Can Sandy cook? Does he wash the dishes? Is he neat, methodical? Does he drink? Does he have women around?"

Dolly nodded. It was not as simple as he thought, she said to herself anxiously as she took the stand. If she were to answer those questions truthfully, she could not give a Yes or a No. He was neat, for a man, but not as neat as John Sinnott or some of the painters she had studied with. The house was fairly clean. He could cook: yes. But most of the time she had been cooking for him. He washed dishes, she supposed, when he was alone. And he was methodical, in his way. He drank, but not as much as many people. In the course of an evening, starting before dinner, he would drink about half a bottle, she had noticed. But lots of the men up here started drinking at ten in the morning. And she had never seen him as tight, for instance, as Martha and Miles Murphy had been, the night of the play-reading. As for women, he had *her* around.

Everything was relative, she reminded herself, as the questioning began. It was like what the anthropologists told you: Sandy had to be measured by the mores of the culture he was in.

She cleared her throat. She had known the plaintiff, Mr. Gray, about one month; she had rented the house next to him and saw him frequently, in a neighborly way. "Would you say that you knew his habits?" As far as one could, in a month. "Speak louder, please," said the judge. Did he have women around? Not so far as she knew. "How do you know, Miss Lamb?" the judge interrupted. "Because I was with him," Dolly replied. The courtroom laughed. The judge rapped with his gavel. "At night, Miss Lamb?" said Barney. "Yes, at night," said Dolly. "Explain the circumstances." "We both were living alone; we have a good deal in common." "You are a

236

painter, Miss Lamb? And Mr. Gray is an art critic?" "He used to be," said Dolly. "He knows a great deal about painting." "And he was interested in your work?" "He doesn't like my work," admitted Dolly, in a meek voice. Another laugh rang out. "But you saw him just the same?" the lawyer proceeded, with a smile. Dolly nodded. "Speak up," said the judge. "Yes. We often had dinner together." "And who did the cooking?" "Sometimes I did. Sometimes he did." "Would you say he was a good cook?" "Oh yes." "What did he give you to eat?" Dolly searched her memory. "Spaghetti with clams. Rice and Portuguese sausage. Oysters. And salad," she added quickly, though in fact it was she who had brought the salad, the two times she had let him cook for her. "Sounds good," said Barney. "Did he open a can or did he cook these dishes himself?" "Oh, *himself*," said Dolly.

"Does he drink?" Dolly hesitated. "He drinks socially," she said at length. "What is 'socially,' Miss Lamb?" the judge wanted to know. Dolly turned stricken eyes on him. "When he's with other people." "He doesn't drink alone, you mean," said the judge crisply, provoking a laugh. Dolly said nothing. "And when he's with you, Miss Lamb?" encouraged Barney. "He drinks a little," said Dolly. "What is 'a little'?" exclaimed the judge. "Be specific. One drink, two drinks, five drinks?" "One or two," quavered Dolly. She was not really lying, she thought; she was only interpreting Sandy's daily consumption in the judge's terms; what would be five drinks to the judge would be one or two to Sandy. And wine did not count. "Sometimes a nightcap," she added. "And that's all?" said Barney. Dolly nodded. "Speak up," said the judge. "Yes." She looked up and saw Clover's little blue eyes staring harshly at her from across the room. A faint feeling came over her; she swayed and steadied herself on the stand. "Go on about his habits, Miss

Lamb," she heard Barney say. All she could think of was that she had just perjured herself and that Clover and her lawyer knew it. The judge was looking at her curiously, waiting for her to say something, but she had forgotten where she was in her testimony: had they asked her yet about his housekeeping? "Is Mr. Gray's house clean?" prompted Barney. "Oh yes," she said, swallowing. "Very." "Dishes washed? All that?" "Oh yes," said Dolly. He seemed to be expecting her to say something more. "He does his laundry," she volunteered. "You've seen him?" "Yes," she said. "In the pond." Again there was laughter, and she could tell from the lawyer's expression that she had said the wrong thing. "In the pond? What pond?" said the judge. "The pond we live on," said Dolly. "The water is very soft, which makes it good, Mr. Gray says, for washing."

In the courtroom, the philistines roared. She could feel their hatred of Sandy, of anything simple and different from themselves, spill out of their braying throats. And she could feel him crouched in his seat behind her, powerless to defend himself, with his white shaven face, a shorn, piteous Samson. The blood rushed to her cheeks; she flamed with temper. "Make them stop laughing," she said, obdurately, to the judge. "I won't testify any more unless you give Mr. Gray a fair hearing." She set her chin. "Order!" cried the sheriff, standing up. "Go on, Miss Lamb," the judge said gravely. The courtroom was absolutely still. "Mr. Gray," said Dolly, "is not an ordinary person. You all think he's strange because he tries to live naturally. He knows all about animals and birds and trees. But he doesn't go out bird-watching, with a book, like me. He just does it naturally, the way he sleeps and eats. He hates any kind of dishonesty or compromise; that's why he doesn't like my painting. He knows the woods the way Thoreau did or the scouts in

Fenimore Cooper. He can set traps and shoot and whittle and make bows and arrows. That's why he'd be a good father; he could teach the children a lot of things that children don't learn any more. Fishing and hunting and making things. He taught me how to open oysters, with just an ordinary knife. And how to scale fish and clean them. But he's not a crank, either. He doesn't want to turn the clock back, artificially. He reads comic books and listens to radio serials; he thinks they're much more real than modern novels and poems. He's not afraid of violence, though he's very gentle himself. He'd teach the children not to be afraid of life. That's what he's taught me, and I'm grateful for it." "Can he sew?" said the judge, drawing another laugh, deliberately, from the courtroom. "Yes, he can," said Dolly, defiantly. "Why shouldn't a man be able to sew? He can knit too; he learned in the Merchant Marine, when he was a boy. Is that something to be ashamed of? Don't you want a man to be self-sufficient? Isn't that the American ideal?"

"That was great, *great*," said Sandy, when she came back to her place. The other witnesses nodded. Clover's lawyer had not even tried to cross-examine her seriously. He had only one question: "Are you in love with Mr. Gray?" The judge said she did not have to answer that, but she had said no, in all honesty, and left the stand in a blaze of glory. "You've won the case," Sandy told her, and Barney made a little pantomime of clapping, when the judge was looking the other way.

Dolly was so flushed with these tributes and with her own extraordinary temerity that she could hardly listen to Sandy, who followed her on the stand. She sat with her own voice echoing in her ears, in a trance of wonder and pride. Vaguely, she heard Sandy testifying to his concern for the children, and how he was fixing up the house for them. He hoped, he said, to marry again, to give the children a mother, but in the meantime he was going to employ a woman to take care of them, after school, in the afternoons, while he was working. He made a good impression—Dolly felt, on the whole—simple and straightforward. But her mind kept drifting off, back to her own testimony, and contrasting it with his. Hers was better, she felt certain. He was a little too apologetic, and his voice was monotonous. People coughed while he was talking; when *she* was on the stand, you could have heard a pin drop. She was the best; she almost wished Martha could have heard her and seen the lawyer applaud. Even if John and Martha disapproved, they would have to admire her *performance*. She almost wished that she could be called back on the stand; a second time she would be more sure of herself, from the outset—she had stumbled badly at first, until she found the right note. "How was I?" said Sandy, coming down from the stand and interrupting her reverie. "Marvelous," said Dolly, mechanically, her conscience smiting her for the vanity and self-absorption that had kept her from paying attention to him. "Marvelous," she repeated, more enthusiastically. But her mind was still on herself, and all she could hear was the iambs of Sandy's voice pounding in her inner ear: "You've won the case," "You've won the case."

Compunction pricked her when Clover took the stand. She was pitiable, *pitiable,* Dolly said to herself, appalled by the life-history that unfolded. Poor Clover had been a baby-sitter since she was eleven years old, and she had worked with retarded children before she married Sandy, at the age of nineteen. She was wonderful with children, all her witnesses had averred, and her lawyer had affidavits from the summer people who had sent their children to a little play group she had run for the past

three summers. She was a poor housekeeper and manager, she conceded, under questioning, but she could not
keep the house tidy when it was full of dogs and cats
and youngsters. Nearly every night, her children had one
of their friends staying with them. They were doing
well in school, and last year they had got more Valen-
tines than any other children in the middle grades. She
went to the P.T.A. and made costumes for the school
plays and played the guitar at school entertainments.
Her lawyer presented affidavits from the children's
teachers. And she had a big heart, as Mrs. Viera had
said: she had taken in an orphan, a spastic child, whose
mother had died of tuberculosis. The child was now in
an institution, but Clover went to see him almost every
week. She went to see her father, too, who was in the
state hospital, and brought him magazines and candies,
though he used to beat her horribly, according to her
ex-stepmother. "She always slips him a bottle," the man
in the white suit contributed in an undertone.

Barney was brutal in cross-examination. Was it true,
he wanted to know, that there had been complaints and
some parents had removed their children from her play
group because she let the boys and girls go naked? It was
true, Clover admitted, but the children were small,
under school age. "That's a lie," whispered Sandy.
"Some of them were sprouting breasts." Then Barney
began to ask her about what he called "a little episode"
at a beach picnic two summers ago. Hadn't she tried to
drown herself after a few drinks? No, said Clover, in a
low voice; she had just wanted to be alone and swum out
to sea. The others had got frightened and gone after her.

When he got to the truckdriver, finally, Clover insisted that he was paying board, but she burst into tears
when Barney wondered whether she had ever listed his
rent as income on her tax return. Naturally, she hadn't,

and she lost her head altogether during the next questions, when Barney was pressing her about where the truckdriver slept and whether the little room she claimed he slept in had a clothes closet. She whirled around and called Sandy a moocher and announced that the real trouble between them was that he had fallen behind on the maintenance payments and would not settle with her when she needed the money. That, she cried, was when he had decided to get righteous about the truckdriver. He was all paid up now because his lawyer had made him do it, before coming into court. "Ask him, *ask* him, if it isn't true," she begged the judge, pointing her stubby finger at Barney. But the judge told her that a lawyer could not be a witness to what passed between him and his client.

To satisfy her, however, he called Sandy back on the stand. "Is it true that you ceased to make payments until the time this action was begun?" "No, it is not true," said Sandy, wearily. "Mrs. Gray is a pathological liar. I was short of money during the summer, when Mrs. Gray was getting paid by her play group. By mutual agreement, we decided that I could wait until fall to catch up with the maintenance." Clover was put back on the stand. "Is this true?" said the judge. "If you mean he told me he couldn't pay and I said yes, let it go for the time being—yes," said Clover. "You shouldn't have done that," said the judge sharply. "The court awarded you that maintenance. You should have made him pay it; that was your duty under the law." "But if he didn't have the money . . . ?" "It makes no difference," said the judge. "It is not for you and your former husband to decide whether he shall support his children. That is the court's privilege. When you divorced your husband here, you put those children under the court's protection. They're wards in chancery, actually." The two lawyers wagged their heads respectfully, in acknowledgment of this legal point. The judge turned back to Clover. "You should have brought him down here, into court," he said severely, "the first payment he missed. When was that?" "In June, I guess." "And how long did this hiatus continue?" "Till the end of October." "And when did this boarder come to live with you?" "Last spring. Around Decoration Day."

"Don't you see what you've done?" said the judge, his voice rising. "No," said Clover. "By letting the maintenance lapse, you've practically entered a confession of guilt with this court. You suggest to my mind and to the mind of any reasonable person that you let your ex-husband off paying for your support because you got a new fellow." "That wasn't the reason. Honestly," said Clover. "Look, Your Honor, he had no money. I was making some. I have feelings. I was sorry for him." She had been wiping her tears with a Kleenex; her makeup had come off, and as a result she looked much prettier. "Then," she said, "when I needed the money, for some winter clothes for the kids, he told me that he wouldn't pay me and that furthermore he was going to sue to get them back if I kept pestering him." "There were no witnesses to this discussion?" "No." "Well," said the judge, "in my opinion, you've brought this action on yourself. You gave your ex-husband a right to think that he was no longer bound to support you. Regardless of your motive. You didn't use good judgment. Let me give you a little maxim for general use, quite apart from this case. *Never let a fellow drop behind in his payments. Keep after him.* Ask the stores. Ask the financing companies. Chances are, Mrs. Gray, if you let him get behind, he'll work up a grievance against you, because the longer you don't make him pay, the more he owes you. Pretty soon, it's got so darn big he *can't* pay it." He slapped his hand on the long table. "*Keep after 'em,*" he repeated, addressing the courtroom at large. "That's right, your honor," agreed the two lawyers, grinning. "Where are those children?" he demanded. "Waiting for you, in chambers," said Clover's lawyer, deferentially. The judge got up and went out.

Waiting for him to come back, the courtroom grew very restless. Some of the witnesses wandered out to smoke and fraternized with the enemy on the courthouse steps. The consensus, as reported by the man in the white suit, was that Sandy was going to win. Dolly's testimony, it was agreed, had done him a lot of good, and Clover had queered her own pitch: her tears and accusations gave the truth away. And yet no one seemed satisfied. The thought of the children, closeted in there with the judge, who was going to decide their fate, seemed to weigh on the witnesses' spirits. Faces darkened, moodily; conversation flagged; watches were consulted, repeatedly. A sense that this was *a serious matter* had somehow permeated the atmosphere. The man in the white suit kept grimacing, as if he had eaten something indigestible. Dolly was sick at heart. If Clover lost the children, it would be *her* fault: she had "won the case," they all thought. But now that she had heard Clover, she began to pray that Sandy would lose. She did not want to be answerable for all the little lies she had told on the stand. She gritted her small teeth and tried to send thought-messages to the judge, begging him to ignore her testimony. Clover was not an ideal mother—anyone could see that—but Sandy was not an ideal father, either, despite the picture Dolly had sketched of him. Uncomfortable memories stirred in her: she remembered how cross he had been when she woke him up, one day, at ten o'clock in the morning. He liked to sleep late and he was often brusque and short-tempered. And he was hardly ever on

244

time. It was a little unfair of him, moreover, not to have told her that Clover had "a hand" with children. But she herself was at fault in this: she should never have agreed to testify without hearing Clover's side. At the very least, she could have asked about her from Martha or the Coes.

She wondered whether she could retract her testimony. But what would they do to her if she got up and confessed that she had lied a little under oath? And what would Sandy say if she betrayed him after he had been lauding her for her "courage"? "The court favors the mother," she repeated to herself, under her breath. The way the judge had scolded Clover, about the money— wasn't that a sign that he really favored her and blamed her for endangering her case?

The judge mounted the bench. His face was very stern, and he summoned the social worker, who talked to him in whispers, glancing back at Sandy and Clover. Dolly's stomach turned over; she did not dare look at Sandy. Then the judge announced his decision. Clover was to keep the children! *Jubilate!* Saved! She could feel the man next to her exhale, as though in relief. He winked. On her other side, Sandy stiffened; his elbows pressed into his body and his shoulders hunched. Dolly stole a look into his shaved face. He was crying. Guilt smote her. She could not bear the thought that she was selfishly glad while he was suffering. He pulled off his white evening scarf and buried his face in it.

The judge was giving Clover a very stiff lecture. He was going to put her on probation, he said, and have the social worker make reports on her. He was not at all satisfied with the conditions in her home as described by Mrs. Viera and the milkman. But no actual evidence of immorality had been presented in court. In his view, she would do well to get rid of her boarder; the maintenance allowance should be sufficient for the household if she planned her budget carefully and did not waste money on drink. Under normal circumstances, he declared, he would have taken the children away from her, but the record of the father moved him to leniency. He believed, despite much of the evidence, that she genuinely loved her children; they had expressed a strong wish to stay with her. If there had been a respectable person represented in the proceedings, a grandmother or an aunt, he would not have hesitated to remove the children from both parents. But he had found, on inquiry, that there was no such person in the offing.

The father would have the right of visitation. He had come into court as the plaintiff, asserting that he had changed his ways, and brought a witness to attest this. But the brevity of her acquaintance with him made it impossible to give any legal weight to her impressions. The courts in this district had known the plaintiff over a period of years. The bench ventured to suggest that the plaintiff might have a motive for pulling the wool (laughter) over Miss Lamb's eyes.

In any case—the judge's voice sharpened—here was a man who had been four times married, deserted by one wife and divorced by two on charges of extreme cruelty. One of these wives now appeared before the court to testify to his character as a father—a very contradictory course of conduct, to put it mildly. The practice of bringing character-witnesses was being abused by counsel. The court was capable of forming its own impression of the character of the litigants. It had its own records and the records of the S.P.C.C. to assist it. To bring in a witness who had known one of the parties "about one month" was an insult to the court's intelligence and would not be condoned if it were ever repeated. The judge glared at Barney.

"Yes, Your Honor," said Barney, but he seemed quite unperturbed. He even grinned at Dolly, as the judge continued, in a more and more sarcastic vein. At the same time, observed the judge, disagreeably, he understood counsel's desire to introduce as a witness a young woman of irreproachable character and fine antecedents, who did not, so far as the court knew, possess a police record. To Dolly's astonishment, both sets of witnesses began to chuckle appreciatively. Yes, the judge went on: so far as the court knew, Dorothea Lamb had never had her license suspended—his gray eye raked the witness —or been arrested for brawling or check-kiting or draft-evasion or assault and battery or drunk and disorderly or vagrancy. "He's kidding," the man in the white suit reassured Dolly. "He's a great bottle- and trencherman himself. Makes allowances for artists and writers. Used to sit in superior court, where these cases come up. Great sense of humor."

Since all the New Leedsians were giggling delightedly, Dolly forced a wan smile, which she slowly let die when she saw that Sandy was unmoved by the judge's sallies. He had stopped crying, but his deep-set eyes were fixed in a cold stare and his long thin body was rigid. Dolly touched his arm, and he began to tremble, all over, like a person in a high fever. As soon as the judge stopped talking, Sandy got up and raced out of the courtroom, without a word to anyone. Dolly followed, alarmed, but she lost him in the press of people. Nobody seemed to care what had happened to him; opinion, even among his own witnesses, had turned against him. He ought to have thought twice, she heard them agree, before washing all that dirty linen in public. That was what had turned the judge against him: a case like that got in the papers and

247

gave the community a bad name with outsiders, which in turn affected rentals and real-estate values. All the judges up here liked to see the lawyers make a stipulation and hear abbreviated testimony. Moral indignation echoed through the corridors. "He's fouled his own nest," cried the old woman in slacks, as she limped up to congratulate Clover.

They were so *changeable,* Dolly thought distractedly. The courthouse emptied, and nobody would help her look for Sandy. They were closing the building before Barney came to her assistance and found him for her, finally, in the men's toilet, where he had been throwing up. He was in a dreadful state. All the way back in the jeep, she had to keep stopping, for him to vomit by the roadside. In Digby, he had her get out and buy him a pint in the liquor store, which he drank from in silence as they jogged along.

This grief terrified Dolly. She was afraid to speak to him, because any word from her would seem false under the circumstances, for she was not really sorry that he had lost the children, but only sorry for him—more awed than sorry, if the truth were told. She felt very remote from him and small, like a fly speck, because she could not share whatever it was he was feeling. This sense of distance was increased when he came into her cottage and set the pint down on the table, two-thirds empty. He took her face between his hands and began to kiss her, wearily, as if he did not want to. An awful smell came from him, of vomit and raw whiskey; his tongue was sour in her mouth. Slowly, he took her clothes off and told her to lie down on the studio couch. But then, when he was naked, nothing happened; he could not get up an interest, though she did as he directed. All night, he kept retching in her bathroom and coming back to lie with his damp head in her bosom. She was terribly hungry, but he would not let her make tea and toast, to settle his stomach. "Stay here," he said, whenever she endeavored to move. "We'll try again in a minute." "It doesn't matter," Dolly would answer, gently, stroking his sweating head. But he could not get the idea of an obligation to her out of his mind. He fell asleep, still fitfully muttering of "having another try." Just before dawn, Dolly faced the facts, covered him with a blanket and a comforter, and crept into her own bed.

ELEVEN

ARTHA's first response, when she woke up one morning in November to find that her breasts were sore, was a canticle of joy. *At last,* she said to herself, with a great leap of her soul. John, next to her, was still asleep; she muted her exultant thoughts for fear they would wake him. It was far too soon to tell him since of course she could not be sure. Yet there could hardly be any doubt. This swelling was one of the recognized signs. She well remembered the terror of waking up in her college bed on bright May mornings to find that her nipples hurt when her nightgown rubbed against them. At that time (she still frowned a little to think of it), she had fought with might and main not to know what was the matter with her. She must have bruised herself, she had kept insisting, during senior play rehearsals, in the fencing scene: she was Hamlet, naturally, and the girl who played Laertes had been clumsy with the foil. You were not pregnant, she had tried to believe, unless you threw up in the mornings. She had not thrown up and she had played Hamlet and graduated, without anyone's knowing. But she had had to have a dangerous abortion, right after Commencement; the abortionist told her she had waited too long. One's physiology, she now assured herself, did not change; the soreness could only mean that.

She began to count back, trying to remember when

her last period had been. She was tempted to wake John and ask him if he knew. But she did not want to trouble him yet. He would be of two minds, she recognized, about the baby. The money part would worry him, and the responsibility; men thought of those things first. And he would fret because the baby would be encroaching on her time. On the other hand, he knew how much she wanted a child and wanted to see him as a father; he underestimated, she was certain, his own capacity for this role. He was a sort of sport in his family, and he was afraid that a baby of his would turn out like his brothers, whom he had never got along with. Indeed, he told her gravely, the chances were that he would dislike it, since he disliked most people. To Martha, as a woman, all this was nonsense. She was confident that their child would be exceptional. Moreover, what John would see was that the baby would be an incentive. For its sake, they would work harder, earn more money, improve their characters.

She smiled at herself for these thoughts but her conviction remained unaltered. They were foolish, romantic notions, but she and John *were* romantics, both of them; they had to have goals and visions. A baby would take up her time; there was no denying that. But Martha had found that the less time you had the more you were able to do. When she had been doing graduate work and acting at the same time, she had accomplished more—John admitted this—than she ever had before or since. It was like the miracle of the loaves and fishes: she had even managed, somehow, to do some theatrical reviews and to cook too, on the days when the maid did not come. She had been happy and newly married; that was perhaps the reason. But she would be happy with a new baby; so would John, if only because happiness was catching. They both, moreover, responded well to pressure from the outside, which was why, doubtless, it had been a mistake to come to the country. But the baby would make up for that.

To bring in extra money, for her confinement (Martha laughed delightedly at the word), she could do another adaptation. Her *Wild Duck* was still earning royalties; only last week, they had got a check from a stock company that was going to do it in Cambridge. A producer had been after her to do a Strindberg; John had made her say no, because of what he called her own work. But the beauty of adaptations was that you could do them at odd moments.

She could translate, between feedings, when the baby would be asleep. And they could save, if they had a real motive. They could give up those two drinks at six o'clock, which were becoming almost regular. And wine, which they always had for company and even, sometimes, when they were alone. She would not be allowed to drink when she was pregnant anyway. And it was bad for the child when you were nursing. They could save on food too. They could live on milk and apples and salt codfish and the various kinds of dried beans and clams and salt pork and cornmeal; there were dozens of ways of doing them, *cassoulets* and *brandades* and *bacalhaes* and *polentas* and *gnocchi,* besides Indian pudding and chowders and baked beans. She might even make bread, which she had always wanted to do. She was naturally extravagant, but she was sure she had a capacity for sacrifice. During the last two years of the war, when she was married to Miles, she had managed wonderfully with ration coupons.

She could do all the laundry herself, instead of taking the sheets and towels and shirts to the laundress. She would make more soups, and they could collect oysters regularly, the way the Coes did. She would sew all the baby's clothes herself. And perhaps she could hemstitch some handkerchiefs for John, as part of his Christmas present. She could even, she supposed, take up knitting, though she hated women who knitted. Could she learn to make chic sweaters and sell them to a luxury market?

Martha shook her head ruefully. She was too enthusiastic: all her ideas tended to become "follies." She would have to curb this tendency or John would think her irresponsible. She remembered one Christmas, when she was married to Miles: she had got the pomander ball craze and had made four dozen pomanders out of oranges and cloves and sweet spices. They were supposed to be an economy; she was going to give them as presents. But Miles thought they were silly and they had all stayed in a drawer, tied up in silk ribbons, till they finally got burned up in the fire. She had not changed a bit. Given the slightest prompting, her mind began to indulge itself in woman's page fancies. She loved domestic chores: the smell of furniture polish, the damp, hot scorch of fresh ironing. And she hated having her time hoarded and rationalized for her, because of her little bit of talent. She did not want to become what she called a *machine à écrire*. Drowsily, defiant, she laid down her terms. She did not propose to feed the child out of horrid jars of baby food; she would make beef teas and custards and purée vegetables herself, no matter how long it took. She had done these things for Barrett, when she was his stepmother. That was the only virtue of being married to Miles: the servants were always leaving, so that she had been able to housekeep without his interference.

Now she could do it again. As these words passed through her mind, John stirred. His slender arm disentangled itself from the bedclothes; he peered sleepily at his watch. Remorse immediately crushed Martha. How selfish she was! What she had really been thinking was that now she would not have to finish her play. The baby was a reprieve. A gloomy look darkened her eyes. John would not let himself see how distasteful the play was to her. Actually, it was almost finished, but she had started rewriting it in order to stave off the moment when she would have to show it to him. Then he would know—what she herself had feared for two months—that she was merely pretending to write a play. But he was not interested in the truth, she had been saying to herself rebelliously, when she heard him go off whistling after he had settled her in her writing room: he was satisfied when he had her penned up in the little white room, going through the motions of writing. No wonder she looked on a baby as an escape into reality.

But perhaps he was right, she hastened now to emend. Perhaps these qualms and doubts were only the natural by-products of artistic production. Perhaps she could really bring it off, thanks to him and his freshly sharpened pencils waiting for her in a glass on her desk, like a bouquet, every morning. Being pregnant, which already deepened her love for him, might make her try harder. There was said to be a euphoria of pregnancy, which might be beneficial to her writing. Yes, she said to herself, firmly: we will have the baby, and I will finish the play too. That will satisfy everybody.

"Hello, darling," she murmured, leaning forward to receive his kiss. All at once, her eyes widened; she swallowed and glanced aside. "What's the matter?" he said anxiously, seeing the shadow cross her face. "Nothing," said Martha, slowly climbing out of bed. "What would you like for breakfast?" In the kitchen, she examined the calendar, put water on for coffee, and then took her clothes into the bathroom, bolting the door. She was trying to remember when the Coes' play-reading had been. On a Friday, she felt certain, and she had started menstruating on a Monday. But was it the Monday before or the Monday after? "When did you go to Boston?" she started to call out, but checked herself in time. It was strange that she could not remember positively and yet not strange, for, having no fear of pregnancy, she no longer kept track of her periods. She started to count on her fingers, ticking off this week, last week, the week before, but she found she could not count straight. Sweat stood out on her pale forehead. She tried to get at the date another way. She had had the curse, she remembered, one day when they had a picnic with Dolly, and John had warned her not to go swimming because she would get cramps. The water had been icy, so that it must have been late in October. Dolly had had the curse too. If John would only go out, she could call Dolly and ask when she had had it; Dolly was the sort of girl who kept track. But Dolly, of course, had no telephone. Warren's mother's death, she recalled abruptly. That would date it. She could call Jane after breakfast and find out for sure.

At once, she began to feel better. There was no reason to worry until she had talked to Jane. She combed her hair and did it up. She looked at herself in the mirror and could see no difference in her face. In the kitchen, the water was boiling. She could hear John in the parlor, shaking down the coals. Everything was all right. She was certain, now, that the picnic had come *after* the play-reading. "What's the matter, Martha?" He had been watching her while she squeezed the oranges. "Nothing," she said, smiling. "Was I making faces? I was thinking about the play." The play, she thought, wryly, was *some* good. He was used to seeing her brood about it.

As soon as the breakfast dishes were finished, she went into her study and shut the door. It was no use calling Jane. Martha knew perfectly well that the picnic had preceded the play-reading. They had not had a picnic since the big storm that week end. She sat down at her writing-table and buried her head in her hands. How was it that she had never even considered the possibility that Miles might have made her pregnant? Without actually forgetting it, she had dismissed that night from her attention; John often said that she had an unconscious as strong as a horse. After the next day, the day Warren had left, she had hardly given Miles a thought. She was through with him for good; he held no further interest or terror for her. He was as dead as a clinker. And, strangely enough, except for the play, she had never felt happier or more secure with John. The air had cleared that night. She had stopped being haunted by the past, and John had stopped being haunted by the future. He had relaxed; she could tell from the way he slept. That was why it had seemed so fitting that they should have been rewarded this month with a child.

It could not be Miles's, Martha said to herself, boldly, hammering on the desk. Her feminine instinct, her very bones told her that it could not be. If it were Miles's, she would be throwing up and rejecting it. She would not have waked up happy this morning. Statistically, all the chances were against it. If she had slept with Miles once during the month, she had slept with John repeatedly. If she *were* pregnant, it could not be Miles who had caused it.

He simply could not be the father of an embryo inside her. Statistically or otherwise, the idea was too unlikely. It was well known that a woman could not conceive right after her period; that was what Catholics called one of the "safe times." She and John had been making love all through the "fertile" days—the ovulation period. If she *were* pregnant, the baby must be John's. It was the reason she had been seeking for their return to New Leeds.

Martha frowned. She had not intended to write this morning. How could she be expected to with this uncertainty weighing on her? Nevertheless, to her surprise, she found herself inserting paper in her typewriter and beginning to type out the second act. It was two o'clock in the afternoon when John knocked at her door, with a tray of sandwiches and milk. "You must have had a good day," he said approvingly. "Yes," said Martha, with a start. It was true. She had had an amazingly good day; her "condition," if it were one, had completely slipped her mind, and it only recalled itself to her, like a shadow, as she began to drink her milk.

She did not think about it again till the next morning, when she woke to find that her breasts were still sore. This time, she was immediately conscious of an unpleasant, disturbing emotion, as if all night she had been having bad dreams. She rehearsed the same arguments, proving to herself that the baby, if there was one, had to be John's. By the time she was dressed, she had convinced herself again. Again, she went to her study and wrote the whole morning, "losing" herself in the characters. In the middle of the afternoon, while she was marketing, she was positive that she had started to menstruate. But when she got home with the groceries, she found she was mistaken. That night they had dinner with the Coes. The next morning, she woke up rigid, literally scared stiff. Her only wish was to go back to sleep and dream that she had dreamed this. But she was wide awake.

A baby was a baby, she said to herself suddenly. What difference did it make whose it was? No one would ever know.

"But *I* would know," she whispered. "Or, rather, I wouldn't know. That would be just it." Supposing, for the sake of argument, she were to let the child be born, without saying anything, what would follow? Assuming the worst, it might look like Miles; it might have red hair. But this was not the worst. If it looked like Miles, then at least she would know; other people would merely find a strange coincidence and somebody would talk about her Viking ancestors—Jane Coe or Miles himself. A new thought made her feel faint. If it looked like him, *Miles* would know! He would try to assert a claim on it, somehow. She would finally be what he had always wanted: the mother of his child. And even, she reasoned, if the child did not look like him, Miles might still decide that it was his. That is, if he thought about the dates. Fortunately, he was unnoticing in such matters: he could never remember that Thursday was the maid's day off, and Sunday and Daylight Saving took him unawares, like giant firecrackers exploding under him as he sat, reflecting, on a sofa. But Miles was inconsistent; this *one time* he might notice and count back. In fact, with his suspicious nature, if a glint of the thought came to him, he would assume that the child was his, without further question. She could not tolerate this, even if it were only an inkling in Miles's brooding mind. He would destroy all of them, given this opportunity. If he were to let on to John, John would probably kill him and go to jail for life. That would eliminate Miles, but she could not permit it. She would have to kill Miles herself.

These melodramatic possibilities were not highly likely, but they could not be ignored. She could not run such risks. It occurred to her that she and John could leave New Leeds, leave the country, even, to get away from Miles. This, she recalled with bitter irony, was exactly where they had started, when she had thought of kidnapping Barrett. It seemed as if there were something preordained in their situation that wished to condemn them to eternal exile, like poor Vronsky and Anna, like the Duke of Windsor: *"Vil spectacle aux humains de la faiblesse de l'amour."* And this was not the worst. The worst would be not to know herself, for certain, whose the child was. If John should ever find out, he would share this misery. She knew very well what they would do; they would set out to have another child at once, just as if this first one were a defective. And this first one, poor waif, would always be a special case. They would always be looking at it for a clue as to whose it was. Whenever it was bad, John would be sure it was Miles's. She herself might love it too intensely, in order to compensate for the doubt. In any case, she could not trust herself to give it a normal life; for her, with her speculative tendencies, that would be impossible, no matter what her intentions. Already, she could feel pity for this unborn being suffusing her, and pity was very unreliable, as a guide to conduct. It signified a conquered repugnance.

But all this, she told herself, was perhaps too abstract. When the baby was born, she might forget all these doubts and simply take it as it was, for its own sake. What if she and John had adopted an orphan, a foundling? They would not care for it any the less because its parentage was unknown. Ah, she replied: but there was a great difference between the totally unkown and a knowledge that has been narrowed to a choice between two possibilities. It would be idle to speculate about a foundling.

By the end of the week, a new, unexpected factor had assumed control of the situation: inertia. Martha felt like a blob of matter decreed by the laws of physics to continue in its existing state of motion unless some outside force interfered. Waking in the mornings to know, even as her eyes opened, that nothing had changed, she promptly fell asleep again. In her dreams, she saw luscious images: white pitchers of milk and sheaves of the reddest roses. The delicious lassitude that was taking hold of her was presumably a symptom of pregnancy. She wanted to do nothing but sleep and let nature take its course. The need for decision lost its urgency. It was surprisingly easy not to think about the problem. And if she simply forgot about it and let the days glide by, as they were doing, she would find that it had all been settled for her. Nature, physiology, would take it out of her hands. She had only to announce, one of these mornings, that she was pregnant, to acquire the status of a privileged person. She would not be *allowed* to worry; the doctor, John, his relations would see to that. She would be carried resistlessly forward, as if on a litter, to childbed—a sensually tempting vision. She was not afraid of labor, and she liked the swollen looks of pregnant women, even the dresses they wore. Her hips were fairly wide, for a small girl; she was healthy. It would all be simple and normal. The lawfulness of the whole picture had a special charm for Martha.

The obstacles in the path were too great, the other way. How could she have an abortion without John's finding out? In the first place, she had no money. In the second place, she had not the faintest notion, any more, of how to set about finding an abortionist. There had been a drive against them since her last operation. Some girls, she knew, got their psychiatrists to certify them for a legal abortion, but she had never been to a psychiatrist. And how was she to go to Boston to start looking for an abortionist? John would want to know why. She did not even dare go to the doctor here in New Leeds to find out whether she was really pregnant. Somebody would be bound to see her in the doctor's office. The next thing, John would hear. An actress she had played with was said to start herself miscarrying with a hatpin, but the thought made Martha quail. She did not have a hatpin, and in her present state of lethargy it seemed as difficult to procure one as to procure the services of an abortionist. Even if she got one, she would not know how to use it.

She felt completely helpless and aware of her dependency on John. If she could only tell John, he would get her whatever she needed: a hatpin, ergot, a psychiatrist, a curettage. But the one thing she was certain of was that she must not do this, not even if she were dying. If everything urged her to have the baby, it was because, if she did nothing, he would never know. The deceit practiced on him would be for his own protection. And if she were to have an abortion, it would be his child she would be murdering, in all probability—the very child she had been yearning for. The word, abortion, coming from her, would blast his faith in human nature. And of course he would guess the reason.

The marvel was that, so far, he had noticed nothing, so far as she could tell. He was full of gentle attentions because he thought she was absorbed in her play. This innocent chivalry was why he must never find out. He was too fastidious; his soul would never recover if he knew. He would not mind the act itself so much as the grotesque fact of pregnancy following on it: the horrible mess, the afterbirth, so to speak, of the act. He could not conceive that she would not have taken precautions. His strictness could not bear even small lapses in her, slips of memory. A lapse on this scale would send his whole world sliding into troll-land. If it had been anybody but Miles that she had slipped with, it would not have mattered so much. But he had saved her from Miles in the first place. Miles, for John, was the Other; that was how they had construed him together, studying his traits with wonder, as if in some old Book of Monsters. And for her to have lain with him, breeding, was a sort of hideous perversion, like sleeping with your wicked uncle.

To Martha, as the person involved, it did not look quite that way, even now. True, she would much rather *not* have slept with Miles, but she could not pretend that the act itself awoke any deep remorse in her. In its consequences, it was horrible, but in essence it was only rather ludicrous, a misadventure. She still could not believe that having slept with Miles could make any difference to the true reality, which was her life with John. This true reality, surrounding her at every moment in the routines of their household, seemed to affirm that nothing could change: if she would only shut her eyes and forget, the bad dream would go away.

Yet all the while the moral part of Martha knew that she would have to have an abortion because all her inclinations were the other way. The hardest course was the right one; in her experience, this was an almost invariable law. If her nature shrank from the task, if it hid and cried piteously for mercy, that was a sign that she was in the presence of the ethical. She knew this also from the fact that she felt no need to seek advice; what anyone else would do under the circumstances had no bearing. The moral part of her seemed to square its shoulders dissociating itself from the mass of weakness that remained. It was almost a social question, she observed with a wan interest: the moral part of her would stop speaking if she did not do what it commanded. But how, she cried out, weeping. How am I to do it, all by myself? There was no answer. The rest of her, the low part, apparently, was supposed to devise the methods. The lawgiver was impractical, a real lady, disdaining to soil its hands, leaving the details to its servants. Martha could have laughed aloud, except for the pride and awe she felt in the acquaintance. She would not have guessed she had so much integrity. In the midst of her squirming and anguish, there was a sensation of pleased surprise.

The first step, she told herself, would be the easiest: merely going to the doctor, which would not commit her to anything. But she kept delaying. As long as she put it off, she could still live in hope and go to sleep at night, half-expecting her period in the morning. Several numb days passed before she found herself in the local doctor's consulting room, having complained to John of peculiar pains in her stomach. At once, she was sorry she had come. The old office she remembered had been redone, in a modernistic style, with chromium and pebbly fabrics and paintings by the local artists. She sat facing the doctor across a blond wood desk. His voice was too loud; she had to ask him to lower it, because John was waiting outside. And right away the explanations began. She had to tell this stout, coarse young man with gold-rimmed glasses that she thought she might be pregnant but that she did not want her husband to know yet. He examined her perfunctorily and took a sample of urine to send away to the laboratory for the rabbit test. She could come back in three or four days. "Three or four days!" cried Martha. "In New York, they let you know in twenty-four hours." A boundless irritation with New Leeds swept through her. It was not modern, only modernistic, like this awful furniture. "Can't you tell me yourself?" She longed for the old doctor, now resting in the cemetery, who used to treat dogs and had no traffic with laboratories. "Why, it's as big as an orange," he always said, when the young wives came to him to learn whether they were pregnant. "Not at this stage," said the young doctor. "I would only be guessing." "What's your hurry?" he went on jocosely. "You'll have a good seven months to wait."

He became very ruffled when she asked him for some medicine. "Medicine?" he exclaimed. "We don't give medicine for what you've got in there." He gestured at Martha's stomach. She had to explain to him, patiently, that she was pretending to have pains "in there," so as not to upset her husband, who did not want a baby, and that *if* she had pains in her stomach, it would be reasonable for him to give her medicine. "Colitis," she suggested. "Let's say I have colitis. You could give me some bismuth." But the doctor seemed upset by Martha's capable manner; she sounded as if she knew his trade better than he did. "I can't give you bismuth when there's nothing wrong," he objected. "Pink pills, then," said Martha. "The old doctor up here always gave pink pills." "I don't have my own pharmacy," the young man replied coldly. Martha was getting angry. "What do you give people who have imaginary illnesses?" she demanded. "You must have *something*." Imaginary illnesses, nowadays, he said, were treated with psychology. He evidently thought she was crazy, but in the end, he gave in and wrote her out a prescription for a mild sedative; her nerves, he acknowledged, were on edge.

What Martha disliked most, during the next few days, was playing the part of a semi-invalid. John's concern was an awful reproach to her; she was reminded, uncomfortably, of how annoyed she had been with him when he had cut his hand. The cut had healed badly, leaving a jagged scar, so that he had a poor opinion of the doctor. It was all she could do to keep him from sending to Trowbridge for another doctor to examine her. This kindness and solicitude, so undeserved, tempted her to reveal everything. She hated to see him deceived in a person, even if it was herself. But when her tongue stirred, to tell him how wrong he was to love her, her lips remained sewed up, as if by a darning needle. And, as she told herself, there was still a chance that she was mistaken.

But of course she was right. She nodded when the doctor told her and was aware of a certain melancholy satisfaction even as her limbs turned icy, sweat broke out on her forehead, and the room reeled and went black. "Nervous strain," she murmured, gripping the cold metal arms of the chair. The doctor had jumped up, to help her to the bathroom. "I'm not going to throw up. I never throw up when I'm pregnant." She blinked the tears from her eyes. He wiped her forehead. All at once, she found herself talking. He was stupid and he could not help her, but she had to tell someone what she was going through. The doctor listened to her account; he seemed less shocked than startled. He had no idea of who she was, evidently; she did not name Miles but spoke only of a "man." The doctor slowly polished his glasses. "And how many times did this happen?" "Only once— I told you," said Martha. "I believe in marital fidelity." The doctor nodded. His portly pink face grew thoughtful. "When was this in relation to your last period?" He looked at the sheet of paper where he had written out the case history. "A day or two after it." The doctor rubbed his jaw. "It seems like you're in the clear, then," he commented. "The chances are a thousand to one against your conceiving at that particular time. You say you had relations with your husband afterward, during the month?" Martha nodded. "The chances are a thousand to one that it's his child you're carrying there." He pointed to Martha's stomach. "Are you sure?" said Martha. Hope surged up; she leaned forward. "We're never sure," said the doctor. "Now and then we get a woman whose ovulation picture is different. You understand, you can't conceive until there's an egg there to be fertilized. That doesn't happen till around the middle of the month, as a general rule." "But how do I know I'm not an exception?" said Martha. "You don't know," said the doctor. "But the chances are that you're not. Go ahead and have your baby. Forget about the other man. He doesn't count, statistically."

Martha sighed. "That's what I've been trying to tell myself," she confessed. "I feel sure it isn't his, somehow." "Well, go ahead then. You're a healthy, normal young woman; you ought to have an easy time. You and your husband want children, you say." "*I* did," said Martha sadly. Her shoulders slumped. There was nothing he could tell her that she had not told herself, without avail. He could not give her certainty, only probabilities, which were no help in the lonely instance. She was listening now merely from politeness. "Go ahead, then," he repeated, trying to infect her with his optimism. "You're not in love with this other fellow?" "God, no," said Martha. The doctor laughed at her vehemence. "You've got nothing to worry about then. Your husband will never know, unless you tell him. This other man won't know. No psychological complications." "You forget about the child," said Martha, abruptly. "I would never have a normal attitude toward it, myself. I *couldn't,* not knowing. Don't you see?" The doctor frowned and straightened a photograph on his desk—his wife and children. "No," he said. "Even if this had happened later, toward the middle of the month, my advice to you would be the same. Don't mess around with an illegal operation. They're dangerous. Your case isn't as unusual as you seem to think. It happens to lots of women, respectable women too. A few drinks; husband's away. . . . *You* know. They go ahead and have the baby and everybody's happy."

Martha looked skeptical. "I don't see how they can be," she said. "Not knowing. Even if it's a thousand to one." "Why do you want to 'know' so much?" said the doctor, wonderingly. Martha threw out her hands in a helpless gesture. "I just do," she said. "It seems natural to me to want to know. How would *you* feel if your wife had a child and you weren't sure whose it was?" "I wouldn't think about it," said the doctor, flushing, as if he were uncertain, underneath. He brought his pale fist down lightly on the desk. "You think too much; that's the trouble with you." Martha smiled. "Is that your diagnosis?" she said. "Absolutely," said the doctor, with more assurance. "What do any of us know when it comes down to it? Even in medicine. It's all a mystery. Why are we here? What does it all mean?" He made a vague, swinging gesture with one arm. "Heredity, what do we know about it?" he continued. "Mendel. Darwin. Then some scientist over in Russia tells us that acquired characters *can* be transmitted. Better not to worry about it. Live your life. 'A little knowledge is a dangerous thing.'" "'A little learning,'" corrected Martha, automatically. She glanced curiously at the doctor. It was on the tip of her tongue to ask him if he knew the Coes. He was not at all a bad sort of person, she decided. He was certainly trying to be kind to her. Yet he took it for granted that she should be willing and able to practice a lifelong deceit on her trusting husband. "You honestly don't understand how I feel about this?" she said in a troubled tone. The doctor shook his head. "I don't get it," he said. "And I don't think your husband would either," he added, in a brusquer voice. "He wouldn't approve of you having a dangerous operation. A criminal operation. You could go to jail." Martha got up. The thought of John steadied her. "No," she said. "You're wrong. He would feel just as I do." Love made her radiant. "So what will you do?" said the doctor, rising too. "I don't know," admitted Martha. "Naturally, I'm scared to death. I'll have to find someone . . ." "I can't help you, you know," he said stiffly. "Remember, if you get in any trouble, I advised you against it." "I know that," said Martha. "You've been very kind, listening." "You don't realize how lucky you are," he burst out. "What if you weren't married? Then you'd have something to worry about. Think it over."

He opened the door to the waiting room. John was not there; he had gone off to get the car checked. Martha sat down with an old copy of *Collier's* and thought of what the doctor had said. She knew what he meant by his last remarks. Next to her, on one of the straight chairs, sat the girl who used to work in the notions shop, big with child. She had been swelling up, month after month, in full sight of the post-office loungers and the old women sitting in their windows on the main street. It was not an unusual case in New Leeds. Every year produced its quota of unmarried mothers. In a few weeks, this girl would go away to have her baby, under the auspices of a charity in Trowbridge, and then she would be back, stolidly pushing her baby carriage down the main highway, while one of the idiots, bearing a special delivery, skipped along beside her, cackling and gabbling. The ceiling of her ambition, if she could not bear the town's impassive scrutiny, would be to board the infant at the local baby farm, a run-down bungalow with a long rickety porch, across from the iceman's, which advertised its business by a long clothesline of diapers flapping in the wind. There the babies could be visited, unseen by anyone but the iceman's incurious family.

Martha sighed, avoiding the girl's eyes, which rested, without expression, on Martha's pale, neat hair and gray cloak and polished black walking shoes. The girl did not detect a sister under the skin. It was strange, Martha reflected: these girls seldom considered adoption, except within the family, with a married brother or sister. The idea of escape did not even present itself; they accepted what had happened to them without making any resistance. Beside her, Martha felt guiltily exotic to be even *thinking* of an abortion. "Behave so that thy maxim could be a universal law." The quixotic thought occurred to her that she *owed* this girl an abortion if she was going to have one herself. But it was not so easy as that. The girl's figure boldly announced that it was far too late. And, in any case, to get the money for herself would be as much as Martha could manage. To indicate fellow-feeling, she smiled affectionately at the girl, who smiled back shyly, disclosing a missing tooth.

TWELVE

MARTHA's hopes had been pinned on Dolly. She could not help thinking that fate had arranged for Dolly to be here, now, when she was needed, instead of off somewhere in Europe. The last abortion Martha had heard of had cost six hundred dollars, but that was in New York; she felt sure she could do better in Boston. Five hundred was as much as she dared ask Dolly for, in any case, since she did not know how or when she would be able to pay it back. Even that much, she feared, might make Dolly gulp a little, for Dolly, though inured to being borrowed from, was scaled, Martha knew, to the small loan. Dolly would be horrified to hear the price of an abortion, just as she used to be shocked to hear what Martha paid for her dresses during the period when Martha was acting. She would feel it was one of Martha's extravagances. Nevertheless, she would have to be asked. If Martha shrank from it, as she drove along the road to Dolly's cabin, it was not because she expected refusal, but simply from shame at what she would have to reveal. She was going to tell Dolly the truth.

Having nerved herself for this, she was conscious, chiefly, of gratitude when Dolly broke the bad news to her before the first, faltering sentence was fully out of her mouth. She would not have to tell now, thanks be to Heaven. Sandy Gray had been ahead of her. It was

Dolly who went red with embarrassment, as though she were making a confession. She had been "helping" Sandy with some improvements in his house. He was putting in heat, for Ellen, who was coming back in a few weeks. Dolly had had to apply to her trustees for an advance. Martha inwardly, so to speak, raised her eyebrows. She and John had had an estimate on heat. Sandy, she calculated, must have nicked Dolly for five hundred dollars, at the very least, if he was only having a floor furnace. She could not but admire his audacity, even while she froze with terror at what this meant for her own predicament. Her mind seemed to split in two, as if she were under an anesthetic that permitted her to watch herself being operated on without feeling any sensation. One part of her was perfectly motionless; the other was listening to Dolly and storing up details and her own commentary, to give John as soon as she got home.

Ellen, she said to herself, impatiently. Ellen will never come back to him. Ellen, in actual fact, if Dolly only knew, was coming back here to stay with the Hubers. Martha had had it from the vicomte, whom she had met just now in the post office. Ellen's return, according to the vicomte, had a purely commercial motive. Her alimony had been cut off, finally, and she was bringing back some Mexican tin bric-a-brac for him to sell. Her hope was to get the Hubers to set her up in a shop of her own, selling Mexican wares to the summer trade. She had found a man in Laredo who would help her smuggle things across the border. The vicomte, who was usually so bland, had turned very malicious this noon. The Hubers were *his* pigeon. He followed Martha out to the parking space, sprinkling libels as he went, like a fat priest with an aspergill. Had Martha heard about the custody case? Did her friend know Sandy Gray was impotent? Martha made a motion of disbelief. "Oh yes, my dear girl, positively," the vicomte assured her, with a cough. He had had it, he attested, from Margery at the grille.

This bit of gossip was printed on Martha's mind as though in blurred type. Warming herself by Dolly's kerosene heater (a new acquisition, she noted absently), she tried to feel concern for what was happening to her friend. Dolly looked badly, very peaked and worn. Her little breasts seemed sunken under her pale-blue shirt and black sweater. Her eyes were sunk back too, and that bright, inflamed look, as though she had just been crying or having her cheeks scrubbed by an angry nursegirl, had become almost too real. Outside, it was a beautiful day, one of those extraordinary days in November, in which the pale-blue sky and the pines reflected in the ponds created a tropical illusion, of palms and blue lagoons. Dolly should have been out painting, but she stood, hugging herself by the stove, with a lackluster air, like a shut-in. Her collections of seashells and fish skeletons had been dismantled; a bunch of cattails stood awry in a milk bottle. The sun's rays showed crumbs on the table. In the kitchen, through the open door, Martha could see a gallon jug, half empty, of the vicomte's cheapest white California. A slight smell of wine was noticeable on Dolly's breath. She had been giving Sandy lunch, she said, as if explaining herself. He was not working at the scallop place any more. He was trying to write an article.

Martha nodded stiffly. Her affective side was not working. She had dragged poor Dolly down; they were both submerging in a horrible quicksand. But this perception sent no message to her sympathies. She could only note and wonder. Her main sensation was one of constraint, which she tried to cover with a manner of formal politeness. Sandy had a writing block, Dolly was saying. "What is he doing?" Martha brought out, with an effort. In her present state, it hardly surprised her to hear that Sandy was supposed to be "discovering" Warren Coe for a women's fashion magazine. Miles had fixed it up. At the mention of Miles's name, Martha felt herself blanch. "Oh?" she said, smiling painfully. Yes, Dolly went on, with brightening eyes. Miles had been splendid. He had such immense energy. He had persuaded Sandy that the time had arrived for him to make his come-back as an art critic. He had sold Sandy and the article in a single, forceful long-distance call. Dolly could see that he must have been a very good editor. He had even managed to get Sandy a small advance.

Ridiculous as it was under the circumstances, Martha immediately felt jealousy of Miles. "Yes," she said curtly. "Miles is very enterprising. He should have been a salesman." "Oh, Martha," said Dolly, sadly. "He *likes* you, really. He asked a lot about you and seemed concerned about how you were." Dolly's coaxing look, pleading with Martha to soften, made Martha tremble with a sense of injustice and betrayal. The vision of Miles, magnanimous, and Dolly, talking her over, was really too much. "Go on," she said tensely. But that was all there was to it; Dolly had seen Miles and he had asked how Martha was. It had come up because they were looking at the portrait. Sandy had wanted Dolly to see it again and take some notes; she was helping him with the article. She was doing the first draft now, to get him started, and then Sandy was going to go over it and put in the ideas.

A peal of genuine, incredulous laughter came from Martha. *"Dolly!"* she began, in fond exasperation. Her voice fell abruptly silent, as a wave of panic struck her. That was the way it had been taking her, during the

273

past few days, in waves, like assault troops. It had happened in the parking area while the vicomte was talking. The reality suddenly grasped her and picked her up and pounded her, like a roller on the beach. But this time it was much worse, for up to now she had had the thought of Dolly to fall back on. It was only now that she fully realized that she would have to go home empty-handed. "Are you feeling sick?" she heard Dolly cry. Martha shook her head and pulled herself to her feet. "No," she said. "I just remembered something. I have to go now." They walked to the door. "It's a beautiful day, don't you think?" said Martha, gazing down at the pond. "What did you want the money for?" Dolly suddenly asked. "Nothing," said Martha. "I'll tell you some time. It was just one of my 'ideas.' Don't tell John I asked you." "Is it the mortgage?" said Dolly, with a face of concern. "If you could get them to wait till next month. . . ." "No," said Martha. "Nothing like that. It was only something I wanted. Don't worry." Martha's natural honesty made it hard for her to hide the fact that something was indeed the matter. But it would be only weakness, she reflected, to tell Dolly now, when there was nothing Dolly could do. To keep herself from giving way, Martha spoke in a dry, half-satirical, almost unpleasant manner that Dolly took as a rebuff. "I'm awfully sorry," she muttered. "If you'd only asked me first." "Never mind," said Martha, warmly. The thought that she was still preferred to Sandy Gray made her feel momentarily better.

That night, for the first time, she could not get to sleep. She lay rigid, thinking, without hitting on a single idea that seemed feasible for more than the instant it took to turn it over. How was she to get the money when there was no one up here she dared tell? Her friends in

New York seemed too far away, and she was afraid to use the mails lest a letter fall into John's hands. Moreover, she had no excuse for going to New York in person. Boston was different. With her adaptation opening in Cambridge, John, she had decided, would not be too surprised if she announced that she was going up to see the final rehearsals. Her own play was almost finished; her spurt of work last week had accomplished miracles. There was one rough spot in the first act left to polish and then she would be done. That was the awful irony of the position. Their purposes in coming to New Leeds had been fulfilled; her play was done, more or less, and she was pregnant. It was like a fairy tale, in which you got your wish, but in such a way that you wished you had not wished it.

Yet out of this recognition issued a new temptation or rather the same one in a "higher" form. When fate, in the shape of Dolly, refused her the money, was this not to be understood as an order to accept what had happened and submit her soul in peace? In straining after an abortion, was she not seeking the impossible: to undo the past? That was precisely her criticism of the people here in New Leeds, the Sandy Grays et al. They refused to acknowledge the reality of the past; they were not *accountable* for their actions. In her case, to be accountable would be to have the baby.

Her head turned restively on the pillow. *No,* she said to herself. The past *could* be undone, in certain conditions. It could be bought back, paid for by suffering. That is, it could be redeemed. The money she had somehow to get was a material token of the price she had to pay for having the past obliterated. Or for having its consequences obliterated; the past itself was indelible. If suffering was the real coin demanded, there could be no doubt, Martha considered, that a genuine transaction was taking place. She was suffering horribly, more than she could have imagined possible. She felt completely exhausted by the struggle that was going on, not so much in her as *on* her, as though she were a battlefield torn by conflicting forces. Every time ground was gained in one place, the action started up in a new spot. Her taut muscles ached, with the effort of lying still, so that John would not sense that she was wakeful. Her head ached; her heart pounded. This very weariness and malaise gave rise to false hopes. A tempter's voice hinted that she might have a miscarriage if she merely kept on agonizing and took no positive steps; miscarriages ran in her family—her mother had had several.

It was the reasoning power of the adversary that she found most intolerable. She was almost ready to have the baby, to put a stop to this arguing. She felt as though she were present, against her will, at an interminable *discussion*. It was like a night at the Coes' raised to a pitch of delirium, with captious voices pleading, "Explain to me, why not? Give me one reason why not." The medieval temptations, with all the allures of gluttony and concupiscence could not, Martha thought, have been half so trying as the sheer dentist-drill boredom of listening to the arguments of the devil as a modern quasi-intellectual. Under this badgering, she could not *prove* she was right, while the devil had proofs innumerable that she was wrong. That was how she knew he was the devil, but she was too tired to demonstrate that. He made chains of propositions; he argued from statistics and from norms and from social history. A Whig lady told her that she was being middle-class: it was vulgar to worry about the paternity of one's children. The vicomte coughed. Sandy Gray announced that she was not "a real woman," in his glowering, miasmal voice.

Miles told her she did not really want a baby and was using this pretext to get rid of it.

In this awful din, Martha found herself reciting phrases from the Bible and from literature. "Father, let this cup pass from me." "All may yet be well." "And is there one who understands me?" Lying beside John, she was conscious of her utter solitude. He was the only one who could divine what she was going through, and he was the only one, alas, in whom she could not confide. She pressed herself close to him, feeling his heartbeat, and wept.

The next afternoon, as soon as John was gone, she started walking rapidly to the Coes'. It was her only chance to see Warren alone. John would be away for several hours, photographing a house down the peninsula for a new piece he was doing on carpenter Gothic. Jane was away too; she had gone to Trowbridge to the dentist. Despite her determination, Martha was nervous. When the Western Union man gave her a lift part way, she had the feeling that she was being hurried onstage before she was ready. She felt suddenly shy of asking Warren because of Miles's "discovering" him. It seemed to her, now, that she should have thought of this herself. Warren was a much better friend of hers than he was of Miles. Why had it never crossed her mind to do something for him? She and John knew editors too. Comparing herself to Miles, she felt that she must appear ungenerous. It was true that once or twice she had tried to awaken some interest in Warren's work among young art critics of the Eighth Street circle, but she had not pursued the effort when she met with no response. Her excuse had been that she was not sure enough of her own opinion. Miles was too grand for such details.

"Let the public decide," was what he had told Warren, it seemed. She found Warren in his studio, with a mourning band on his corduroy sleeve, sitting on the broken sofa in a state of despondency. Contrary to what Martha had expected, he was not at all pleased with Miles's activities on his behalf. His easel stood empty. He had not been able to work, he said, for nearly a week. He did not want to be discovered yet. He was not ready for it. It threw off all his calculations. And it had opened a gulf, he confided, between him and Jane. Jane, being a woman, was pleased as Punch, naturally. They had been spatting for days. He saw Jane's side of it, but Jane did not see his. Miles said the magazine was going to send a photographer, which meant that Warren would have to take all his work out of storage and notify the insurance company. That was only a bother. He could get a man to help him clear out the studio to make room for the paintings; the old bicycles and the washing machine and the deep-freeze and the dishwasher could stay outside, for the time being, under a tarpaulin.

The worst was having to choose what paintings he wanted reproduced. Jane did not realize the seriousness of that. It involved a revaluation of his whole artistic development. To do that honestly, the way it ought to be done, would require six weeks of solid thinking. And just now he had started on a new phase; something the Lamb girl said had set him off. He did not want to interrupt himself to think about his past work. If he were really honest, he might want to reject his past completely.

"You can't reject the past," said Martha, in a somber voice. "You don't think so?" cried Warren eagerly, brushing off a chair for her to sit on. "Explain that a little, will you?" Martha smiled and sighed. "Not now," she said. "Another time." Warren's blue eyes were full of hungry disappointment. Martha made an effort; this, she reminded herself, was very important to Warren. "I think Miles is right," she said carefully. "Let the public decide. Pick out an assortment of the things you think are best, in their own terms. The public may like a style you don't like at all now. But you can't help that. It wouldn't be fair not to show them. That was you once."

Warren nodded. "Jane says the fission ones are too dark to reproduce well technically. How do you feel about that?" "They *are* dark," assented Martha, without interest. Warren leaned forward. "But Miles thinks I should put the emphasis on the fission series. On account of your portrait, I can understand that, of course. But the funny part is, now that that phase is behind me, I feel further away from it than I do from my middle period." He waited. "That's only natural," said Martha, aware that she was supposed to comment. "Is it really?" cried Warren. "Of course," said Martha. "In the theater, I always hated my last performance." Warren sat very still. "I hate to remind you, Martha, but you told me just the opposite a few years ago. Then you said every artist likes his latest work best, like a mother with her youngest child." "Oh," said Martha. "Did I? Yes, I remember." Actually, what she recalled saying was that an artist liked his weakest work best, but she did not want to repeat this on the present occasion. It shocked her a little to realize that, having come to borrow money from Warren, she was only dishing up what she thought he would like to hear.

If he knew this, he would be cast into despair. He was very much upset because Sandy, who was doing the article, had not even come around to look at his recent painting. "How can he write about me when he doesn't know what I'm doing now?" Martha laughed. As always, with Warren, she found herself amused and interested, despite herself. He appealed to her didactic instinct; she could not resist setting him straight. "It really doesn't matter," she now told him, half severely, "what Sandy says, as long as he praises you. You mustn't expect anything more. I learned that in the theater." Warren looked horrified. "But that's just 'puffing,' " he exclaimed. "I can't lend myself to a thing like that. I was counting on some real criticism." Martha grew impatient. "Don't be greedy," she said. "The main thing is for your pictures to be seen. They'll never be seen if you sit here hungering for the ideal disinterested critic to come and discover you. Take what you can get."

Warren's eyes dilated. "I'd rather wait till I'm dead," he said. "That's what I've been telling Jane. I don't want to be recognized in my lifetime. I know that now. My work is here. Some day, perhaps, somebody will find it and value it." Martha caught her breath. Warren's small figure was tense; he held his clasped hands aloft; a noble fire flashed from his eyes. Perhaps, she said to herself, this ridiculous, rapt person will really turn out to have been a great artist, and we are all too earthbound to see it. "But why, Warren?" she said gently. "The man who finds you in the future may be a fake too, like Sandy Gray. There's no reason to think that the breed of art critics has been improving." "That's not the point," said Warren. "I'll be beyond it then. And I won't be influenced in my work by what the public sees in me. That's what I'm afraid of. Of starting to copy myself, like Picasso, because one of my styles catches on."

"That's a danger," admitted Martha, gravely. "But if you're brave enough to paint all alone and wait for posterity, you ought to be brave enough to risk being influenced by the public's response. Every artist faces that problem. Some master it." Warren shook his head. "I might not be one of those," he said simply. "But you have to take that risk," argued Martha. "You're creating a set of very artificial conditions here." She waved her hand about the studio, with its derelict machines. "You might as well be painting in a time-capsule. That can't be right for your work. An artist has to have some reality-check. If you don't get it from nature, you have to turn to an audience." But Warren insisted that he was only interested in his own inner development; what happened outside, he had concluded, was just static.

The thought occurred to Martha that Warren was afraid of being judged by an audience. He had been neglected so long that he now clung to that condition, like a prisoner fighting off attempts to free him. But she liked Warren too well to want to believe this. She preferred to think that he was a martyr to his own literalness and simplicity. It was another case of his taking in a strict sense everything he heard and read; the dangers of fame, the need for dedication had been made too vivid to him. In one way, he had no imagination; in another, he had far too much. He *visualized* too readily; every text sprang into illustrations before his boyish eyes. But of course he was a painter.

Martha gritted her teeth. She had to speak some time. "Warren," she said abruptly. "Have you any money of your own? Any that you could lend me? I'm in terrible trouble. That's why I came to see you today. I don't want Jane to know." Warren hitched himself forward and looked around the room quickly, as if to make sure they were alone. "What is it, Martha?" he whispered. She raised her eyes and met his searching gaze. "I'm going to have a baby." She drew a deep breath. "I don't know whose it is." Warren lowered his eyes; he laced and unlaced his fingers as he sat slumped on the couch. She could hear that he was breathing heavily, like a dog. His face was averted, but she saw, in profile, the white flare of his nostril and the grim set of his lips. She was done for, she presumed. She had foreseen this possibility. Middle-class morality was very strong in Warren. He saw red, as he put it, when a friend exceeded the speed limit. And he was prissy about casual sex. Love, for him, was the only sanction. Yet she had asked him rather than Jane just because he was moralistic. No matter what he thought, he was too high-minded to betray her confidence. Jane would not be shocked, but she would tell the whole village. "Was that supposed to be a *secret?*" Martha could hear her artlessly cry. Watching him now, Martha remembered how fond he was of John and how idealistic he had always been about their marriage. She supposed, without caring much, that she had broken his heart.

Warren unclenched his jaws. "Miles?" he inquired, in a toneless voice. Martha bent her head. "How did you know?" Her head hung heavy; she had never thought that Miles would tell anyone. "I saw it," said Warren. "*Saw* it?" cried Martha, turning scarlet. "At the play-reading," confessed Warren, with a shy, kind look at Martha. "I couldn't help noticing that there was something between the two of you. Miles's nose got purplish; it always does when he's amorous. A painter notices those things. And you were a little high." "High?" exclaimed Martha bitterly. "I was more than high." "Not really," said Warren, reassuring. "You hadn't reached the glassy stage. But I was afraid for you." "Oh," said Martha. "Did Jane notice all this too?" Warren nodded apologetically. "Good God!" said Martha. "I wish I were dead."

Her voice rang out in the big studio. "Me too," said Warren. "I ought to be shot." "You?" Warren's head bobbed. "It was my fault, when you come down to it. I should've let you go home when you wanted to. I was getting such a kick out of listening to you and Miles. I'll never forgive myself, Martha." He suddenly picked up an ashtray and hurled it against the wall. "That's what I'd like to do to myself," he said, in explanation. "Poor Warren," said Martha sadly. "Don't take it so hard. I didn't have to stay. The real mistake was mine. I never should have come to dinner. John and I should never have come here in the first place. I knew that." "You always said so," agreed Warren. "But I never could see why." "Now you see," said Martha, with a mournful stare.

Warren knitted his brows. "Not altogether," he admitted. "Show me the logical connection. Just because this happened this once. . . ." "It didn't *have* to happen. Is that what you mean?" Warren nodded. He was waiting, modestly, for Martha to assemble her thoughts. He wanted a "proof." "No," she said. "It wasn't necessary, in the philosophical sense. It was contingent. Everything in human behavior is contingent." "Then how do you know—?" began Warren. "I don't 'know,' " exclaimed Martha, suddenly out of patience with Warren, who even at this moment had to feed questions to her as if she were an IBM machine. "But I do know, in the plain ordinary sense. *Something* bad was bound to happen, if I had any feelings, if Miles had any feelings. Any fool could see that. That's what's wrong with you, Warren. That's what's wrong with this horrible place. Nobody will admit to knowing anything, until it's been proved. Sandy Gray can pass for a decent man here because the contrary hasn't been proved yet, to the community's satisfaction. He's 'only' had four wives run away from him. That isn't a fair sample, statistically, you can remind me." "Only three," emended Warren. "The first one died, you know."

Martha groaned. " 'Only three,' " she said. "You act as if the human race had learned nothing, as if everything were possible, as if we could all start on a new phase every day. Or a new wife. It's all the same. You take up a doubting posture. But you don't really doubt. You just ask questions, like a machine." Her voice rose, in slight hysteria. Warren looked at her in consternation. "Forgive me," she put in. "But it's true. And the whole world is getting like you, like New Leeds. Everybody has to be shown. 'How do you know that?' every moron asks the philosopher when he's told that this is an apple and that is a pear. He pretends to doubt, to be curious. But nobody is really curious because nobody cares what the truth is. As soon as we think something, it occurs to us that the opposite or the contrary might just as well be true. And no one cares."

"Don't you think that's the effect of advertising?" ventured Warren. "I mean, the companies make all these claims, and nobody believes them, so that when you come right down to it, the ordinary person gets pretty darn skeptical. He wants to question every big assumption that's offered him." He smiled brightly. "I suppose that could be a bad thing if you wanted to look at it that way. I never thought of that side of it. But how would you fit in Socrates?" Martha groaned again. "Socrates," she said, "assumed that the ordinary person *knew* something. The problem was to get the ordinary person to remember what he already knew. Socrates showed that by demonstration when he got the slave boy to work out, for himself, a problem of mathematics." She broke off. "What are we talking about?" she said crossly. "Warren, I have to have an abortion."

Warren nodded. "You see that?" she cried, wonderingly. "Why, yes," said Warren. "It goes with what you've just been saying, doesn't it? You care about the truth. You don't want to have a baby when you don't know whose it is." "Exactly!" sighed Martha, with joy. "I began to think nobody would understand it." "I'm not very bright up here," said Warren, tapping his head, "but I know you, Martha. You couldn't stand a situation like that. From your point of view, that would be hell on earth. A person like Jane"—he twinkled— "wouldn't be bothered at all. When the baby was born, she'd have blood tests to find out who the father was." Martha looked at him in surprise; she had not thought him so perceptive. She laughed. "It would be almost worth it," she said, "to make Miles submit to giving a blood sample. He has an awful fear of the needle." Warren's eyes lit up with boyish glee; sadly, then, he renounced the picture. Despite the gravity of the occasion, he and Martha were on the edge of giggles, like children conspiring, as they started to map out a campaign. The need to be ingenious and secret, in the face of danger, made them lightheaded; it was only when they came to speak of John that they were altogether serious, for they did not look on him as an enemy. To Martha's relief, Warren took it for granted that John should not be told. He applauded Martha's decision as in the interests of the public safety. Twenty years ago, he told her, when he was John's age, he would probably have killed Miles if he had got Jane in this fix.

Warren, unfortunately, had very little money of his own on hand; it was Jane who held the purse strings. His tiny inheritance was managed by her mother's man of business. And Jane, he agreed, had better not know. Miles, Warren said, logically, was the person who ought to pay. Contrary to Warren's principles, he was boldly taking sides. Inside himself, he confessed, he was hopping mad at Miles. Martha was glad to see this, despite her better nature, but she was also mystified, for she had not told Warren a word about the circumstances of her fall. He assumed Miles was in the wrong, and the reason, it turned out, was simple: Miles, said Warren, darkening, had evidently neglected to take precautions.

Martha laughed, but actually she had to admit that her own view was not so different from Warren's except that it was herself she blamed, not Miles. It was an explanation but not an excuse to say that, trying to have a baby, she had got out of the habit. She ought to have thought. This failure to *think* was what she could not forgive herself. And it was what John would not forgive her if he were ever to find out. Warren did not agree. That was the man's duty, he said sternly; the woman was at his mercy. "Amn't I right?" He folded his arms.

"I guess so," said Martha, weakly, not wanting to lose her champion over a quibble. But she would rather die, she declared, than have Miles know what had happened. If Warren told him, she would kill herself. It was a question of her honor, as John's wife, that Miles should never know what straits he had reduced her to. Her tears suddenly gushed out; she cried from self-hatred and an abrupt conviction of the hopelessness of her efforts to salvage a little honor—for that was all it amounted to—from the abominable mess she was in. Warren drew out a handkerchief. "I'm not going to tell him," he repeated, soothingly, as he wiped her face. He had a better idea, he confided, when he finally could get her to listen.

Miles had not paid for the portrait yet. Tomorrow, without telling Jane, Warren would go to Digby and collect the purchase price from him. This would more than pay for the abortion. Warren would bank the rest under his own name; later on, if Martha could not pay him back, he could tell Jane some fib to account for the difference. Miles would never suspect and it was not Jane's business, Warren announced heroically, how he spent his own money.

But it was Helen who had bought the portrait, objected Martha, looking up. Warren might find it very awkward to ask her under the circumstances. She was not the guilty party. Warren shook his head. Helen, he said, had the money, but Miles was the real arbiter. If Helen did not pay for it, Warren would take the picture back. Miles would not want that because it might frustrate his scheme of discovering him. Warren's enthusiasm gradually persuaded Martha. She sat up and rearranged her hair while Warren ran into the house to fetch her a cigarette. The possibilities of collecting a large sum of money from Miles seemed unreal to her, on the face of it, but everything seemed unreal: her condition, her visit to the doctor, this cabal in the cobwebby studio. And it was true, as Warren said, that Helen Murphy had money and that they did owe for the portrait. Why should it seem unnatural that Warren would expect to be paid? If there was a lingering strangeness in the situation, it was the strangeness of New Leeds, which submitted everything that passed here to its own angle of distortion. She could not help feeling, moreover, that there was a kind of convincing poetic justice in what Warren proposed. Warren's very goodness and simple, open heart made her trust in him, like some visionary little friar. It was right that Miles, who had been treating himself like a Renaissance condottiere, pillaging the countryside from his stronghold, should finally have to pay up. Warren was one of those people, God's disinterested innocents, who had a right to appear humbly at the doors of the mighty demanding reparation.

In Digby, the next morning, Warren was directed to Miles's study, up above the gymnasium. Downstairs, where the portrait hung, the baby was standing in a play-pen, in charge of a native girl. Helen was busy, taking dictation from Miles. In his role of creditor, Warren felt a little uncomfortable, claiming to be a friend to see Mrs. Murphy. When Miles heard his voice, he yelled at him to come up. In trepidation, breathing quickly, Warren appeared at the head of the spiral staircase. But Miles was in high good humor, freshly shaved and scrubbed and smelling of lotion. He was wearing rimless spectacles and a big white wool dressing gown, with a green cord; his feet were in brown suede booties with a fleece lining. He sat at a huge table, which was covered with books with markers in them. Helen, in a plain dress, was in a low chair beside him, holding a pad in her lap. The tower room was lined with bookcases and filing cases. There was a dictionary-stand and a pair of library steps, as well as a bird-cage, containing a strange black bird, like a raven, Warren thought. The room was rather cold, and a revolving electric heater stood by Miles's side, warming his bare calves. Little dishes of water were placed all around the room: Miles had a phobia about the air being dehydrated. Glass jars full of something that looked to Warren like mold stood on a shelf; lately, Miles had been interesting himself in natural history, which doubtless explained the bird. Miles was probably observing its habits.

Warren could not help feeling excited by the scholarly apparatus of Miles's sanctum. "I don't usually see people in the morning," Miles explained, with a kindly look over his glasses. He supposed, naturally enough, that Warren had come about the article. "See Sandy about it," he advised. "Get him to go over your pictures with you. Tell him what to write, if you want. Don't let him patronize you. When it's finished, I'll look it over and fix up the spelling and punctuation." Warren tried to indicate that this was not his purpose in coming, but Miles did not seem to hear him. "Don't worry," he genially roared. "It's going to be a great thing for you. But you don't want to let it distract you from your work. You ought to be home, at your easel, at this hour, instead of gadding around. What are you painting now? I'll be down to see you one of these days. Give my love to Jane." Having fired these remarks at Warren, he settled his glasses on his long nose and picked up a book from the table. His lips moved slightly as he read. It was plain that Warren was supposed to be off now. So as not to disturb him, Warren began to talk to Helen in whispers.

"Money?" Miles exclaimed, immediately looking up. "What money?" Warren blurted out that he had come to be paid for the picture. Miles stared. Helen's hand went out impulsively to a checkbook that Warren could see lying on the table. She started to look for a pen. "Of course," she murmured. "Right away." Miles raised a hand. He was smiling. "Just a minute," he said. "Jane told Helen there was plenty of time. I don't know that we can swing it this month." He glanced affably at Warren. "Why don't you leave me your bill?" he proposed. "Then Helen can take care of it when she does the accounts next month." Warren swallowed. Owing to Martha's condition, the word, *month,* had acquired a terrible significance for him. He did not know what to say. Miles was looking at him in such a friendly, unconcerned way, as though the subject were closed. "But

I need it now, this month," Warren declared, in a thin, squeaky voice, turning humbly to Helen. Helen's long thin hand went out again, capably, for the checkbook. "Nonsense, old man," Miles interrupted, with a slightly irritable laugh. "You and Jane are rolling in it. I'm a poor man, comparatively, with a lot of expenses. I've still got the car to finish paying for and I'm still buying books for my work." A testy note came into his voice; he fitted a cigarette into his holder. "You can see for yourself," he went on, flourishing the holder. "I've had to advertise for most of this stuff. I've got a couple of rare-book dealers running things down for me."

Warren felt like a moneychanger as his eyes, following Miles's gesture, took in the array of books on the shelves, most of them in foreign languages, Greek, German, French, Latin, Italian, rare editions, doubtless, and all in fine bindings. These books must have cost Miles a fortune. And they were necessary to Miles's work, for which Warren still felt a keen respect. His eye lit on a tiny volume of Kierkegaard: *"De omne dubitandum esse,"* he read. His loyalty to Martha wavered for an instant. He remembered how good Miles had been to him, how generous he had been with his library. Jane was a bit stingy about books. They were dust-catchers, she said. It was cheaper, according to her, to join a library that would send you any book you wanted. But she always forgot to send them back, so that Warren was ashamed to use their memberships. He yearned to borrow that Kierkegaard. If he asked for it, Miles would press it on him. People said Miles was mean about paying his bills, but perhaps he was really strapped, as he was saying now. Warren's gaze went wistfully to Helen. "But if Warren needs it, dearest," she murmured.

Miles pulled up his dressing gown and put his hands on his hips. "Why would he be needing it?" he said, with a suggestion of a brogue. Warren blinked. He had not been prepared for Miles to ask him his reasons. "I have a lot of expenses too," he said gamely, "in connection with my mother's estate. My uncle needs cash to settle it. He doesn't want to sell now, with the market down." He felt a momentary pride in this story, the first he had ever invented; it had just the right amount of truth in it, he considered. "Why don't you ask Jane?" inquired Miles, sensibly. Warren gulped. Now that he thought of it, it seemed a logical question. "I can't," he said wretchedly. "I can't ask her to sell stocks, either, till the market comes up again. She's done so much for me." "She married you," said Miles. "Why should you turn to me instead of her?" "Because you owe it to me," Warren brought out faintly, blushing up to his eyes. He could see Miles's point of view perfectly. From Miles's point of view, he looked a real son of a bitch, yes, a son of a bitch, coming down here to dun Miles, just to save a few filthy dollars on the stock market. He would not blame Miles if he never spoke to him again.

A nerve began to twitch in Miles's shaved pink cheek. His foot came forward in its bootie and kicked the heater off. "Look here, Warren," he went on, still patiently. "You're going to make a lot of money thanks to Helen buying that portrait. Sandy's article is going to put you on the map. As soon as that piece comes out, dealers will be beating a path to your door. Wait and see. I know how these things work. Why, man, you ought to pay Helen for her vision in buying that picture. A picture of Martha, mind you, my former wife. It took generosity for Helen to do that." "I know that, Miles," put in Warren, sadly. His fifty summers turned to fifty winters; he was withered with shame at his importunacy. He could see that he was putting Miles's back up every time he spoke. "By the way, how *is* Martha?" he heard Miles say in his most Jovian tones. "She's fine," said Warren, coloring again. All at once, he remembered that it was Miles who ought to be blushing. This thought, when he concentrated on it, brought his blood to a boil. "Why, yes, you might say," Miles continued, winking, "that you owed Helen money. It's the turning point of your career. Now don't get excited," he added, pacifically, noticing that Warren's fists had clenched. "I don't mean that Helen isn't going to pay you. That was just a *jeu d'esprit*. Let's say she gives you a couple of hundred next month and a couple of hundred the month after. That'll see to your Christmas stocking." "No," said Warren.

"Perhaps I could give him something now, Miles," Helen intervened. "No," said Warren. Hectic spots burned in his cheeks. "A couple of hundred won't do."

Miles cinched in his robe. Under Warren's fascinated gaze, a change began to take place in him. He swelled, as if inflating with air, like a balloon slowly distending. As he swelled, his cheeks got redder and his eyes, two green gimlets, receded into their fleshy upholstery. "Why, you're off your chump, man," he said. "Nobody buys pictures that way. Ask any dealer. They sell them on tick. Don't you know that much about your own trade? I'll tell you what's the matter with you." "Hush, darling," said Helen anxiously. "You mustn't let yourself get excited. Warren doesn't mean——" "Hush, yourself," said Miles, in a strange, rough voice. "Don't try to run me. Go on downstairs, to your child. Tend to your knitting." Helen retreated, with her pad, smiling fixedly at Warren, as if apologizing for herself. She did not go all the way down. Warren heard her footsteps pause, somewhere in the middle; she was listening. Tears stood in Warren's eyes; he wanted to punch Miles and make his crooked nose bleed, for the way he behaved toward women. "I'll tell you what's the matter with you, Coe,"

Miles repeated. "Your head's got too big for your hat. You're suffering from delusions of grandeur. I ought to have expected this. When Helen told me the price you were trying to put on that painting, I set it down to temporary insanity. I was sorry for you. Here, I said, is a decent, modest little chap who's so starved for recognition that his first sale unhinges him. 'Don't argue,' I said. 'Just keep the painting and let him come to his senses. The price is merely symbolic; he's too much of a gentleman to play a friend for a sucker.' Frankly, I thought you'd consider yourself lucky to collect on the quarter-dollar. He needs ego-satisfaction, I said to myself, and I drummed up this magazine piece for you. Sandy thought I was bats when I first put the idea up to him." He paused to let this sink in; his thin lips were set in that narrow, cruel line they had when he was drunk. Warren, across the desk, accepted blow after blow to his vanity without flinching; the only thing that hurt him, really, was to be called "Coe."

He did not mind what Miles thought of him as an artist; it was his friendship that was bleeding away, in this eyrie, while the silent bird swung in its cage and the gold lettering of the books shone. "Mind you," Miles continued, in even tones, "none of this affects my attitude toward your work. I can see you for what you are, as a man, without losing faith in your picture, downstairs. As a human being, you're a wretched little *rentier* and a leech. I've put up with you for ten years, having you pick my brains whenever you and your frau invite me over to put on the feedbag. But you're a damned fine draughtsman. I always said so. I say it again. And I'm going to pay you for the picture. Don't think I'm going to default on it. I'll pay you what I think it's worth, in my own sweet time. If you don't like that, you can sue me. Now, go on, peddle your papers."

He took up a book and pencil and swung sideways in his swivel chair. Warren did not move. Miles finally looked up, as if casually, and discovered him still there. "Well?" said Miles. "Give me my money or I'll take the picture back," said a low, threatening voice issuing from Warren. He was re-testing the theory, which had not proved true in boarding school, that all bullies are cowards. Miles leapt up. "Helen," he yelled. "Come up here, damn it! Get this *bill-collector* out of my study." Warren's fists, which had doubled up in self-protection, did a little dance. "Helen!" Miles bellowed. "Coming," a faint voice answered. They heard her footsteps on the stairs. Warren's fists fell; his shoulders slumped. He could not hit Miles in front of his wife. And Miles would probably refuse if Warren invited him to step outside. "I'll take back the picture," he declared wildly, as he cast a last vengeful look at Miles and started to run down the stairs, nearly bumping into Helen, who swerved aside to let him pass. He came pounding into the gymnasium and rushed up to the portrait, which seemed to look askance at him with its curving ironical smile. His threat, he recognized, had been perfectly idle. He could no more remove the picture than he could beat up Miles. It was too big.

Even as he tugged at one corner of it, he admitted defeat. The picture began to teeter. Carefully, Warren set it straight. He was afraid that if it fell, in the heavy frame Miles had put on it, the crash would disturb the baby. He smiled wanly at the little creature, wiggled his ears, and softly took his departure. His heart was downcast, because he had failed Martha, but he could not help feeling a mite of satisfaction. Just for one minute, Miles, with his dumbbells and his Indian clubs, had been afraid of him.

He sat, conscientiously warming the motor, in the

Murphys' driveway. He was not thinking, yet, of the terrible things Miles had said to him, which made him feel sorrier for Miles, almost, than he did for himself. He was concentrating on the money. And all at once he saw, very simply, how he could get it.

THIRTEEN

Yet nothing connected with money was easy, Warren discovered. When he drove up to the bank in Digby to try to borrow on his mother's estate, he found that Jane's signature would be needed. The best thing, he decided reluctantly, was to call up his aunt's husband in Savannah. The old man, as the executor, was still pottering around, paying the debts and the taxes, but he certainly ought to be able to advance Warren something on his share of the principal. Warren got a pocketful of change and settled himself in the pay-phone booth in the Digby drugstore. As usual, the circuits were busy, and the first connection was bad. Then his aunt's husband, when Warren could finally hear him, was not much nicer than Miles. In his mock-courteous Southern style, his uncle wondered that Warren should be in such a hurry to get his mother's little bit of money, when he had not troubled to hurry to her funeral. Warren, his uncle observed, was quick enough to use the long-distance today, but when his mother died, a little old night letter had been good enough.

Warren had grown up on his aunt's husband's obscure sarcasms, which had been aimed at his artistic tendencies, and he now felt like a boy again, charged with crimes he was not aware of having committed. "Night letter?" he cried, over the humming of the wires. "I don't know what you mean, Uncle Chet." He ransacked his memory.

"Jane sent a telegram." "Your aunt got a night letter," Warren's uncle retorted. "Seemed to us you might have telephoned, instead of waiting all that time." "There must have been a mistake," yelled Warren. He would have to ask Jane about it when he got home. But then he remembered that he could not ask her: he could not let her know that he had talked with his uncle. "Why didn't Aunt May mention this when I was down there?" he piteously wanted to know. He was fond of his aunt, and it desolated him to think that she had been harboring a grudge against him. "She didn't want words at the funeral," replied his uncle. "Tell her there was a mistake," pleaded Warren. These misunderstandings had been typical of his boyhood, as the only child of a widowed lady, with cousins and in-laws ceaselessly putting their oar in to trouble the waters. It was this very uncle, childless himself, who had decreed that Warren should go to military school. These memories, of bafflement and helplessness, made Warren nearly drop in the phone booth.

"Uncle Chet," he cried. "Listen. Forget about that, just for a minute. I have to have some money, right away." "What you need it for?" his uncle's voice came sharply. It was the same trigger-tone that Warren could remember, from thirty-five years ago, when Warren had asked his mother for extra pocket-money to buy, it was revealed, drawing materials. He had lacked the gall to lie and say he wanted a baseball mitt or any of the manly articles that his in-law would have approved of. "I can't tell you," he said now. "But it's awfully important. A matter of life and death, just about." His uncle made a dissatisfied sound. "You'll have to give me more than that to go on, Warren," he said grudgingly. "I've got my duty to the estate. I'm not going to go and sell shares just to please you." "You could borrow from the bank," argued Warren. "You got banks up there, I suppose," said his uncle, satirically. "Your mother always claimed you married a wealthy woman." "I can't tell Jane," said Warren, instinctively lowering his voice. "What's that?" said his uncle. *"I can't tell Jane,"* repeated Warren, as loudly as he dared. "It's a private matter. There's a girl up here, a friend of mine, in trouble."

"In trouble?" exclaimed his uncle. "You mean. . . ?" "Yes," desperately cried Warren. There was a silence. Then a dry chuckle came from the other end of the line. "Well, well," said his uncle. "I didn't think you had it in you, Warren. I guess you've reached the dangerous age." "It's not me, Uncle Chet," protested Warren. "No, no," chuckled his uncle. "It was two other fellows, I suppose. No call to apologize. I won't let on to your aunt. How much do you need?" Warren reflected. It was up to him, he saw, to accept his uncle's mistake. "Five hundred dollars," he said bravely. "You better make it seven." "Sounds like you're being blackmailed," commented his uncle. "No," said Warren. "Oh, no. This girl is what you'd call a lady, Uncle Chet. Things are more expensive up here—doctors and all that." "How far gone is she?" inquired the old man. "About six weeks," said Warren. "Maybe seven. I'm not sure." He whitened as he saw the implication: did his uncle realize that Warren's mother had died just over six weeks ago? "Umm," said his aunt's husband. "You're in a hurry then. How shall I get the money to you?" Uncle Chet's *savoir faire* stunned Warren; he had never thought of this difficulty himself. Any letter that came, Jane would open as a matter of course, if she found it in the post-office box. "Golly," sighed Warren. "I don't know what to tell you. This is an awfully small place." "I could send a bank check," ruminated his uncle, "in a plain envelope, addressed to some friend of yours. You got any bachelor friends?" Warren canvassed his circle of acquaintances. There was Paul, he decided. Paul was supposed to be trustworthy; Jane said he knew everybody's secrets. "Paul de Harnonville," he spelled out the vicomte's name for his uncle. "Airmail, registered?" said the old man. Warren hesitated. If it were registered, they would notice it at the post office. But they might notice it anyway. Still, what if Jane were to come by while Paul was signing for it? "Better plain air mail," counseled his uncle. "I'll try to get it off this afternoon." "You've been a prince, Uncle Chet," said Warren, warmly. "Don't mention it," said the old man. "You should have told me right off, instead of beating about the bush."

Warren was wringing wet when he emerged from the phone booth. His knees wobbled as he came out into the sunlight and started to cross the street. In the distance, he recognized Harriet Huber, with a shopping bag, and he ducked behind a telephone pole. He was afraid to be seen coming out of the Digby drugstore; it might be guessed that he had been making a telephone call there. He felt that his complicity with Martha was written all over him, and he attributed unusual insight to every native he saw. He was not known in Digby, but this very fact, he feared, would imprint him, as a stranger, on the minds of the Digby population. They would all remember that a small gray man in corduroy had been in the drugstore an exceedingly long time.

It was only one o'clock when he parked in front of the New Leeds liquor store. Warren felt he had lived centuries since he had got up in the morning. His experience with Miles, just by itself, would take him a lifetime to digest. Miles had told him some home truths in the course of his tirade. Was he really a leech and a brainsucker? He supposed he was, as a matter of fact. Martha had implied something like that, though in a politer way. But Miles had killed a precious part of him—the nerve of intellectual curiosity. He would never be able to ask a serious question again. Some time, much later, he would talk all this over with Jane. She would be bound to find out, before long, that he had tried to collect for the painting. And he would have to produce some reason to explain his behavior, without implicating Martha. The number of lies he was already committed to made him question his sanity. Was this he, he asked himself wonderingly. He wanted to call up Martha, to tell her what had happened, but if John answered the phone, he would have to prevaricate again. If he called here, from the drugstore, the girl at the fountain would hear him, while if he called from home, when Jane was in the village, there were the neighbors on the party line. Yet he was not sorry for what he had undertaken. It was worth it, to know the truth, worth it, to help Martha. He felt honored that she had asked him.

Paul was out to lunch. Warren found him in the grille and indicated that he would like to speak to him, alone, when he was finished. Warren was too excited to eat anything himself. The vicomte nodded and handed him a rusty key. "Meet me in the shop." Waiting in the dark antique shop, amid the dust of marble and the smell of worm-eaten old furniture and moldy upholstery, Warren felt very adventurous, though a little queasy inside. The shop, he thought, had a secretive, almost criminal atmosphere, as though any shady deal could take place here. It occurred to him, suddenly, that the vicomte would know where to find an abortionist.

Paul, when he came in, was not at all perturbed at being asked to serve as a letter-drop. "It is not the first time," he said equably. "You would be surprised. This little shop is very convenient, for all kinds of business.

You have a little *affaire*, I suppose, something you do not wish to tell Jane." "Not exactly," said Warren. "It's more of a commission, you might say. Something a friend has asked me to take care of. I can't tell you without betraying his confidence." "Of course," said the vicomte. "I have no wish to pry. It is very serious, this commission?" "Very," said Warren, with feeling. "I see that," said the vicomte. "A check will come in the mail," explained Warren. "When it comes, will you call me up? We ought to have a signal, I suppose." "Naturally," said the vicomte. "That goes without saying. When the letter comes, I will telephone that I have a new shipment of wine I want you to try. I will have the letter in the liquor store." "I don't suppose you could get the check cashed," said Warren. "It'll be made out to me, a bank check." The vicomte pondered. "If you indorse it, I could take it to Digby. Or Trowbridge, if you prefer."

"I'll pay you for your trouble," volunteered Warren. "If you wish," said the vicomte. "It doesn't matter. I am always glad to do a service for my friends. Living here, all alone, I can so seldom repay hospitality. How much is the check, if I may ask?" "Seven hundred dollars," said Warren. The vicomte raised his fair eyebrows. "Someone is to get a present, perhaps?" Warren studied his sneakers. "Don't tell me," said the vicomte. "I prefer to guess. It has to do with a lady. Possibly a married lady who is to get an expensive present her husband doesn't know of. That is Maupassant—a little out of fashion. Or possibly it is not a lady. Someone has stolen something, and restitution is to be made, on the q.t." Warren said nothing. Paul, he perceived, really meant it when he said he did not wish to be told. He closed his blinking eyes, like a medium, and put a fat finger to his forehead, seeming to relish, voluptuously, the sense of mystery with which he himself was enveloping this request. "Or could it be a girl? An unmarried girl who finds herself in trouble, as we Americans say. *Pauvre fille*. I am sorry for her. Possibly I can help. There is a doctor, a refugee, in Boston, who will sometimes take such cases." Paul took his wallet from his pocket and slowly thumbed through a grimy collection of business cards. "Here," he said, handing one to Warren. "This is the man. A nice old fellow. A Jew. His father was physician to my family. The son cannot get a license to practice in this country; he is too old to pass the examinations." Warren gave the card a gingerly inspection before handing it back to Paul; the doctor's name and address were firmly stamped on his memory. "Thank you, Paul," he said. "But it isn't that kind of trouble, this time." He gave a daring laugh. "Ah well," said the vicomte, indifferently, "so much the better. I will not have a sin on my conscience. Blackmail, could it be?" He continued his ruminations. "Some little irregularity, a taste for young boys?" His round blue eyes revolved over Warren, who had a painful sense of shock. Between his uncle and the vicomte, he stood convicted as a regular Cellini. What horrified him most was the way it was taken for granted that anything was possible, for a respectable married man. He thought of what Martha had said yesterday, about how everybody mistrusted appearances and yet no one really cared what the truth was. "Blackmail," mused Paul, still studying Warren with an air of connoisseurship, "is rather rare here, in New Leeds. It is many years since we have had a case of it. Emotional blackmail, yes. The other kind, no. The community is so tolerant that a blackmailer could not make a living here. I've often thought of this, Warren, in a speculative way, to pass the time. I am ideally situated, you might say, to make a profession of blackmail here. As a Catholic, I receive many confessions; you atheists take me for a priest, though I cannot give absolution, naturally. Then there is my work in the liquor store and my work in A. A. When I go around to buy furniture for the shop, I see a good deal. But if I were to try to capitalize my knowledge, I would not make a penny." He lifted his huge shoulders. "It is a community of glass houses. One can only sit by and watch. Now and then there is a soul to be saved."

"Excuse me," ventured Warren. "But how do you reconcile your religion with what we were just talking about? I mean, that card you wanted to give me. I thought you Catholics were against that sort of thing." "Officially—*ça va sans dire*," said the vicomte. "But I am not the church, my dear Warren. I am only one poor sinner. I believe in works of charity. Here is a poor Jew in Boston who is deprived of his means of livelihood. It is only a work of charity to put him in touch with a poor girl who will be disgraced if she bears a fatherless child. The church frowns, but God is merciful. He winks, I think, at such cases. I commit a little sin, but God will forgive me, probably. I do not pretend to know. Only God knows what he will do with my soul. I will have to wait and find out. I am not in a hurry." "That's awfully interesting," said Warren. "Do you really believe in a life after death?" "Naturally," said the vicomte, with an air of astonishment. "I am a Catholic." "But how do you reconcile that—?" "Reconcile, reconcile," pronounced the vicomte, impatiently. "That is all I hear from you atheists and Protestants. 'Paul, how do you reconcile . . . ?' I do not need to reconcile; I leave that to God. On earth, I am agnostic, though I keep the sacraments. In Heaven, I will be a believer, for then the meaning will be revealed to me. In Hell, if I am sent there, I will have to believe too; that will be my punishment, to know that I am a scoundrel for all eternity." He sighed. "What is the expression? It will all come out in the wash." He looked at his watch; it was time to open the liquor store. Warren followed him out of the shop.

Three days later, in the waning afternoon, John Sinnott sat in Martha's study, trembling with anger. The front door had just banged; she was hurrying down the hill to the garage. For the first time in months, they had had a violent quarrel. Martha had provoked it, deliberately, out of nothing. The phone had rung while she was typing out her manuscript, and she had jumped up to answer it, though he had told her over and over to leave the phone calls to him, when he was in the house. It was never anything important enough to justify her interrupting her work, especially now when she was almost finished. She had promised to let him read the play before she went to Boston, the day after tomorrow. But she would not have it ready if she kept jumping up and down. This time, it was only Warren on the phone, with an invitation to tea, which Martha immediately shrilled at him to accept, though they were already committed to have dinner with the Hubers. One invitation a day, they had agreed, was enough; there was no reason why they could not see the Coes tomorrow instead. But Martha had flown into a passion when he, paying no attention to her, told Warren to make it tomorrow. "You don't have to go if you don't want to, but I'm going," she had breathed, defiantly, snatching the telephone from him to tell Warren she would come, alone.

This frantic avidity for social life seemed disgusting to John; it was unworthy of Martha. If she could have seen how her pretty face looked, contorted with rage and terror at the idea of missing a social engagement, she would have bowed her head in shame. Beside himself, suddenly, John had tried to force her to look at herself in the long mirror in the parlor. But she had twisted out of his grasp and fled to the bedroom. It was the nearest they had ever come to blows, and he had felt instantly sickened. Half remorseful and half sullen, he had waited for her to make up with him. But when she came out of the bedroom, finally, all dressed, she said she was sorry yet she made no effort to coax him to come to the Coes' with her. In fact, he got the impression that she was secretly glad to be rid of his company. She was itching to be off, and when he pointed out that there was no hurry, that if she would wait, while he dressed and shaved, they could stop in at the Coes' for a minute, on the way to the Hubers', Martha said coldly, "I don't want to wait for you. You always take so long." His anger had risen again. It was almost dark, already, and she was not a good driver; he hated to have her take the car over these roads at night. "I'll come back for you," she said, "in time to start for dinner." And now that she had made sure he was not coming, she had reached up to give him a kiss. "I know it's dull for you," she murmured, "listening to me and Warren." "Go on," he said icily, pushing her away. "Enjoy yourself. I bore you. I 'always take so long.'"

Then the door banged, and he had rushed furiously into her writing room, minded to do something destructive. He pulled her manuscript page out of the typewriter, flung it to the floor, and started to type out the heading of a letter. He was going to write to the real-estate agent to put the house on the market. When Martha came back, she would find him packed to leave. He was not going to dinner with the Hubers under any circumstances. Martha had been too peculiar lately, running off to visit people the minute he was gone, complaining of being ill and then insisting she was well

305

again, wanting to go to Boston, and dropping into fits of abstraction several times a day. She had even, Dolly had told him in confidence, tried to borrow some money from her. And now she could not wait a minute while he changed his clothes and shaved. The sound of his electric razor irritated her, probably, though she had delighted in it when she had first known him, as a contrast to Miles's lather and old Gillette. All this restlessness must mean that she was finally tired of him; after seven years, he was no longer a novelty for her. What she really wanted, probably, though she did not know it, was a new man. The thing they had always said, about the seven-year term, was true. He could tell it himself. As his anger subsided, and he could examine his feelings for her, he discovered only an emptiness, a great hollow of disappointment. He could see her virtues, objectively, but they did not speak to him any more; another man, who did not know her as he did, might find her attractive and winning. He picked up the manuscript sheet from the floor and carefully smoothed it, glancing idly at the lines of dialogue. The temptation to read her play, to punish her, was very strong for a minute, but he set it aside. It would not be fair to read it, when he felt so sad about her. He added the sheet to the pile of manuscript on the writing-table.

Just then the door opened, and Martha appeared. She hurried across the small room and flung her arms around him. "I love you," she said. "You were thinking I didn't." John nodded somberly. "I couldn't go off and leave you thinking that," she said. They looked at each other steadily. "I really do," she said. Her eye fell on the typewriter and traveled to her manuscript. She mistily smiled. "You were going to read my play, to get back at me," she announced. John laughed unwillingly. "I thought of it," he admitted. "But you couldn't be so cruel," she said reproachfully. "No," he agreed. "I can't hurt you, Martha. You're too vulnerable." He put his arm around her, lightly, resigned to this fact. "And is that such a deprivation?" she asked, with a faintly quizzical look. "Yes," he said, speaking honestly. "I'd like to feel free to hurt you." "How strange," said Martha, thoughtfully. "That's very different from me. But I can see how it might be dreadful, never to be able to hurt somebody, like a horse being hobbled. That's why you feel so shackled. It must make you hate me." "Sometimes," he confessed. Martha hesitated. "If I gave you good reason to hate me, would it help, would you feel liberated from these constrictions?" "Possibly," said John, dryly. She gave him a very searching look and sighed. He distinctly read her thoughts. Her poetical temperament was wondering whether she could "drive him away" from her, like some great tragic heroine, while her prosaic self balked, like a little mule. He laughed. This conscientious transparency of Martha's was why he could not hurt her. "Go along," he said, and Martha went, with a troubled backward glance.

He sat staring mechanically at the sheet of paper in the typewriter, on which he had written the date. All at once, everything was clear to him. He had the clue to Martha's strange behavior. It was December, and she was thinking about Christmas. That was why she was going to Boston; that was why she had tried to borrow money from Dolly. She set foolish feminine store by anniversaries and holidays and loved to prepare surprises. She had been sad and abstracted lately because they were short of money and because she was determined, nevertheless, to buy him some extravagant, absurd Christmas present. Their first Christmas in their new house! That was precisely how Martha would think of it. She had made herself sick with worrying over her romantic contrivances; that was probably what had been wrong with her stomach. And now, undoubtedly, she had some scheme cooked up with the Coes, which was why she had been in such a hurry to answer the phone and to go off there, herself, without him.

He was torn between relief and exasperation. It lightened his spirits to realize that Christmas was the only thing that was the matter with Martha. At the same time, he could have screamed at how typical this was of her. She had always made a fuss over Christmas. In their little apartment in New York, they had always had a Scandinavian-style Christmas tree, with round Swedish cookies and colored candies and gingerbread men and walnuts gilded by Martha, and real candles, of course, burning in holders that had belonged to her grandmother and had been sent on, from Alaska, when her mother died. It had been extremely pretty, but dangerous; their apartment was a firetrap, and whenever the tree was lit he had had to stand by with a bucket of water and a fire-extinguisher, which Martha laughed at. And the candies and cookies on the tree invariably attracted mice; she insisted on keeping the tree up until Twelfth Night. There were always heaps of presents, expensive ones, from the very best shops. She rejoiced in having things specially made for him. And there was always a Christmas dinner party, with a goose and snappers for the guests. He could not deny that he liked this passionate festivity, but only because of her, because it transported him into the northern fairy world of her childhood, with real elk and reindeer and icicles. But he did not care at all about getting presents. This year, her play would be present enough, if she gave it to him in manuscript covers, with a dedication. He had told her this months ago, and she had agreed, but now she had gone back on her word, obviously, and was borrowing money they could not afford to give him something he did not want. He wondered, irritably, what it was she had in mind. An expensive phonograph, perhaps, like the one the Coes owned? Or some foreign books bound specially in violet bindings? Or could she be thinking (he shuddered) of giving him heat for Christmas, so that he would not have to fix the fires and the stoves? John shook his head; that was not quite right. Martha always preferred to give something solid, that could be opened under the tree.

And what was he to do? To stop this folly, peremptorily, or let her have her way and pretend not to notice what she was up to? She would grieve if he prevented her. For Martha, a bare Christmas would immediately become symbolic of the notion that their love had fled. He remembered, now, certain mournful, deep looks she had been casting at him, when she thought he was not observing her. These looks he could now decipher; they meant that she was being sorry for him because she had not yet thought up a way of getting money for his Christmas. Her obstinate, childish heart refused to learn that he was really indifferent to such things. It was only with her brain that she philosophized. A rueful tenderness plucked at his sleeve. Martha's dreams and discontents, her plans and projects, were those of a young girl, whom he could still picture, on roller skates, with her bookstrap. To her, reality still spoke a "little language," like the language of the flowers, or of precious stones or apple seeds. Sooner or later, she would have to grow up, he reflected, but in a way he would be sorry to see it. The child in him, even in anticipation, fought against losing its playmate. Would he accept a "womanly woman," calm as a Roman matron, in exchange for this precocious, learned, bold sister, who was always outshining the other pupils, thinking rings around them, as Dolly had once said, describing Martha in the classroom? For some reason, John suddenly felt melancholy grip him, like a pain in the heart. He saw them all as children, like babies pickled in bottles: Warren, a wizened boy, Jane a middle-aged schoolgirl in bloomers, Dolly, prim, in a hockey dress, himself on a rocking-horse charger, Martha. He put a fresh piece of paper in the typewriter and wrote: "Martha, I love you, but life is serious. You must not spend any money on Christmas." He drew a heart and signed his name. She would find it in her typewriter in the morning.

Martha had the money in her pocketbook, and the name of a doctor in Boston, which Warren had written out for her. She was in an exalted mood. The night was bright and starry, though there was no moon. She was almost at the end of the ordeal, she said to herself calmly and joyfully as she backed out of the Coes' driveway, with Warren's flashlight beaming "Good luck" at her. They had urged her to stay and have cocktails with Eleanor Considine, the local poetess, who was coming to have dinner with them. But she wanted to get back to John. Eleanor Considine, a woman of fifty, with dyed red hair and a long amatory history, was a cautionary example of everything Martha was trying not to be. She had run away from a conventional husband, out west in Cincinnati, and married a young man, who had died of tetanus, all alone, in Mexico, from a cut she had neglected to have attended to. She had been married again several times, once to her original husband, who supported the several children she had picked up en route. She was now after the vicomte, who could give her a title, she said; she had set her cap for Miles and gone to him as a patient, after Martha had left him. Nothing fazed Eleanor, as her friends delightedly remarked. She had a rough, ringing laugh and an artless, witty candor; she confessed her misdemeanors to everyone, on first acquaintance; her truthfulness excused her, it was commonly felt. And she was always scribbling something, plays in verse, mock epics, love poems, elegiacs, *vers de société;* when she was on the wagon, she came to parties with a notebook in which she took down the conversation. Like Martha, she had a good ear, and many people still nervously agreed that she might do something eventually, even while they smiled at her pretensions to seriousness. But she insisted on regarding Martha as a rival, and Martha did not want to see her, even though, as the Coes said, she was getting old and deserved pity.

Tonight Martha could not tolerate the presence of anything petty. She was very much moved by what Warren had done for her. All she had heard from Warren, until today's telephone call, was a hurried injunction to stand by: the money would be coming. Just now, while Jane was in the kitchen, he had related to her in an undertone the events of the past seventy-two hours. A gentle pride had emanated from Warren: he was proud of his aunt's husband, proud of the vicomte, proud of his own subtlety in eliciting the name and address of the doctor, proud, even, in a curious way, of Miles, for behaving so terribly. Everybody, including Miles, had been prodigious.

This was what Martha felt herself, a sort of wondering gratitude, not only to Warren personally but to life itself, which suddenly revealed a new dimension, like Warren's outer space, beyond the shining galaxies. She could not help thinking that she was in the presence of the sublime, which was of course the verge of the ridiculous. Happiness misted her eyes as she drove along the

311

sand road; a hymn tune came to her lips. Despite the doctor's caution, she was not in the least afraid. Abortionists, she had always heard, did their task much more proficiently than licensed doctors, and why shouldn't they—they had more practice at it. In two days, it would be over. After it was over, she might possibly tell John. Perhaps she owed him the truth, so that he could hate her if he chose to. For a moment, back in her writing room, she had almost spoken. But now, with her mind very clear, she saw this impulse as sentimentality. Once it was all over, John would not hate her for what she had done; in fact, he would admire her resolution and fortitude. The only person he would hate would be Miles. Therefore, there was no reason to tell him unless she wanted praise at the price of peace in the community. Yet it would be good to have truth between them again.

In any case, she did not have to decide yet, and however she decided, it would be all right. She suddenly knew this, without knowing how she knew it. But it was an unmistakable certainty. In a matter like that, she could trust herself. For the first time in years, since the summer she had married Miles, she could say this aloud. She said it, and her wonder grew. She had changed; she was no longer afraid of herself. That was the reward of that fearsome decision, which no longer seemed fearsome, now that it was behind her. She laughed and stepped on the gas. *"Integer vitae, scelerisque purus,"* she sang, thinking of Warren. Around a blind curve ahead, she saw the faint reflection of the headlights of a car, coming rapidly toward her: Eleanor Considine, doubtless. Martha slowed down and hugged her own side of the road. As the car crashed into her and she heard a shower of glass, she knew, in a wild flash of humor, that she had made a fatal mistake: in New Leeds, after sundown, she would have been safer on the wrong side of the road. "Killed instantly," she said to herself, regretfully, as she lost consciousness. This succinct appraisal, in the wavy blackness, became a point of light receding until she could find it no more.